Fallen

a novel

Mia Sheridan

To Christi. The lingering grace of your friendship remains with me always.

PROLOGUE

Thirteen Years Ago

Kandace cried out as her foot caught on a thick root, pitching forward before catching herself, glancing back, and stumbling on. The moon above was round and bright, but it only shone in feathery pools, mostly blocked by the ancient, towering trees that swished and moaned in the gusting wind.

She could hear the men behind her, crashing through the forest in pursuit, their breathing labored, heavy, a word or two drifting to her here and there as they gave each other instructions.

Up ahead. There! Goddammit, don't let her get away!

Kandace's lungs burned, the agony of the gunshot wound in her upper back screaming in pain with every desperate twist and turn of her escape.

Please, please, don't let them catch me.

She was dead if they did. She had no doubt of that. They hadn't hesitated in shooting her in the back as she'd run from Lilith House. She might be dying anyway. There was so much blood. She felt it streaming down her back, pooling at the dip of her spine. She was weak, terrified, but she could still run. Obviously, nothing vital had been hit—she hoped. If she could just find a place to hide, wait them out . . .

She had been so sure she could get away undetected. She'd had a *plan*. How had they known?

Kandace broke right, ducking through the vegetation that grew thick between two trees. She ran, hopping over impediments in her path that the moon highlighted, swerving around trees, ducking under branches that seemed to reach out and grasp at her, slow her down, too afraid of those pursuing to waste fear on the fact that she was being swallowed up by the forest where a horned demon was said to roam.

Through a break in the trees she saw something swinging, there and gone in the blink of an eye. She slowed, glancing back once, terror seizing her throat, making it even more difficult to pull in air.

Yes, supposedly a demon lived here. Even Dreamboat had said this forest might be haunted. She hadn't quite believed it. But she'd been different then. Now . . . *now* she could believe anything. Lilith House had assured that.

My utmost for His glory!

She fell to her knees beside a towering fir, going still as she attempted to catch her breath. Her heart beat loudly in her ears, blood whooshing, sending waves of throbbing pain to her wound. Her hand found the rough bark of the tree and she gripped its solidity, leaning against its trunk as she listened. Their voices were farther away now, but she could still hear them. They were coming closer. She had no time to waste.

But she needed to rest. So badly. She had to lie still for a moment. Her eyes darted around, searching for somewhere she might hole up like a wounded animal until the threat was over.

The leather bag she had strapped across her body rubbed against her wound and she adjusted it as she pulled herself to her feet.

A soft noise to her right made her startle and she whirled toward it, assuming a defensive crouch. A red fox stood in a thin clearing, staring, its amber eyes soft and knowing. She released a harsh exhale, straightening as she blinked at the animal. She thought of the injured creatures the kid had treated, hiding them in the shed behind Lilith House until they were well enough to be set free. At the thought of the kid's tender heart, regret slammed into her chest like the bullet in her back had done. *Little Dreamboat. I'm sorry I left you behind. I'm so sorry.* She'd be back for him though. Her hand went to her round stomach. She had someone more helpless to protect now. The kid could handle himself. He was stronger than he knew.

The fox's ears pricked as the sound of the men coming closer bounced off the trees. The voices were suddenly very close and she didn't remember leaning back against the tree. Had she drifted off? The fox stared at her for another moment

3

and then darted in the opposite direction from where she stood.

"There!" one of the men shouted. Feet crashed through the brush, following the movement of the fox.

Kandace didn't hesitate. She ran the other way, weaving, stumbling, terrified that she was growing weaker by the moment. She clutched the leather bag to her body as she moved, tripping over something on the ground and going down with a painful jolt. For a moment she considered not getting up. She considered lying right there on the forest floor and just . . . giving up. It would be so easy. She rolled to her back, gazing up at the stars through a break in the branches.

Don't give up on yourself. I haven't. She heard her friend Scarlett's passionate tone in her head, the words she'd said to her not so long ago and the memory bolstered her. Kandace pulled herself slowly to her feet. She *had* given up on herself. She'd made so many mistakes, had so many regrets. She hadn't listened to Scarlett then, the only real friend she'd ever had, but she'd listen to her *now*. She wouldn't give up, not when it mattered most.

There was a large rock near where she'd fallen and Kandace took off the leather satchel, taking in a deep breath before using what strength she had left to push at the rock. Sweat and blood dripped down her spine as the rock slowly rolled, leaving a large crater in the dirt where it'd been. Kandace went down on her knees, using her hands to dig a deeper hole. She folded the leather satchel up, using the strap to wrap around it, placed it in the fresh hole, and then pushed the rock back where it'd been, scattering pine needles and dead leaves around it. Standing, she used her feet to smooth out the ground. She took a moment to assess the hiding place, and then satisfied it didn't look as though it'd been disturbed, she turned and moved on.

Despite being unencumbered by the bag, Kandace was slower now, but still she traveled forward. The trees began to thin, making movement easier, the terrain turning rockier, large boulders as tall as people, outlined by the moon. When she came to a clearing, she stopped, panting, turning in a slow circle. A canyon was in front of her, the forest behind. There was nowhere to travel forward, but she couldn't turn around. Something shrieked overhead causing her to jump and let out a terror-laced squeal. Her heart pounded in her head . . . only, no, no, the pounding was coming from outside of her. Slower, steadier than the panicked rhythm of the blood pumping in her veins. A drumbeat, drawing closer. Cold dread settled in her gut. Tears spilled out of Kandace's eyes and tracked down her cheeks as fear vibrated through her. *No, no, this can't be real.*

A dark shadow with large, curved horns moved behind a tree to her right and she stumbled backward, her head pivoting as the shadow appeared between two trees to her left. The world tilted, swimming before her eyes. She felt hot and cold, shivering and burning. Her teeth began to chatter. The shadow appeared again and again, moving impossibly fast, seeming to be everywhere at once, the drumbeat rising, a slow chant echoing words she didn't know. Words from another place, another time. Kandace let out a choked sob stumbling backward, away from that unknown horror.

MIA SHERIDAN

She turned back to the woods, toward the enemy she could identify, the enemy she had a chance of fighting, of hiding from. A blow smacked into her flank, causing her to whirl around, clutching at her midsection as she fell. Shouts. More voices. Blearily she saw the man who'd just shot her turn and raise his arm toward the sky to signal the others forward.

A bolt of lightning streaked across the heavens and before the coming thunder rumbled, a fur-covered creature surrounded her from behind, and Kandace jolted, opening her mouth to scream but unable to utter a sound.

"Holy fuck! Did you see it? The *thing!*" said a man's voice—one of *them*—high and panicked.

Weakly, she attempted to fight, but whatever it was, it was too big, too strong—*inhuman*—and she was so tired, so weak. Dying. It picked her up effortlessly and ran, something clanging at its side, chanting as it moved, its voice gritty and unused. She caught one word, garbled but recognizable because of its strangeness: *Novaatngar.* She'd heard it before, recognized it from the legend the kid had told her. *The Dark Place.*

Oh God no. No no no.

Fat droplets of rain hit her face as another spear of lightning ripped the sky in two, shaking the ground and rattling her teeth.

But God will strike you down once and for all! He will pull you from your home and uproot you from the land of the living!

Perhaps Ms. Wykes had been right. Perhaps she was wicked after all. A sinner. And if the devil who had captured

6

her allowed her to live, God Himself would strike her down. Kandace struggled weakly, the arms around her increasing their pressure. She felt them descending, the thing's footsteps steady and sure as it maneuvered them down and over, navigating a steep incline. Her eyes cracked open and her equilibrium tilted dizzily so that she snapped her lids closed. She'd been looking into a bottomless pit, the entrance straight to hell.

The creature stopped suddenly and prickly brush scraped across her exposed flesh before she was laid down on hard, packed dirt. Kandace's head swam, white pinpricks of light obscuring her vision as she grappled for something to cling to. Her head hit the ground with a soft thud. Her eyes closed and then cracked open, the stars that had danced in her vision fading momentarily. She looked straight into the face of the thing that had captured her and carried her there. Her stomach cramped and a scream rose to her throat that emerged as nothing but a horrified squeak. *Oh God no. No. How could it . . .* She tried to think. She tried to *think* but her thoughts scattered like dry leaves on a windy day. Kandace leaned over and wretched on the ground, moaning as she rolled back, her head hitting the ground again.

Behind her, the brush rustled as it was moved back aside and then the foliage fell back into place, closing out the moonlight to the space where she'd been left . . . alone.

The shock that had ricocheted through her at the sight of its face calmed to a dull throb of faraway concern. Her limbs felt weighted, her vision growing hazy again. *Dreamboat. Little Dreamboat.* The wind screamed past and the rainfall

7

intensified, mixing with the retreating drumbeat. Competing noises echoed around her, blending, fading, growing louder and then fading again, lulling her to sleep. A pain ripped down her abdomen and she emitted a low moan.

Mommy, I want my mommy. She *craved* the safety of her mother's embrace. *Yes,* she could admit to that longing now. She should have acknowledged it sooner. She should have grieved it and let it go. Oh, if only . . . if only.

Her hand went to her rounded stomach, which was drenched in blood. Another pain tore through her. *I'll do better,* she thought. *If given the chance, I'll do better. For both of us.*

Kandace used the final vestige of strength to curl her body, bringing her knees upward, and closing her eyes.

The drumbeat faded, along with everything else.

CHAPTER ONE

Present Day

"*I*s that it?" Haddie asked.

Scarlett glanced in her rearview mirror to see her seven-year-old daughter leaning forward, gaze focused on the statuesque white mansion, its gables rising proudly into the blue, California sky.

"Yes," Scarlett said, stopping the car and staring at the structure. It'd seemed less imposing in the pictures she'd looked at online. "Lilith House," she muttered. "Or at least it was. We can give it our own name though—anything we want. We can call it . . . Sunnyside Manor, or Happy Hill House . . . Haven Cottage maybe?" She shot Haddie a grin. "What do you think about that?"

"I don't think you can just change a thing's name," Haddie murmured, her eyes still glued to the house. "Can you?"

Scarlett turned to look at her daughter's serious expression. Haddie was always serious though. Too serious, Scarlett sometimes worried. *An old soul,* her friend Merrilee called her. She smiled, smoothing a lock of white-blonde hair away from her child's angelic face. So serious. So beautiful. "I'll check my rulebook on that, okay, kiddo? For now"—she unhooked her seatbelt—"let's go introduce ourselves."

"Okay, Mommy."

Scarlett set their suitcases down on the front porch as she input the code the bank had given her for the lockbox. The door let out a long, piercing squeak when Scarlett pushed it open, as though it had been rudely awakened from a deep sleep and was voicing its complaint at the intrusion. Maybe it was. After all, the house had sat empty and abandoned for the last thirteen years.

Haddie walked stoically next to her as Scarlett entered, stopping in the middle of the two-story foyer and looking around. A grand staircase curved upward directly in front of them, cobwebs stretching from the railing to the walls and glinting in the sunlight pouring through the large arched window above. The wallpaper—what she assumed had once been bright pink and yellow roses—was now dull and peeling. It gave off the sinister effect of dead flowers climbing the walls. A series of squeaks sounded from above and Haddie moved closer to her mother's side. *Surely ghosts reside here,* she thought, or at least, that was the overall effect of the house where time had apparently stood still for over a decade. *I've moved my daughter into what appears to be the quintessential haunted house,* she realized with an internal grimace.

Her childhood friend Kandace had been here once. To think of that felt surreal. What was her reaction when she'd first stepped into this foyer? Had she thought it elegant? Probably not. Kandace had been used to homes far more opulent than this one.

"People died here, Mommy?" Haddie asked, bringing Scarlett from her wandering thoughts.

Scarlett's gaze flew to her daughter. She must have heard her talking to Merrilee. *Damn.* She paused for a moment. "Not in the house, baby. But yes, there was a fire in a building out back. The students and the staff living here at the time were in that building and they didn't get out."

Haddie's forehead screwed up uncertainly. She glanced at Scarlett as though she was only telling her a partial truth. Scarlett opened her mouth to offer some reassuring words when Haddie spoke first.

"What's that smell?" Haddie wrinkled her pert little nose. Apparently, her daughter had moved on from the fire . . . and the deaths. Scarlett was only too happy to change the subject, even if the new topic was unpleasant as well.

"I don't know," Scarlett said, though she'd noticed it too. "Something might have died in the walls a long time ago. We'll have to get an exterminator out here." Or maybe it was just the mildew-ridden carpet she spotted through the open door of the room to their right. She set down their suitcases and went down on one knee in front of her little girl, looking

11

into her wide green eyes and giving Haddie her most cheerful smile. "We've got a lot of cleaning up to do around here, but I promise you this is going to feel like home before we know it, okay?" She held up her hand, curling all her fingers inward, except her pinkie. "Pinkie promise."

The glint of a smile lit Haddie's face. A pinkie swear was like gospel to Haddie. She raised her own hand, linking her pinkie with her mother's and shaking.

****

$\mathscr{A}$n explosion of dust burst before Scarlett's face and she sputtered, flapping her hand around in an effort to dispel it. "God, this place is a mess," she muttered. Still, there was life left in the old girl and she'd found it in an attic suite of rooms, rich with exposed beams and what she assumed were original hardwood floors that would be gorgeous once they were re-sanded and stained. There was only one window in the bedroom she'd designated her own, but it had a lovely view of the gazebo and towering conifers behind the yard, and featured a beautiful stained-glass transom window that made rainbow-colored light flood the space.

Haddie's new room was much smaller, but spic and span now that she'd spent the morning cleaning it, and the shared bathroom—though rusty and under about seven layers of grime—was in working order.

They'd found the livable space after wandering what felt like an endless labyrinth of hallways and corridors, some doors still locked from within. Scarlett had mentally added a locksmith to her list of professionals to call, eyeing the antique glass doorknobs that featured large keyholes. When she'd bent and squinted one eye, pressing the other to the small opening, she'd discovered that a keyhole cover concealed her view.

The door to the attic stairs had stood wide open, that rainbow light shimmering on the walls, and drawing them toward its source. It had felt *right* the moment they'd entered.

Temporarily, she'd set them both up in what would be her bedroom and then started cleaning as soon as they'd woken up and disentangled themselves from the sleeping bags and blankets they'd snuggled under to camp on the floor. There were repairs over repairs to make, walls to repaint, fixtures to replace, furniture to buy, but for now . . . it was livable and that's all they needed to get the more major work underway. Which was a boon because before they'd arrived, she hadn't been sure the place was habitable, or whether they'd have to rent somewhere nearby as the remodeling work was being done. This attic space was going to save her a good amount of money—money that could be well used elsewhere.

At the thought of money—*the* money—a spear of guilt pierced her stomach, but she ignored it. She'd gone down this route. Too many times to count. She'd made her choice and she *wasn't* going to spend the rest of forever beating herself up over it.

She focused back on the room around her. Yes, this space would be perfect once there were events at Lilith House that would spill out to the surrounding grounds, some of which might go late into the night. She'd considered the idea of having a small house built on the property, but this was better, and she'd be spared another expense. The expansive attic space was practically soundproof with its thick walls and solid-wood floors, and being so far away from the main floor of the house. Another white noise machine or two, and she and Haddie would still have their own quiet privacy.

Scarlett had contacted a handyman in Farrow, the town beyond Lilith House, and he was supposed to be by that afternoon. She wasn't sure of the extent of his skills, but she hoped he could at least get the water running in the kitchen, tell her if the wiring seemed sound, and recommend a company that would do the heavier lifting of the substantial renovation she had planned, and a landscaping company that would help beautify the grounds.

The grounds were crucial to the success of the business she had planned.

Scarlett gave the top shelf of the closet another swipe, her hand bumping into something that slid backward, hitting the wall with a soft clink. Frowning, Scarlett went up on her toes, reaching blindly for the item, her fingers meeting what felt like cool metal. She gripped it, bringing her hand out and holding the item up in front of her.

A silver crucifix, darkened with tarnish.

Scarlett frowned, turning the item this way and that, taking in the fancy scrollwork, the lifelike metal rendering of Jesus, and the gemstones decorating all four points. They appeared to be diamonds, but Scarlett figured they were probably just cubic zirconia. Who would have left something as valuable as a diamond-encrusted crucifix behind?

For reasons she couldn't quite explain, a chill moved down her spine. She had the strange urge to drop the crucifix as though if she held it too long, it might scald her flesh. She'd thought of this place as a haunted house just the day before, and this discovery definitely did nothing to diminish the creep factor.

Just as she was about to toss it right back on the top shelf where she'd found it, she caught sight of something at the top of the cross where two winged angels were entwined. She brought it closer, studying the dark red substance staining the grooves of their wings. She used a fingernail to dig a speck of it out, looking at that too. Was that . . . it looked like dried blood. "Creep factor, officially heightened," she mumbled.

Scarlett placed the crucifix back on the highest shelf, pushing it all the way into the corner. For a moment she just stood there, considering . . . wondering if the creep factor might translate into good marketing. She'd read there were vague spooky legends about the canyon nearby, and of course, the fire in what had been a small chapel that killed the young women and staff who'd once lived here was absolutely tragic. But she hadn't thought about using any of those stories to her advantage. She hadn't thought about whether it could be an advantage at all . . . but *maybe*. Or was it obscene of her to even consider using the story of the lives lost on this property and whatever spooky tales may exist about the area for financial benefit? Scarlett stepped down off the stepstool. *Probably.* She'd have to learn more about the area and think about all that later. Because at the moment, there was nothing at all to market anyway.

At the moment, the place was only barely livable.

And likely haunted.

By benevolent spirits, if any at all, please and thank you.

Scarlett picked up the bottle of glass cleaner which was on the floor with the other sprays, sponges, scrub brushes, and old rags and took it to the window, misting some on the thick windowpanes and beginning to wipe them clean.

Through the glass she spotted Haddie in the dress she'd picked out that morning. Scarlett smiled, always enchanted by her girl's penchant for dresses, the frillier the better, clothing that seemed so at odds with her almost . . . somber personality. To see the way pink satin or white eyelet—or in today's case, blue gingham—made her daughter's green eyes widen with delight never ceased to bring forth a grin from Scarlett. She smiled now, watching as Haddie moved forward, stepping slowly into the trees. Her smile faded and she raised her hand to knock on the glass, to attempt to get her daughter's attention, to call her home, when she saw Haddie bend down and pluck something from the ground. A yellow flower. Haddie was being a little girl, collecting wildflowers. She'd never had a yard before. To Haddie, this must feel like one giant park.

Scarlett bit at her lip for a moment, conflicted as she stared at her child through the glass, watching her from afar. In some ways, it felt like a metaphor for her relationship with Haddie. She knew most mothers had a hard time letting go, but Scarlett had always had this vague sense that she couldn't hold on to Haddie even if she tried. It would be a useless attempt. In some way she couldn't explain, not even to herself, she knew Haddie existed on a plane all her own. She could walk beside her daughter through a mist she had no name for, she could love her fiercely—and she did, *oh she did*—but there was too much inexplicable distance between them to ever truly grasp the whole of her.

It worried her. On some level it broke her heart because she suspected she wasn't enough for Haddie. Her very deepest fear was that she wasn't the mother her child needed.

Haddie turned her head slightly and Scarlett drank in the angelic perfection of her. Even from this distance, Haddie was beautiful. Otherworldly. Not like Scarlett, who was pretty enough in an ordinary sort of way, but not stunning like her child. A beloved little alien girl who had somehow come *through* her but was not *of* her.

She brought her knuckle to the window, hesitating again just as her skin touched the cool glass. And yet . . . Haddie had always been a cautious child—*overly* cautious if anything. It wasn't her physical safety Scarlett obsessed over. So then . . . why not let her explore their new property a little? Haddie wasn't perfect, no seven-year-old was, but she'd always understood boundaries. She wouldn't venture far—it wasn't in her nature—and she'd likely be back in ten minutes, her fist full of flowers, a rare look of carefree happiness on her lovely face. At that thought, Scarlett's lips turned up. Slowly, she dropped her hand as her daughter slipped into the darkness of the trees.

CHAPTER TWO

$\mathcal{A}$ prickly bush caught on Haddie's pretty dress and she stopped, using her hand not holding the yellow flowers to pull out the thorn. The branch fell away as she continued on through the trees of the forest that stretched out behind the house.

Lilith House. Mommy had said they could change its name, but that felt wrong to Haddie. The house already knew its name. And anyway, even if someone changed *her* name— if they called her Emma or Sarah or something else—she'd still be who she was. Changing a name couldn't change anything else about a person or a thing. Haddie was very sure of that.

Mommy had funny feelings about the house, but Haddie didn't think her mommy knew why. Maybe it had to do with her friend who ran away from there, and the fire that happened afterward. She'd heard Mommy talking to Aunt

Merrilee about the girl named Kandace when she thought Haddie was sleeping. Haddie wasn't sure if the house was bad or not, but she got a heavy feeling in her bones when she looked at the doors at the end of the second-floor hallway. She didn't know if the house was mad or sad. She couldn't tell what the house was saying because it was still only waking up. Lilith House was confused, the same way Haddie sometimes felt when she blinked her eyes open after a dream and didn't know where she was.

The same feeling hung in the forest, but something else had pulled Haddie here. The shadow of the thing she'd seen darting through the trees as she'd stood in the window of her room. The thing that kept drawing closer and closer as if it wanted to get a look at the new people who had moved into Lilith House. It'd come right up to the burned-up building— the place that made Haddie's bones feel like lead—in the back before disappearing into the trees once more. It was like it was curious about them.

Haddie was curious too.

She stepped gingerly over a cluster of wild mushrooms, careful not to touch them because she felt their heaviness, glancing over her shoulder when she heard a soft crunch. Whatever was moving behind her slipped into the shadows. She only got the impression of darkness and the sharp edge of a horn or a tusk. Haddie's heart thumped and she swallowed, trying to pull forth the weight of the thing. Not the weight of its body, the feeling wasn't about that. Haddie didn't have a better word for the sense she got about things. She only knew that when her bones got heavy, when her whole body felt full-up with the weight of a person or a thing so that she couldn't even move, that there was badness in it. The opposite of her mommy who felt as light as a feather to Haddie. So light that when Haddie was around her, she sometimes felt like she was floating. Her mommy was good and . . . *light*. As weightless as the sparkly bubbles Haddie blew with the big yellow wand Gram gave her.

She stood still, trying, *trying* to measure the weight of the thing behind her, but could not. Something was wrong. Or . . . different. She couldn't get a sense of what and that made Haddie's skin prickle even while her curiosity kicked up.

What are you? Why can't I feel you?

She'd experienced this before. Sometimes with people she passed on the street, and once with a little boy who was in her music class. Mostly, she got it with very, very old people. Sometimes those old people died very soon after, like Mrs. Klaus in the apartment building where she used to live. She wondered if the thing behind her was very, very old and about to die.

She stepped forward, and the thing followed. She bent down to pick a white flower with a black center growing in the shade of a giant tree, adding it to the yellow ones clutched in her fist. Mommy would like these. That worried look she got on her face sometimes when she stared at Haddie and didn't know Haddie could see her would vanish momentarily. Mommy would smile and put the flowers in water on the windowsill the way she did when Haddie used to bring a rose home from Gram's garden, and their new house would feel a little more like home.

As Haddie stood straight, a slow drumming sounded behind her along with words, said in a low, scratchy voice. It wasn't singing . . . but more like the way the men in the church had sounded at Mrs. Klaus's funeral as they walked with smoking sticks down the aisle behind her casket.

Haddie didn't know what the words the thing behind her meant, but they made her bones heavy. They made her bones so heavy they *ached*. The words were bad words. They meant something bad and terrible. Haddie barely noticed the flowers drifting to the forest floor as, trembling, she turned around to face the thing saying the words she didn't know but could *feel*. Her chest rose and fell rapidly as the drumbeat and the words grew quieter, moving away from her in the other direction, deeper into the cool darkness. Whatever had been following her was leaving.

Haddie stood still for several moments, the ache in her bones subsiding. Movement to her right caught her attention and she turned to see a red fox staring at her, its head cocked to the right. The red fox felt light. It didn't mean her any harm. She wondered if the dark thing did. Haddie let out a slow breath, turning toward Lilith House and making her way back to her mother.

CHAPTER THREE

Scarlett set the box of dishes on the kitchen counter and wiped her hands down her thighs. That was the last of the boxes, all they'd shoved into the trunk of her SUV before leaving their small rental apartment in the Playa Vista area of Los Angeles. The moving truck would arrive in a few days with their beds, mattresses, and a few other pieces of essential furniture. But all their other possessions now resided inside Lilith House. Or . . . Sunnyside Manor. Only, it was as though the house had silently declared its original name to her, planting it in her brain, because she couldn't stop thinking of it as such.

So, fine. "Lilith House it is," she told the walls of the estate. Haddie had been right. You couldn't just change a thing's name.

She turned, heading out of the kitchen toward the stairs when she caught sight of a man, standing stock-still in the foyer, his gaze fixed on her, expression filled with what could only be described as hostility. She let out a startled breath, bringing her hand to her chest. "My goodness, you scared me." She released a nervous laugh as she shook her head, attempting to shrug off the fear that had spiraled through her veins. "You must be Louis. Thanks for coming." No *thanks for not knocking and scaring me half to death. And mean mugging me before we've even met.*

The man narrowed his eyes even further. "I'm not Louis. Who are you?" he demanded.

Scarlett frowned, unease lifting inside her. She eyed this stranger. He was tall and broad-shouldered. Handsome in a rough sort of way, though maybe the roughness could mostly be attributed to his expression and surly attitude. "Excuse me? This is my home. Who are *you* and why are you here?"

"Your *home?*" He glanced around as though he might be checking whether or not he'd stepped inside the wrong dwelling.

Perhaps he'd mistakenly ended up at *this* abandoned mansion in the middle of nowhere when he'd meant to end up at another.

Scarlett cleared her throat. "Yes, my home. I bought Lilith House and moved in yesterday. Now I think you better tell me who you are and why you're in my house, or I'm going to have to call the police." She pulled her cell phone from her pocket and held it up, her thumb poised to dial 9-1-1. She glanced at it, suddenly noticing she had absolutely no service.

"There are no cell towers in Farrow," the man said. "Didn't anyone tell you?"

"Uh, no," she said, looking stupidly at her phone again as if he might be lying and those three bars would suddenly appear.

He stared at her for several beats before a muscle in his cheek ticked. "In any case, I am the police." He let out a long breath, running a hand through his short dark hair. "Deputy West."

"I see." She lowered her eyes to his T-shirt and downward to his jeans, landing on his boot-clad feet and then raising to his eyes once again. *Green.* While Haddie's eyes were a pale sea-glass green, this man's eyes were the green of pine trees in a sunlit forest. *Beautiful.* His lashes were thick and curled upward. Too pretty for a boy. Too soft for such a hard-looking man. Yeah, he was handsome, she'd give him that. But she didn't trust handsome men—in her experience, it was too easy for them to lie.

Or maybe she was just gullible.

Anyway.

"Off duty," he explained, and it took her a moment to re-follow the trail of the conversation. He'd obviously read her unspoken question as to his lack of a uniform.

"Is it typical that members of the police department around here walk into private residences without knocking?"

"Sheriff's department. And I hadn't heard that anyone bought this place."

Scarlett returned her useless phone to her pocket. "Was I supposed to make an official announcement to the authorities?"

That muscle tic again and a slow release of breath. "We got off on the wrong foot. I apologize for entering without knocking. I saw your car and, well . . ." His words dwindled. *Thought someone was breaking in?* she surmised would have been the end of that sentence if he'd finished. He walked toward her and though she was tempted to step back, she held her ground. Deputy West extended his hand. "Welcome to town." His tone conveyed anything but congeniality.

"Gee, thanks," she muttered. She eyed his hand warily and then reached out her own. His hand enfolded hers easily, his skin browned and slightly calloused, fingers masculine and sturdy. An unwanted shiver moved through her blood. "Scarlett Lattimore."

He nodded once, dropping her hand. "Just you?"

"What?"

"Just you living here?"

"Oh, um, no. I have a daughter, Haddie. She's seven."

He kept watching her as if waiting for her to continue, noting, she was sure, that there was no *Mr.* Lattimore. Much to her dismay, heat rose in her cheeks, and she hated herself for it.

Being a single mother is not *a scarlet letter.* Though if it was, she'd been aptly named to play the role.

A knock sounded at the door, causing Scarlett to jump, bringing her hand to her chest *again.* God, she must seem like a scared deer. "Come in," she called, a little too exuberantly.

Deputy West turned as the door swung inward and a wiry, dark haired young man entered, his face breaking into a smile. "Hey there, Cam. Didn't expect you to be here."

"Louis," Detective West—*Cam*—greeted, his tone several shades warmer than when he'd addressed her, Scarlett noted. "How are you?"

25

"Well now, can't complain much. How's that hot water heater?"

"Better. Thanks for helping out with that."

Louis nodded and then looked at Scarlett. "Mrs. Lattimore?"

"Scarlett." She stepped forward, grasping Louis's outstretched hand. "Thanks for coming."

"You bet. Damn near fell over when I heard someone bought the old girl. Musta been a quick sale, no one's buzzin' about it in town." He looked around, his eyes going from the stairway to the walls to the ceiling and then back to Scarlett. "Sure do have your work cut out for you, sprucing the place up."

"I'm hoping that's all it needs—some heavy sprucing. That's why I called, so you could tell me exactly what I'm looking at here."

"You didn't have the place appraised before you bought it?" the deputy asked, raising a dark brow.

"Louis is right, it happened quickly," Scarlett said. As if it was any of his business *why* she'd bought this place. "It seemed like a deal whether it needed major fixes or not. So I jumped on it. The property itself is pretty fantastic."

The deputy glanced out the window, a shadow of something Scarlett didn't know how to identify darkening his features for a moment and then smoothing out. He offered no comment.

"Course the place does have a history," Louis said, eyeing the deputy. "Figure that's why it's sat empty for so long. People hear what happened here and shy away, you know?" He scratched at his cheek. "That and it being so remote and all."

Deputy West shot Louis what looked like a warning glance. "Well," Scarlett said, "I was looking for remote. And I've heard there are stories about this place—some of them bad—but that sort of thing doesn't bother me. Houses have history. People have history too, some of it unpleasant. It doesn't make any of us less valuable." She glanced back and forth between them. Deputy West narrowed his eyes, staring at her with even more directness. She looked away from that laser focus.

"True enough, I guess," Louis said. "So, uh"—he held up the toolbox in his hand—"should we get started?"

"I'll show myself out," Deputy West said.

"Yes, absolutely. Feel free to come and go as you please," Scarlett said, adding a note of overly sweet sarcasm.

The deputy's full lips twitched so quickly that if Scarlett had blinked, she'd have missed it. Perhaps the man had the smidgeon of a personality after all—somewhere deep down inside. Deep, deep down. He gave a short nod. "Ma'am. Louis."

"See ya, Cam."

She watched him walk away and Scarlett tamped down another wave of annoyance as the door shut behind the deputy. She mustered a wide smile, turning to Louis. "Okay then, how about we start with the plumbing? Also, are you able to get me set up with Wi-Fi?"

CHAPTER FOUR

Thirteen Years Ago

$\mathcal{K}$andace stepped into the foyer of Lilith House, glancing disinterestedly around. Stuffy. Expensive. She yawned. God, if one lavish hellhole had turned her into what she was, what made them think another was going to reform her?

What a joke.

The man who'd picked her up at the airport set her suitcase down and gave her a stiff nod. "Good luck, ma'am."

"Catch ya later, Eddie." She winked and took satisfaction from the blush that burned his ashen face. "Yes, ma'am." He turned with an awkward shuffle and exited through the front door.

Kandace stood there for a moment, an unfamiliar feeling of doubt settling in her limbs. What the fuck was she supposed to do? Go looking for someone to greet her and tell her where she would be sleeping?

Her gaze moved over the wall to her right where a large crucifix hung next to the portrait of a severe-looking man. Her eyes lingered on him for a moment, the hairs on the back of her neck rising. She looked away, leaning slightly to the left so she could peer down the hallway beyond.

She cupped her hand over her mouth. "Helloooo," she called. "Anybody home?" For several beats only silence filled the space, but then she heard the slow click of footsteps coming toward her on the polished wood floor.

For some unknown reason, nerves fluttered in Kandace's stomach and she brought her hand to her midsection as though she could press it away. *This place is fucking creepy,* she thought.

A moment later a slender, older woman appeared in the doorway, stopping and perusing her slowly, a look of pure disdain on her pinched face. She was wearing black from head to toe—skirt, sweater, and shoes—but had a string of creamy white pearls around her long, pale neck. Her hair, a deep silver, was pulled up into a tight chignon and she didn't appear to wear a stitch of makeup, her lips thin and bloodless, the only color in her face, her startling golden eyes, the color of which Kandace could see even from where she was standing. She moved forward slowly, and Kandace watched the woman who somehow seemed to both glide and move stiffly as though she was standing on a wheeled platform and someone had given her a push. "You must be Ms. Thompson. I'm Ms. Wykes, the headmistress of Lilith House."

Kandace smirked and reached out her hand. "How do you do?" she said sarcastically.

Ms. Wykes tilted her head, her lips turning upward, though the rest of her face remained unchanged.

"Oh dear." She clicked her tongue. "Insolent, aren't you? No mind. We've dealt with worse than you here at Lilith House. You'll be following rules like a good little girl before we all know it. Follow me now." And with that, she turned, doing that stiff glide as her short heels clacked on the floor.

A good little girl? This bitch had to be kidding. Kandace had half a mind to turn on her tennis shoe and take her insolent behind right out of this weird-ass place. But there was the court order . . . and the fact that she'd basically burned every bridge she'd once had access to.

Nine months, she reminded herself. She just had to complete one semester of school here at Lilith House and then she could resume her life. *This is your final chance,* her mother had said. *After this, there'll be no more.* And for whatever reason—instinct, the tone in her mother's voice, pressure from Kandace's new stepfather, or likely all of the above—Kandace knew her mother meant what she said.

Kandace followed Ms. Wykes through the foyer and down a long hallway beyond. The older woman disappeared through an open door and Kandace entered after her into what was a relatively large office, featuring a bay window that revealed a view of the forest behind the house. A tall, well-muscled brute of a man with a shaved head and a keloid scar running down his cheek stood next to an ornate mahogany desk, while Ms. Wykes stood in front of it, her hands clasped. Off to her right was a wall of built-in shelves filled with hardbacked books, and in the corner stood a black metal birdcage with two bluebirds perched on a branch that extended from one side of the cage to the other. In the midst of the heavy furnishings and almost-masculine feel of the space, the soft-colored winged creatures were especially lovely and an inexplicable mournfulness rose inside Kandace.

Lovely things are not meant to last here. Kandace's expression twitched with the unsettling thought that seemed to come both from nowhere and everywhere around her like a whispering chorus of ghosts in the walls.

"Put your cell phone in that box," Ms. Wykes instructed, pointing at a wooden box attached to the wall next to the door, a slot in its top.

"I prefer to keep my phone."

"Your preferences are no longer relevant, Ms. Thompson. Put your phone in the box. Technology is a tool of the devil and we resist its temptation here at Lilith House. Your phone will be returned to you upon the completion of your term."

A tool of the devil? What the fuck was this woman smoking? "What if I want to contact my parents?"

"We have paper and pens. I personally deliver the outgoing mail to the post office every third Monday of the month. In addition, I will be sending a bi-weekly update to your parents concerning your performance here at Lilith House."

Paper and pens? Outgoing mail? *Jesus.* They may as well have shipped her back to the 1800s.

You can do it. It's temporary. Who was she going to call anyway? Her service had gone out completely several miles up the road. Not only that, but because of that whole *burnt bridges* thing, she couldn't think of one person who would miss her much. Aside from her dealer.

Kandace narrowed her eyes, hesitating, but finally pulling her phone from her pocket, turning it off, and dropping it in the box. She'd play the game—for now. It was always easier to break the rules if you were flying under the radar. And clearly they were big on *rules* here.

Ms. Wykes nodded to the burly man and he approached her, grabbing her arm as he used his other hand to pat her down. "Hey!" she yelled, attempting to twist out of his grasp, but he was far too strong to fight against. He pulled out the baggie of five joints and several ecstasy tablets she had in her pocket and tossed them backward onto the desk before releasing her. Kandace glared at him, straightening her clothes. *Shit.*

Ms. Wykes picked up the baggie, holding it up for a moment, and then placing it back on the edge of her desk without comment. "Sit down," she said, indicating a chair in front of the desk. Kandace hesitated, glancing at the man who was watching her with a small smirk on his face, his arms now crossed over his square chest. Kandace's gut gave a slow roll. Something felt very off. She sat in the chair, crossing her legs, as Ms. Wykes turned and walked to the birdcage, opening the tiny door and removing one of the bluebirds. It sat perched on her hand as she pet its shiny head slowly with one long-nailed, bony finger.

"Do you know the story of Lilith, Ms. Thompson?"

"Lilith? Lilith who? Never heard of her."

Ms. Wykes gave her a small, cold smile. "I *have* never heard of her," Ms. Wykes corrected. "We speak in full sentences here, Ms. Thompson." She paused, running her finger over the bird's head again. "I'm speaking of the original Lilith, of course. Adam's first wife." She sighed. "Regrettably, she was a sinful and assertive woman who didn't understand her place, instead choosing to rebel against God and her husband."

"Sounds like my kind of girl."

"Indeed," she purred.

Ms. Wykes fingered the pearls at her neck for a moment. "Of course, God saw her for who she was and replaced her with another woman, a woman of purity and grace. A woman suitable to stand by Adam's side."

Ms. Wykes stepped forward and drew a large pair of shiny silver shears from a cup holder on her desk. Kandace's heart leapt and her muscles tensed, and for the first time since she'd stepped into the house, she felt a frisson of real fear.

Ms. Wykes used the pointy tip of the scissors to stroke the bird's head, once and then again. The bird stared at Kandace with one wide black eye as if imploring her for help. Kandace's fingers curled around the wooden arms of the chair, body held taut. "You see, Ms. Thompson, women such as Lilith simply cannot be allowed to fly free and spread their depravity. They simply cannot infect men with their sin and filth." She brought the scissors up and in one quick movement, captured one of the bird's wings at the place where the wing met the body and clipped it off. The bird screamed in agony as Kandace let out a shriek of her own, drawing back, while simultaneously reaching for the bloody bird Ms. Wykes was now holding by its feet as it tried desperately to escape, flapping its one wing frantically, its shrill squeals filling the room. Ms. Wykes moved the scissors to the other wing and Kandace jumped up. "No!" she wailed, reaching forward as the muscled man who had stood to the side of the desk grabbed her, and effortlessly held her back as Ms. Wykes clipped the bird's other wing. Then in one quick flick of her wrist, she whipped the bird's body away. It hit the wall with a hard smack, falling to the floor where it lay bleeding, its scream diminished to only a small whimper, its breast rising and falling with its final quickened breaths.

"What's wrong with you, you crazy bitch?" Kandace screamed just as the man holding her threw her forward so she collided with the desk. Before she could even begin to turn, he was behind her, slamming her upper body onto the hard wood and holding her down by her hair. It felt as though a steel bar held her still and all she could do was flail helplessly just as the bluebird had done.

On the floor in a puddle of blood, the now silent wingless creature stared, its eye cloudy, chest still rising and falling, but slowly now. So very slowly. *Oh God, oh God.* Kandace's soul shuddered, though she refused to cry in front of this evil bitch and her bloodhound. She *refused.*

Ms. Wykes stepped into her line of sight, blocking the bird and bending down so that her face was level with Kandace's. *I will not cry. I will not cry.* Kandace stared icily back at Ms. Wykes, and Ms. Wykes regarded her for a moment. "Mm," she hummed. "I can see you're more defiant than some, more difficult to break." She brought the still-bloody scissors up. "But mark my words, Ms. Thompson. You will break. You will break in ways you never imagined. And when you leave Lilith House, you will return to your parents the obedient little girl they've been promised."

Terror pooled in Kandace's stomach as Ms. Wykes raised the scissors and then brought them down toward the back of her head. Kandace let out a shocked cry as they snapped shut with the same loud metallic snip that had sounded when she'd used them to clip the bird's wings.

The pressure lifted on her head and she realized that the man was no longer holding her by her hair. Ms. Wykes tossed something on the desk next to her as Kandace struggled to rise. She blinked, reality crashing in around her when she realized what it was: her long blonde ponytail.

The man yanked her by the back of her shirt and she stumbled upright, taking a step backward, her hand going to the empty spot at the back of her head. She gasped out a breath. "You cut my hair." The words sounded breathy, disbelieving.

"Vanity will not be tolerated here, Ms. Thompson, nor will sinful behavior of any sort."

Kandace stared at her. She couldn't remember the last time anything had shocked her. Ms. Wykes was right about one thing: Kandace had become desensitized to sinful behavior, hers or anyone else's, but she could honestly say she was shocked now. Stunned and deeply frightened. Her eyes darted to the large man, a glint in his eyes that told her he'd be only too happy to exert whatever physical force was necessary to ensure she was cooperative.

But Kandace was seldom obedient. She let out a slow, controlled breath. They didn't know who they were dealing with. Not yet. But they would. She swore it. They would.

"I'll report this," she said. "I'll tell them what you did today. Everyone will know. They'll shut you down."

Ms. Wykes smiled and for the first time it met her eyes, her expression one of genuine amusement. But as quickly as that, it vanished. "You will? Oh dear," she said, her tone dripping with sarcasm. "I'm sure your mother will believe you. I'm quite certain you've never lied. I imagine her trust in you is veritably unshakeable." She tapped a bony finger against her thin, blanched lips. "You, a disappointment who showed up here at Lilith House high and practically hallucinating"—she nodded to the baggie of marijuana and pills—"when the court has made it clear that should you be caught with drugs, the chance you've been given here at Lilith House will be rescinded in exchange for jail time. In exchange for a permanent record."

Kandace stared at her, wondering if jail time would be better . . . or worse. She knew what her mother would say. *God, you're such an embarrassment.* The words came back to her now, cutting, the same way they had when her mother had hissed them at her.

"Now," Ms. Wykes said, brushing her hands together as though what had happened was no more than a casual, though slightly unpleasant, welcome that should be brushed aside. "You are in the attic with two other young women. Jasper will show you to your room."

Kandace's mind raced. She had to find a way out of here . . . she needed to talk to the other young women and find out more about this place, find out if this was the regular welcome wagon, find out . . . everything she could. "My suitcase is still in the foyer," she said.

"Your things have been burned," Ms. Wykes responded. "You will be given a uniform, and a modest sleep outfit, no more." She grabbed something off her desk—*a silver crucifix*—raising it high in both hands, her voice booming, eyes burning with sudden passion. "And He said to them, 'Take care, and be on your guard against all covetousness, for one's life does not consist in the abundance of his possessions!'" The gemstones on the crucifix flashed in the lamplight as she lowered her arms, her eyes narrowing as that cold smile turned her lips up again.

Kandace moved her gaze slowly from Ms. Wykes to the bird lying on the floor in the pool of blood. It was no longer moving.

It had died.

The other bird sat alone behind its bars, staring longingly out the window at the forest beyond.

CHAPTER FIVE

$\mathcal{S}$carlett took a sip of wine, glancing at Haddie across the card table she'd set up in the kitchen—along with two metal fold-up chairs—where they could eat meals. They'd dined on canned chili and crackers for dinner and had been living off items from the small box of non-perishable food she'd brought from their old apartment for the last few days. She'd have to venture into town in the morning to stock up on some more, especially now that the gas line was working and they had an operational stove and running water in the kitchen. The electricity had checked out, though Louis had had to reset several of the breakers, but once that was done, the old refrigerator had hummed to life. It was smelly and dirty inside, but it wasn't anything some elbow grease and a quart of bleach couldn't fix, so she'd take on that task right before she grocery shopped.

Haddie was deeply focused on her drawing tablet on the table in front of her, her colored pencil scraping softly over the paper. Scarlett clicked the mouse on the laptop in front of her, opening the program she was using to design the planned remodels on the house. She raised her gaze, glancing around the room. The size would work for her needs, but the entire layout would have to be reworked, the space gutted. Then she'd bring in industrial appliances, a prepping station . . .

The scraping of Haddie's pencil drew her attention, the back and forth motion growing ever faster as her daughter worked diligently to color something in. Scarlett focused on the picture, what looked to be a page almost completely covered in black. She frowned, leaning forward. "What are you drawing, honey?"

Haddie blinked, her hand stilling as she looked up at her mother. Scarlett frowned, taking in the drawing from upside down. "Are those . . . horns? What is that, baby?"

Haddie glanced down at her drawing, looking at it curiously as if seeing it for the first time, as if she hadn't been the one to create it. She tilted her head. "I don't know."

Scarlett watched her for a moment. Her daughter's imagination had always been vivid. But though her drawing looked particularly morose, she didn't appear distressed and Scarlett released a slow breath, and then took a sip of wine as Haddie went back to her work.

"See anything cool while you've been out exploring the property?"

Haddie stilled for a moment. "Just the flowers I brought you. And . . . something with horns." She gave a small nod down to her picture, her lashes lowering. "And a fox."

Scarlett frowned. "Oh . . . honey, maybe you should stay out of the trees. There are probably lots of wild animals that live in there."

"The fox didn't want to hurt me, Mommy." She said it with the surety of a sage, as if it was an inarguable fact. As if she'd communicated with the fox and it'd told her of its intentions.

Scarlett regarded Haddie. She'd always seemed to sense things about people, and yes, even animals. Sometimes she went right up to a dog, kneeled down, and began petting him, and other times, she'd pull Scarlett to cross the street if one was coming toward them. She responded the same way with people. She either liked them immediately, or never warmed to them at all.

Merrilee had once asked Scarlett if she thought Haddie might be on the autism spectrum, but Scarlett had rejected that. It wasn't that she was in denial, it was just that no one knew Haddie better than she did. Haddie had a vivid inner world, that was true. But she was *overly* emotional if anything. She felt things deeply and was keenly intelligent. She could be . . . secretive, but she also wore her heart on her sleeve. Plus, she had never had a problem with eye contact as many children on the spectrum did, in fact she seemed to seek it out. Sometimes Scarlett was sure the little girl was looking straight into her soul. Haddie was . . . unique, but Scarlett didn't think her uniqueness could be tested or quantified. Haddie was just . . . *Haddie*.

She'd like to ask Haddie's father about the things that made their daughter special, to find out if it might be something genetic, but of course, that ship had sailed. She'd promised never to contact him again and signed her name on the dotted line.

Very literally.

"Maybe from now on just . . . keep to the edge of the woods, okay? I want you to be able to hear me if I call."

"All right, Mommy." The pencil sounded on the page again, this time with less intensity. Without looking up from her drawing, Haddie asked, "How long did your friend Kandace live here, Mommy?"

Surprised by the question, Scarlett paused. Had she told Haddie that? Well, obviously, she must have. Or once again, maybe she'd overheard her talking to Merrilee about Kandace. Haddie could be so quiet it was easy to forget little ears were always listening. *Kandi.* "Only a short time. Less than a year."

"When this was a . . . school?" The pencil continued to scratch softly on the paper, a lulling sound now that Haddie moved it more slowly, more steadily, and with less fervor.

"Hmm-hmm." She glanced out the window behind Haddie where the forest met the sky, thinking of her childhood friend. Her first real confidante. When Scarlett's father had passed away suddenly and unexpectedly, Scarlett's—mostly unskilled—mother had had to go back to work. She'd taken a housekeeping position at the Thompson family estate, and Scarlett, often trailing along behind her, had befriended Kandace, the only Thompson child, who was three years Scarlett's senior. Scarlett had been grieving her father, and with his passing, had been thrust into what felt like an entirely different life. Kandi had taken her under her wing and offered the healing gift of friendship. While Scarlett's mother cleaned, Scarlett and Kandace would play make-believe and dress up in the expansive attic, usually donning one of the five wedding dresses Kandace's mother had gotten married in over the past thirteen years of Kandace's life.

Despite Kandace's older age, and her often seemingly indifferent attitude, Scarlett knew that deep down, Kandace was tender and kind. She'd been desperately looking for validation—attention and affection—and never receiving it from the one person who should have given it naturally: her mother.

It was no wonder she'd made the choices she had. It was no wonder she'd sought "love" in all the wrong places. It was no wonder she'd ended up at Lilith House, a reform school for wayward girls.

Even after Scarlett's mother took a new position with a different family, she and Kandace kept in touch—even if months would pass between phone calls—until right before Kandace left for Lilith House. Lilith House where Kandace had eventually run away from, never to be seen again. Scarlett had known that Kandace had headed down a dangerous path, she'd known that Kandace was skating the razor's edge of decisions that had consequences she'd never come back from. She'd hoped . . . along with Kandace's mother, she was sure, that Lilith House would help put her back on the straight and narrow. *Instead . . .*

Scarlett's eyes again went to the edge of the vast forest beyond. *Where did you go?* she wondered. *Where are you now?* They'd searched the woods. She wasn't there. But being *here* made Scarlett feel somehow closer to the troubled girl who'd shared her heart with her, and few others.

"Tell me about Ruby Sugar."

Scarlett smiled. Haddie knew about Ruby Sugar, the name Scarlett had chosen for her business, but like all of Haddie's favorite stories, she liked to hear it being retold. "Kandace and I played a game where we were wedding designers. We used our names to create the company name. Ruby is another word for Scarlett, and sugar is the main ingredient in candy." *Or . . . Kandi.*

Haddie smiled. "I like that, Mommy."

Scarlett smiled back. She did too. Especially because when she'd seen the ad for Lilith House and recognized it as the school Kandace had been banished to, and then run away from, she'd gotten a feeling that was so strong, so absolute, that she'd picked up the phone before she even made a conscious decision to do so.

A sound caught her attention and she turned her head toward the wall where she thought it was coming from, listening intently. It sounded like . . . faraway screaming, the rising wail of human misery. Scarlett stilled, goosebumps rising on her skin. The noise subsided, but another one picked up. This time it sounded like crying—the very distant sobs of an infant.

"What in the world?" she whispered. "Haddie, do you hear that?"

Haddie looked up from her drawing. "What, Mommy?"

"It sounded like crying. It must have been the wind, but . . ." She shook her head, mustering a smile for her daughter. "Wow, kind of spooky the way a breeze sounds coming through these old walls, huh?"

"It's just a memory, Mommy."

Scarlett frowned. "What do you mean, Haddie? *My* memory?" Did Haddie think she was hearing things coming from her own mind?

"Lilith House's memory."

Those goosebumps rose higher. "What do you mean, baby?"

Haddie shrugged, focusing back on her drawing, humming softly.

Scarlett stared at her daughter for a moment, opening her mouth to demand that she explain her comment further, but Haddie seemed perfectly content and Scarlett didn't want to push her child and potentially alarm her when there was really nothing to be alarmed *about*. Add that comment to the list of hundreds like it she'd heard from her over the years. She turned her head, staring out the window, mostly unseeing for another few minutes, attempting to warm from the chill that had settled under her skin as Haddie continued to draw. No more sounds came from the walls. Trees shifted outside, swaying gently. There was definitely a strong breeze.

Finally, convinced she'd heard nothing more than wind rattling the rafters, she looked at her computer screen, rubbing at her eye as she tried to find the motivation to do some more work on the remodeling plans. She drummed her fingers on the table for a moment, instead opening a browser window and typing in the name of their new house. Several links popped up immediately. *Thank you, Louis, for bringing Lilith House into the modern century.*

She'd looked Lilith House up once before from their apartment in LA, but more so to view as many pictures of the interior as possible . . . to determine if it was right for what she had planned. In all honesty, part of her had been hoping it wouldn't be. She'd come upon the sale so unexpectedly, and the idea that had almost immediately planted itself in her head felt far too ambitious . . . ill-advised . . . crazy, even. But also . . . *right.* She'd never been particularly impulsive, and when she had been, she'd usually ended up regretting it in at least some way or another. But the more she'd clicked through the available pictures, traveling remotely from room to room then each outdoor space, the more her excitement level doubled, tripled, *soared.* It was as though someone was quietly, but urgently, nudging her along.

At the time it was the physical attributes of the house and property she'd been most interested in, so she hadn't taken much time to find out more about the history. She did that now, perusing slowly through the websites that mentioned the house, gathering its history.

Before the California Gold Rush in 1849, hunters had flocked to the state to take advantage of its enormous wealth of resources. One such man, Hubert Bancroft, made his fortune as a fur trader and in 1876, then built what was later named Lilith House. Though the family—who only grew wealthier as trade increased and they delved into other business ventures—would eventually build on and expand the dwelling, it was considered one of the finest mansions of its time, especially in a part of California that remained relatively poor.

When more recent generations, apparently lacking the same ingenuity and grit as their forefathers, all but squandered the family fortune, Black Monday was the final nail in the coffin of their wealth, and in 1987, Wendell Bancroft, now penniless, walked into the forest and hung himself from the branch of an ancient ponderosa pine. The bank took possession of the house.

In 1988, the leader of the Women's Ministry in Farrow reported receiving a directive from God that they purchase the Bancroft house and turn it into a Christian girl's school to house troubled young women. The Women's Ministry members pooled all of their resources, and with the townspeople's help, they raised the money for the purchase of the property. They named it Lilith House, and began accepting applicants in the fall of 1989.

Scarlett clicked on the image of an old brochure, a logo at the top with a tagline beneath: *My utmost for His glory!* She read it once and then again. What did that mean? Some Biblical phrase, she assumed. There was a block of copy below and she zoomed in on it: *Lilith House seeks to mend and rebuild the characters of girls who have consistently turned toward Satan and away from their Savior.*

Scarlett squinted one eye. Maybe she wasn't the most religious person—though she'd count herself as spiritual—but that copy sounded downright disturbing. Who read that and thought, *that's where I'm sending my child?*

Parents at the end of their ropes, she realized with a sigh.

She zoomed in on the photo on the cover. It was a group of twelve girls standing stoically in front of what was now Scarlett's home. As her eyes moved from face to face, a chill moved through her, born of *what* she wasn't entirely sure. These were supposedly defiant troublemakers, and yet each one of them looked empty-eyed and slack-jawed, staring vacantly at the camera. Her eyes were drawn to two young women at the edge of the group, one with vibrant red hair, and the other tall and dark haired. An older woman stood just next to them, wearing a gray dress and a choker of pearls. She was unsmiling, but there was an out-of-place . . . almost . . . perverse satisfaction in her expression that caused Scarlett to instinctively lean away from her photograph.

She glanced quickly through the rest of the brochure that talked about programs and amenities, and then looked back at the photo, averting her eyes from the gray-haired woman. The students were wearing burgundy uniforms and they all sported the same short haircuts devoid of any real style— which, was it just her, or was that sort of odd?—so Scarlett couldn't tell what year the photo might have been taken. Kandace wasn't in it, so it had to be taken prior to her arrival. She'd run away from Lilith House just before the fire broke out and the school shut its doors forever, so no brochure would have been created after Kandace left.

If it *was* taken just before Kandi arrived, these might be the twelve students who died tragically in the fire. Scarlett swallowed, her shoulders drawing up as her gaze again bounced from one unsmiling face to another. *Troubled girls, sent off by their families, never to return.*

She tried to picture beautiful, stylish Kandi in one of those boxy, nondescript uniforms, a choppy haircut, and no makeup and couldn't. Kandace, who had always favored tight jeans and bright lip gloss.

Scarlett did another Google search about the fire that had occurred in the small chapel that had once sat behind Lilith House. She knew the twelve young women living there at that time had died tragically in the fire, along with five staff members. *Seventeen souls had perished.* What she didn't know was that it was thought a lightning strike had caused the fire. "How awful," she murmured.

"What, Mommy?" Haddie asked.

Scarlett brought her head up. She'd become too involved in her search, fallen down the rabbit hole of Lilith House's past. But what a past it had. "Nothing, honey. But guess what? The movers are going to be here tomorrow with our beds and our other things," she said to Haddie with a smile.

"No more camping?"

Scarlett smiled. "No more camping." She tilted her head. "You know how I told you I thought we needed a whole new fresh start?"

Haddie nodded.

"Well, I think this house does too. Do you get that feeling, Haddie?"

"Yes, Mommy," she whispered.

Scarlett smiled, reaching across the table and taking her daughter's hand. "Then let's make it happen. Do you think we can do that?"

Haddie's expression faltered and she glanced out the window. "I hope so, Mommy," she whispered.

CHAPTER SIX

Thirteen Years Ago

$\mathcal{K}$andace stepped into the room where Jasper had led her up a narrow set of steps, the door clicking closed behind her as his heavy footsteps descended. She was in the attic. A wide-open space with a peaked, beamed ceiling and a partially stained-glass window at the end, the nighttime forest stretching as far as the eye could see.

Two girls sat on beds, their bodies still, staring at her with wide eyes. One of the girls, a chubby redhead nodded to an empty, twin-sized metal bed by the window. "That's yours, I guess," she said, her voice barely above a whisper.

Kandace looked at it, noting the clothes draped over the thin gray blanket: two all-red uniforms, two white nightgowns, two pairs of white cotton underwear, and a white bra. Sitting on the floor was a set of black penny loafers.

"Are you kidding me?" Kandace muttered softly, fingering the stiff fabric of the calf-length uniform skirt.

A red uniform? Seriously? *Dark* red, but still. She was sure it signified *something*. "Is fucking *red* the color designated to fallen women, or what?" she asked the other two girls, thinking of the story of Lilith Ms. Wykes had told.

"Shh," the tall girl with black hair hissed. "If they catch you swearing, there'll be a punishment."

Kandace looked back and forth between the girls, noting they had the same short, shaggy haircut she now had. Evidently, violent, forced haircuts were status quo at Lilith House. "What's with this fucked-up place?" she asked, lowering her voice as she swore again. "Is everyone here like Ms. Wykes? Because if so, we need to get PETA out here, stat."

The girls glanced at each other. "Not exactly but . . . they all follow her lead. They do whatever she says. Unquestioningly," the girl with black hair said. "The bird?" she asked.

Kandace nodded. "Is that part of every greeting?"

They shook their heads in unison. "We didn't experience that. Apparently, she saves it for the girls she thinks need an immediate lesson in compliance. But we've heard talk of that and . . . well, we were walking by her office earlier and heard the . . . noises."

Noises. That seemed like an insufficient word to describe the bird screams that still rang in her head.

Kandace turned toward the window, mentally shaking off the memory of what had been done to the poor creature . . . the awful sounds it had made as it died . . . She refused to think about it anymore, though. It had been done to control her, to horrify her, and Kandace refused to be controlled.

"Ms. Wykes told us about the natives who used to live in those woods," the redhead said, and when Kandace turned toward her, she glanced at the black-haired girl who nodded. "She said one's still out there, a war-mongering demon hungry for human flesh."

Kandace laughed, but when the other girls did not, she put her hands on her hips. "You can't be serious."

The black-haired girl shrugged. "I don't know, but a few girls have reported hearing drumming noises coming from the woods, and others have spotted . . . horns on walks around the property."

Kandace resisted rolling her eyes. "So we're not always kept on leashes?"

"The better your behavior, the more privileges you receive."

"Of course," she muttered. *Just like any proper prison.* She moved the clothes aside and sat down, the metal bedsprings squeaking. She sized up the girls, wondering if they were trustworthy or not then decided to risk it. "I'm Kandace Thompson, seventeen, from Los Angeles. I'm here because, according to my mother, and several judges, I'm a substance abuser and a thief. I flunked out of the sixth school my mother forced me into, and Lilith House is my last chance to straighten up, or I receive jail time for my most recent crime of stealing my latest stepfather's Lamborghini, taking it on a joyride while high on ecstasy—that I purchased by pawning several pieces of my mother's jewelry—totaling the car, and almost killing an eighty-year-old pedestrian. In my defense, that old lady came out of nowhere and was so hunched over, she barely appeared above my windshield."

Neither girl looked particularly impressed, which meant she was in good company. Unless they'd been broken in *or rather broken down.* The girls seemed so . . . meek. *That will never be me.*

"Who are you and what are you in for?" Kandace asked.

The red-headed girl spoke first. "I'm Aurora Duncan. I'm sixteen, from Arkansas. I got here three months ago. I'm a chronic cutter." She lifted her nightgown where seemingly hundreds of short red scars crisscrossed her milky thighs. "I'm self-destructive, socially awkward, and a rebellious academic failure, to name just a few."

"Wow. You sound like a royal mess."

"The mess part? Yeah." Aurora pulled her nightgown back down and drew her legs to her chest.

"How long are you here for?"

"Until I show improvement."

Kandace's eyes widened. "No specific end date? Wow, that's rough."

The girl nodded. "Some girls stay here for years. I'm pretty sure my parents would be just as happy if I never returned at all."

"I relate. My mother's latest husband is a judge and they're both worried sick that I'm going to publicly humiliate him and ruin his chances for re-election." She picked at a hangnail for a minute. "They sent me here as much to *reform* me as to hide me away." Kandace paused for a moment and then looked to the other girl. "And you?"

"I'm Sydney Dennison. I got here a few weeks after Aurora. I'm seventeen, from San Diego. Drugs, alcohol, chronic sexual promiscuity, general lowlife behavior."

"Nice." It seemed Kandace wasn't the only lowlife, after all. She leaned back on her elbows. "So . . . no one's ever reported this place? At the very least, seems like an animal cruelty charge would stick."

Sydney shrugged. "If they have, no one's believed them. We're not exactly . . . trustworthy people."

The truth of that statement trickled down Kandace's spine like a slow drip of ice-cold water. Damn, that truth hurt. Of course, Sydney was right. "No," Kandace murmured. "I get it. My mother wouldn't believe me at this point if I said the sky was blue. If I told her what happened when I got here, she'd say I was lying because they took my drugs." And truthfully? That was far from beneath her. She'd done a lot worse than that.

Aurora lowered her feet to the floor. "You brought drugs in?" She shook her head. "You're on her radar then. Fly low."

Kandace sat up too. "It's not like she can do us actual harm. That would leave marks, evidence."

The girls exchanged a look. "Like we said, we haven't been here long so we don't know if it's true. But there are rumors . . . they do things that will heal before we leave or that make it look like we did them to ourselves. Ms. Wykes's trained dog is only too happy to carry out her sadistic punishments. That's what we've heard anyway. And sometimes there are . . . screams and then one of the girls is absent from class for a couple of days. When she comes back, you can tell she's been smacked around."

"Seriously? Jasper?"

They both nodded. "Another student told us about this girl named Beth who got sent home right before we arrived. Apparently, she was making trouble about something, and then all of a sudden, she was found in her room, having overdosed."

"She smuggled drugs in too?"

"That's the thing. We all know no one smuggles drugs in here. But they put out a story that she'd had someone secretly meet her on the property and that person had supplied her. Addicts will be addicts, and all that. Sneaky bastards who go to great lengths to get a fix."

The sad thing is, Kandace thought, *that's the truth.*

Another wave of coldness moved through her. And it very suddenly occurred to her that perhaps she wasn't as tough as she'd made herself believe. Perhaps, instead, what she'd done was turn herself into the perfect victim.

Just like every single one of the girls here at Lilith House.

"She didn't even bother telling anyone the truth later," Kandace guessed. "Because no one would have believed her."

"Probably," Aurora said. "Or maybe she was so happy to be home that she did whatever she had to do not to be sent back here."

"Do you know what she was making trouble over?"

The girls glanced at each other. "She said someone had molested her."

"Molested her? Who?"

Aurora shook her head. "She didn't know. She just said she could *tell.*"

Kandace raised an eyebrow. "And we're sure she really wasn't on drugs?"

Aurora shrugged. "I wouldn't stake my life on it or anything."

The lights in the room suddenly went out. "Damn," Sydney whispered.

"Why did the lights go out?" Kandace whispered back.

"They shut off the lights at nine o'clock. Our bedtime. There's a nightlight in the bathroom if you need it."

What the actual fuck? Nine?

"I don't even have a toothbrush. They took all my things."

"There's a clear cosmetic bag on the sink for you," Sydney whispered again. "Just the basics. We're not allowed makeup or lotion or anything like that."

"Right," Kandace muttered, her hand going to the back of her shorn hair. "Vanity will not be tolerated. Ashy skin all around."

The squeak of bedsprings suggested that both girls had turned over to sleep. She sat there in the dark, leaning toward the wall cautiously, a chill sweeping through her. *Whispers.* Coming from within the walls. One, then another. *No. Just the wind outside,* she told herself, *or some strange acoustics in this old house that causes voices to carry from one floor to the next.* Yes, it had to be one of those two things. Even so, as Kandace's eyes adjusted to the dark and the unfamiliar features of the room shifted into focus, that chill remained.

CHAPTER SEVEN

$\mathcal{A}$ loud knock echoed from below and Scarlett frowned, standing upright from where she'd been scraping wallpaper off the lower portion of a wall in a hallway in the west wing and wiping her hands down her thighs. She used her forearm to smooth the sweaty pieces of hair that had fallen loose from her ponytail away from her face and headed toward the front door.

When she pulled it open, Deputy West was standing there, holding a box in his hands. Her brow lowered and she eyed him warily. "Deputy West. Hi. What brings you out here?"

"I appreciated your offer to come and go as I please," he said, a note of dry humor in his voice. "But I thought it better that I knock and, you know, give some fair warning that you have company."

She squinted one eye at him. *Huh.* So the guy wasn't the humorless stick in the mud she'd originally thought him to be. "I appreciate that." She used her arm to indicate her sweaty, messy hair, and her face she was pretty dang sure had dirt smudged on it, baggy ripped jeans and old, stained T-shirt. "Gave me just enough time to put on my finest."

He grinned and she smiled back, and for a moment, time stilled. Scarlett's heart kicked up but then so did her unease. *No,* she cautioned herself. *Don't even go there.*

The deputy seemed to read her discomfort because he cleared his throat and looked away, holding something up. "Uh, I brought something by. I was going to install it, with your permission of course."

She looked at the box he was holding, reading the print. "A security front door lock set?" She met his eyes, confusion wrinkling her brow. "Why?"

He looked to the side, squinting into the trees for a moment and then back at her. "Listen, this place has been empty for a long time. Kids use it for any number of things. Entertainment. A crash pad. I've made it a habit to drive by and make sure nothing dangerous or illegal was happening, which is why I was here the other day. If *I* didn't know someone had moved in, others won't either. I'll install it."

Scarlett leaned a hip on the doorframe, crossing her arms. "Seems like a pretty excessive *welcome to the neighborhood* gift. Is this a service Farrow provides all its new residents?"

"No, but it's not only for you. It'll save me the work of having to make a report when some stoned kid tries to enter without knocking and scares you and your little girl."

Scarlett chewed at her lip, glancing at the box again. "All right. But I insist on paying for the lock set. It looks expensive."

"No need. My friend's dad owns the hardware store. He's the one who picked it out. He has better taste than I do. Anyway, friend discount. I practically got it for free." Scarlett eyed the beautiful aged brass set on the photo. It was simple, yet elegant, and perfect for the arched wooden door she planned to have sanded down and re-stained. Honestly, if she'd gone shopping for one herself, she'd likely have chosen that exact one.

"All right. Well, thank you. I accept. But you'll have to let me at least repay you with a glass of lemonade and some cookies."

For a moment it appeared he was going to turn her down. His mouth opened, but then he pressed his lips together and nodded once. "Sounds nice. Thanks."

There was an awkward pause. "Okay then," Scarlett said, backing away. "I'll leave you to it. Oh! Do you need any tools? I have all the basics . . ."

"No. I brought what I need. I'm all set."

"Okay, great. I'm going to . . . uh"—she hitched her thumb over her shoulder—"get back to work, but just holler when you're done."

"Will do."

Scarlett shot him one last smile and then headed back to the hallway where she'd been working. She stepped into the bathroom nearby and cringed at her reflection in the mirror. *God, it was worse than I thought.* Not *only* did she have dirt smears on her face, but there was white dust from the dried wallpaper paste in her hair and eyelashes, and a tiny piece of wallpaper stuck to her cheekbone. She looked absurd. She was surprised he'd been able to speak seriously with her at all.

She used a wet piece of toilet paper to clean her face as best as she could and then brushed the white dust from her hair. She sighed. Without a shower and a vat of makeup, this would have to do.

Scarlett went to the window at the end of the hall and looked outside where Haddie was still lying on her belly on a blanket, her elbows propped up, a pile of books next to her. Scarlett knocked on the glass, not really expecting Haddie to be able to hear her, and was surprised when she looked up, waving at her mother. Scarlett smiled, waving back and watching as Haddie looked away, focusing on her book.

That was one thing they shared in common. Both she and Haddie could get lost in books for hours. Sometimes they spent entire Sundays in their PJs, lazing under blankets and reading.

Scarlett went back to her scraping for a while but was too distracted, listening to every small bang and clatter from where Deputy West was working below, so after about twenty minutes, she put down her scraper yet again and headed toward the kitchen. She made a pitcher of lemonade and popped open a Tupperware container of the chocolate chip cookies she'd made earlier that day and put several on a plate.

She wrapped a couple of cookies in a napkin, poured a plastic cup of lemonade, and went out the back door to take the treats to Haddie.

"I thought you could use some sustenance," Scarlett said when she'd made it to where Haddie lay, dropping onto her knees next to her daughter, placing the lemonade on a flat square of grass and the cookies on the blanket.

"Thank you, Mommy." Haddie reached for a cookie. "What does sustabance mean?"

"Sustenance. It means a source of nourishment. I know how easy it is to forget to eat when you're involved in a good story." She nodded to the open hardcover on the blanket in front of her daughter. "How are you liking *Charlotte's Web*?"

"I love it. Templeton's very selfish, but he makes me giggle too."

Scarlett grinned, picturing the childlike reaction to a funny fictional character. "Who is that again? It's been a while. The rat, right? The one who'll only help Charlotte for food?"

Haddie nodded, her expression growing thoughtful before she glanced into the woods. "Yes, that's him," she murmured, looking back at her book. "He'll help Charlotte for food."

Scarlett stood. "Bring the blanket and the cup and napkin in when you're done reading, okay?"

Haddie nodded, already immersed back in the tale of friendship and farm life.

She made her way to the front entry where the deputy was putting tools back in the red toolbox on the floor. The shiny, aged brass door lock set glinted from the dull, patchy wood. The deputy glanced up. "All set," he said, straightening.

"It looks great. Thank you."

He closed the door and engaged the deadbolt, then unlatched it, using the handle to pull it open. "There are two locks, nice and sturdy. No one's going to get through this front door without a battering ram."

Scarlett let out a breath. "I doubt anyone will go to that much trouble for the use of a crash pad and place to get high."

"You'd be surprised," he murmured. "Anyway, better safe than sorry. From what I remember, the back door lock is still in working order, and the French doors all have crémone bolts. Those are old, but still strong. You should go around and make sure all the lower-level windows are locked and get them inspected as soon as possible."

She nodded, though to her, he seemed overly concerned about the safety of a stranger. Then again, maybe that came with the job. Safety was his business after all. Perhaps it was part of his nature too. She was having a difficult time getting a read on the man.

"I've got lemonade made if you're still up for a glass."

He followed her to the kitchen and washed his hands, and then at her suggestion, they went out to the gazebo behind the house where she poured the lemonade and offered him a cookie.

He thanked her and took a big bite of the cookie, chewing, swallowing, and then nodding toward Haddie, lying at the edge of the woods in the distance. "That's your daughter there?"

Scarlett took a sip of lemonade and then nodded. "Haddie. She's seven going on seventy-seven." She breathed out a smile.

He glanced at her and then down at the hand sitting on the wood-chipped Gazebo bench. "You're divorced? From her father?" He appeared almost confused for a moment and then grimaced. "Shit. I mean, darn it. I'm sorry, that's none of my business."

A feeling not unlike affection twisted through her. He was handsome, yes, but he was not one of the smooth charmers she was used to. She'd thought him surly and rude the day before, but today, now that he'd let his guard down, she was getting this sense of . . . awkwardness, as though his social skills were unpolished. Not because he was impolite but because he didn't have much practice using them. He was . . . unexpected.

His uncertainty confounded her, especially considering his good looks. She figured good-looking men had plenty of opportunity to hone their charm. It was just a fact of life. Why hadn't he? She glanced at his ring finger, noting he was unmarried.

"It's okay," she murmured. "I don't mind the question. Haddie's father and I were never married. He's not in the picture."

He studied her for a moment and then his gaze moved back to Haddie, an expression she didn't know him well enough to read crossing his features and then disappearing. He held up the chocolate chip cookie. "These are really good."

"Thanks. They're Haddie's favorite."

For a moment they were both silent as he finished the cookie and took a long sip of lemonade, and she stared off in the distance, watching him from her peripheral vision. He was so close and she was so keenly aware of his presence. It made her feel twitchy, exposed somehow. She hadn't found herself attracted to a man in a very long time. "So um, can I ask you something, Deputy?" She turned to face him.

"Sure," he said, setting his glass down and leaning over to pluck a long blade of grass growing through the slats in the gazebo floor. "But call me Camden."

Camden. "Okay. As long as you call me Scarlett." She paused. "You said kids use the house for entertainment. What exactly did you mean by that?"

The deputy—*Camden*—glanced at the house and then away. He used both hands to fiddle with the blade of grass in his fingers, pausing for longer than felt comfortable as though he was taking the time to choose his words carefully. Was he worried about scaring her? Making her feel unsettled in her new home? He'd already done that by showing up and installing security . . . "There are stories about the house. You might already know some of them given that you can find them online."

"Yeah," she confirmed. "I looked up the house's history. Spooky stuff."

"The kids think so too. They set up dares . . . you know, *'spend the night in the scary house and I'll pay you a hundred bucks,'* that kind of thing."

"Ah. The old sleep in the abandoned haunted mansion dare. A classic."

His lip quirked. "I guess it's a classic for a reason."

"True." She paused. "I read up on the Bancroft family. Tragic ending to that story."

"Tragic beginning too, depending on whose point of view you're telling it from."

Tragic beginning? She hadn't read about that. "What do you mean? I thought Hubert Bancroft made a fortune in fur trading and built this grand house."

He shook his head, appearing suddenly regretful that he'd brought it up. "I'm not much of a storyteller," he said haltingly, bending and twisting that blade of grass. "There's probably . . . something online." He slid his eyes away and his cheekbones tinged pink like a child who was telling a falsehood. But why would he?

She cocked her head. "If there is, I didn't come across it. I read about his son and the loss of the family fortune that his great-grandfather made from the fur trade."

He looked down at the blade of grass again, now looped and twisted into some sort of shape. He was quiet for several awkward beats. "He wasn't only a fur trader, he was also an evangelist."

"Oh," Scarlett said. "I didn't read about that."

Camden's brows knit as he stared off behind her. "His mission was to convert all the savages who lived in these parts to Christianity."

"The . . . savages?" She frowned. "You mean the Native Americans who lived here?"

Camden nodded. "The Serralinos. They were considered heathens, evil-doers, and Hubert Bancroft thought it his Godly duty to save their fallen souls." He looked at her, his expression grave as though he was recounting something that had happened to people he knew personally. "If they cooperated, they were spared, though enslaved, used as trappers for the furs he sold to enrich himself. If they didn't, the men were pushed into the canyon and if the fall itself didn't kill them, the elements or wild animals would. If it was a woman who refused, she was made a whore for Hubert and the other male leaders in his ministry."

"No," Scarlett breathed, swallowing thickly. "That's awful. God, the things people do in the so-called name of religion."

Camden's gaze speared her, and something that looked like deep sorrow moved through his eyes. "Yes," he said. He was quiet for several long moments, his fingers still now, and Scarlett wondered if he'd go on or if that was the end to the tale, so when he began speaking again, it startled her. His fingers began twisting the blade of grass once more.

"One such indigenous woman was named Taluta." He gave her the ghost of a smile. "The name means red, like yours, but she was named for the color of her hair," he said glancing at Scarlett's light brown ponytail. "Anyway, Taluta refused to convert, and apparently violently rejected the advances of one of Hubert's men. They were able to restrain her, however, and threw her over the canyon cliff, but not before raping and brutalizing her."

Scarlett blinked at him in horror, rendered mute by the unthinkable hypocrisy of men proclaiming to act in the name of God, when in actuality, they were committing atrocities against people whose only "crime" was to be different than them.

He stared off into the tree line, reciting the story as if from memory. "When they left her, she lay at the bottom of the canyon in a pool of blood and brokenness. Her husband, only just returning from a hunt for their tribe, learned what had happened to his wife. Refusing to allow her to die alone, he donned his horned war garb, painted his face the way a warrior does when he knows he's heading toward his certain death, and then scaled the canyon wall as far as he could and dropped to the earth, crumpled beside her, his own injuries surely extensive as well.

"But when Bancroft's men returned the next morning to sate their depraved curiosity, neither one was there. Instead, a red fox, its fur the exact color of Taluta's unusual auburn hair, with eyes the precise amber shade as hers, darted from the bushes at the top of the canyon and escaped into the forest."

"They thought she'd turned into a red fox and climbed out of the canyon?"

"That's what the legend says."

"And him?"

"They say he still roams the forest, his cold heart full of vengeance. People have reported hearing his war chant carried on the wind and seeing the shadow of a horned dead man searching to avenge the wrongs committed against his love with the sacrificial blood of others."

"That's . . . quite a story," Scarlett said.

"They called it Novaatngar after that," he murmured. "The canyon. It means, the dark place."

She repeated the name softly, a chill causing her shoulders to rise and the tiny hairs on the back of her neck to prickle. And what he'd said about himself was wrong. He was a very good storyteller. He'd *moved* her, not just with the words that conveyed the tale, but with the emotion he'd infused in the telling.

"Are there any Serralino people still left in these parts?"

He shook his head. "The very last of their tribe died a couple of years ago and took their language with her. An old woman named Narcisa Fernando who lived in a small, one-room house a few miles from here. She was a midwife once, but in her old age, she sold dried herbs and soaps, things like that. She'd catch a ride with a local fisherman who came up this way once a month or so. He'd drop her at the edge of town and then she'd walk to the center, despite a severe limp. When no one had seen her through the winter, the sheriff went to check on her and found her dead in her bed."

For several moments, Scarlett could only sit in silence, the sadness of the story, and the idea of dying alone in your home and not being discovered through a long winter, both a heavy weight in her gut. Narcisa Fernando's death was merely lonely, though. The story of what had been done to her people a century before was pure evil. She cringed internally at the specific example of the abomination of things humans did to each other. When she looked over at Camden, he was watching her in that intense, studious way, as though trying to decipher her. Only unlike Haddie, who truly seemed to be able to see into her soul, Camden appeared frustrated that he could not.

She cleared her throat, gave her head a small shake, and glanced over at the back of the house. "The Internet made Hubert Bancroft sound like a hard-working hero. A total success story. But really . . . the man who built this house I'm living in, attempted to convert people he viewed as savages," she mused aloud. "And *he* was the true savage. Wow." She gave her head another disbelieving shake. History really did depend on who was telling the story.

Camden turned his head toward the house as well. "Later, I suppose the house served the same purpose. The attempted conversion of savages."

"The girl's school?" she asked. "That's a harsh way to put it." Scarlett frowned, tilting her head, picturing Kandi, remembering the good-hearted person Scarlett had known her to be. Full of life . . . vivacious. Yes, she'd made poor choices later but . . .

He paused a beat before removing his gaze from the house and meeting her eyes and offering a small humorless tilt of his lip. "My poor attempt at humor. It was harsh. I shouldn't have said it."

"No, I'm sorry. I just . . . got prickly because I had a friend who attended Lilith House for a short time."

He cocked his head to the side. "A friend?"

Scarlett nodded. "Yeah. My friend, Kandace, was sent here not too long before the fire happened and the school closed." Scarlett stared unseeing at the back of the massive structure, her mind's eye full of Kandace's laughing face. She felt her lips tip slightly and then just as quickly fall. "She got into some trouble and was sent here. She ended up running away though and there hasn't been a sign of her since. It's like she just disappeared into the ether." She moved her eyes back to him and stilled at the look on his face. He looked almost . . . stunned. She frowned. "You okay?"

He drew back slightly, shaking his head. "Yeah. That's . . . terrible. I'm sorry to hear it. I didn't know you had a personal connection to the place."

She shrugged. "Well, sort of, I guess. I spoke with her right before she left for Lilith House, but I never talked to her while she was here. Apparently, they had strict rules on cutting off all outside influences. But when I saw the property up for sale, it immediately caught my attention because of Kandace."

He pulled his full lower lip between his teeth for a moment. "So," he said haltingly, "what are your plans for it? It's a pretty big place for just two people."

As Scarlett watched him, noted the subtleties of his posture, the way he held his expression, she got the strange sense that this right here was the only reason he'd agreed to the lemonade and cookies. It was this question he'd wanted to ask. It was the only reason he'd stayed—he'd wanted to prod her for information. It made suspicion kick up inside her again, the feeling that this house meant something more to him than he was letting on. And a small piece of her felt— *stupidly*, she told herself—hurt. His agreeing to spend time with her was due to an agenda. *What,* she had no idea. *And why do you care anyway?*

She picked at a piece of chipped paint beside her thigh. Despite her mildly hurt feelings, there was no reason to keep her plans for Lilith House a secret. In fact, if her business was going to succeed, she needed the word to spread as far and wide as possible. She needed to make connections—however casual—with the townsfolk in Farrow. And one of its officials wasn't a bad place to start. Her hesitation, though, was not only because she was suspicious of this handsome stranger with far too many secrets in his eyes, but because she'd only spoken of her dreams with her mother and Merrilee. She'd only said it out loud to the people she trusted deeply. Saying it now made it feel as though she was giving something sacred to someone she may or may not be stupid to trust. "I . . . uh, I'm a pastry chef. A baker. Before I found this place, I was hoping to someday open my own cake shop—wedding and event cakes mostly—in LA. I unexpectedly came across the sale of Lilith House and my dreams sort of"—she let out a small, nervous laugh—"started spiraling, I guess." She felt the blush rise in her cheeks and hated that it did. Vulnerability made her nerve endings feel raw. "If I can make it work, it will be perfect for an event venue. It's only a couple of hours from LA, but provides the feeling of being world's away. Swept into an earlier era." She smiled. "There's a ballroom on the second floor at the back of the house with these wrought iron verandas that are just stunning. Or they will be, with some work. There's already a communal restroom area for bridal parties to use, even if it does need to be completely re-tiled. The grounds, if brought back to what I imagine was their original splendor, will be perfect for outdoor ceremonies, or simply strolling under the moonlight. Even this gazebo . . . once the broken boards are fixed and it has a fresh coat of paint, I can just see the photographs that might be taken with this as a backdrop." She picked another chip of paint from the bench. "It needs repairs and remodeling, and refreshing, of course. All the appliances have to be updated. I know I have a lot of work ahead of me. But with an industrial kitchen and—" She stopped, realizing she was starting to spiral again as she always did when she started dreaming of Lilith House's potential. When she started envisioning the life she might carve out for Haddie and her. Scarlett let out a small laugh and brought her hand to her cheek. "Anyway, my goal is to start the work as soon as possible and wrap it up in a year with a spring opening." She looked down—away—not wanting to see his reaction, telling herself it didn't matter anyway. She didn't even know him. Had no real idea what kind of person he was.

When she peeked up at him, she saw that he was gazing at her thoughtfully. She saw no disapproval in his eyes and she let out a slow breath, her shoulders relaxing. Camden glanced at the house and then back at her. "Weddings. Parties," he murmured as though almost speaking to himself. "Those are good things." He looked back at her. "Maybe it's exactly what this place needs."

Scarlett smiled. *Yes,* she thought. *Love. This place needs love.* It suddenly seemed so very clear, and the idea bolstered her dreams that much more. It gave her purpose. "I hope so," she said. "I'm going to do my very best."

He was quiet for a moment before he said, "That friend in town I mentioned whose father owns the hardware store? He does some remodeling on the side, you know, if you're looking for bids." Camden squinted and looked away. His body seemed to have stilled as though he nervously awaited her answer.

"Yeah, that'd be great. Louis gave me the name of someone as well. Carl Dover?"

"He's good too. Not as good as Mason."

"I'll give both of them a call."

Camden dug in his pocket, pulling out his cell phone with the hand not holding the folded piece of grass. "Give me your number and I'll text you his. That way you'll also have mine in case . . . you know . . ."

"Those kids show up with a battering ram?"

Camden laughed, an expression mixed with a note of surprise, and it transformed his face from handsome to devastating. She stood quickly, wiping her hands free of the dust and particles of paint chips that had stuck to her skin and he followed suit. "I should get back to work . . . see if Haddie needs . . ." Her words faded when she glanced over to where her daughter had been, only to see an empty blanket, her pile of books scattered across the vacant spot. Apparently reading had been set aside for more exploring. "Well, I'd better go. By the way, do you know if there's anything wild I should be concerned about? You know, other than old indigenous zombies?" She gave Camden a wry tilt of her lips. "I've been letting Haddie explore the property and she told me she saw a fox and something with horns. I know so little about wild animals so . . ."

Camden squinted at the empty blanket for several beats. "Probably a deer. And yes, there are foxes, a black rat snake or two. All harmless."

"Unless you're a rat."

He smiled again. "Exactly. Well, thank you for the lemonade and cookies. Now I know why they were so good. You're a professional."

She let out a laugh on a breath. "At the moment I'm just the unemployed owner of what could very well turn out to be a money pit." She shot him a smile. "By the way, thank you for the safety that new lock will bring. It was kind of you."

Camden nodded, handing her the folded blade of grass the way Haddie sometimes handed her an empty gum wrapper. Confused, she automatically took it from him. "Call if you need anything," he said, only turning his head back toward her, showing her his profile, his jaw rigid. And with that, he strode through the weed-ridden gardens toward the front of the house.

Scarlett looked down at the folded piece of grass held between her thumb and index finger. It wasn't something he was discarding as she'd originally thought. She brought it closer to her face, marveling at the intricacy of the thing he'd created right in front of her without her even knowing. It was a fox, with tiny feet and tiny ears, it's snout in perfect proportion to the rest of its body. How in the world had he done it? *At all,* but much less while simultaneously holding a conversation? *And it's a fox.* Scarlett gazed at it for another minute, delight spreading through her. "Taluta," she whispered, recalling the name from the legend he'd shared with her. She looked up just to see him rounding the house and disappearing out of sight.

CHAPTER EIGHT

*H*addie dropped a red Skittle on the pine-needle-strewn forest floor, moving slowly and deliberately, creating a trail of colorful breadcrumbs in her wake.

When her mother had mentioned that Templeton the rat was convinced to do things for food, Haddie had suddenly wondered if she could lure the thing in the woods with a sweet treat as well. Maybe this was a way to let it know Haddie wanted to be . . . friends? Was that what she wanted? No . . . not necessarily. She didn't even understand this thing yet. She just wanted to know what it *was.* She wanted to understand the creature that had no weight. Curiosity burned brightly inside her, and the flame had only grown bigger since she'd arrived at Lilith House and spotted it. She'd stood at the window in their new attic home the night before and stared out into the dark forest and she swore she could feel the pull of the thing somehow, but different than she'd ever felt a pull before.

She reached inside her pocket where she had a large-sized package of Skittles Mommy had bought her at the gas station on the drive to Lilith House. Haddie had fallen asleep before she could eat them, and now she was glad for it. They were the perfect lure. *Everyone* liked Skittles.

A cloud went over the sun, darkening the forest, and an iciness traveled over Haddie's skin. A shadow shifted in her peripheral vision. She was being watched.

Movement in the other direction caught her eye, something swinging from a tree. She turned quickly but there was nothing there. She let out an exhale.

Just the forest's bad memory.

There and gone before she could fully understand it.

She stepped forward, dropping another Skittle on the ground, turning slightly so she could head back in the direction of her house. She had walked in a wide arc, moving nearer to her home, hoping that when she came out of the forest, she might turn around and see the thing that followed her.

A loud caw rose up, the fluttering of wings spooking Haddie and causing her to jump. Shadows seemed to move and shift all around her as though there was not just *one* thing tracking her, but a whole forest full of creatures she had no name for. Ones she couldn't *feel*. She hurried forward, walking faster now, dropping Skittles haphazardly. She heard the crunch of pine needles behind her as the thing drew closer, and with her heartbeat thumping, Haddie began to run, abandoning the package of Skittles on a pile of dead leaves.

Scratchy laughter echoed through the forest and the footsteps picked up behind her. Haddie screamed, the shrill sound bouncing from tree to tree and disappearing into the patchy sky above.

Haddie slipped, falling to her knees and letting out a cry of pain and alarm as something sharp punctured her skin. She jumped to her feet and continued running as the scratchy howls of laughter grew higher in pitch. It was pursuing her. It would catch her and eat her alive!

Haddie burst out of the forest, her head turned back toward the thing chasing her, colliding heavily with . . . her mommy. Haddie sobbed, gripping her mother's waist, turning her face into her stomach.

"Haddie, baby, what's wrong? What happened?" She let go of her, sinking to her knees and smoothing back her hair, wiping away the tears coursing down her cheeks. Haddie glanced back at the forest behind her, a stream of sunlight filtering in and making the woods hazy and green. *Magical.* There was nothing there except trees and rocks and bushes of wild berries.

A bird exploded from the trees in a burst of flapping wings and rustling branches, its cry sudden and sharp. Just a normal, harmless bird. Haddie felt its lightness as it lifted into the sky.

She let out another shuddery sigh and stepped back, pointing down at her bloody knees. "I fell," she said.

Her mother's brow lowered. "Is that all? It sounded like . . . you sounded terrified."

Haddie looked at her mother's beautiful, concerned face and lied to her. "I was afraid you wouldn't hear me."

"Oh, honey." She smoothed away another piece of hair and then stood. "Let's make a pact that you never go so far that I wouldn't hear you if you called for me, okay?"

Haddie nodded.

"Now, let's get those knees washed and bandaged, and scrub that stain out of your dress." She stood, taking Haddie's hand and leading her toward the house.

Haddie didn't glance behind her toward the forest. The thing had already moved far away. She couldn't feel its weight, but she could sense its retreat.

CHAPTER NINE

Camden stood at the window, a cup of coffee in one hand, watching as the sun rose over Farrow. He heard a door open down the hall and footsteps approaching. Georgia came up next to him, laying her head on the side of his shoulder. "Morning," she said, her voice groggy.

He leaned over and kissed the top of her head. "Morning. How'd you sleep?"

"Okay. Thank you for staying."

"Anytime. You know that."

She yawned. "It's too damn early to get up."

His lips tipped. "You know me, Georgie."

He heard her smile and turned his head to meet her eyes. "I do. Better than anyone. Always up with the sun." She gazed up at him and he saw the hunger in her eyes. He took a sip of coffee, turning back to the glow of dawn on the distant horizon.

He knew this wasn't a good idea, but he couldn't seem to say no to her. How could he?

She cleared her throat. "So, what'd the sheriff say when you met with him yesterday?"

Camden paused, thinking of the meeting he'd had with his boss, picturing the subject of that meeting. The woman who'd just moved into Lilith House, the one who kept popping into his mind though he didn't invite the thoughts. Why had he told her all those stories? He still wasn't sure. He wondered what she thought of him, wondered if he seemed awkward to her. He had limited practice interacting with people. Still, even now, he was never sure he got it quite right. "He wants me to keep tabs on Scarlett Lattimore and report back. They're suspicious."

"Yeah. Well, I'm pissed. Who is she anyway?" Georgia stepped away, crossing her arms over her chest.

He glanced at her to see her eyes had hardened, her mouth turned into that familiar pout. "Just some woman who plans to turn the house into a business."

"A business?" she spat. "We've waited thirteen years for this, Cam. We earned it. There's no way some bitch is going to take what's rightly ours."

His muscles tensed. "She already has, Georgia. Unknowingly. Like I told you and Mason, we're going to have to modify—"

"Oh, bullshit."

He turned to her. "We'll talk about this later, okay? With Mason. I have to go home and get ready for work."

Her expression registered hurt. She reached out to him. "Okay. We'll talk about it later. I just—"

"I *know*, Georgie. I know." He sighed. "She has a daughter. She's only seven."

Georgia blinked. "A daughter?" She chewed at her lip a moment, finally shaking her head. "It doesn't matter. Changes nothing."

"Her mother told me she's seen horns in the woods." He'd mentioned it to the sheriff. He shouldn't have. He regretted it now. It'd made a spark of interest light in the sheriff's eyes and a heavy feeling of guilt settle in Camden's stomach. He didn't know what that might mean to the man, but he hadn't liked the expression on his face.

Georgia laughed. "Horns? *So?* It's a forest." She rolled her eyes. "Oh God. That legend?"

"I think they believe it. Sometimes I wonder too . . . I used to . . . see things."

Georgia let out a small huff of breath. "We need to *forget* the things we saw at Lilith House. The things we experienced there. Isn't that the whole point?"

He regarded her for a moment, finally nodding. "Yeah. Yeah, it is." He owed her that, that and so much more. He leaned forward, kissing her forehead, letting his lips linger there. He heard her let out a small sigh and then he stepped away. "See you later."

"Bye, Cam."

Camden stepped out of Georgia's house, jogging down the steps, the vision of Scarlett Lattimore's face as she'd laughed in the shade of the gazebo filling his mind.

CHAPTER TEN

$\mathcal{D}$owntown Farrow struck Scarlett as both sleepy and old-fashioned, as though both pace and time had slowed at some point in the recent past and the rest of the world, having not received the same memo, had continued to speed right on by. Although there were several large estates that looked to feature every modern amenity including swimming pools and basketball courts, sprinkled on a hill overlooking the town, the rest of Farrow was completely at odds. Scarlett drove down Main Street, noting the quaint ice cream parlor with outdoor seating, the theater with the hand-lettered marquee, and the white, domed bandstand at its center.

There was a sense of charm in Farrow, but to Scarlett, the small town situated in a valley between two mountains also gave off a strange feeling, possibly because such a vital example of a modern urban landscape existed less than two hours away.

However, despite the odd feeling, there were plenty of examples that modern life was very much being lived there. Cars and trucks were parked in the spaces along Main Street, people were out walking dogs and simply strolling the neighborhoods, and the bells rang from the church tower as Scarlett pulled up in front of the white steepled building with the emerald-green doors. The parking lot was mostly full, and a few stragglers hurried toward the short set of steps.

"Ready?" she asked Haddie as she got out of the car and went around to open the back where her daughter sat strapped into her booster seat.

Haddie nodded as she unbuckled, stepping down from the car, her gaze moving between the church and the cemetery behind it and to the left, her expression morphing quickly from concern to placid and back again. "Are you okay?" she asked, taking Haddie's hand.

"Yes," Haddie said. "Lots of things happened here. Good and bad."

Scarlett glanced at the church. Haddie said these kinds of things sometimes and she never knew what to make of it. She'd asked her to explain what she meant dozens of times, but the questions always seemed to cause Haddie to withdraw. So rather than pointing them out and making Haddie feel self-conscious, she'd learned to take them in stride, labeling them "Haddie-isms" that maybe someday her little girl would have the vocabulary to describe to her. Or maybe not. Maybe she'd simply outgrow this phase, the same way other children eventually left their imaginary friends behind. "Yes," Scarlett confirmed. "That's a good way to describe a church." They began walking toward the door, Scarlett spotting a sign that said, *Office,* with an arrow pointing toward the back of the building. She stepped onto the path that led there. "Joyful occasions take place in churches like weddings and baptisms, but people also gather in churches for sad events like funerals and memorial services."

Scarlett saw Haddie nod her head from her peripheral vision as she pulled open the door on the back of the building with a small placard that told her she was in the right place. They entered a back stairwell and followed it down, stepping into a wide-open area, stacks of folding chairs and tables against the far wall next to a darkened hallway, and a basic kitchen area to their right. The smell brought back memories of school events after hours. There was a room off to the side with a large picture window where you could observe children playing, the muffled sounds of their laughter echoing through the glass.

Scarlett squeezed Haddie's hand and walked to the door, rapping on it. When it swung open, an older woman with close-cropped gray hair and a wide smile stood there. "Hi," she said, looking between Scarlett and Haddie.

Scarlett smiled. "Hi, my name is Scarlett Lattimore, and this is Haddie. We're new in town, and I was hoping someone here would have some information about locating childcare for my daughter? It would only be on an as-needed basis."

The woman nodded and opened the door wider. "Oh yes. I'm Ruth. Come on in. This is the childcare room that's only open during services. But I'm sure Sister Madge could help you. She knows everyone in the community. Let me give her a call."

"Thank you."

Ruth picked up a phone on the wall by the windows that faced the cemetery and Scarlett nudged Haddie as they waited, nodding toward the bookshelf and encouraging her to check it out. Haddie walked slowly to it, picking up a book as Ruth came back. "Sister Madge lives on site, and has her own office-slash-residence right behind the church. If you go back out the way you came and follow the path in that direction, you won't be able to miss it."

"Great. I appreciate it." She glanced over at Haddie who had opened the book in her hands and already seemed engaged. A little girl sitting nearby looked up and Scarlett noticed that her eyes were strangely spaced, one slightly larger and higher than the other. The child lowered her head, going back to the bead maze she was playing with.

"Haddie's welcome to stay here with the other children while you speak with Sister Madge," Ruth said.

"Oh, okay . . . well, that would be good. I'll only be a few minutes, I'm sure."

"Haddie?" she called to her daughter, who looked back at her. "I'm going to be back in a few minutes okay?"

Haddie looked slightly unsure, but nodded. "Okay, Mommy."

Scarlett thanked Ruth and headed back outside, taking the cement path to the back of the church where she immediately spotted a very small white house. She walked to it, knocking on the glass pained portion of the door, and turned the knob, pushing it open when a pleasant voice singsonged from within, "Come in."

Scarlett stepped directly into a front office, featuring a sitting area off to the side.

An older nun stood up from where she'd been sitting at her desk, smiling kindly at Scarlett. "Well, hello. Scarlett Lattimore, right? How wonderful to welcome a new family to our community." She brought her hands together in front of her face in a silent, singular clap.

Scarlett walked forward, extending her hand. Sister Madge took it, her skin cold and smooth, her fingers as delicate as a bird's wings. "Thank you," Scarlett said, letting go and taking a seat at the leather chair in front of the desk. "We're so happy to be here."

"Where in Farrow are you living, dear?"

"We're actually outside town, at the old Lilith House?"

Sister Madge's expression did something funny, but it was so fleeting that Scarlett wondered if she'd imagined it. The old woman smiled broadly. "Isn't that wonderful? I daresay I never thought the old girl would see life again. I must hear all about what you and your husband plan to do with it."

"Oh, um, there's no husband, that is, it's just me and Haddie."

The same smile remained on Sister Madge's face, unmoving for several beats. "Oh, I see."

She told herself she might be imagining the sister's disapproval. Then again, if anyone was going to be a stickler for doing things the "proper way," she supposed it'd be a nun. Scarlett glanced away for a moment, clearing her throat. "So, I'm in the process of acquiring quotes for a full remodel. If all goes according to plan, I'll be opening a wedding and event business on the property in the spring."

"Weddings," Sister Madge sighed, clapping her hands together the way she'd done moments ago. "Such happy events. So many young women gracing our little town. How lovely." She lowered her hands, folding them on the desk in front of her. "I imagine you've heard about the tragedy that occurred at Lilith House thirteen years ago."

"The fire?" Scarlett asked, for the other tragedies Camden had spoken of had happened long before that, and not necessarily on the house's property, but in the forest beyond. That canyon of death. *The dark place.* "Yes. I did. A lightning strike? Is that right?"

Sister Madge nodded sadly. "There was a terrible storm that night that came on very suddenly. The staff and students of Lilith House were in the chapel enjoying a service when a bolt of lightning struck the building." She shook her head, appearing as though she was barely holding back tears. "Of course, I've imagined so many times what it must have been like for them as the chapel filled with smoke, the old wood igniting too quickly for anyone to escape. It's almost too terrible to comprehend."

A lump had filled Scarlett's throat. "Yes," she managed. She knew Kandace had run away from Lilith House a week before the fire—she'd learned about it from Kandace's mother when she'd attempted to get in touch with her friend—and though no one knew what had become of her, whether she'd decided to begin a new life where she could leave her problems and responsibilities behind, or whether some form of trouble had found her, Scarlett had to feel relieved that Kandace hadn't been there that night to burn to death as chaos and screams filled the acrid air around her. *She was too vibrant, too full of life to have died like that. Trapped. Crushed.*

It'd been years before Scarlett had stopped hoping Kandi would appear back in her life, full of stories about all the adventures she'd been on during those missing years. Grown up, matured, another "aunt" to richen her daughter's life.

She offered Sister Madge a weak smile. "I like to think Lilith House and I are alike," she said. "We both need a second chance. Perhaps we can provide that for each other."

Sister Madge tilted her head, a small smile lighting her thin lips as she studied Scarlett. "What a nice sentiment, dear." She leaned forward slightly. "Now, what can I do to help you get more settled in our community?"

A muffled crash came from the back of the house and Scarlett frowned, her gaze shifting to the short hallway where she could see three closed doors.

"Cleo," Sister Madge said. "My cat. I live here as well, if Ruth didn't mention that," she explained. "Just enough room for the two of us." Her smile grew. *A cat?* What had it done? Knocked over a piece of furniture?

"Ah," Scarlett said. "Um . . ." She worked to pick up the string of the conversation again. *What can I do to help,* the nun had asked. "I'm actually looking for someone with childcare experience. There will be a lot of work taking place at Lilith House over the next year, and I'm going to need someone to look after my daughter on an as-needed basis until school begins. I was hoping you might be able to suggest someone? It'd be nice if the person could come to the house sometimes, but I'm also happy to drop Haddie off on the days I know I'll be overseeing the renovations for a good part of the day."

"Yes, of course, and I think I have the perfect candidate in mind. Amelia Schmidt helps out in our childcare center and she's just the loveliest girl, and wonderful with young people. Many of our parishioners use her for babysitting, but with it being summer now, I'm sure she'd relish more work. She doesn't drive just yet, but if you're willing to drop Haddie off, like you said, or pick Amelia up, it could work out just fine. Here." She pulled a pen and pad forward and jotted something down on it, handing it across to Scarlett. "Here's her number. Her father died a few years ago, God rest his soul." She closed her eyes and made the sign of the cross. And when she opened them, she waved over to a photograph on the wall of a group of men, all in white suits, standing stoically for the camera. "He was a member of the Religious Guild here in town." She sighed heavily. "But anyway, Amelia's mother is a true pillar of the community herself."

"The Religious Guild?"

"Oh, yes. It was formed right after the town was founded. The sons of Farrow have held the moral line for centuries."

The moral line? What line was that? And why did *they* get to decide where any particular moral boundary began and ended, simply because of their bloodline? No one man was more righteous than another by virtue of his birth. That sort of belief system was rife for all sorts of corruption.

Scarlett's gaze moved from the photo of the group of men to the one next to it. It looked like a Biblical rendering of a man standing while a woman, mostly naked lay at his feet, reaching for him beseechingly. "The Fallen Woman," Sister Madge sighed. "Of course, there have been many famous ones throughout history. I like this depiction, because she's seeking atonement by reaching for the blessing of a righteous man." She lowered her voice as though sharing a secret. "So many do not, you know. Atone."

For a moment, Scarlett didn't know what to say and so she kept her eyes on the painting as though studying its tones and shadows. Fallen woman? *Atonement?* What was she supposed to say to that? Was Scarlett considered a fallen woman? Was the sister suggesting that *she* should atone? *You're being paranoid and defensive,* she told herself. *She's a nun. So her ideas are antiquated. So what?*

"It's a beautiful painting. The symmetry is . . . quite masterful. Not that I know anything much about art. Just . . . well . . ." She glanced at the slip of paper in her hand and then back to Sister Madge. *Stop rambling. You sound like an idiot.* "Thank you so much. I'm grateful for the contact." Although now she couldn't help question the referral. If the teen— Amelia—started talking about *atonement,* she would have to pass.

"I hope it works out." Sister Madge stood and so did Scarlett. The old nun came around the desk and opened the door. "I need to head downstairs as well. I'll walk you back to fetch your little girl. Haddie, was it?"

"Yes," Scarlett said as she stepped through the door of the simple house after Sister Madge, and they walked side by side down the path, through the back door, and downstairs, stepping out into the wide-open space Scarlett assumed was used for church business events and socials, and came to stand in front of the large glass window. "That's her right there," Scarlett said, pointing to where Haddie sat in a chair against the wall, her face focused down on the book in her lap.

"Hmm," Sister Madge hummed, her head tilted as she gazed at Haddie. "Beautiful child." She looked up at Scarlett. "So many would give anything to have such a precious gift."

Scarlett nodded, smiling even as additional unease pinched her chest. Odd thing to say. "She is a gift."

"Indeed. We'd just love to have her as part of the church youth group. Of course, that won't be for some time as she'll need to be thirteen, but you keep that in mind."

Scarlett couldn't even begin to imagine her daughter as a teenager. Not yet. Still, she smiled at the nun. "Oh. Absolutely. I will. I'd love Haddie to be very involved in the community."

Sister Madge's smile widened. "I do hope so, dear."

"Thank you again, Sister."

"Of course. If you need anything, just call. Farrow has always come together for its residents during any time of need, big or small. We take pride in a long history of caring for our own." And with that, Sister Madge gave her one last smile and then turned, heading for the stairwell.

Scarlett opened the door, seeing Ruth on the other side of the room and shooting her a smile that faded quickly when Ruth didn't smile back, but instead gave her a thin-lipped look of disapproval, heading to where she stood. Scarlett glanced quickly at Haddie, who was still sitting with her head bowed. It was only then she noticed that her shoulders were shaking very slightly as though she was crying. That pinch of unease gripped tighter. She took a step toward her child, turning back at Ruth's voice directly behind her.

"Ms. Lattimore."

"Ruth, what happened? Is everything okay?"

"I'm afraid not. Haddie said something quite cruel to Mikey." She nodded her head to a little disabled boy propped in a chair by the window, his legs encased in metal braces, head tilted, a thin line of spittle running down his chin.

Confusion swept through Scarlett. Haddie had said something cruel? "What did she say?"

"Robby heard her tell Mikey that he was nothing. Nothing at all. Bullying is not tolerated here, Ms. Lattimore. She is not welcome back."

CHAPTER ELEVEN

Thirteen Years Ago

$\mathcal{S}$he needed a cell phone, *any* cell phone. And not because she intended on making a call, even if she *could* find a spot where there was service. Like she'd told her new roommates, no one was going to believe a word she said. The past few years had ensured that. She had a feeling the greeting she'd received from Ms. Wykes was only the tip of the iceberg around here as far as abnormal—and perhaps *illegal*—practices occurred. What she needed was *video.*

The sounds of dishes clattering softly behind her faded as she made her way down the hall, ducking into the bathroom, waiting a few minutes by the door, and then peeking out. No one had followed her. She walked quickly toward Ms. Wykes office, glancing behind her every few steps to make sure she wasn't spotted. She had slipped out the side door when the other girls at her table rose to dish up their plates. Thankfully the table she'd been assigned to was near the back of the room, somewhat obscured by the other tables. She'd slip back in when the other students were busy clearing the tables and bussing their dishes.

She heard the sound of footsteps from above and halted, waiting as they faded away, moving toward another wing of the second floor. A staff member most likely. She was still new enough that she could fake being lost, but the longer she was here, the flimsier that excuse would look.

She took a deep breath when she'd made it to the door. She'd waited almost two weeks, biding her time, acting like a good little girl, but it was now the third Monday of the month, and she was ready. She'd watched Ms. Wykes leave out the front door as they'd been heading to the dining room, a small, black purse held over one arm. She'd glanced out the window as the long black car pulled away from Lilith House, but still, her heart beat harshly in her chest. *This will only take a minute. That's all I need.* She raised her hand and rapped softly on the solid wood door on the very off-chance someone was inside. All was silent. She tried the handle. *Locked.* Of course. She'd known it would be. But her mother's door had always been locked too, and Kandace had still managed to steal a good portion of her jewelry, designer purses, and any expensive clothes the pawn shop would take for cash.

She reached in her pocket and brought out a hairpin, sticking it in the lock and maneuvering it until she heard a small click. "Yes," she whispered softly, turning the handle and ducking quickly inside. Her eyes darted around the office, her nerve-endings trembling. In the corner of the room, the one remaining bluebird eyed her silently. Kandace swallowed heavily, taking one step toward the winged prisoner but then stepping back. *Sorry, buddy. If I try to spring you, you might give me away. Another time, okay?* She hoped birds were mind readers and he'd understood the message she'd sent.

She turned to the box on the wall, moving quickly toward it and using her pin again to work the small lock holding the top closed. She had it open in mere moments, her hands shaking as she unhooked the key lock and pulled the top open. Empty.

"Goddammit." She let the top drop, looping the lock through and clicking it closed. She glanced around the office, a droplet of sweat rolling down her back. She didn't want to know what Ms. Wykes would do if she caught her in her office, much less rifling through her drawers. Her eyes bounced from the bookshelves, to the two file cabinets, to the desk, and all its numerous drawers. *Where do I begin?* For all she knew, the cabinets held nothing more insidious than student files. Ms. Wykes had told Kandace her phone would be returned upon her departure from Lilith House, but more likely, the phones she confiscated were smashed under her sensible shoes or Jasper's heavy boot.

And she was out of time. The girls would be finishing their meals now. She could only pray her absence hadn't been noticed by the staff, or that they assumed she'd gone to the bathroom without asking. This mission would have to be rescheduled.

She opened the door, glancing in both directions down the hall, turned the lock on the inside of the door, and then pulled it closed behind her.

Her heart slammed to a stop when she heard the sound of voices directly around the corner. Kandace scurried to the first doorway she came to, turning the handle—*it was open, thank God*—slipping into the darkened interior and pulling it closed behind her. Blood whooshed in her head as the conversation grew louder. Kandace's ears pricked, her muscles held taut as she attempted to control her breathing, struggled not to make even the tiniest noise. It sounded as if the two women talking had stopped nearby and were engaged in an argument. Kandace couldn't make out the words, but she listened as their voices rose and fell in heated debate.

Kandace took a small step back so she could lean more fully against the wall and the ancient wood beneath her feet creaked loudly. The voices outside the door ceased and Kandace cringed. *Shit.*

Now that her eyes had adjusted to the dark, she saw that she was standing at the top of a set of wooden steps that turned the corner halfway down, traveling lower into some space she couldn't see from where she stood.

Footsteps were approaching the door. Kandace stepped as carefully as she dared while still racing to beat whoever was about to open the door. She ducked around the stairwell corner just as the door above was pulled open, a wide shaft of light filling the space and spilling around the bend where she now stood, back pressed against the wall, breath held.

"This door is supposed to be locked at all times." A woman's voice, one she didn't recognize.

"One of them must have forgotten," the other woman murmured. "We'll let Ms. Wykes know."

"Don't," the other woman whispered. "I mean . . . don't they have it rough enough as it is?"

The other woman didn't answer but Kandace heard the click of a lock being turned and then the door was pulled closed, shutting out the light. Kandace blew out a slow breath. The stairwell was dark, dank. It smelled like mildew and dirt. It must lead to some sort of a basement storage area. There had to be a back way out, right? A window? Even a small one? Something . . .

God, I'm screwed. She needed to get out of there as quickly as possible and pray to God her absence hadn't been noticed.

She stepped down into a wide-open space, the floor concrete, the walls open rafters, a dim light coming from somewhere beyond and barely illuminating the space enough so that she could see where she was stepping.

Boxes and random pieces of furniture littered the area. Several beds, their springs rusty, were piled near the wall, with a few pieces of luggage in front of them. Kandace stepped toward the suitcases and backpacks, attempting to spot her own. She turned away. What did it matter anyway? Other than the drugs, which she assumed had been flushed the day she'd arrived—*and what a shame because she sure could use to get high right about now*—the only thing she'd brought were clothes and toiletries, and those would be useless here at Lilith House.

Kandace scurried between two piles of rotting boxes, heading farther into the recesses of the basement, toward that seemingly faraway muted glow of light.

An eerie snickering sound came from the darkness to her right where the light didn't reach and she whirled toward it, her pulse jumping. For a moment she simply stood there frozen, her heart thumping as she stared into the pitch-black. Something shifted and Kandace jerked backward as it came rushing at her from out of the gloom. *A skull. White bones.* The scream on her lips ended in an expelled whoosh of air as she hurled herself backward, tripping and falling onto a pile of boxes and refuse, raising her hands in defense as the thing hurtled toward her, attacking.

A flood of adrenaline threw Kandace into fight mode, and she shoved the thing away with her arms and kicked at it with her legs, panting with terror as she crawled quickly from beneath it and jumped to her feet, whirling back around, prepared to fight it off again. Instead . . . she blinked, still panting, but leaning closer, a small hysterical laugh rising in her throat. She leaned forward and grabbed the thing, pulling it upright.

It was a fully intact anatomical skeleton like the ones used in classrooms, standing on a pair of rickety wheels. "Holy shit," she muttered, pushing it away from her. It rolled backward toward the gloomy corner. "Holy shit," she repeated.

She didn't think anyone could have heard her scuffling about with the skeleton in this below-ground space that must be well insulated and was hopefully far enough away from the others in the house. Still, she needed to get out of there. And she *wanted* to get out of there. Despite that she now knew the skeleton was nothing but an old teaching tool, she still felt shaken and anxious. As rattled as the bones that had just sprung from the gloom and fallen over her.

With an intake of musty air, she turned back toward that light. She made it across the large room, glancing behind her every few steps, and when she rounded another tall pile of storage boxes, she saw that a single bulb hung from the rafters of what was a sort of hallway off the main open area with rooms on either side. *More* storage? And at the end of the hallway, she saw a wooden door with a thin sliver of daylight showing beneath. Relief filtered through her. Sunshine. *A way out.*

As she tiptoed quietly past an open door, the light reached inside the room to reveal three desks all in a row, and a chalkboard at the front. It looked like a classroom—the desks small and childlike—but for who?

A loud rustling sound made Kandace halt abruptly as she sucked in a startled breath. The sound had come from the room just past the small classroom. Slowly, tentatively, she stepped forward, soundless on the concrete floor. She heard more rustling and the squeak of what sounded like bedsprings. Her eyes rose to that door at the end of the hall. Should she make a mad dash for it? No, that might catch the attention of whomever was inside the room just ahead of her, whereas if she peeked inside and saw that the person making the noises was turned away, or occupied with some task or another, she could quietly sneak by.

Kandace took in a big breath, mustering all her courage and leaned around the frame. Inside the room, a boy sat hunched over on a bed, headphones over his ears, books spread out around him, as he wrote on a notebook on his lap. Kandace slowly let her breath out, pressing her lips together in indecision. He only looked to be a kid, thirteen, maybe fourteen, tall but skinny, from what she could tell in his sitting position. *Slight* but for his height, with the smooth skin of a young teen who hadn't yet sprouted his first whisker. She didn't think he necessarily posed a physical threat if push came to shove. But who was he and would he call someone who *was* a threat? Would he scream when he saw her so that Jasper the hellhound came running?

Perhaps she should make a break for the door, hope it was easy to fling open and escape before he'd even gotten a good look at her face? They all wore the same uniform and had the same God-awful short, shaggy haircut, even if he came out of the room and saw her from the back, would she really be able to identify her later? *Yes, if it's already been noticed that you're missing.*

As though he sensed her presence, the boy's head came up, his gaze clashing with hers, eyes widening with surprise. He ripped the headphones off and leaped to his feet. Kandace drew back, glancing once at the exterior door and then back at him.

As they stared at each other, Kandace saw not only the surprise in his gaze, but fear as well. Her shoulders lowered and she raised her hand as though attempting to calm a frightened animal. "It's okay. I'm just . . . lost." She inclined her head toward the door. "I see an exit, so I'll just—"

"You're not supposed to be down here."

She nodded. "I know. I'll be in trouble if I'm caught. Don't say you saw me, okay?" She tilted her head, giving him her most flirtatious smile, but she could feel that it fell flat. She didn't exactly feel like a girl who could convince anyone of anything using her feminine wiles at the moment—even a boy in the throes of puberty.

Vanity will not be tolerated.

Oh yes, they'd stripped her of that, no doubt there.

He narrowed his eyes at her, appearing torn. "I'm *supposed* to tell if I see one of you in a place where you shouldn't be."

One of you. She nodded. "I get it, and I'd ordinarily never ask someone to be dishonest, but . . . I'm really not doing anything wrong, and if they get the idea that I am—"

"You're *sinning.*"

"Yes."

"You'll be punished."

Kandace bobbed her head. "Yes. I will."

His expression registered another flash of confusion, but it melted into what appeared to be concern. He wet his lips, pausing for several beats. "Don't go out that door," he finally said in a rush of words, nodding toward the one she'd been headed toward. "Ms. Granger has a direct view from her classroom and she might see you. If she does, she'll report to Ms. Wykes. I know a better way."

Relief made Kandace's breath come easier. He wasn't going to rat her out. In fact, he was going to help her. "Are you a . . . student here?" she asked, curiosity overwhelming her as she stepped into the room. "I was told there weren't any boys."

"There aren't. That is . . ." He cleared his throat, embarrassment flashing in his eyes. "We, I mean, myself and two others . . . we weren't sent here. We were born here."

"Born here?" she breathed, her eyes roaming his young face. She'd thought him a good-looking kid when she'd first caught sight of him, but she could see now that he was beyond that. He was a beautiful boy. "What do you—?"

His fingers clamped down on her arm at the sound of a door opening and shutting, and then feet descending the wood steps. Kandace's heart rate jumped. Shit, someone was coming down the same set of steps she'd taken ten minutes before. Someone looking for her?

The boy pulled her, putting his finger up to his lips as he met her eyes. *Shh.* Kandace nodded, letting him lead her toward the door, where he then turned right. From there, he walked her toward a wall and pulled at a board. What had just looked like a planked wall, had a small secret door that swung outward on hidden hinges. He pointed inside, indicating that she should crawl in. Kandace hesitated. She'd thought she could trust this kid, but how did she know he really wasn't just some nutjob? There seemed to be quite a few of them at Lilith House. And she wasn't talking about the students. How screwy did you have to be to teach at a place like this anyway?

The footsteps were getting closer, the gait slow, but steady. They sounded like men's shoes. Jasper? The boy nudged her. "Go," he whispered, an edge of anxiety in his tone. She had so many questions, but there was no time for that. Not now. Kandace took a deep breath and climbed into the small space and the boy climbed in after her and pulled the hidden door shut. The footsteps rounded the corner and stopped. Kandace held her breath, the boy's body pressed against her own in the mostly dark space, the only small amount of light coming in through the tiny gaps between the slats.

After a moment, the person began walking again, but she could hear that he had turned around and was heading back the way he'd come.

"Go," the boy said, and now that her eyes had adjusted to the dark, she could see that there were rungs attached to the wall that she could climb. "Climb all the way to the top. You'll exit into a back hallway near a utility room that rarely ever gets used. Turn right at the end of that hall and it'll take you to a set of stairs. From there, you should be able to find your way." He opened the latch and stepped out, beginning to close the small door.

Kandace looked up into the pitch-black above, placing her hands on the rungs. "Hey," she whispered to the boy just as the door was about to shut completely. He pulled it open, revealing one eye in a small shaft of light. "You're a dreamboat, you know that?"

She couldn't see his full expression, but she thought he'd smiled, one that was both slightly shy and mildly astonished. The door clicked shut and Kandace began to climb.

CHAPTER TWELVE

$\mathcal{A}$s they pulled out of the church parking lot, it began to rain. *Fitting,* Scarlett thought. She glanced at her daughter in the rearview mirror to see her staring out at the water-streaked glass, a look of pure misery on her face. She looked up, and their eyes met. Scarlett's heart squeezed painfully. "What happened, Haddie?" she asked. "Why did you say that to the little boy?"

"It's not what I meant, Mommy." Her voice was little more than a whisper, laced with the same distress Scarlett saw in her expression.

"What did you mean then?" *You're nothing, nothing at all,* Ruth had reported Haddie saying to the disabled child. Scarlett still couldn't even imagine her pure-hearted daughter saying something like that.

Haddie paused, her brow knitting. "I don't know," she finally said.

Scarlett exhaled a frustrated breath. "*How* can you not know what you meant? It came out of *your* mouth."

"I know but . . ." Her words faded away and again, she looked out the window. Scarlett gripped the steering wheel, tears threatening. She felt so damn upset . . . with Haddie, but mostly, *mostly* with herself. She felt incompetent . . . alone.

She saw the sign for the hardware store Deputy West had mentioned and pulled into the lot. The rain was dwindling now, white rays emerging from behind the heavy clouds that had recently shed their weight.

She turned off the car and turned to her daughter. "Haddie, did you think less of that boy because he has braces on his legs?"

Haddie shook her head, her expression so *earnest*. "No, Mommy."

"Did he . . . scare you? Were you frightened of him because he's different?"

Haddie paused but then shook her head. "No, Mommy."

Scarlett watched her little girl, so much going on behind those sea-glass eyes, so many things she longed to know, to understand. She released a slow breath. *Be patient. She's just a child.* "Haddie . . . sometimes I talk to myself when I'm trying to work through a problem or . . . even just my own tangled thoughts. Sometimes it helps to speak things out loud. They sort of . . . sound different than when they're just bouncing around in my own head. Was that what you were doing back at the church?"

Haddie seemed to mull that over and then nodded. "Yes, Mommy."

"So you weren't speaking to that boy so much as you were talking aloud. You didn't mean to hurt him or say something cruel."

Haddie nodded her head vigorously. "Yes, Mommy. Yes, that's it."

Scarlett nodded slowly. "I understand that. I bet if someone heard me speaking my thoughts aloud, they'd question me too. Those thoughts are . . . well, they're unfiltered." She looked off to the side, trying to put these ideas into childlike terms so she knew they were on the same page. "They're really just for you so you don't stop to consider how they'll sound to others."

Haddie nodded again, her eyes filling with relieved tears. "Yes," she said, the word emerging on a choked whisper.

"Oh, Haddie." Scarlett's heart gave another painful squeeze and she grabbed her purse, opened her door, and went around to the back where she pulled her daughter into her arms. For a few minutes they stood just like that by the side of the car, both squeezing each other tight. When Scarlett pulled back, Haddie gave her a sweet, tremulous smile. "It's important to be mindful about what you say out loud, and what you work through in your own head, okay? You don't ever want to accidentally hurt someone's feelings, right? Especially someone who might already feel self-conscious about the things that make them different?"

Haddie nodded, hugging her mother again. Scarlett gripped her tight and then set her down, giving her a smile as she grasped her hand. "I love you."

"I love you too," Haddie said, but her smile slipped. "They won't let me go back to that church now."

"Well," Scarlett said, giving her daughter's hand a squeeze as they approached the door to the store. "We don't need people who don't believe in second chances, now do we?"

Scarlett squatted in front of Haddie and held her pinkie up and Haddie released a gust of breath that turned into a small grateful smile, looping their fingers together. "No, Mommy. We don't," she said. Scarlett nodded, giving her a quick kiss on the cheek before standing.

A bell over the door jingled when Scarlett pulled it open and they both stepped into the dim interior of the relatively small store, a stand of paint samples directly to their left and a front desk to their right. A woman, who had been bent over something to the side of the counter, straightened, offering them a smile. "Good afternoon. Welcome to Grady's"

"Thanks," Scarlett said, stepping forward and catching sight of what was in the box. "Oh my goodness," she practically squealed. "How old?"

"Six weeks," the woman said. She looked at Haddie. "You wanna hold one?"

Haddie's eyes grew wide with delight. "Can I, Mommy?" she asked, looking up at Scarlett.

Scarlett grinned. "Sure, if it's okay."

As the woman picked up a tiny orange kitten and handed it to Haddie, Scarlett glanced toward the back of the store where she heard the muffled sounds of what she thought was arguing, a male and a female voice rising and falling in urgent-sounding tones. She looked back to Haddie who took the kitten gently and then held it against her chest, delicately running a finger over the tiny head. Scarlett watched her, noting the pure, unguarded love on Haddie's face, the fierceness of her mother's love rising up inside her so suddenly, she almost gasped. Her girl was not a cruel child. She was pure and good, her spirit filled with gentleness. It was *normal* for children to question that which was different, but she hadn't done it to be unkind. How could Scarlett have ever doubted that for even a moment?

The woman who had been smiling down at Haddie as she held the kitten, glanced up at Scarlett. "I'm sure you didn't come in to hold kittens. What can I do for you?" she asked with a warm chuckle.

"I'm looking for Mason Grady. He was recommended for some potential remodeling work."

"Oh sure. He's back in his office." She glanced toward the rear of the store, worry crossing her features. "Let me just give him a ring. What's your name, honey?"

"Scarlett Lattimore."

"I'm Sheila by the way." She picked up the phone next to the register and dialed, turning away slightly. "Hey, Mason, someone's here to see you. A Scarlett Lattimore."

She paused, obviously listening. "Yeah, I know. Do you want me to . . . right, okay. Sure, I'll tell her." She hung up the phone. "He'll just be a minute. He's got a couple people back there now but he said they're about done."

"Great. Thanks." She watched Haddie love on the kitten for another minute and then heard the sound of a door open and footsteps on the linoleum floor coming toward the front. She looked up as an attractive man with curly, light brown hair appearing to be in his mid-to-late twenties rounded the corner, followed by a younger, pretty dark-haired woman and . . . Deputy West. Her heart gave a strange twist. His eyes met hers and though his expression seemed placid, she swore she saw anger simmering in his mercurial eyes. Had his been the raised voice she heard from the back? Or had Mason Grady been the one yelling . . . and about what? Scarlett shook the questions off. It wasn't any of her business and she really didn't care.

"Ms. Lattimore?" the man who had to be Mason Grady asked, extending his hand. "I'm Mason Grady. I hear you're looking for help with some renovations?"

She took the man's hand and shook, noticing that his eyes were two different colors, one brown, one blue. "Uh, yes." She glanced at Deputy West who had stopped and was standing off to the side watching them. "Deputy West," she murmured.

A muscle jumped in his jaw, but he nodded. "Ms. Lattimore." So they were back on more formal terms now. All right then. Strange, unreadable man.

The young woman had walked ahead of them and was holding the door open. Scarlett noticed she had a hairline scar above her lip as though she'd once had a cleft palate. It made her no less lovely. "You coming, Cam?" she asked, shooting Scarlett what could only be described as a hostile glare. That attitude, however? It definitely detracted. *What the heck?*

Deputy West paused, looking as though he was considering saying something to Mr. Grady, but then, apparently having changed his mind, muttered, "Yeah," and walked toward the door without a second look at Scarlett. *Okay then.* He and the woman left, the store growing dim once more as it shut out the momentary blast of sunlight.

"Come on back to my office and you can tell me about your project," Mr. Grady said.

Scarlett focused back in on him. "Thank you, Mr. Grady—"

"Mason, please. Mr. Grady's the man who raised me. And we look nothing alike." He grinned, his smile wide, teeth white and straight.

Haddie had turned away with the kitten, and her shoulders were hunched as she cradled the small creature to her chest. "Haddie, sweetheart, put the kitten down and come with me."

"She's welcome to stay out here and visit with the kittens while you attend to business," Sheila said. "I have a granddaughter just about her age so I'm used to kids."

"Oh," Scarlett murmured. "Well . . ." She went around to Haddie and leaned over her shoulder, a smile tugging her lips at the sight of the sweet little face of the kitten.

She wasn't sure about leaving Haddie with Sheila, even if she was just in another room, because just a short time before, Haddie had been in tears over how Ruth had chastised her. And although Haddie was such a resilient little girl, and looked completely at ease in Sheila's presence, she was still

Scarlett's baby. "How about if you come with me and we'll visit the kittens again on our way out?"

Haddie glanced at Sheila and gave her a small smile. "I'm okay staying here," she said.

Scarlett paused again. "Well, all right. I'll be back shortly, and if you want to come join me, you just tell Sheila, okay?"

Haddie nodded, completely engrossed with the kitten.

Scarlett thanked Sheila and then followed Mason to the back of the store where he showed her into a small, tidy office.

When she emerged twenty minutes later, it was with a smile and an appointment for Mason to come to the house the next day and work up a more precise bid. But he'd seemed enthusiastic about the project, and his ideas were both on par with her own, and offered exciting possibilities she hadn't considered. "Thank you so much for allowing me to interrupt you without an appointment. I can't wait to walk you through the place," Scarlett said, reaching her hand out.

He shook, smiling brightly. "I appreciate the opportunity. Lilith House has sat empty for far too long. I'd love the chance to be a part of bringing her back to her former glory."

"See you tomorrow then," Scarlett said, turning and heading back to the front to tear her kitten-obsessed daughter away.

"Sheila said in two or three weeks they'll be ready to go to new homes, Mommy," Haddie said when they'd pulled out of the lot and were heading back toward the road that led out of town and toward Lilith House.

Scarlett glanced in her rearview mirror and gave her daughter an amused eyebrow lift. "New homes?" she asked. "Wow, I hope someone will want at least one."

"Can we take one, Mommy" Haddie breathed. "Please?"

They hadn't been able to have pets in their small apartment in LA, but now that they lived on so many acres of land, what trouble would it be to adopt a kitten, or even two? They'd probably be helpful in keeping the field mice population low too, which certainly wouldn't be a bad thing. "Maybe," she said secretively. "I'll think about it." The idea of surprising her daughter with two kittens of her very own in two or three weeks sent a jolt of happiness through Scarlett. And Lord knew, every little bit helped toward the effort of making their new house feel like home.

The gravel crunched under her tires as she came to a stop in front of the house, getting out and taking Haddie's hand as they walked toward the front door.

She gazed up at the massive structure, the ideas Mason had discussed filling her with excitement as she saw the house, not as it currently was, but as it could be. And not just because *she* saw its potential, but because someone else did too. His ideas had rolled so effortlessly off his tongue, it was almost as though he'd already had them formed long before she showed up. They were that natural, and that *good*.

Scarlett startled when Haddie let out a loud yelp, turning to her daughter and instinctively reaching for her. Before she even had a chance to ask Haddie what had scared her, she saw the bony, plucked-looking body of a baby bird sitting on the first step. "Oh no," she breathed, pulling Haddie in to her side. "Oh poor thing." Scarlett looked up and around at the tops of the trees that sat at the periphery of the house. They all seemed too far away for the helpless creature to have dropped from, but she supposed it could have attempted to fly . . .

Haddie's thin shoulder trembled against her body and she dropped down in front of her daughter, shielding her from the creature. But when she saw that Haddie was looking with something akin to horror, not at the bird, but something else behind her to the left, she glanced back, a concerned frown on her face. A Skittles wrapper lay discarded near one of the front pillars. She stared at it for a moment. She'd bought Haddie Skittles on the drive there. The wrapper had obviously been dropped during one of the many trips inside. Haddie must have looked away from the sadness of the dead baby bird, her gaze affixing to the bright candy package.

"It came right to our door," she heard Haddie murmur behind her.

She turned back to face her daughter to see Haddie had moved her gaze to the forest. "The bird? No, Haddie. It must have dropped out of a tree somehow, or maybe it tried to fly. An animal could have gotten hold of it and then dropped it here . . ."

Haddie was looking at the bird again, seeming to only be half listening to Scarlett. Her eyes suddenly grew wide. "It's alive," she breathed.

"What?" Scarlett turned around, looking at the still creature. "No, honey. It's not."

Haddie nodded her head. "I can feel it," she said. Scarlett opened her mouth to speak when, sure enough, she could see the bird's tiny breast rising and falling slowly.

"Mommy, it is. It's alive. We have to help it!"

Scarlett only hesitated a moment before standing and going over to the helpless baby and very delicately scooping it up into her hand. It was so tiny, it fit right in her palm. "Come on," she said to Haddie. They could at least get it out of the sun, make it comfortable.

Inside, she went into the kitchen and found a square Tupperware container, using her one available hand to line it with a clean, soft, kitchen towel. She laid the bird gently inside and then handed it to Haddie, who took it, gazing down at the baby. "Is it going to die, Mommy?"

"Probably, honey. We should expect that it will, okay?"

Haddie looked up at her, her gaze so somber and adult-like. "Okay," she said. "But we can love it before it does."

Scarlett's throat felt tight. "Yes, baby, we can do that."

CHAPTER THIRTEEN

$\mathcal{S}$carlett pulled the string connected to the bare bulb hanging over the basement stairs, the narrow stairwell flooding with light and exposing decades of cobwebs. She screwed up her face as she batted a few away, taking the rickety steps slowly, one hand gripping the rail which—miraculously—still remained solidly connected to the wall.

As she rounded the corner and stepped into an enormous space littered with boxes and old castoff furniture, her phone rang, making her jump. "Jeez," she murmured to herself, pulling her phone from the pocket of her sweatshirt. She was surprised she got any reception down here.

Merrilee's name and photo displayed on the screen brought a smile to her face. "Hey," she said, hitting the speaker button.

"Scar!" Merrilee's voice rang out in the dead, still basement. "How are you?"

"Good," she said, leaning precariously over an open box and peering inside. A part of her expected something to jump out and scare the living daylights out of her. This place was spooky in the way all old, dark, unused spaces filled with the relics of other people's lives were. But only dusty fabric greeted her . . . old curtains, or clothing, or linens that might very well be nesting mice if she reached her hand in to find out. Which, no thank you very much. "If I sound echo-ey," she told Merrilee as she moved on from the open box, "it's because I'm down in the basement."

"For what reason, pray tell, are you digging around in the basement of an old, dusty mansion?"

Scarlett let out a soft laugh. "*My* old dusty mansion. And I'm just looking around. I have a contractor coming out tomorrow and I wanted to get a better lay of this land, so to speak, before he starts drafting plans. This place is huge, Merrilee, and it feels like a mausoleum right now." She walked through a makeshift aisle, weaving between junk, her eyes peeled for anything that might be of interest. Something that could potentially be salvaged and brought back to life for posterity's sake.

"What does Haddie think of it?"

Scarlett sighed, stopping for a moment. "She seems a little wary of everything right now." Scarlett frowned. "I'm not sure, Merrilee, it's like . . . she's keeping something from me . . . or, oh I don't know. You know Haddie. She's secretive."

"I don't think she's secretive, Scar. Or at least . . . not because she doesn't trust you. I think it's just that Haddie feels things more deeply than most children and she has to let those things simmer before she finds the right words."

Warmth filled Scarlett's chest. Merrilee was right. She knew she was. And how wonderful it felt to discuss her concerns about her daughter with someone who loved her too. "Thanks, Mer. You're right. Sometimes it's hard for me to wait for those words to come."

"I've told you before, they'll come easier the older she gets."

"Yes, I think so." She paused as she moved forward, heading toward where the open area turned into a narrower corridor. "Something weird happened in town today."

"What, honey?"

She told Merrilee about the church playroom and the disabled little boy with the leg braces. She told her how she'd questioned Haddie who had insisted she hadn't meant what she said. When she'd finished, Merrilee was quiet for a moment. "Haddie's never been cruel. I'm sure . . . well, I can't say what that was about, but this is all a big change for her too. Maybe she's a little confused . . . not exactly herself. That would be natural."

"Yes, I know. I believed her, I just . . . well, you're right. It's going to take time to adjust. Everything here is new and strange for both of us. This house and the town . . . it has a strange vibe to it." Scarlett leaned into a room, the door half-open. Inside was empty except for a metal bed. She frowned. Had someone once slept in this basement? A strange chill skittered up Scarlett's spine.

"A girl from *LA* says a place has a strange vibe? Now I'm concerned. What could possibly shock you that the City of Angels doesn't already provide? In spades. Although," she said, dragging the word out, "you *are* used to the big city and moved to the boondocks."

She acknowledged what Merrilee said with a chuckle. Her friend was right. But it was more than that too, although Scarlett didn't know enough about Farrow yet to say exactly what.

"Met anyone interesting?" Merrilee asked.

"Hmm," Scarlett hummed. "I met the Deputy Sheriff of Farrow. He's . . . interesting."

"Ooh, cute interesting, or creepy interesting?"

Scarlett laughed. She would have said cute interesting before today. Before he'd scowled at her and walked away without saying goodbye. "The jury's out. He's got a bit of a strange vibe too."

"Well, I expect you to get back to me on that."

"Ha. I will. He might have a girlfriend, so there really won't be much to mention."

There was a short pause and when Merrilee spoke, the laughter had faded from her voice. "You know," she said, "if things don't feel right, now or . . . at any point . . . well, you can come back anytime."

"I know," Scarlett said quietly. Only really, she *couldn't*. For *so* long, she'd had this feeling her life was somewhere else, waiting to begin. She'd felt it inside herself, not as a rush on her part, not as an action to fulfill, but as a . . . *promise*. Something that would make itself known to her when the time had come. Such overwhelming *certainty* had gripped her when she'd seen the ad for Lilith House. Here. Here it was, *finally,* the promise that had been waiting to be fulfilled.

Her mother had always said Scarlett had a sixth sense, but Scarlett had written that notion off long ago after making one bad decision after another. If she really had such sharp instincts, why in the hell did she keep making such pitiful choices? At that thought, her daughter came to mind, her chest pinching. One of those "poor choices" had resulted in her beloved girl, so how could she think of it that way? "I'm going to stick it out though, Merrilee. There will be challenges, but I feel like this is the place we're meant to be. At least for now."

She heard the smile in Merrilee's voice when she said, "Then I trust that it is too. And," she went on, "I'm going to come visit you just as soon as I can get a few days off. Maybe in a couple months?"

"Anytime would be wonderful. I miss you already."

"I miss you guys too. Give Haddie a kiss from me, okay?"

"I will." They said their goodbyes, and Scarlett dropped her phone back in her pocket, nudging the next door open. Inside was another bare bed. When she peered inside the third room, the same sight awaited her. *Weird.* Would the school have put students down here for some reason? Seemed odd and . . . disturbing. Like she'd stumbled upon the school's version of solitary confinement. *Stop letting your imagination run away with you,* she admonished herself as she turned back toward the stairs. *They're probably just storage rooms.*

She made her way quickly through the piles of boxes and what looked mostly like junk. She'd have to make arrangements to have this hauled away once demo started on the house. As she was about to turn the corner and head up the stairs, she spotted something in the corner to her left. Could it be . . . she yanked the white sheet covering the object and let it drift to the floor, waving her hand to disperse the cloud of dust that had covered it. Just as she'd thought, a birdcage! *How perfect.* Haddie would love it, and it'd be a place she could safely set her little patient while the baby bird—*she hoped*—recovered.

She picked it up by the base and carried it up the stairs. She stopped in the kitchen to wipe the cage down, admiring the beautiful scrollwork of the bars. Scarlett didn't necessarily love the idea of birds in cages, but for their temporary purposes, it would work nicely. And they'd leave the door propped open as a sign of their abiding belief that beautiful, feathered things should not be locked away, unable to fly as God intended.

She took it to their attic room where Haddie sat on the floor, her stuffed animals in a circle, the box holding the injured baby bird directly in front of her. Scarlett set the cage down and grinned at Haddie. "Look what I found in the basement. A recovery hospital for our little patient."

Haddie stared at the cage for a moment, her eyes widening momentarily as her forehead creased in a frown. Her gaze moved to Scarlett, her lips parting slightly as though she was about to say something, but changed her mind. Haddie's expression was so . . . strange.

Confused, Scarlett looked from the birdcage to Haddie. "We can leave the door open, baby. I just thought it would be a good temporary home. He'll be right at your eye level and you can check on him easily . . ."

Haddie picked up the baby bird gently from the box, cradling him against her chest. She turned her shoulder outward as if . . . shielding him. Haddie moved her eyes to the cage, that same peculiar look on her face as she shook her head. "No," she asserted. "I'll just keep him with me."

"Are you sure?" Scarlett glanced at the cage, wondering if it appeared scary for some reason to her daughter. "It's perfectly—"

"No." She lowered her face. "No, thank you," she whispered.

Scarlett paused. Haddie was . . . Haddie, but all kids got strange ideas in their heads sometimes. She supposed the cage might look sort of imposing, especially to such a small girl. "Okay, then. I'll just put it back."

Haddie nodded, laying the baby bird back in the box.

"How's he eating?"

"Good," Haddie said, using a finger to smooth the downy fluff on the top of his head. Scarlett had looked online and found that softened dog food or well-mashed hard-boiled eggs could be fed to orphaned baby birds, so she'd prepared the eggs. If the little guy was eating well, it gave her even more hope that he'd survive. "How about you get all your friends ready for bed," she said, smiling around at the circle of—primarily—fur-filled, non-egg-eating pals.

"Okay, Mommy," Haddie said, shooting the cage one last wary glance. Scarlett picked up the apparently offensive piece of furniture and set it outside their room, shutting the door on it.

Half an hour later, Haddie was snuggled up in her bed, the baby bird next to her on the bedside table. Scarlett sat down on the bed and pulled the blanket to her chin. She stroked her daughter's silken hair and leaned down and kissed her forehead. "I love you," she murmured just as a loud creak sounded from a floor below. Haddie's eyes widened. "It's okay," she said, smoothing Haddie's hair back calmly even as her pulse quickened. "It's an old house. There are going to be lots of creaks."

"I think it's waking up, Mommy," she whispered, but there was no fear in her voice.

Scarlett's gaze moved over her daughter's features. "I suppose even houses sleep sometimes if they're left all alone."

"Yes," Haddie agreed. "They do." She yawned, turning toward where the baby bird slept, its bony breast rising and falling.

Skittering sounded somewhere in the walls. *Mice,* Scarlett thought. *Great.* She wondered if there might even be a bat or two. She'd move that exterminator up higher on the priority list. "Sleep tight," she whispered to Haddie as she stood, picking up the bird in its makeshift nest so it wouldn't wake her daughter later, turning on the white noise machine, and heading downstairs.

In the kitchen, she stood at the window, staring at the deepening nighttime sky, the silvery stars as clear as scattered diamonds on a bed of azure silk. Movement near the edge of the woods caused her to suck in a startled breath, but then she saw a small red fox duck around a bush. Her heartbeat slowed. *Taluta.* Her lips tipped as the red fox disappeared into the dense trees beyond.

Her gaze moved to the edge of the windowsill where she'd set the blade of grass Camden had miraculously fashioned into a fox. The grass had stiffened as it died, its color fading from emerald-green to brownish-gold. She picked it up, holding it in her fingers and marveling at it again.

Behind her, she heard the sound of a door softly closing. Scarlett whirled around, a startled breath escaping in a soft gasp. She placed the grass-shaped fox on the counter and moved cautiously toward the kitchen door that led to the hallway, and the foyer beyond. What had that been? A shutter flapping maybe? But no, it'd sounded distinctly like an internal door clicking closed. And it'd been close.

Scarlett leaned forward as she walked, peering around the corner to see into the foyer before she stepped into the open space. It was empty, the gas lanterns that she'd turned on earlier that evening emitting a soft glow, the flickering light making those flowered vines on the wall stretch and grow.

She heard a soft bump and turned toward the noise, her eyes fixed on the wall that held the bannister. She swore it sounded as though someone was climbing the stairs, but the grand staircase was devoid of human life. A shiver moved through her. *Calm down. It's just the age of the house. Stop spooking yourself.*

But even as she attempted to explain the sound away, it continued upward, somewhere behind the wall. Something was there, moving. Something with *weight*. She pictured a strange ghoul, its black body climbing up the inside of the wall. Scarlett stood, frozen, listening to the soft taps of the thing climbing, heading up and away from where she stood, though—thankfully—in the opposite direction of where her daughter slept. Tentatively, she took a step, and then another, gathering her courage and following the sound, pressing her ear to the wall and then pulling quickly away, lest whatever it was reach through the planks and grab her. *Which is ridiculous,* she tried to reassure herself, and yet still the feeling of barely tempered dread persisted. There was *something* there. She could *feel* it on the other side of the wood. She could feel its menacing.

Her breath came short as she walked beside the soft thumps of climbing coming from within the wall until it moved upward, seemingly into the ceiling, the noises fading away. Scarlett waited, her heart thumping, as the sounds of another door opening and closing overhead could be heard. Her heart sped even further as fear spiked within. *What the hell?* Someone or *something* was in her house.

A board squeaked above as though whatever she'd heard was now walking the hall and Scarlett turned, bolting down the stairs and running to the kitchen where she picked up her phone and called for help.

CHAPTER FOURTEEN

Thirteen Years Ago

Kandace couldn't sleep. She stood at the window, watching as the sun came up over the trees. Even though she'd left Los Angeles less than a month ago, the world felt so far away. Real life seemed so distant. Ever since she'd arrived at Lilith House, she'd felt as if she had slipped and fallen down some rabbit hole that transported her into a skewed past. Lilith House felt . . . ancient somehow. Ancient and *off*. There were things she could pinpoint that were strange and even dreadful, but there were other peculiarities that she couldn't name but sensed all the same. As if something lay in wait for her just around each long and twisted hallway.

Kandace leaned forward when she spotted a blur of movement within the trees. Something large and seemingly *tall*. Or was it just a trick of the hazy lighting? Her blood chilled. *Ms. Wykes told us about the natives who used to live in those woods. She said one's still out there, a war-mongering demon hungry for human flesh.*

"Stop it," she whispered to herself. She refused to give credence to dark fairy tales. She knew very well that was just a story used to keep the girls in line. Keep them from attempting to venture off the Lilith House grounds. She squinted, trying to make out what it *actually* was when suddenly something else to her right caught her attention. It was the kid. Kandace turned her head, watching as the boy paused for a moment as though listening to make sure he didn't hear anyone nearby, and then ducked around the chapel and headed for the forest.

What are you doing, Dreamboat?

Kandace turned, looking at her roommates who both slept soundly. Then she pulled on her uniform, left her room—committing the sin of breaking curfew—and tiptoed quietly down the stairs. For a moment she stood still, listening for any sounds, but all she heard were the creaks and moans she'd grown used to. The students and teachers were still in bed, but Lilith House? Lilith House never slept. Lilith House had stories to tell, especially in the dark. She crept toward the back stairs. If she returned before anyone woke, no one would be the wiser.

When she made it to the first level, she checked quickly behind her, and then ducked out the back door, closing it very gently.

Kandace took the same route the boy had, entering the woods at the large gray rock where she'd seen him last. She expected that she'd have to travel more deeply into the forest to find him—if she was able to locate him at all—and so when she practically stumbled upon him just a few feet from the edge of the tree line, she almost screamed.

The kid, obviously shocked to see her, jumped to his feet, eyes wide, face filled with fear.

Kandace held her hand out. "Whoa, sorry. It's Kandace. Remember me?"

He stared at her another few beats before bobbing his head and swallowing. "Yes. I remember you."

"Okay, good." She didn't lower her hand, still attempting to calm him, to wipe that startled expression from his face. He looked like a frightened animal who'd just been cornered in the wild. Could she really blame him? If he'd grown up at Lilith House . . . *Geez*. She didn't even want to think of what sort of life he'd led. She'd be a chronic nervous wreck if she'd spent her life in that hellhole too.

He swallowed again, his eyes darting to the ground and then back to her. She followed his gaze to the place he'd just looked. "Holy shit. What is that?" She lowered her arm, going slowly to her knees so she could get a better look.

The boy dropped down beside her, still looking at her warily. "A baby fox."

Kandace tilted her head. "What's wrong with it?"

"Twisted leg," he murmured. "Probably born that way. His mother abandoned him. Nature doesn't tolerate imperfection. It's a weakness. And in nature, weakness equals death."

She stared at him for a moment. He had mumbled it, but his eyes shone with passion as though the words he'd said were very personal. "How sad," Kandace murmured, her heart giving a small twist as she took in the tiny creature with what looked like a miniature splint on its leg. She knew what it felt like to be motherless, despite that her mother was very much alive. And maybe that made it worse. She looked from the small, curled-up creature to the boy. "Where'd you find it?"

He glanced down at the baby animal he'd been mending and then back to her before shrugging. "They come to me."

Kandace frowned. "They come to . . . what does that mean?"

He shrugged again. "They seem to . . . find me. Sometimes here . . . sometimes closer to the back door of my room. They're sick or injured—imperfect—and I help them."

"How often?"

His eyes met hers. "All the time."

Confusion swept through her. Had no one ever seen this boy? The others he'd mentioned? Or if they had, had they been explained away as one of the staff member's children? She thought of the crawl space where he'd helped her hide. Were *they* the whisperers in the walls? The source of the sounds she'd heard on her first night at Lilith House, convincing herself it was merely the wind? As she stared at him tending to the baby animal, she felt both disturbed and . . . awe-struck. As though the forest sent its faulty babies to be mended by this dreamy boy who sometimes existed as nothing but a hidden whisper. Weird and . . . wonderful, especially considering the trauma of watching the bird be tortured and killed in Ms. Wykes's office. It was like the discovery of Dreamboat here and what he did on a seemingly regular basis, righted a terrible wrong, if such a thing were even possible.

Even more, to find anything gentle and kind in the midst of such depravity felt like a small miracle.

Kandace raised her head and looked deeper into the forest. She swore she heard the soft beat of a drum but wrote it off as the wind or the soft pitter-patter of hooves somewhere far away.

"I wouldn't touch those if I were you," he said.

Her gaze followed his to where her hand was on the ground, her pinky finger next to a cluster of white mushrooms. She hadn't even noticed them in the midst of the scattering of pale, dead leaves and other forest floor debris. She pulled her hand away, looking at him questioningly.

"Toxic," he said. "I ate the tiniest piece of one once out of curiosity and was sick as a dog for a day and a half."

Kandace frowned, moving aside. She'd be sure to wash her hands the moment she went inside.

He looked away from her, petting the animal. "Don't tell, okay?" He nodded down, and with his words, his voice broke slightly, his thickly-lashed eyes imploring her.

Sensitive kid. Too sensitive for a place like this. She suddenly felt scared for him.

"I won't tell, Dreamboat."

He smiled a bashful smile before scooping up the injured baby and holding it to his chest. They both stood. "I have to hide this one in the old shed until it's healed. *If* it heals." He touched the splinted leg gently. "Some things can't be fixed," he said, his face troubled.

Kandace didn't ask him what would happen if the helpless thing couldn't be healed. Truthfully, she didn't really want to know. "What if they find it?" she asked, nodding to the animal, a shiver of worry making its way down her spine. To her limited knowledge, animals didn't fare well behind the walls of Lilith House.

"No one ever goes in there except me and the others. It's just filled with old junk."

She thought of the three rooms she'd passed in the basement. "The other kids who were born here?"

He nodded. Before they stepped from the cover of the trees, he looked at her. "You should get back. If they catch you . . ."

She waited a moment for him to finish, but he didn't. "I know, Dreamboat."

He gave her that shy, surprised smile again and she couldn't help smiling in return. She liked his reaction to her compliment. He was a cutie, and he didn't even know it. "I'll walk with you to the shed and then I'll head up the back stairs. Can I ask you a question first though? It's sort of personal."

The kid paused, nodded. "Your mothers . . . were they students here?"

He shrugged. "I think so." A cloud moved across his expression. He glanced down at the tiny animal clutched against his chest and then back to her. "They didn't want us."

"How . . . why? How do you know that?"

"Our tutor told us. We all came out damaged, just like him"—he ran a finger down the fox's back before meeting her eyes again—"and so they left us here."

What in the world? That didn't sound . . . three girls had given birth at Lilith House and then left their "damaged" babies behind? How exactly did *that* work? And this boy? He appeared anything but damaged.

She opened her mouth to ask him more, but he pulled at her sleeve. "We have to go. It's almost time for chapel. They'll expect you there."

Shit. She'd forgotten about chapel. Yes, yes, they would expect her there.

She followed him to the edge of the forest and then walked in his wake as he wove from one landmark to another, obviously dodging the windows where someone might look out and spot movement. The sun cast a pale glow across the silver sky, shadows dissipating as dawn turned to day. When they made it to the small shed on the other side of the property, they both took a moment to catch their breath. A bluebird swooped down, causing Kandace to leap back and duck her head. But the thing landed easily on the kid's shoulder and he tilted his head toward it, nuzzling it with his hair. "Hey, Rocky," he said. "Go on. I'm busy right now." He gave his shoulder a small shake and the bird flew away, soaring smoothly into the morning sky.

Kandace took a step forward. "What are you? A bird whisperer too?"

He made a small sound of humor. "He fell out of his nest when he was a baby. I fed him and now, he doesn't know how to be a wild bird. It happens sometimes. I'm not sure why, but it does."

"Huh," Kandace said. This kid was interesting to say the least. She glanced around. The door to the shed faced the trees and was hidden from the view of the house. The kid eased the door open, and she followed him inside. Dusty shafts of pearly light floated from the one window high on the wall, and Kandace looked around at the piles of old tools and paint cans. She looked up, noticing that the ceiling was clean of cobwebs and dust, and the floor was swept of dirt and debris. Upon closer inspection, it appeared as though the kid had cleaned it, and then re-piled the junk to make it look unused.

A secret hospital in the midst of a war-torn land, that treated nature's children.

The kid ducked behind a pile of rusty junk, bending to set the fox down somewhere safe and hidden, and then straightened, joining her near the door.

When they turned, Kandace let out a startled gasp. A young girl stood there, staring icily at her. Kandace blinked, the fact that the girl had a cleft palate registering. "Hi."

The girl said nothing, her eyes finally sliding to the boy. "Another one?" she asked, her expression warming.

"Yeah. A fox," he murmured, his gaze moving nervously between Kandace and the girl.

The girl looked back at Kandace. "Can she be trusted?"

Indignation filled Kandace. Who did this little shit think she was? As quickly as the thought came though, her ire slipped. This girl was the abandoned kid of some teenage runaway. And she didn't have to wonder what this girl's "damage" was.

"I think so, Georgia." the kid muttered.

"I can be trusted," Kandace asserted, a cloud parting and a ray of sun causing her to squint. "I have to go though. Now." She pushed past the girl. "Bye, Dr. Dreamboat," she called. She glanced back once to see that the girl—*Georgia,* was that what he'd said?—had turned to watch her leave, that same frosty stare stuck firmly to her damaged face. And not for the first time, Kandace wondered how a place that demanded sinlessness could mistreat and discard children . . . in any way.

CHAPTER FIFTEEN

*G*ravel flew as Camden's truck skidded to a halt. He yanked the keys from the ignition, jumping from the vehicle and jogging toward the door where he'd installed a new lock a few days before.

Raising his fist, he pounded harshly on the door and a second later, Scarlett pulled it open, her eyes wide, skin pallid. "You okay?" He looked off behind her, searching for something specific he might battle that would result in banishing that look of fear from her face.

"Come in," she said, stepping aside so he could enter. "Thank you for coming." She closed the door and wrapped her arms around herself, glancing up at the staircase and then back at him. "I feel kind of silly now. And you're obviously off duty." Her gaze flickered down his body, noting, he figured, his lack of uniform. "I thought I heard something . . . well, in the . . . in the *walls*. I . . ." She shook her head as though embarrassed. "I think maybe I spooked myself. It could have been mice. It probably was, right? I mean, it had to be."

"What do you mean, in the walls?" he demanded, a sinking feeling in his gut. *Damn them to hell.*

For a moment she appeared torn, but then she pointed at the wall that curved upward with the staircase. "I heard something there, on the other side of that wall. It was almost like something was . . . climbing. The sound disappeared up there"—she pointed at the ceiling over the staircase—"and then I heard, like, a door closing."

Camden swore under his breath. *They'd promised.* "Where's your daughter?"

Scarlett's brow dipped. "She's sleeping. I checked on her after I called you. The door to our room is locked."

"Okay. I'm going to check things out. Why don't you head back to your room and stay there? I'll call you when I'm done."

"You think there's reason to be concerned." She said it as a statement, not a question, so he didn't answer her. Instead he repeated, "I'll call you when I'm done."

"O-okay," she said, pausing for a moment and pressing her lips together as though she was holding back from saying more. Apparently having decided not to question him further, Scarlett nodded, turning and walking to the stairs. He watched her disappear up the curved staircase and then he turned to begin his search of the rooms and halls he knew well.

An hour later, Scarlett found him, nailing the final board into place. "I told you I'd call you when I was done," he muttered, dropping his hammer back into the toolbox he'd retrieved from his truck after he'd conducted a search of the house and felt confident no one was hiding in some dark corner.

Scarlett crossed her arms over her chest, squinting at the boards he'd just nailed to the wall. "What's that about?"

Camden faced her fully. "There are crawl spaces in the walls of the house. They can be accessed by hidden doors in the walls."

Her eyes grew wide. She stared at the boarded-up spot for a moment, her gaze finally drifting to him. "You think someone was in the crawl space in my house? Who?"

"Kids." And God, he hoped he wasn't lying, although he was pretty sure he was. His gut tightened. "Word gets around about things like secret crawl spaces in the local haunted house." He rubbed at his eye. "I think I found the entry point, a window on the first floor in the back with a broken lock. I boarded it up and checked the rest. They seem sound, although like I told you, you should have all your windows checked by a professional as soon as possible."

She was still staring at the boards he'd nailed in place, a crease between her eyes. "Why would kids sneak into my house and climb through *crawl spaces*? That goes a little beyond trying to find a party spot, or a crash pad."

He shrugged. "Why do kids do anything?" He picked up his toolbox. "Like we talked about before, a dare. For kicks. The thrill of scaring you."

She blinked at him. "So . . . you're sure you nailed all the openings shut?"

"Yup." Camden turned, beginning to make his way downstairs. He heard Scarlett's footsteps behind him.

"What if you . . . well, what if you locked some kid carrying out a dare in the walls? What if they're still in there and they can't get out?"

He turned to face her, a strange thump in his chest at the earnest expression on her face. *Dammit* she was pretty. It made him feel off balance each time he stared at her for too long, so he looked away. "You hear someone might have broken into your house to terrorize you and you're concerned for *them*?"

She raised her gaze as though considering. "Yes. I mean, can you imagine?" She glanced at the wall. "It would be like being buried alive."

He considered her for a moment. He'd only known her a handful of days, her presence was a damn inconvenience to him to say the least, and yet he found himself intrigued by her, interested in the things that came out of her mouth, the way she viewed the world. And of course, there was the way she made his body feel, both clumsy and electrified just by virtue of the way she looked. He stared at her a moment longer. Yeah, so he was definitely attracted to her.

Didn't matter. He had one goal in mind, and she wasn't going to get in the way. But not at the expense of her safety.

She had a little girl, an innocent child.

And she'd known Kandace. He was still having a hard time wrapping his mind around that.

Hey, Dreamboat. He still heard her voice in his head sometimes, that nickname that had both embarrassed him and filled him with pleasure.

Camden turned, heading away again. "Call me if you smell something dead coming from the walls."

Behind him, Scarlett gasped, rushing to descend the stairs next to him. "You're *not* serious."

They stepped into the foyer together and came to halt, Camden turning toward her, feeling a twinge of humor at the mild outrage on her face. He *hadn't* been serious. He'd checked the crawl space—shone his flashlight up and down it on each floor—and knew no one was in it, but he took another moment to enjoy her reaction. He had the feeling that if he told her there was likely some drug-addled teenager locked up in her walls, she'd take a sledgehammer and make it her job to free him or her. Dumb woman. She was going to get herself hurt. She was going to get her child hurt.

Farrow was no place for her.

Lilith House might prove dangerous.

And what will you do about it, Cam? Come up with an excuse to board up every window and crawl space? Sit on her doorstep with a pistol? Wouldn't it be easier just to let them do what they want, so long as they don't hurt her?

Yeah, yeah it would.

He'd tried to remind himself of that as he'd walked through her mess of a kitchen to check the window, spotting the drawings of cakes she had hanging up on one empty wall underneath a logo that read Ruby Sugar. The colored sketches were so outrageously beautiful and unique that they had

140

stunned him for a moment. And Camden wasn't a man generally impressed by spun sugar and frosted flowers.

So she was beautiful and kind and ridiculously talented. So what?

Where exactly do your loyalties lie? Those had been Georgia's words and they rang in his ears now.

With you, Georgie, he'd answered. *Always with you.*

"There was no one in the crawl space," he said. "When you start with the renovations, you might want to have them sealed up permanently though."

Her eyes ran over his face as though she could see under his skin. It made him nervous. It made him feel like she knew things about him he didn't want her to know. *She doesn't. How could she?* "What was the original purpose of those crawl spaces? Any idea?"

"I don't know if anyone knows for sure. I've heard Hubert Bancroft had them created as hiding spaces for his family should there be an invasion of some sort. It was a lawless time back then. Wealthy people often had hidden spaces in their homes where they might hide people or things worth stealing."

"Things worth stealing," she muttered as if mulling over the phrase. Scarlett's gaze moved away for a moment and she nodded her head. "Not to mention Hubert Bancroft considered himself judge, jury, and executioner in the murder of innocent people. I might be paranoid too if I was a stone-cold devil any fair-minded person would relish seeing dead."

Like that, he thought, a small chuckle moving up his throat at her phrasing, true though it was. She said things like that and it made him want to protect her, not just from physical harm, but from anything that might distress or scare her, or even make that small frown line appear between her eyes. Because she was perceptive and caring and *decency* poured off her like a tangible thing.

Christ Almighty.

He scrubbed a hand over his face, opening his mouth to tell her to lock the door behind him. He didn't want to spend another moment with this woman. It was shaking things up. It was going to ruin everything.

A shrill chirping came from the direction of the kitchen. He turned toward it. "What was that?"

Scarlett sighed. "Our temporary guest." She turned, heading toward the noise and, unable to resist, Camden followed.

When they arrived at the kitchen, Scarlett went immediately to a Tupperware container sitting on the counter, picking it up and turning toward him. Inside the container, nestled in a kitchen towel was a baby bird.

"He ate a little bit of mashed egg earlier, but he won't take any water."

"Good. A nestling can easily drown if you give it water."

"Oh," she breathed. "Okay. Well, good to know." She ran a finger over the back of the baby bird. "Sorry, little guy." She looked at Camden. "How do we hydrate him?"

"He'll have gotten enough from the food. You can get some baby bird formula at the pet store in town tomorrow." He pursed his lips. This situation needled at him, felt all-too familiar. "Where'd you find it?"

"By our front door." She shrugged. "I'm assuming it fell from a nearby nest and an animal dragged him near the house. He's lucky to be alive."

"Seems like a suitable name, then. Lucky."

She smiled. "Lucky. Yes, I agree." She peered over at the bird. "You have been christened."

"Once you name something, it's harder to see them die."

She appeared to consider that for a moment. "Yes, I can see how that's true." She sighed. "It's too late in any case. Haddie's already attached." She paused. "I'd hoped Haddie would be able to care for him, but he's making that sound every hour and so I suppose I'm on night duty."

She looked tired. It didn't diminish her beauty, in fact, if anything it enhanced it, made her look soft. Vulnerable. The way she might look first thing in the morning, after a night of— "They eat frequently," he said, watching her watch the baby bird. "If he seems reluctant to take food from you, tap on his beak right here. He placed a finger over the spot he meant, careful not to tap now that the small thing had fallen back to sleep, buying her—and him as long as he was here— some temporary quiet.

"Okay. Thanks." She looked up at him. "You know a lot about wildlife."

"Some. You can't grow up in a town surrounded by wilderness without acquiring some knowledge about its inhabitants."

She smiled. "I appreciate the help. I'm a city girl who never owned a pet. I know very little about animals, wild or otherwise." She gently placed the container back down in a darkened corner of the counter, turned around, opened her mouth to speak, closed it, and then opened it again to say, "Do you want a nightcap?"

He stared at her, his gaze flicking briefly to the helpless baby contained snugly and safely in a Tupperware container. She'd be up every hour on the hour tonight. She seemed resigned to it. And for what? For some pitiful creature who'd probably die anyway because she didn't know what she was doing? *Go,* he told himself. *Staying is a bad idea. Very bad.* His eyes returned to her pretty face, expression expectant. "Sure," he sighed. "I'll have a nightcap."

CHAPTER SIXTEEN

$\mathcal{S}$carlett retrieved two glasses from the cabinet, mindful to be as quiet as possible so she didn't wake the sleeping baby. That chirping sound was enough to set any new mother's hackles on edge.

"Is whiskey okay?" she asked, nodding to a bottle on the counter. "It's all I have. My best friend is a liquor distributor and she gave it to me. I'm not much of a whiskey drinker, but she gifted it because of the label." She picked up the bottle and turned it around so that the Rebel Yell label was facing him. "Private joke," she said, her lips tilting in a wry smile as she thought of the night she'd withdrawn the first of the money she'd deposited seven years before and they'd gotten drunk and danced to Billy Idol in her living room. Later, she'd cried herself to sleep in a heap of tears and shame, but for a few minutes there, she'd been strong, she'd let the world—or at least the four walls of her living room—hear her rebel yell.

That rebel yell had quickly faded to a quiet sob, but the whiskey had been on her counter since Merrilee had given it to her, a reminder to grasp that strength when she could, however tremulous and temporary it might be.

And the further reminder that Merrilee believed in her strength and supported her dreams.

"Sounds like a good story," he said.

"Not really," she answered too quickly, carrying the glasses and bottle to the table. They both sat down and she twisted off the cap, pouring them each a finger. She held up her glass. "To empty walls, sleeping babies, and those who arrive when you call for help," she whispered.

He smiled, raising his glass and clinking it lightly to hers. Their fingers brushed briefly and they both pulled their glasses away quickly, making her suspect he'd also felt the zap of energy move between their skin, though his expression indicated nothing. He took a sip of his whiskey, making a face as the liquid fire slid down his throat. She grimaced along with him. "It gets better the more you drink," she said, her voice strained.

He let out a soft chuckle. "That's usually the problem."

She smiled, dipping her head in agreement just as the tiny thing with the—apparently—*massive* lungs let out that bone-chilling chirping sound. "Oh holy hell, little one," Scarlett murmured, beginning to stand.

Camden's chair scraped across the floor as he came to his feet. "Let me," he said, moving around her and picking up the baby bird in his makeshift nest.

Scarlett grabbed the mashed egg she'd made earlier and handed it to Camden who sat back down. He used one finger to rub the bird's beak right where he'd shown her earlier and the tiny thing opened its mouth widely, accepting the food he offered. "Amazing," she said, noting the ease with which he fed the bird after she'd struggled to get even the smallest bit into its mouth. "Were you a mama bird in a past life?"

He smiled at her and her chest felt tight to see this big, strong man holding the delicate creature with so much gentleness. "Could be. Maybe that's why I'm so restless," he murmured, watching the bird as he ate from his finger. "In some past life I used to be able to fly and now I merely have feet."

She tilted her head, taking him in, her curiosity spiking again, the question rising up inside her: *who are you?* "You're restless?"

He looked up, appearing almost confused for a moment as if he hadn't realized he'd made that statement out loud. "Sometimes. Who isn't, I guess."

She took another sip of whiskey, watching as he fed the bird. *She* was restless too. It'd come on in the last few years, this . . . feeling that she was supposed to be *doing* something, only she had no idea what. This notion that she was walking through mist and someone was calling for her only she couldn't see them, couldn't *get* to them, didn't know what they wanted. The feeling had dissipated slightly with the purchase of Lilith House and the new sense of purpose at starting a business, but she had to admit some of it still lingered. "Yes," she said. "Yes, I know what you mean."

Their eyes met, gazes clashing, heat flowing between them. *God.* Chemistry was a bitch of a thing. It didn't care about timing or convenience. There was no shutoff button, no dial with which to lower the damn temperature. She'd given in to it before and it'd almost ruined her. She was still picking up the pieces of her self-respect. She didn't need, nor want to be attracted to this man. And yet, the feeling was so alluring, so *good.* It was like a thrilling drug that made you come alive.

And she was pretty sure he felt it too.

And yet . . . she'd sensed such bitterness in him at Grady's earlier that day. Had she misunderstood when she'd assumed it was directed at her? She did have a tendency to second-guess her own responsibility for other people's reactions. It was the people pleaser in her.

He nodded over to the sketches on her wall. "Those are good." He shook his head as though he'd misspoken. "No, they're not just good, they're incredible."

She felt a warm flush of pleasure at his compliment, and the sincere expression on his face. "Thank you. They're brand-new designs, all my own. As soon as I have a proper kitchen up and running, I'm going to create each one and do a photo shoot. Then I'll have a brochure made . . . some initial advertising. It seems like a lot when I start thinking about all the to-do items on my multitude of lists."

He squinted at her teasingly. "You have more than one to-do list?"

"Oh my gosh, yes. I have lists upon lists. I have *binders* of lists. I even have a master list of all my lists so I don't accidentally forget about any of my sub-lists."

He chuckled, a look of true amusement flashing in his green eyes. "One thing at a time, right?"

She nodded. "Yes. That's my motto."

There was a weighted silence before he cleared his throat softly. "So how'd you find this place anyway?" he asked, looking around the kitchen. "I didn't think the bank advertised its sale anywhere outside town. It's been empty for a long time."

She tapped the pads of her fingers on the table soundlessly, tilting her head, recollecting. "It was the most random thing actually. I had just left work. I was working in this restaurant in Beverly Hills. The commute sucked and I sort of hated my boss." She let out a short laugh, taking another sip of her drink, enjoying the burn now. "Anyway, I was walking to my car, tired, irritable, flour in my hair, you know, just living the glamorous life of a pastry chef, when a breeze picked up and this piece of trash—or so I thought—blew up off the street and stuck to my shirt. Well, I peeled it off and took a few steps to toss it in a trash can, when I happened to glance down at what it was. A flyer. This newsletter, with meeting times and whatnot, a church thingy, I think, and at the bottom was a picture of Lilith House and information about the sale. Well, I recognized the name because my friend Kandace had attended the school here. I stood there in the middle of the sidewalk just . . . stupefied." She looked off to the side, remembering the feeling that had filled her chest, this sudden, overwhelming . . . *fire* to do . . . *something*. "I went home and looked up the pictures online and it just seemed . . . perfect." She gazed behind him. "I mean, it had literally plastered itself to my body. It felt like fate."

Camden had stilled, his eyes latched on her face. "What are the odds?" he murmured.

"Exactly. What are the odds?" Her gaze moved behind him as she pictured that unexpected moment. That flyer, it was like . . . it was the permission she hadn't known she needed to make the first move to see her dream become reality.

"You believe in fate then? You think that brought you here?" He looked so serious, like every cell in his body was hanging on her answer.

She thought about it for a moment, gave it the consideration it deserved. "Yeah. I do." She swirled her drink. Her body felt warm and loose. "I've felt it before too. I felt it the night I met Haddie's father." She looked down, feeling shy suddenly talking to this man she barely knew about such personal things but well, he was sitting across from her with a baby bird in his hands, and the alcohol had loosened her tongue. "Things obviously didn't work out between us, but when I met him . . . it was like I felt this *pull*, some master plan, that almost seemed to come from outside of myself, moving me toward an unplanned fate. I know that sounds dramatic but it's the truth. It was like . . . Haddie was meant to be created, she was *meant* to be here, despite everything falling apart once that happened. She was the *point* of it all and so there should be no regret." Emotion welled up inside her, the love she felt for her daughter, and she let out a soft laugh. "My goodness, I'm a loose-lipped drunk, aren't I?"

Despite her embarrassed smile, Camden's expression remained intense, almost pained. "What are you thinking?" she asked.

He glanced down at the bird, his muscles visibly relaxing. He appeared almost sad. "I was thinking that I like that idea . . . that everyone who's here is here to serve a purpose."

She nodded, her heart giving a sharp kick. She thought again of that night, how even with the fateful pull she'd just described, she'd almost talked herself out of it. She remembered how she'd gotten up the nerve by channeling *Kandace,* her free-spirited friend who she knew would tell her to throw caution to the wind and *live.*

Seize the day, Scarlett. She could practically hear Kandi's voice in her head, even now.

The bird was asleep again, his ravenous appetite sated for the moment. Camden got up and returned his container to the dim corner of the counter. Scarlett took another sip of whiskey, enjoying the warm flush of relaxation as it spread to her limbs. She had to be mindful not to drink so much that waking up through the night would be difficult. When Camden sat back down, she nodded to the baby bird. "Seriously, I have a new respect for mama birds. Even Haddie didn't wake that frequently when she was an infant."

His lips tipped. He swirled his drink, silent for several minutes, his expression registering conflict. "Can I ask why Haddie's father isn't in the picture?"

She liked that he was curious about her too. But from the expression on his face, it almost appeared he didn't want to be.

She took a quick sip of the whiskey. She'd been telling the truth when she said that the more you drank, the easier it went down. She was indeed feeling loose-lipped. Still, out of habit—and by threat of legal ramifications—she opened her mouth to give her stock answer, that Haddie's father had been a one-night stand, that when she'd told him she was pregnant, he'd said good luck and goodbye, which was true. Mostly. Instead, she found she *wanted* to tell this man the truth. She didn't even really know why. Maybe, like she'd just thought, it was the liquor, or the way he'd held the baby bird so tenderly in his strong, masculine hands. But now, she realized, even more than those two things, it was that he'd come so quickly to her rescue tonight. It was the way his eyes tracked over her features like for that singular moment, his world revolved around the mystery of her thoughts. Maybe all those things combined made Scarlett relax her shoulders and tell this man—this virtual stranger—the truth when she'd divulged it to no one else except Merrilee and her mother. "Haddie's father is Royce Reynolds."

He tilted his head slightly, no recognition in his expression.

"Seriously? You don't know who Royce Reynolds is?" Momentary amusement bubbled up in her chest. She'd finally told someone her "big secret" and he didn't even know who the mega-famous superstar was. Hollywood's golden boy. *People's* Sexiest Man Alive.

"No. Who is he?"

"He's an actor. No, more than that. He's a star. Big time. When I was twenty, I was working for a catering company that had been hired to host this party in LA. Royce Reynolds was there and he struck up a conversation with me. He was charming. I was star-struck. I knew he had a girlfriend—they were constantly splashed across the tabloids, but . . . he mentioned they'd recently broken up and I believed him." She took a quick sip of her drink. She liked to think she'd have declined his offer to go back to his room had she known he was lying about the breakup, but . . . well, she'd been young and dumb and giddy over his attention. And like she'd said, there had been that *pull*. "He invited me back to his room and one thing led to another." His jaw tightened for a moment and then loosened. If she'd blinked she might not have seen it. Had that been . . . *jealousy?* Or disapproval? It made her doubt her decision to be this open with him. She took a deep breath. She was already in the middle. May as well cross to the other side.

"Anyway, a couple months later, I found out I was pregnant and I called to let him know." She cringed internally when she thought about the hoops she'd had to jump through just to get a message to him. She'd honestly been surprised he called her back at all. Or remembered who she was. "He seemed rattled . . . all but hung up on me. I was scared. Alone. But I thought, well, he doesn't want anything to do with this and so I'm on my own. Next thing I know, though, his *wife*—the girlfriend he said he'd broken up with, who he'd married the week before in some secret ceremony—is at my door. She

153

kindly requested that I sign a non-disclosure agreement saying I would never make Royce's paternity public and if I did so, I would be sued."

"He sent his wife to confront you?"

Scarlett nodded. Yeah, that had been humiliating. Royce hadn't even had the balls to come meet with her himself, to look her in the eyes, ask if she was okay. She would have signed the paperwork either way. She was capable of caring for her baby, even if it meant barely making ends meet. She wasn't going to try to force him to acknowledge their child if he had no interest. Yeah, she would have signed the paperwork either way. She just might not have taken the money if it'd been *him* who came to see her.

She didn't tell Camden about that though. She still felt such deep conflict on that subject. He might look at it as selling out her own daughter. And why shouldn't he? Wasn't that sort of what she'd done?

He was looking at her in that way again, but now she didn't welcome it. Now she wanted to hide.

"Is that why you moved?"

"No. Royce and his wife live in New York City. I only met him because he was filming a movie in California. I wasn't . . . you know . . . running away from him or anything." Although in a small sense she'd done just that. She refused to even glance at tabloids in the grocery store, she no longer watched shows that included entertainment news, and she rarely went to movies, and if she did, she made sure to show up after the previews had aired.

"Does Haddie know who her father is?"

"No, and now I have to swear you to secrecy, because . . . lawsuits and all. If you tell anyone, I'll deny it."

His eyes softened. "Scarlett, your secret's safe with me." He watched her for another minute before saying, "I should go."

"Right. Yeah, of course. I should try to get some sleep anyway before . . ." She nodded back to the sleeping baby bird.

Camden stood, picking up their glasses and placing them next to the sink. Scarlett headed out of the kitchen toward the front foyer and he followed. When she got to the door, he was suddenly right next to her. Her breath stuttered and she looked up at him. He was so close, and though it was dim in the foyer, the flickering light of the gas lamps picked up the lightness of his eyes, mesmerizing her. Her gaze washed over his features, the perfect combination of hard and soft. She took in the rigid set of his jaw, and the fullness of his lower lip, the sharp line of his cheekbone, and the velvet fringe of his lashes. His eyes went to her mouth and for a heartbeat she swore he was going to lean in and kiss her. Her pulse jumped, her ribs tingling. She wanted it, his lips on hers. Instead, he took a small step back, though his gaze didn't waver. "You won't be able to let him go," he said.

"What?" The word was barely breath.

"The nestling. He's at the stage where he'll imprint on you if you care for him."

"Imprint?"

"Consider you his."

She broke eye contact, her gaze sliding away from his intense stare. "Oh," she murmured. "Should I—?"

"There's nothing to do about it. It's just nature. He can't control it any more than you can."

Their gazes tangled. *Just nature . . .* She'd thought something similar earlier, about the chemistry that sizzled in the air between them. *Just nature.* Indeed. "So . . . he'll be mine forever?" she asked.

He paused a beat, his gaze narrowing very slightly. She got the odd sense that something akin to anger stirred within him. They were communicating with each other in a language she didn't fully recognize, the uttered words barely scratching the surface. "Is anything forever, Scarlett?" His hand covered hers on the doorknob and at the feel of his warm, rough palm, she pulled away, swaying slightly now that she had nothing to hold on to. Apparently, the question was rhetorical because without waiting for her answer, he turned the knob and walked out into the night.

Scarlett engaged the lock quickly and leaned back against the door. She brought her hand to her heart, feeling its steady beat under her palm. She startled at the sudden high-pitched chirping but then let out a slow, steady breath, grateful for the distraction from her chaotic emotions.

CHAPTER SEVENTEEN

Haddie stepped gingerly through the grass, dropping the last of her Skittles as she made it to the far side of the shed. She had collected the bag left near their front door when her mommy had gone inside with the baby bird, and there had still been a few handfuls of candy left. She scooted around the small, wood structure, moving quickly to the other side, before pressing her body against the rough, splintery wood.

Overhead, the sky was alight with stars. She needed to get back inside as quickly as possible before Mommy noticed she wasn't in her room playing on her iPad anymore.

Her heart gave a jump when she heard the soft crunch of grass. The thing was nearby, just at the edge of the woods behind the old structure where she stood. Haddie closed her eyes, trying again to feel its weight and letting out a frustrated gust of air when she, again, sensed nothing at all.

She stepped carefully over the dirt beneath her feet, cautious not to make a noise and let the thing know she was there—if it didn't already. She had no idea if it'd been watching her from the darkness of the trees. Maybe it knew exactly where she was. Out here in the night, all alone. Her skin prickled, fear rising inside her. Maybe this was a very bad idea, following her curiosity this way. She couldn't tell if the thing meant her harm or not. She couldn't even tell what it was.

She very suddenly wanted her mommy. She glanced up at the house, the attic windows filled with the soft glow of light from within. The safety of her mommy's arms seemed a hundred miles away. The darkness closed in on Haddie and her heart began pounding. The sound of footsteps grew closer . . . closer. There was a shaft of moonlight cast on the ground next to the shed, and from where Haddie stood at the back, she could see the shadow of looming horns, growing ever larger as the creature approached.

She clenched her eyes shut for a moment, frozen with fear. She thought of the bird the thing had left at her doorstep. She'd decided it was a gift, but maybe it was a warning. Maybe the thing was telling her what it was going to do to her—take her far, far away from Mommy and leave her for dead in a heap of skin and bones.

Haddie swallowed, mustering her courage as she pushed herself off the wall of the shed, turning in the opposite direction from which the thing was approaching. She crept quietly along the perimeter of the structure, but her shadow moved with her, reaching outward and giving her away. Her heartbeat quickened. The creature let out a rusty-sounding laugh, its large, horned shadow following hers.

Haddie picked up her pace. She just needed to make it around to the other side and then she could run for her mommy. If she ran into the open now, she'd have to race for the woods. And that was where the creature lived.

The thing let out a snorty high-pitched sound, halfway between a giggle and a cough and Haddie shivered, moving ever faster. The creature picked up its pace as well as though it was playing a game with Haddie—her fear exciting it as it took chase.

The thing was directly behind her. In her terror, she pictured its head lowered as it raced to spear her with those long, sharp horns.

She raced around the shed, her previous courage dipping as she came to the side where she could make a break for the open grass. The creature was too close though, it's heavy, flat footsteps right on her heels. Haddie raced around the building again, the creature chasing, that high-pitched snorting sound mixing with its loud puffs of breath. It was so close she could smell it now. It put off the pungent scent of dirt and sweat. As she rounded the corner again, she let out a squeal of fear, looking behind her and directly into the moonlit face of the creature.

Their gazes locked for one startling moment as horror washed through Haddie. *Oh! Oh!* With another squeal and a burst of adrenalin, Haddie sprinted away from the shed, rounding the corner and fleeing into the open grass toward the house where her mommy waited.

She couldn't sense the weight of it. She couldn't tell where it was. And she didn't understand what she'd seen.

When she made it close enough that the soft glow from the windows above lit the ground, she dared a look back.

There was nothing there.

Nothing at all.

CHAPTER EIGHTEEN

$\mathcal{T}$he banging was music to her ears if not to her utterly exhausted brain. After approving the—pleasantly reasonable—bid for the first phase of the project, Mason had been true to his word and said he could get a couple of guys over ASAP to at least begin some of the demolition. As Scarlett and Haddie descended the stairs, Scarlett waved at the two men Mason had sent, already busy tearing up the warped portion of flooring in the foyer. They spared her a quick salute and went back to work.

She grasped Haddie's hand, leading her toward the back door, to avoid the work being done near the entrance. They stepped out into the warm summer morning, the sun a bright orange orb in the cloudless blue sky. Haddie pulled her hand away and peeked in at the sleeping baby bird, and seemingly content with his comfort level, dropped the dark cloth back over him.

Scarlett would have loved to take a break and leave the little guy at Lilith House, but she'd learned well that he wasn't keen on missing any of his hour-on-the-hour meals, and so if she didn't want to terrorize the work crew, she had to cart her new charge with them, along with a baggie of food.

Next time she saw an orphaned baby bird on the ground, she was going to avert her gaze and walk right on by.

That's your exhaustion speaking, and you know it.

Yeah, she did. She'd never be able to abandon something in need, but darn it, staying up to feed someone else's demanding—and let's face it, *butt-ugly*—baby hadn't exactly been on any of her lists, master or otherwise.

As they made their way around the side of the house, Scarlett noticed what looked like a green Skittle every few steps, slightly melted and blending into the patchy grass. She stopped, looking behind her and ahead to see that they traveled in a straight line to form a trail that led toward the old shed near the tree line. The shed she hadn't yet been brave enough to look inside. Who knew what manner of mess it contained?

"Haddie"—she turned to her daughter who'd stopped beside her—"did you do that?" Scarlett nodded down to the widely spaced line of green Skittles.

Haddie paused but then nodded slowly, her expression blank. "Yes, Mommy," she said. "I was trying to . . . catch something."

"What? Like a bunny? With candy?"

Haddie swallowed and Scarlett got that internal buzz she felt when Haddie was having trouble communicating something or leaving information out. "Yes, Mommy." She looked behind them and then ahead. "I left a trail of all the colors."

Scarlett frowned in confusion. Something had eaten most of the candy. It couldn't have been a bunny, could it? More likely a scavenger such as a raccoon. Those things would eat anything. A small nervous laugh emerged. "Well, whatever it was that ate your trail, decided it didn't like the green ones." *Odd.* Scarlett took a step forward, heading for the front of the house and their car as Haddie walked beside her. "I guess I can't blame it." She smiled down at her daughter. "Everyone knows the green ones aren't any good."

Haddie's expression remained mostly blank, though her eyes were alight with interest. Or . . . wonder. A curiosity that stayed burning in her gaze even as they got in the car and pulled away from Lilith House. A curiosity that Scarlett could see had stolen her away, at least temporarily as she pondered things available only to her own mystifying mind. "It doesn't like green," Scarlett thought she heard Haddie murmur under her breath.

Scarlett pulled her eyes away from where she'd watched Haddie for a moment in the rearview mirror, focusing on the windy, single-lane road that weaved through the forest toward town. The drive to Farrow took about thirty minutes, but to Scarlett, who was from Los Angeles where it could literally take two hours to go twenty miles, the drive was nothing. If anything, it was relaxing, a chance to think, to get lost in the quiet of her own head as the road disappeared beneath her tires. Haddie, similarly, seemed happy to quietly stare at the woods outside her window, caught up in her secret thoughts.

As she drove, Scarlett's mind turned to Camden West and the moment she'd thought he was going to kiss her two nights before. At the memory, a kaleidoscope of unwanted butterflies stirred to life in her stomach. *Speaking of curiosity.* It seemed she and her daughter were alike in that they both were in possession of far too much of it.

She was slightly embarrassed that she'd been so forthcoming with him, but then again, he'd made her feel like he was deeply interested in her, like he was almost . . . hanging on her every word, and it'd felt good. He'd made her feel *interesting*, and God, it'd been a long time since she'd thought of herself as such.

Is anything forever, Scarlett? His words reverberated through her mind. She wondered what sort of life he'd lived to make him ask such a cynical question.

She followed the directions the girl named Amelia Schmidt had given her when they'd spoken on the phone. The girl had been peppy and engaging and Scarlett had liked her immediately. She'd seemed enthusiastic about the idea of looking after Haddie, so she'd set up a meeting for the three of them that morning.

The house where Amelia lived with her parents was in a quaint residential neighborhood in Farrow. Scarlett admired the vining pink bougainvillea that grew up the columns of the front porch. Other than the lush, bright blooms, the house was small and somewhat plain, though it was obviously well-maintained, the paint fresh, the porch swept clean.

Haddie held the bird in his "nest" in one hand, and gripped Scarlett's with the other as she rapped twice on the door. A moment later, a woman who looked to be in her mid to late fifties pulled it open, offering Scarlett and Haddie a pleasant smile. "You must be Ms. Lattimore."

"Yes, but please call me Scarlett. And you're Amelia's mom?" She hesitated in asking the question. The woman seemed a tad older than she'd expect Amelia's mother to be, but she certainly wasn't going to ask if she was her grandmother and find herself with her foot in her mouth. Better to err on the side of youth when making assumptions.

The woman pulled the door open so they could enter and as they stepped over the threshold, she smiled and said, "Yes. Victoria Schmidt. Call me Vicky."

She closed the door behind them and said, "You must be Haddie."

Haddie nodded shyly. Vicky glanced at the container in Haddie's hand, but didn't ask about it.

Scarlett glanced around, noting the large painting of Jesus's crucifixion on the wall to their left, and a wooden crucifix on the portion of wall next to the staircase. It made her think of the crucifix she'd found in the closet at Lilith House and a slight shiver of unease moved through her, for what reason she had no idea.

When Scarlett looked back at Vicky, the woman gave them a tepid smile, twisting her hands together as though she was nervous. Or perhaps just shy with strangers. "Welcome to town. Amelia can't wait to meet you. She's just out back watering. She loves gardening. She planted everything in our yard. Um, let me go get her." She nodded to a living room to the right of the hall. "Please make yourselves at home." She twisted her hands nervously again. "I do hope this works out. I've been encouraging Millie to become more independent. That's important." Her features twisted slightly and then her expression became placid again. "Millie has always been wonderful with children. I can't imagine that she won't be a teacher someday."

"That's so great to hear," Scarlett said, trying to put the obviously socially awkward woman at ease. "We can't wait to meet her."

Vicky bobbed her head. "I'll tell her you're here. She'll be in in a minute."

Scarlett led Haddie to a green couch in the living room with another picture of Jesus—this image of him walking on water—hanging over it. Scarlett appreciated Jesus as much as the next semi-religious girl, but really, this seemed excessive.

Then again, perhaps the world would be a much better place if more people loved Jesus with the same devotion Victoria Schmidt obviously did.

"She's sad," she thought she heard Haddie whisper, glancing over to see her daughter peeking under the fabric at the bird.

The sound of the back door opening and then slamming closed broke Scarlett from her thoughts and a moment later, a pretty, blonde teenage girl appeared around the corner, offering them a large smile, her braces glinting in the light streaming in through the front window. "Hi. Scarlett?" She reached out her hand as Scarlett stood to greet her, shaking her hand exuberantly. "I'm Amelia."

The girl was all legs, her limbs long and slender like a baby colt still growing into its form, and her smile was sweet and infectious. She was bright-eyed and happy, and Scarlett found herself grinning back. Amelia threw herself onto the couch in that way teenagers do, across from where she and Haddie sat. Amelia leaned forward. "Haddie, right? I love that name. As soon as I heard it, I thought you and I might make a good team. Millie and Haddie. We sound like a matching pair, don't we? Like we just go together?" Amelia's metal grin widened again, a dimple appearing in her left cheek.

Haddie's return smile was instantaneous, one of those open, child-like ones that were so rare. She nodded at Millie, her smile morphing into an expression of bashful delight.

Scarlett let out a breath of relief. Haddie liked this girl. She'd liked her immediately and without doubt. And really, that was all Scarlett needed to know. Anything more would be purely about formalities.

"What have you got there?" Amelia asked, pointing to the container Haddie had placed on the coffee table.

"It's a baby bird," Haddie said, drawing the dark piece of fabric back slightly.

Amelia leaned over farther and let out a soft gasp of breath. "Oh my goodness. It fell out of its nest?"

Haddie paused but nodded. "We think so," she said, glancing at Scarlett. "We have to take care of it now. We thought she might not make it because she's tiny and hurt, but my mommy said she's a fighter." There was a gravity in Haddie's tone that Scarlett had never heard before and, with surprised interest, she glanced over to see her gaze glued to Millie as though she was in a semi-trance.

"Poor little thing," Amelia murmured, putting her hand over her heart. At the gesture, Haddie blinked and looked down. "How do you know it's a she?" Scarlett had wondered that too when Haddie said it. Scarlett had been referring to the bird as a he, but really, she had no basis for that.

"I just . . . feel it," Haddie said.

Amelia smiled at Haddie. "Ah."

"She eats egg," Haddie explained. "But we're going to stop at the pet store after this and buy some baby bird formula."

Scarlett watched as the two girls—their golden heads bent together over the tiny bird—discussed its care. She marveled at the fact that there was something so immediately comfortable about Amelia, as though she was a long-lost friend they were catching up with. What a sweet girl she seemed to be.

When Haddie gently placed the cloth over the bird, Scarlett said, "Well, speaking of that little guy, or, I mean, *girl,* we'd better get going before she wakes up hungry. It was lovely meeting you, Millie. I'd love it if you'd watch Haddie. I think you two get along great."

"I'd love to," Millie said. "Especially now after meeting Haddie." She offered a smile. "My parents had me later in life—sort of a surprise baby, you know?—so there were no siblings, just me." She looked at Haddie. "I've always wished for a little sister."

Haddie smiled back shyly at Millie.

"Then this works out perfectly," Scarlett said. "Right, Haddie?" She pushed a lock of hair off her daughter's forehead as she nodded. When she looked back at Millie, she asked, "Your mother is okay with Haddie coming here some days?"

"Oh definitely. She's shy, but my mom's really nice." She nodded up to the picture of Jesus and leaned in closer. "Very involved with the church if you didn't already guess."

Scarlett smiled. "You must be part of the youth group? Sister Madge mentioned it earlier."

Millie shook her head. "This fall I will be. But there's a separate group for the original town members. Stuck-up, right?" She rolled her eyes and Scarlett breathed out a laugh.

"Um . . . I'll go with"—she squinted one eye—"traditional."

Millie grinned. "Oh!" she said, turning her attention to Haddie. "I forgot to tell you I have a craft room upstairs with everything you can imagine. We can color and make friendship bracelets, and do all sorts of things. Maybe we could even make a little cradle for your baby bird so she doesn't have to sleep in a box."

"A craft room," Scarlett repeated, smiling at her daughter. "That sounds right up Haddie's alley, right?" Haddie's eyes had lit up as Millie described the room and now she nodded enthusiastically at Scarlett.

"And do you feel okay watching Haddie at Lilith House some days?" she asked Millie. "I'd pick you up, of course."

"Promise there are no ghosts there? That's what the kids say." She let out a soft laugh.

Scarlett forced a smile, thinking about the fear she'd felt the night before at the sounds of someone climbing up the inside of the wall. *Kids, just kids.* She resisted a shiver. "Ghosts? No. We haven't seen any, right, Haddie?"

Haddie nodded, even as her eyes slid away.

Millie let out a small giggle and shrugged. "We're not afraid of ghosts anyway, right, Haddie?" She winked at her.

"Sometimes," Haddie said softly. "But not *all* the time."

Scarlett set up an appointment to pick Amelia up for a few hours of childcare the next day and they said their goodbyes to Millie.

As they stepped back out into the sunshine, Scarlett felt as though a weight had been lifted from her shoulders, and this feeling of peace had descended, Millie's sweet cheer a balm to her soul that she hadn't even realized she'd needed so desperately. So many things in Farrow felt so *odd*—disconcerting—but here was this girl, this breath of fresh air.

The move was a major adjustment for both of them, and Scarlett had felt guilty for taking her sensitive child away from the only home she'd ever known, from Merrilee's love and affection, from Gram's steady presence. So to see the joy in her face as she interacted with Millie was the best gift she could possibly receive.

CHAPTER NINETEEN

Thirteen Years Ago

*K*andace was having the strangest dreams. Only the weirdest part was, she really couldn't remember anything about them. All she knew was that she would wake up with this odd sort of *heavy* feeling, but when she'd tried to piece together the dream that left her with those sensations, she couldn't remember a single thing about them.

It was the school. This damn house where an oppressive feeling of doom suffocated them. The way she felt both lost in time and utterly aware of every tick of the clock.

The way screams sometimes echoed from the floors below, and then one of the girls would be missing from class for the next few days. She wanted to ask them about it, to get their account, but socializing with anyone other than your roommate—or in her case roommates—was not facilitated.

Somehow it was all the more horrifying to let your own mind wander as to what was happening in rooms beyond your own. She wondered if Ms. Wykes knew that and figured she must. Everything here was calculated.

"What happened to you?" Aurora asked quietly, her words mumbled around a mouth of toothpaste.

Kandace looked at her in the mirror in front of where they were both brushing their teeth at the large farmhouse sink in their shared bathroom and then followed her gaze to her arm where there were several small, round bruises.

For a moment she frowned in confusion, but then she remembered the kid grabbing her arm as he'd pulled her from the forest. She hadn't thought it'd been with enough strength to cause bruising, but obviously it had been. She wasn't going to mention the kid to Aurora though. It wasn't that she didn't trust her. It wasn't that she *did* either, it was just that she wasn't going to risk getting the boy in trouble after he'd put himself on the line to help her.

"I was late to class yesterday. One of those old bitches pulled me into the room like I'd personally insulted her with my tardiness."

Aurora's eyes widened and she glanced behind her in the mirror nervously as if one of those "old bitches" might walk in unexpectedly at any moment. God, everyone walked on eggshells around here. She was beginning to as well. The rigorous academics, hours of Bible study, the rigid schedule, strange sounds in the walls, secret, forgotten children living in the basement, and of course *those screams*. She felt like she was walking through a different life, one she had no compass for, one in which every step felt precarious and uncertain.

"Play by the rules, okay, Kandace?" Aurora said, leaning over to rinse her mouth. When she stood, she laid her hand gently on the fingerprints on Kandace's arm. "I don't want to see anything bad happen to you. Let's do whatever we have to do to get out of here."

She offered Aurora a weak smile. God, she had a headache. Those damn dreams. She really hadn't slept well at all. "I will, I promise," she lied. Because while she realized doing anything other than "playing by the rules" was risky, her curiosity was spurring her to learn *more*. Whatever she could. She did plan on getting out of there, but she'd also like to send a whole team of law enforcement officers *back*. Those who would *expose* Lilith House and all its dirty secrets.

All three girls dressed in their uniforms and left the room together, headed for their first class. As they stepped down onto the first floor, bells began clanging.

"Holy fuck," Kandace swore softly.

"Line up, girls," one of the teachers said loudly from somewhere up ahead.

"Fire alarm," Sydney said, a worried line forming between her eyes. The small group of girls in front of them started moving toward the front exit.

"There's been a grease fire in the kitchen," the teacher ahead explained. "We have it under control, but the fire department is on the way nonetheless. Single file, girls. No need to panic."

Kandace took hold of Aurora's arm and tugged at her gently. Her roommate gave her an astonished glance and shook her head. *Please,* Kandace mouthed.

The girl glanced in front of her, but the staff members were all around the corner, only the group of girls they'd come down the stairs with shuffled ahead of them, those at the front of the line rounding the corner toward the front door. "Cover for me," she whispered when Aurora widened her eyes in question. "Please." She didn't give the girl time to agree or disagree, turning and rounding the corner behind them, hurrying toward the back hall and those basement steps that led to the rooms below.

This time, however, the door was locked. "Dammit," Kandace swore, reaching up and taking the pin that held her bangs back out of her hair. The hum of voices grew dimmer as did the retreating footsteps. Kandace wiggled the pin in the lock, letting out a frustrated breath when it slipped from her fingers and fell to the floor.

A lone set of footsteps suddenly sounded on the hardwood, drawing nearer. "Is everyone out?" a voice called. Ms. West, she thought, but she couldn't be sure. A swooshing sound filled her head and that damn headache still throbbed. Kandace glanced around desperately, but there was nowhere to hide, only a long empty hallway in front of her. She dropped the pin again, the small dark object disappearing onto the dark mahogany floors. "Hello? Anyone?" the voice called. "There's been a fire. All students must gather out front." Kandace dropped to her knees and grappled blindly for the pin, the feel of the small tool meeting her fingertips. She grasped it and stood quickly, sticking it in the lock.

You can do it, you can do it.

With a very small click, the lock disengaged. Kandace grimaced as she opened the door as slowly as she dared, only one tiny squeak emerging. She prayed whoever was coming hadn't heard it, or that it had been disguised beneath her own clicking footsteps.

She slipped through the crack of the door and pulled it closed quickly behind her, engaging the lock from the other side.

As Kandace stood stock-still just like she'd done the first time she was behind this particular door, the footsteps moved past, not stopping. She let out a long, slow breath and headed down the steps.

When she reached the bottom, this time she didn't linger. She headed straight through the piled furniture and boxes, rounding the corner into the dim hallway beyond.

The first room was empty as was the second room. As she approached the open doorway of the third, she heard the very distant sound of fire engines approaching Lilith House. *Please let the arrival of the trucks cause enough distraction that I'm not missed.*

In the last room, the three children sat together on the bed. Dreamboat was sitting with his back against the wall, the girl—Georgia—was at the end, and another boy was sitting on the right edge. All three of them looked up as she appeared, their eyes growing wide with surprise.

"What are you doing here?" Dreamboat asked, setting down the hefty-looking book in his hands. *A Bible.* He'd been reading to them from the Bible.

"There's a fire," Kandace said. "Did anyone tell you?"

The girl's crooked mouth set in as thin a line as it could being that her lips didn't—*couldn't*—meet. "We already have a caretaker," she said. "You should go." Well. Wasn't she a pleasant little thing? Kandace identified, but it didn't mean she appreciated the nasty attitude directed straight at her.

Even so, she couldn't help feeling some pity for the girl. Despite the unlucky hand Kandace had been dealt in some respects, she'd always had a pretty face. And she hadn't hesitated using it to her advantage. This girl didn't even have that.

Kandace narrowed her eyes at the girl briefly just to show her she didn't care for her, shifting her attention to the other boy sitting on the edge of the bed. "Hi, I'm Kandace."

"Mason," he murmured, his shoulders curling slightly as he looked down.

Kandace looked at Dreamboat. "What if there's a serious fire? You're just supposed to stay down here?"

He shrugged. "Ms. West would make sure we got out. It's not like we're locked in here." Still . . . if something happened to the school—if a fire really erupted and burned the place to ash—where would they go? She had a feeling that at least on paper, these kids didn't exist.

"Where's Ms. West now?"

"She had a class upstairs. She used the intercom to tell us what was happening." He nodded to an ancient-looking receiver on the wall—one of those antique intercom systems that had once been used to summon servants. So these kids weren't even considered important enough to leave the premises during a kitchen fire? Her own problems, her own grievances with life, the fact that she felt invisible to her mother unless she was disappointing her, suddenly seemed sort of . . . *pathetic.*

"You're just supposed to stay out of sight?"

"Yeah."

"Have you ever left Lilith House?"

The three of them glanced back and forth between each other. "No," Dreamboat finally said.

God. They'd spent their lives in these three, small basement rooms? Kandace studied the teens for a few seconds. She needed to find out more about them. Because when she left, she might not have proof that the people who ran this school were batty as shit. Maybe no one would believe a word she said about her own experience. But maybe, if she produced some evidence about these children, they'd do something about the fact that three kids had been hidden away from the world, outcasts through no fault of their own. And yet, *they* seemed to simply . . . accept that this was normal. *To them, it is.* They weren't asking for help. They were just existing. *Are they allowed to see the sunshine? Or do they always have to sneak?* Too weird. So wrong.

The girl—Georgia—stood. "I'm not sure why you're down here. We're *not* your business."

Dreamboat rose to his feet. "She's just being nice, Georgie." He squeezed Georgia's shoulder as he walked past her. Georgia's eyes softened and her hand went immediately to the place he'd just touched. When Kandace moved her gaze to the other boy, he was watching Georgia as well, only his expression was sad, sullen, as though he'd noticed her reaction to Dreamboat and it caused him a measure of heartbreak.

Huh. Interesting. There was a little love triangle going on down here. A soap opera playing out between three abandoned teens in the basement beneath Lilith House. Oh, the pitiful angst. Especially considering love triangles never ended well.

"You really shouldn't have risked coming down here again," the kid said, leading her out of the room.

"I was concerned about you."

He looked briefly confused, as though he didn't know what to make of the idea that anyone would be concerned about them.

They walked to the back of the basement, turning where she remembered the hidden door was.

He began to reach for it. "Can I ask you a question?" she said.

He paused, his hand dropping momentarily. "Sure," he answered warily.

"Do you have any idea who your mothers were? Their names? Anything?"

He shook his head just as noise sounded from upstairs. Footsteps, voices. *Damn.* It sounded like the girls were heading back into the school to return to class. If she hurried up the ladder in the wall, came out in that empty corner on the top floor, she just might make it back down again in time. The kid pulled the hidden door open and Kandace crawled inside.

She turned back to him. "Hey, Dreamboat, that girl, Georgia, is she trustworthy?"

The boy paused, but then nodded. "She'll do what I tell her to do. She won't say a word about you."

Kandace recalled the way she'd looked after he'd touched her so briefly. Yeah, Kandace could believe she'd do whatever this little dreamboat told her to do. She started to climb but then paused again. If she was going to find out more about these three, she needed to know as much about them as possible.

She had a feeling they were the key to bringing this place down.

She'd enjoyed the blush on his face every time she teased him with the nickname, but it wouldn't be enough if she hoped to uncover more information. "What's your real name, Dreamboat?"

His eyes moved away and then back. "Camden."

"Camden what?"

He shook his head, eyes lowering. "Just Camden."

Then he shut the door behind her and she heard him walking away.

CHAPTER TWENTY

Camden knocked loudly on the front door, hoping his own pounding could be heard over the steady bang of hammers from within. After a few minutes of no answer, he tried the door, leaning inside. "Hello?" he called, stepping into the foyer of Lilith House.

A handyman who often worked for Mason stepped around the corner, gripping a crowbar in his hand. "Hey, Cam."

"Hey, Kenneth. I'm looking for Ms. Lattimore."

The man pulled a bandana out of his back pocket and wiped the perspiration off his forehead. "She left about an hour ago. Asked if there were any bodies of water nearby. I heard Mason mention Hermosa Creek."

"With her daughter?"

"I think the daughter's with her sitter in town."

"Is Mason still here?" he asked. He hadn't seen his truck out front, but maybe he'd ridden with one of his team.

"Nah. He left right after Ms. Lattimore."

Camden pressed his lips together, that disquiet that had been his constant companion since they'd fought in Mason's office the week before gripping him tightly.

"Thanks, Kenneth."

Kenneth gave him a small salute and Camden exited the house, heading for the path that led to the shallow creek about a quarter mile from the house. Hell, at this time of year, it might not just be shallow, it may have dried up completely. But if she hadn't returned to the house yet, maybe she'd found something worth lingering for.

She's not your responsibility, yet here you are. He'd promised himself he'd stop checking on her. *And he would.*

He swore beneath his breath, even while his feet kept moving down the dusty, dirt road that his young legs had traveled so many times when it'd been safe for him to sneak away for an hour or two.

He'd heard it said that some roads steal your time, some steal your comfort, and some steal your heart. Where had he read it? He couldn't remember, but it had stayed with him the way quotes sometimes do. He'd thought of it that first day he'd made the winding drive that led back to Lilith House. He'd pondered on the question of what else the road that took him back to the place of his birth could possibly steal from him when it'd already taken those things. *Nothing,* he'd thought. *There's nothing more Lilith House can take from you.* Now it was *his* turn to retrieve what he could. Until the other night, it had been thirteen years since he'd been in that basement. And the darkness . . . the damp smell . . . the familiar creaks of the house . . . it brought back too many memories. Conjured up the echoes of the screams from above, ones he could do nothing about. Strengthened his resolve to *own* those ghosts . . . *that pain.*

As he moved quietly through the forest, he heard the soft trickle of water up ahead. It drew him as that same sound drew all creatures, great and small. *Life.* He could smell the clean sweetness of it before it even met his eyes.

When he stepped through the trees, he stopped short, his ribcage tightening and his breath falling short. There she was, her skirt drawn up her legs, her feet submerged in the clear, shallow stream, her hands behind her on the ground and her face tilted toward the sun.

Something wild and ancient inside him responded. He didn't know exactly what it was. Instinct? Some primal law of attraction? Whatever it was, it was simply part of nature's order. Cam had studied math and English and science—Ms. West, the woman who'd eventually shared her name, had been an excellent tutor—but he'd also made nature part of his education by spending every second he could in the woods beyond the school, the only place where his soul felt truly *free.* The only place he'd ever felt he mattered. Not to any one person, but maybe just to some . . . system, or plan that was bigger—*loftier*—than the small world he'd been relegated to for his whole life up to that point.

What are you thinking?

I was thinking that I like that idea . . . that everyone who's here is here to serve a purpose.

Their conversation came back to him. She'd put into words the things he'd felt—yearned so desperately to believe about *himself*—when speaking about her daughter, and it'd filled him with a wild hope, lit a small fire in his belly. It'd also caused turmoil, uncertainty, because it didn't align with his well-laid plans. It went in opposition.

He drank her in, his eyes moving over the feminine lines of her body, her profile lifted to the sky. He'd meant what he said to Scarlett about the nestling—though he was pretty sure she knew as well as he did that he'd also been referring to himself—those primal responses determined by nature could not be avoided, nor changed. They simply were. That part he couldn't fight, even if he tried.

Scarlett lowered her head slowly, her eyes opening and meeting his gaze. She startled slightly, sitting up straight and bringing her hand to her chest. "You've really gotta stop doing that," she said on a small laugh.

"Sorry," he murmured, stepping out of the trees and walking to the other side of the stream from which she sat facing him. He could have taken three steps and walked across it, but instead he sat down on a large rock next to him, leaning forward and resting his elbows on his knees. "One of the guys working at Lilith House said you were headed this way." He squinted at the crystal-clear water rolling steadily over the rocks in its bed.

"Yeah?" she asked, eyeing him, obviously questioning why he'd decided to come in search of her through the woods.

What reason did he have? *I'm drawn to you. I can't seem to stay away. I think about you far more than I should.* Those were all true, but he couldn't tell her that. Wasn't ready or willing to admit any such thing. He'd admitted far too much already. He needed to be drawing away, and instead, he was seeking her out. "I, uh"—he reached forward and scooped up some water, drank it from his cupped hand—"was really thirsty." He gave her a wry smile, hoping his humor had worked to deflect her question.

She laughed. "Seems like you could have quenched your thirst in any number of more convenient ways."

He squinted off behind her, smiling. "More convenient, but not half as refreshing. There's nothing quite like flowing stream water."

She eyed him, acquiescing with a smile. "You are correct there. I tasted it. It is indeed refreshing," she teased.

He chuckled and for a moment they simply smiled across at each other, the chemistry in the air between them as much a moving current as the rolling water.

A hawk cried out overhead and the trees rustled in the breeze. "Peaceful out here, isn't it?" he murmured.

"Yes, except the bird calls, which have me running for the nestling formula. I've apparently already been programmed like one of Pavlov's dogs." She laughed. "Either that or it's PTSD." She shook her head. "Haddie's on day duty with her new sitter, Millie Schmidt. Do you know her?"

Cam smiled. "Yes. She's a nice girl. You deserve the break. I'm sorry I interrupted your quiet time."

Scarlett shook her head. "No, I'm glad you're here." Her cheeks colored slightly as she looked up at him from under her lashes, and if he'd questioned it the other night, he suddenly knew without doubt that she felt the same electric charge flowing between them that he did. Damn it felt good. And terrible. His eyes roamed her face, her body. He'd thought before that she was pretty, but it was more than that. She was beautiful, from her shiny golden-brown hair to her perfect unpolished toes. He leaned over and pulled a long reed of grass from the ground, needing to busy his hands.

Scarlett wiggled her feet. "It feels wonderful," she sighed and at the sound of her pleasure, his body tightened. He welcomed it. This moment . . . it felt good and . . . innocent. *This is how it's supposed to feel,* a voice whispered inside. He thought of the natives who had once drank from this very stream, carrying containers of the cool, clean water back to their tribe. It amazed him that when he was in her presence for short bursts of time, it felt as if nothing else existed, only her. And that feeling was especially vivid here where there was only the earth below and the sky above. No Lilith House. No *plan.* No promise. No past, and no future. Only them. Only *now.*

It made him feel like the man he wanted to be. Not the one Georgie and Mason believed he should aspire to. Certainly not the vision Lilith House had had for him. Just his *own,* the one he rarely explored, the one who lived inside him like a secret garden just beginning to grow.

His thoughts caused his mood to sour, bursting the peaceful bubble he'd been in so briefly. He looked down, focusing on the practiced movement of his fingers.

"This feels like the first time in forever I've just sat still and done nothing," she said.

He regarded her, noted the serene expression on her face, the way her body looked relaxed and pliant. The sun was shining on her exposed thighs and he could see a light brown birthmark mostly hidden by the raised hem of her skirt. Every muscle in his body primed to lift that skirt higher, to discover the mystery of her birthmark. Did it look like a crescent moon, or maybe a state? Maybe there was nothing to compare it to. Maybe that birthmark was a shape that was completely specific to her, like a fingerprint, or the curl of the hair on her scalp. He wanted to know it. He wanted to trace it and commit it to memory. Damn but he was attracted to her. "I imagine, being a single mom, you rarely get breaks."

She nodded, sighed. "It's true. It can be really hard not having someone to split the workload with." She chewed on her lip for a moment as if considering. "In lots of ways, things are easier now that Haddie isn't a baby. No diapers, no crazy sleep schedule." She paused for a moment. "But Haddie . . . well, you haven't met her, but she's . . . she's different." She frowned slightly as though regretting her own words.

"How do you mean?"

"Well, my friend Merrilee calls her an old soul, and I guess that's a good way to describe it. She's the most serious kid you'll ever meet. It's like she has this very intense inner world that so far, she hasn't shared with me."

186

Cam tilted his head. He could relate to that. For different reasons of course. He'd been isolated from the world at large, his early existence mostly narrowed down to three basement rooms. He'd been deeply shamed by the fact that he—*they*—were considered such an embarrassment that they had to be hidden away like a dirty secret. Then later, tricked, used . . . Yes, that was all different, but even now, he had trouble sharing his inner feelings with anyone. Sometimes he wanted to, he did, but he simply didn't know how. Nor had there been anyone he *could* tell, because his thoughts and experiences seemed too unusual, too strange and overwhelming to hand over to another person and expect them to even remotely understand. To handle them gently. Except for the people who'd lived it with him. Those who were also discarded . . . "Maybe she just doesn't have the words yet to describe all her feelings," he offered.

She nodded. "Yes. Yes, that's what I've thought too. Hoped. It's just . . . in the meantime, I worry about her. I worry that she keeps secrets from me."

"What sort of secrets?"

Scarlett shrugged. "I don't know." Her gaze moved away again, a worried frown creasing her forehead. His fingers moved more swiftly on the blade of grass, folding and looping.

"I'm probably not one to give advice on kids"—he glanced up at her momentarily—"but what I do know is that you're a loving mom who cares deeply for her daughter. Anyone with two eyes in their head could see that. And I don't think there's anything more important for a kid than that. She'll find the words, eventually. And you'll be the first person she brings them to."

She smiled softly. "Thanks, Camden, I appreciate that." She closed her eyes momentarily, breathing out a small sigh. "This is a good place to bring your troubles to. Do you feel that way as well?"

He nodded. "Yes. The peace of this place feels bigger than anything else."

"Yes, that's exactly it. I've been sitting here thinking about the natives you told me about, the ones who were so brutalized by Hubert Bancroft. You said there are legends about horned devils in these woods seeking revenge." She shook her head. "But I only feel peace here, the way they must have once upon a time. It's like it . . . lingers in some supernatural way. I think maybe it's their gift and their legacy. Not vengeance, or hatred. Just peace."

He watched his fingers working the grass for a moment. "I like the thought," he said. "But after what was done to them, who could blame them for wanting vengeance? In one life or another. Don't they deserve it?"

She tilted her head, her eyes moving over his features as though she'd heard something in his voice he hadn't meant for her to hear. "I heard this story once about an old Cherokee. He said to his grandson, 'There is a battle between two wolves inside us all. One wolf is evil and angry. Jealous and resentful. The other wolf is good. It is filled with love and hope, humility and empathy.'" She paused and he leaned toward her unbidden. "The little boy thought about it and asked,

'Grandpa, which wolf wins?' And the old man quietly replied, 'The one you feed.'"

Camden felt an odd rush of breeze move through him as though a door somewhere deep inside had just been opened. *The wolf you feed is the one who wins.* But was it possible to stop feeding one wolf to feed the other? And was it too late for him? He let out a slow breath. "I like that. I'll remember it."

She smiled. "I've talked a whole lot about myself. Tell me about you."

He squinted down at the grass, creating a loop and threading the end through it. He didn't want to lie to her, but he couldn't tell her the truth either. "Not much to tell. I grew up here, moved away for a while, came back, applied for a job at the sheriff's office, and now here I am."

He felt her gaze on him but didn't look up. "That just told me a whole lot of nothing."

Cam smiled. "I wish I was more interesting but sadly, if I went into all the details of my life, you'd fall asleep right here on the riverbank, risk rolling into the water and drowning. Whatever the opposite of glamorous is, that's me."

Scarlett laughed. "That dull, huh?" She narrowed her eyes at him. "I'm not sure I'm buying it. Although as you know, I had a bad run-in with 'glamorous,' so the opposite sounds like a welcome change." She paused. "Maybe someday you'll go into more detail about your terribly mundane existence."

He chuckled. They were both silent for a moment. Speaking of her bad run-in with glamorous . . . "I looked up that actor," he admitted after a moment. "Haddie's father."

She grimaced. "I was hoping you'd forget I told you all that."

He hadn't forgotten. In fact, as he'd googled the guy, jealousy had pumped through his veins. *So stupid, so stupid.* He didn't want to feel that way, but he did. He'd wanted to put his fist through the screen when the guy with the megawatt smile had popped up. "I told you your secret's safe with me."

"I believe you." She paused. "Why'd you look him up?"

Camden focused on his fingers for a few beats. "I was curious about what sort of idiot spent time with you, then crawled away like a spineless coward," he said softly. When he dared look up at her, her expression was a mixture of surprise and pleasure. Camden stood up and stepped across the stream, using three exposed rocks for stepping stones. He dropped down on the bank beside her and handed her the grass blade, now formed into something new.

She took it from him, their eyes holding as their fingers brushed. Scarlett's gaze fell to Cam's mouth and his gut clenched with need. She was so close. He could see the freckles on her nose and the tiny black dot in the blue of her left eye. He could smell her delicate, sun-drenched scent. She looked at what he'd given her and then back up at him, her expression morphing into utter delight.

"A girl," she said, drawing in a breath. "Me?"

He nodded, feeling momentarily shy but pleased by her joy.

"How do you do it?" she asked, nodding to the re-formed blade of grass.

He shrugged. "Practice." *Lots of time on my hands when I was younger.*

She glanced at it again. "It's incredible. I'll cherish it."

She spoke so seriously, and with so much reverence, that his heart jolted. It was only a blade of grass and she was acting like he'd given her the Hope diamond. Still . . . he'd so seldom in his life been recognized for any accomplishment, he'd so seldom felt seen by anyone, and he couldn't deny the pleasure that swam inside him at the knowledge that he'd made her happy.

She glanced at his lips again and he couldn't help it, he leaned forward and kissed her. The kiss was soft, gentle. It was the slow brushing of velvety, sun-warmed lips. It was his fingers on the nape of her neck, sliding upward to grip her scalp as she moaned, his body giving an answering jolt of pure lust. It was her tongue sliding into his mouth and his meeting hers. It felt like the most natural thing in all the world, and the most extraordinary.

It was delicious mindlessness as she fell back onto the dry grass and he came over the top of her, tilting his head so he could explore her mouth more deeply. He molded his groin to hers, pulling back and then pressing forward, a groan of pleasure rumbling from his chest. His body felt incredibly *alive* in a way it never had before. The sunshine warmed his back, the softness of her curves cradled the long, hard planes of his own. For one sweet moment, there was nothing but beauty and rightness before all the old shame began flooding in. Camden pulled away, his eyes widening momentarily as he imagined a look of fear on her features, breath expelling in relief when he saw only calm, only need, and then the blink of confusion. "Is everything okay?" she asked.

He nodded, giving her a small smile. His hang-ups weren't her fault and he wouldn't let them sully what that kiss had been: sweet perfection. He wanted to do it again. He wanted to take it further. So much further. He wanted to lose himself in her. He wanted to, but he couldn't. If only he could. God, if only. So he pulled away, sitting up. She sat up as well, taking a moment to smooth her hair and lower her skirt from where it'd ridden up. He spotted a small, oval green-gray stone at the edge of the water and picked it up, running his thumb over its perfect smoothness.

He thought about Georgia and a modicum of guilt rose inside of him. Damn it. *This,* this had felt so good for a time, but with the kiss, reality had steamrolled back in, and there was nothing he could do about it. He'd made his choices, he'd sealed his fate. He'd fed his wolf. "Yeah." He mustered another smile, squinting over at her. "I was just thinking we should probably get going."

Scarlett ran her hand over her hair again. She looked embarrassed. Hurt and regret pooled in his chest. "Right. Yes." She began to stand and he jumped up first, offering her his hand. She wobbled slightly, laughed, as he pulled her up. "I guess I do have a project I should be managing back at the old homestead."

The homestead. Lilith House. *Keep focused, Cam.*

He dropped the stone in his pocket and they began to walk through the woods, shafts of sunlight beaming through the breaks in the trees. Their fingers brushed, and he wanted to take her hand but he didn't. Instead he grasped the stone in his pocket, running a finger over its time-worn edges. It had been pummeled and tumbled, its coarseness knocked away until it washed up on the sunny shore, smooth . . . soft. The time at the stream with Scarlett had felt that way too . . . gentle, *peaceful,* in an existence that had only rarely experienced such things. It would be a reminder of what that'd felt like, even if it could only ever be temporary. Hell, maybe it'd serve as a wish that perhaps *he* could be made softer from the hardships he'd endured as well. Interesting thought, foreign even. Each instance he spent time with Scarlett *shifted* something different inside of him. He wasn't sure he liked it.

After another few minutes, she turned to him. "By the way, you didn't tell me why you came by in the first place."

"Huh?"

"You stopped by Lilith House and one of the men told you where to find me. But why'd you stop by?"

"Oh, uh, I was just checking in. Making sure everything was okay after the other night."

She glanced at him sideways and he sensed some disappointment in her expression. "I appreciate it, I do. But you really don't have to feel responsible for my safety. I'll call you if I require your professional services."

He held back a smile. He'd ruffled her feathers by suggesting his visit was for purely professional reasons. He liked that it bothered her. It meant she was hoping his visit was personal. And the truth? It had been. He'd wanted to see her, plain and simple. The professional check-in was going to be his excuse. "Actually, the check-in was really more for the bird."

She stopped, putting her hands on her hips. He stopped too, turning to look at her. "The *bird?* There was some kid crawling around through the walls of my house, and you came back to check on the bird?" His lip quirked. She looked so damned indignant and so damned beautiful.

At the movement of his lip, her brow dipped. "You're joking."

"I'm joking." He wasn't very good at it. He knew that. And now he'd made her mad.

She made a soft huffing sound and continued walking. He caught up with her, grabbing her hand and swinging her around. "I came to check on you because I wanted to make sure you were okay, but also because . . . I wanted to see you." *Damn, no, I shouldn't have said that.*

She tilted her head, watching him. "You're very hot and cold, Deputy."

Deputy. He released a breath, ran a hand through his short-cropped hair. She was right. He was. He was up and down and all over the map. He had reasons for that. He wanted her, and he shouldn't. He was fighting himself because he *had* to. "I know." He sighed. "Things are . . . complicated right now. I need to focus on my job." Excuses. Shit, she was looking at him like she saw right through him. She probably did because he was a shit liar. There went that softness between them. He'd ruined it.

She nodded slowly, taking her lip between her teeth for a moment before letting it go. "Well." She let out a loud whoosh of air. "Things are complicated with me too. I've got a lot going on." She waved her hand in the general direction of Lilith House. They'd moved close enough now that they could hear the soft echoes of banging from the work crew. "I really don't have time for . . . well, anything. So . . ."

He glanced at her. "Just bad timing," he murmured.

"Right. Bad timing." She lifted her chin as they stepped from the forest, looking both accepting and determined.

Desperation clawed at his insides. She was drifting away from him, and he was letting her. He opened his mouth to say something, what, he didn't know, but—

"Haddie's back," she said happily, picking up their pace. "Mrs. Schmidt very nicely offered to drive Haddie home," she went on as they drew nearer. It seemed like she was talking more to fill the awkward silence than to make any real conversation. "Said she was going to be out at a church meeting . . ."

He looked ahead to see a white Camry parked in front of the house.

"Scarlett—"

"Thanks for coming by, Deputy," she said, stepping ahead. "Haddie!"

He stopped next to his truck watching as Scarlett turned, waving to the Camry as it drove away. Dismissed. He'd been dismissed.

Get in your truck, Cam. Drive away. Mason has access to the house now. There's no reason for you to be here. But his feet kept moving, walking to where Scarlett stood with the little blonde-haired girl he'd seen lying on the blanket the day he'd installed the lock on her front door. Before he'd made it to them, Scarlett turned, the box he knew contained the baby bird held in her hands. "See for yourself, Deputy." She pulled back the black fabric to reveal a tiny portion of the sleeping bird before covering it again. "Alive and well. And due for a feeding so I'd better get to it." She turned from him and stopped short, a gasp emerging as she went to her knees. "Haddie?"

Camden's heart jumped as the hair on his neck rose. The angelic-looking little girl was standing in the gravel, visibly trembling, a look of shocked horror on her face as she stared up at him, unblinking. Beneath her, a pool of urine was seeping into the stone.

"Haddie, baby, what is it?" Scarlett's voice held a note of panic. "Oh, honey. You've wet yourself." She stood, turning and thrusting the bird at Camden. He took it as Scarlett turned back to her daughter and scooped Haddie up in her arms and practically ran for the house.

For a moment, Camden simply stood there, watching them disappear inside Lilith House, his gut churning. She'd looked terrified of him, so terrified that she'd lost control of her bladder? *What the hell just happened?*

He practically jumped out of his skin when the bird in his hands started screaming to be fed.

CHAPTER TWENTY-ONE

Thirteen Years Ago

She'd been living at Lilith House for two months. Eight weeks of nothing but school work, worship services, chores, lights out at nine p.m., and waking with the sun. The only bright spot in an otherwise dismal existence, were the times she could manage to sneak away and check in with Dreamboat and his menagerie of patients. She rarely stayed for long, not only because she couldn't take the risk herself, but because she wasn't willing to chance the kids getting in trouble.

Look at me, Mom, two months at Lilith House and here I am making unselfish choices for the first time in my lousy life.

I'm reformed after all!

My utmost for His glory!

She really hated this weird—and yes, she could admit it, scary—fucking place.

She hated the stupid rituals, the meaningless ceremonies, the complete lack of technology, an absence of even the smallest pleasures, those devout weirdos in white suits who had joined a few of their services, and all the endless talk of a god that was unrecognizable to Kandace.

Two months down, seven to go. She needed to make the most of her remaining time there so when she left, she was armed. She needed to gather some information about the kids in order to take something with her that had a chance at helping them escape Lilith House. What kind of a life was it for them? She was practically climbing the walls after eight weeks. What must it be like to live there permanently? No, something was off with their situation and she needed to find out what. She needed to be brave. She'd successfully snuck into Ms. Wykes office once, and she'd successfully visited the kids on several occasions now. There weren't cameras in the walls. After all, technology was a tool of the devil. No one had eyes in the backs of their heads. Jasper roamed the halls like the hellhound he was, but with his big, cumbersome body, she could hear him coming a mile away. She'd watched. She'd learned *everyone's* routine in her short time there. This was *worth* the risk.

And on the off chance she got caught, she could take what they dished out. Even the girls who were absent from class after a night where she heard screams from below, always showed back up eventually, even if their eyes were a little extra shifty, and she spotted a bruise or two. Yes, she could take the possible consequences. Kandace just prayed she wasn't potentially putting any innocent birds in harm's way.

Thank God *that* whole event was fading from her mind. Sometimes she even questioned if it had really happened. It had been a bluff of sorts, something to shock and horrify her right out of the gate so she'd remain wary and docile. *Well, fuck them.* It wasn't a bad strategy, actually. Do something like that once, and you might never have to do anything like it again. Look at her roommates for example, so-called "bad girls" afraid of swearing too loud.

Once Kandace was excused from her final class of the day, she headed to her after-school work detail, cleaning and disinfecting the classrooms. Sometimes a teacher leaned her head in and checked on her, but mostly, she was left on her own. They knew she was there doing the job by the fact that the job was done.

She'd just have to hurry today. She needed to buy herself some time.

Ms. Wykes would be in the Tuesday afternoon staff meeting.

Fifteen minutes, she estimated. No more.

Kandace hurried through the chores in the first classroom, gathering her supplies, and rushing to the second room, giving the other girls just enough time to get to their work detail, or to their rooms where they were expected to study.

Kandace left her supplies in the second classroom and headed down the hall. She startled when a classmate named

Lucille turned the corner and almost bumped into her. "Oh sorry," Kandace said, smiling widely.

The girl, a rail-thin brunette who rarely said a word, but rather watched the other girls from beneath her highly arched brows, narrowed her eyes, transferring a bucket of cleaning supplies from her right hand to her left. "Don't worry about it," she said, giving Kandace what looked like a phony smile.

Kandace cocked her head. "Ladies' room," she said. "Excuse me." As she walked away from the girl, she cringed internally. Why had she explained where she was going? It'd made her sound guilty. *You're losing your edge here, Thompson.* Yeah, she was losing a lot of things at Lilith House, another being her sanity.

She glanced behind her but the hallway was clear, Lucille apparently having moved on to whatever task she'd been assigned. Kandace blew out a breath of relief, making turn after turn until she came to Ms. Wykes office once again.

Of course, it was locked. She removed the pin from her bangs and went to work. This time it only took her about thirty seconds. At least she was keeping her breaking-and-entering skills sharp. Kandace slipped into the room, shutting the door quietly behind her and locking it from the inside.

Her gaze landed on the now-empty birdcage. She wasn't going to let herself guess at what had happened to the remaining bluebird.

She headed directly to one of two file cabinets behind Ms. Wykes's desk, using the pin to open the lock at the top left of the first cabinet. Then she slipped the pin back in her hair and opened the top drawer.

A noise sounded outside the office and Kandace froze, holding her breath and listening intently. Nothing. She turned around and started rifling through the files, each clearly labeled with a girl's first and last name. They didn't appear to be in alphabetical order . . . but instead, arranged by year. *Yes!* It was what she'd hoped for. Though he appeared younger, the kid had told her he was fifteen, which meant his mother would have been there sixteen years before or so, which meant . . . she was probably in the first filing cabinet? She bent down to pull open the next drawer when another small noise met Kandace's ears and again, she froze, her ears straining to pick up any sound that might indicate someone was coming closer. But after a moment, she turned back to the cabinet, opened the second drawer from the top and saw that the dates on those folders were of the correct—she *hoped*—year.

She pulled the first one out, rifling through it. A whole list of the girl's offenses was at the front along with her picture. The rest of it was . . . class assignments, work detail information, and . . . date of discharge. *Damn.* She pulled out the next one. There had to be thirty files from that year. Lilith School didn't house that many girls, but perhaps some had only served a short sentence, with the rest being full-time students like Kandace, and her roommates. She had hoped—

A key rattled in the lock and before Kandace could even fully whirl around, the door swung open, banging against the wall and bouncing back with a piercing squeak. Ms. Wykes stood in the doorway, her beady eyes locked on Kandace.

Kandace's heart drummed with sudden panic, her mouth going dry. *Oh God.*

"Well, well, well," the woman singsonged, moving forward in that inhuman glide.

Kandace swallowed heavily and then slammed the cabinet door closed. "Where's my marijuana?" she demanded, pretending self-righteous bravado she didn't feel. "It's mine and I want it back."

Jasper, Ms. Wykes's constant shadow, entered the room, coming to a standstill near the door. There was something predatory in his eyes, some sort of . . . excitement. It caused a deep tremor of fear.

She knew men like him. He got off on pain. Even in her most self-destructive moments, she'd always avoided that type. She'd kept a wide arc between her and Jasper since that first day, but now? There was no avoiding him.

Kandace knew then she'd been lying to herself about the bluff. The bird had been a warning, and she had not heeded it.

"Drugs are a tool of the devil, Ms. Thompson. Do you think I would store such a thing in my office? Do you think I would keep such a thing at all?" Ms. Wykes moved closer as did Jasper. "I'm severely disappointed, Ms. Thompson. *Severely.*" She put a finger on her lips. "Now what to do with such dishonesty. Such *sinful* behavior."

Fear zinged through Kandace like a downed live wire. She threw her head back and let out a shrill scream that surely the whole house could hear.

"Jasper," Ms. Wykes hissed. "Restrain this girl now."

"Yes, ma'am," Jasper said, his thick lips turning upward as he drew near. Kandace upped the level of her wails, flinging herself away from Jasper so that her back hit the file cabinet behind her. She tried to duck, to move under his grasp as he came at her, but he anticipated her move and went low, grabbing her around the waist and spinning her around. He was like a boa constrictor. All muscle coiled around her so that she could hardly breathe.

Kandace thrashed in his arms. She had no real plan. But maybe if she fought aggressively enough, they'd throw her in a room by herself rather than be bothered with the theatrics.

Or maybe they were enjoying it. Maybe she'd taken the wrong tack. Maybe begging for her blackened soul would have appeased them.

No, something inside her whispered. *Nothing will appease them. It's too late.*

Jasper dragged her out of the room, quite literally, Ms. Wykes following behind. She was reciting something, a religious incantation, as though they were heading for an exorcism, and she was the one possessed of a demon.

"To the showers, Jasper," Ms. Wykes said. "I see this one needs a cleansing. We will wash the evil from you, girl."

Kandace thrashed harder, to no avail. "Help!" she screamed. "Somebody help me!" But from the way it seemed, Lilith House was very suddenly abandoned, the other girls and the rest of the staff sitting still and silent behind the closed doors they passed.

Hers were the screams echoing through the hallways now.

She'd never come to anyone else's aid. Why should anyone come to hers?

Jasper carried her effortlessly through the corridors and up the main set of steps, and though she fought mightily, it did no good. She seemed to be the only one exhausted when he finally set her down on the tile of the large communal bathroom floor. Cold tile. Kandace glanced down, noting that somewhere along the way, she'd lost both her shoes.

She cried out when her uniform was very literally torn from her body, the fabric splitting down the back with one hard yank of Jasper's hands, as though they'd been constructed to do so. Kandace grabbed for the cover of the material, but Jasper ripped it away. "Stop it. Stop it!" she screamed, crossing her hands over her chest to cover her bra. "You're all sick! My mother's going to hear about this! My *lawyer* is going to hear about this!"

Ms. Wykes's laugh was a scratchy, unused sound pulled out of the mothballs in the storage area of her shriveled heart. She turned on the shower with a quick flick of her wrist. They were going to make her *bathe?* While they watched?

Kandace could hardly catch her breath. Her eyes darted to the doorway of the bathroom and quickly back to Jasper who moved toward her. She attempted to duck around him but, despite his size, he moved like lightning, going low and grasping her by the legs, hurling her up and over his shoulder. Kandace kicked at him and pounded at his chest, letting out an ear-shattering shriek directly into his ear.

Jasper flung her off his shoulder and her back hit the tile wall of the shower, sliding down the hard surface before her butt smacked into the floor. Kandace let out a choking scream. It felt like her tailbone had cracked in two.

"Careful now, dear, you'll hurt yourself," Ms. Wykes said in a calm, soft whisper, somehow all the more horrifying for the serenity in her tone.

Kandace moaned, her sobs echoing around the large, open room. The water pounded on the floor just in front of her where Kandace was curled against the wall, unwilling to move. *Oh God, this hurt.* Something was broken, it had to be. "Please," she moaned. "Please."

"That's better," Ms. Wykes said, steam curling around Kandace and wafting into the air where Ms. Wykes and Jasper stood staring mercilessly down at her. "Some obedience. That's it. You want to be saved, don't you, sinner? You want redemption from the Lord, you just don't know how to achieve it. That's why we're here. To assist you. To help you atone. Jasper, the brush, please." She put out her hand and Jasper handed her a pair of long, rubber yellow gloves and a scrub brush.

Kandace's pulse leapt, fear drumming within to the same tempo as the pounding water on the tile floor. She brought her hand up, attempting to push off the wall as Ms. Wykes donned the gloves. Kandace's lower back screamed in agony and she let out another sob, tears pouring down her cheeks. Ms. Wykes reached up and redirected the showerhead so the water was directly on Kandace. Kandace screamed again, raising her arms and turning her face from the scalding water that suddenly rained down over her mostly nude body. *It burns, oh God, it burns. Somebody help me, help me. Pleasepleaseplease.*

She flailed, then when more of the burning water hit her skin, she tried to roll into a ball, then push upward, using her hands for leverage against the wall, but Jasper pushed her back down. Ms. Wykes reached in with her bright yellow gloves and began scrubbing mercilessly at Kandace's scalded skin.

It was agony, red-hot, indescribable agony.

Kandace screamed and thrashed, slipping and flailing as Jasper used his place of higher ground to keep her from gaining traction on the slippery tile while Ms. Wykes used the wire scrub brush to scour every inch of Kandace's burned and blistered skin.

It lasted forever. Kandace drifted in and out of consciousness, the pain of what was happening to her never allowing her to escape for long. Just when she thought she might go crazy from the pain, from the cruelty these two monsters were inflicting on her, the scrub brush was suddenly lifted, the pounding noise of the water ceasing. Kandace dragged her shaking legs into her body, her arms coming around her legs, but yelping as soon as raw skin met raw skin. Her moans continued, one after the other, short pulses of sound that she couldn't manage to stop.

Half-conscious, she was dragged upward, her moan erupting into a scream as some fabric was wrapped around her ruined skin.

Ms. Wykes's voice sounded directly against her ear. "Now then, Ms. Thompson. There will be no more sneaking into my office? Will there?"

In response, Kandace could only manage another moan.

Jasper picked her up and, with the contact, Kandace sobbed brokenly. The world around her faded in, then out. She was being carried somewhere. Her bed? The infirmary? Home? *Please, please let me go home. I'll do better. I'll do anything you want. Please, Mom. Mom. I just want to go home. I'll be good. I'll be so good.*

The world went black.

She came to slowly, attempting to move her limbs. Her body *burned.* Oh God, it burned. And it ached. A shudder ran through her as she attempted to crack her eyes open, but it was too bright and she drew back, trying again. Reality swam in front of her and for a moment, she wondered if she was simply having a horrific nightmare. Her brain grasped to understand, to put her reality into context.

She was in the chapel, her arms strung up to each side of her, feet just touching the ground. Twelve students all sat in the pews in their red uniforms, heads bent. The teachers sat stoically in chairs against the opposite wall. Some stared at her nervously, others with contempt.

Her back burned so badly she didn't think she could bear it, the light from the window behind her streaming in and heating her already scalded skin.

Kandace let her head loll forward, another deep shudder running through her body, nerve endings zinging with intolerable pain. Tears coursed down her cheeks and she let out a barely perceptible cry as the salt of her pain ran over her raw skin. Her gaze moved over the girls. *Please don't look up. Don't see this.* She could only imagine what she looked like, strung up like some alternate version of Christ, wearing only

207

a bra and underwear, skin bloody and ruined. But she knew they'd be made to look. After all, she was there as an example for the rest of them. *Repent. Obey. Or this will be you.* Apparently, whatever injuries the other girls who'd been disciplined had sustained while she was there, hadn't been enough of a show. This though? This was plenty.

"Please rise," came Ms. Wykes's voice. She was standing somewhere on Kandace's right but Kandace didn't bother trying to lift her head to see her. She didn't have the strength. The girls rose slowly, lifting their gazes to her, some visibly drawing back, others standing in shocked silence while tears rolled down their cheeks.

The heat from the window beat into her injured flesh and a memory enveloped her, causing the pain to recede momentarily. Light had streamed into the attic where she and Scarlett used to play. It'd been beautiful, like a spotlight God had made just for them, not the god Lilith House described, but the one she'd felt in her spirit, and she and her friend had danced in its glow, twirling and whirling and dreaming the dreams of little girls whose lives stretched before them—wide open and full of possibility. She'd been innocent then, no mistakes, no failures. No regrets. Just unending grace. Why had she let go of that? Why had she given it up so willingly?

Kandace closed her eyes and pretended she was there now. She heard the words Scarlett had said, so long ago, when she'd found Kandace crying after her mother had rejected her once again: *You're stronger than you think you are*, she'd whispered, taking her hand.

You're stronger than you think you are. The words repeated in her head now, like a mantra, like a life raft in a sea of misery and pain.

Because the thing was, Scarlett had offered her that same grace even after she'd fallen. She'd reached out her hand but Kandace hadn't taken it. Not that time.

She'd eventually been sent to Lilith House. And there was no grace here, only shame.

"If we confess our sins," Ms. Wykes's voice broke through her thoughts, "He is faithful and just and will forgive us and purify us from unrighteousness. Isn't that right, Ms. Thompson?"

Kandace moved her eyes toward her but didn't answer.

"Are you ready to confess your sins?"

You're stronger than you think you are. "Yes, Ms. Wykes."

She smiled. "Good. Tell the other girls what you have done, and why you required cleansing."

Kandace moved her eyes toward the other girls. Her gaze met that of Lucille, the girl she'd passed in the hallway and the girl lowered her eyes, a flash of guilt moving over her expression. She'd followed Kandace. She'd seen her entering Ms. Wykes's office. She'd told on her. Which meant . . . it was all they knew? She pulled her shoulders back very slightly, holding back the sob of pain. *You're stronger than you think you are.* She looked from one classmate to the other, hoping they could see in her gaze that though she was bent—burned and bloodied—she was not broken. "I snuck into Ms. Wykes's office to find the drugs I brought with me," she said. "Drugs, a tool of the devil." She let her head fall slightly.

"Yes, drugs, a tool of the devil, indeed," Ms. Wykes said. "Will you cast away all tools of Satan from this moment forward, Ms. Thompson?"

"Yes, Ms. Wykes."

"Why? Why will you do that?"

She looked at her in confusion for a moment, and then realized what she wanted from her. "Because," her voice cracked, "my utmost for His glory."

Ms. Wykes nodded proudly, like one of her students who had formerly been severely lacking suddenly showed a sign of possibility. "Yes, Ms. Thompson. All that you are. All that you must cast away. All that you must relinquish and forsake. Your *utmost* for His glory. Do you understand?"

"Yes, I understand. My utmost for His glory," Kandace repeated weakly. Behind her, the sun blazed. On her wrists, the cord bit into her bloody flesh. She cringed and shook, biting the inside of her cheeks to keep from passing out. Her eyes, so, so heavy, lifted slightly to capture Ms. Wykes in her fiendish satisfaction.

"Repeat after Ms. Thompson, girls," Ms. Wykes said, turning toward the other students. They repeated the words in a low monotone.

Ms. Wykes, a pleased smile on her lips, raised her arms in the air and sang out the words herself, throwing her head back as though in ecstasy. "Now then. Shall we begin our service?"

Kandace wavered in and out of consciousness as the service droned on, but she didn't let the pain make her cry out again, and not a tear slipped from her eye. Instead, she repeated the line Scarlett had whispered so lovingly to her all those years ago, drawing strength not only from the memory, but from the fact that her friend had said them with such conviction. She had believed in Kandace, and she had hoped Kandace would believe in herself too. She hadn't then.

I will now, she promised her friend. *I'll try.*

When at long last, the service was over, Kandace was untied and lowered gently, almost reverently. She bore her own weight, testing her tailbone that still ached terribly, but was not nearly the worst of her pain. Kandace let out a slow exhale as a light cloth was wrapped around her body.

They helped her shuffle back up to her room and then one of the other instructors came in, not meeting her eyes as she slathered burn cream over her skin. She lay down on her bed with a groaning sob and was tucked in under the sheets.

A few minutes after the door had shut behind them, her roommates came into the room, kneeling down next to her, their eyes red and puffy, their expressions full of anguish. Sydney reached out tentatively to touch her, perhaps to smooth the strands of hair back that had fallen over Kandace's brow, but pulled away, her hand trembling. "My God," she whispered. "What did they do to you?"

"I'll be okay," Kandace said, voice gritty with pain. She hadn't looked in a mirror. She didn't know what she looked like, but she had to figure her skin would scab over and heal, that they hadn't gone deep enough to scar. She was going to feel like she had the worst sunburn of her existence for a while. She was going to be unable to sleep for at least a week as her raw skin stuck to her sheets. Her bruised tailbone was going to cause her to cry out each time she sat up. But she *was* going to be okay.

A tear rolled down Aurora's cheek. "Hey," Kandace said, "think of it as a free chemical peel. They basically gave me a cosmetic procedure that some women pay thousands for. When I leave this place, my complexion is going to be as soft as a baby's ass."

Both girls' eyes darted to the door and then back to her. "Butt," Kandace whispered. "Baby's *butt*." The girls both managed tremulous smiles.

Kandace adjusted herself on the bed, grimacing as a wave of nausea passed through her. "Oh God, I'm going to throw up," she moaned.

Sydney jumped up and was back a few seconds later with the bathroom trash can. She slid it next to the bed in the nick of time as Kandace leaned over and vomited, the movement and the acid in her throat making her moan in pain once the worst of the stomach cramps had passed and she once again, came to rest on her pillow.

Aurora got her a glass of water and helped her drink and then, exhausted beyond anything she'd ever imagined, Kandace closed her eyes and miraculously managed to fall asleep.

CHAPTER TWENTY-TWO

" All buckled?" Scarlett asked, looking at Haddie in the rearview mirror. Haddie met her eyes, nodded.

Concern washed over Scarlett for the tenth time that morning. It appeared Haddie hadn't slept at all the night before, lavender smudges marring the porcelain skin beneath her eyes, making the green of her orbs that much more startling.

As they began driving toward town to pick up Millie, Scarlett turned on the radio, adjusting the volume down low. Her gaze flickered to Haddie again, staring out the window at the forest rushing by. "You sure you feel better?" she asked. She'd questioned Haddie extensively the night before about wetting herself. Her daughter hadn't peed her pants since she was twenty months old. She'd potty-trained early, and once she'd started wearing "big girl undies," she hadn't had one accident. That she'd wet herself the evening before was extremely concerning to Scarlett.

Of course, Haddie had brushed it off, saying she didn't feel well and it was just an accident. She'd looked confused, torn though, and Scarlett got that feeling again that she was keeping something from her. Scarlett felt teary, frustrated. Alone. She'd slept like crap the night before too.

Of course, it didn't help that even after she'd decided to schedule a check-up for Haddie, to rule anything physical out, then managed to convince herself that Haddie was a kid and kids sometimes had accidents, Camden West kept popping into her mind.

Was Haddie's loss of bladder control related to *him?* No, surely not. Haddie was always very clear if she didn't like a person. To Scarlett's knowledge, her daughter had *never* pretended to like someone she didn't.

Only problem was . . . Haddie seemed to Scarlett to be growing more secretive by the day. Something was weighing on her, she *knew* it, and yet try as she might, question her as she did, Haddie wouldn't be straight with her.

You're a loving mom who cares deeply for her daughter. Anyone with two eyes in their head could see that.

His words had consoled her, ministered to her. *Damn him.* Speaking of secretive. Damn Camden West and his evasive answers and vague statements.

Not much to tell. Things with me are complicated.

Right. Like *her* life was the picture of simplicity.

Scarlett glanced in the mirror, wondering if it was possible that he had a problem with the fact that she had a daughter. That could be a lot for a single man to take on . . . Disappointment rose inside her. Their kiss had been . . . *magical.* It really had been. He'd felt it too, she could tell by the awestruck look on his handsome face, and yet he'd pulled away. Why? *Damn it, I don't have time for this,* she thought, a burst of frustration causing her to grip the steering wheel even more tightly.

God, why had she told him about Haddie's father? Sure, she'd been mildly tipsy, but that didn't excuse it. She'd sworn an oath—on paper and in her own mind—that she'd never reveal Royce's identity, ever.

Scarlett *refused* to fall for another man who regretted touching her. Another man who made her feel half-crazy in the head. Like now. And perhaps there was no *half* about it.

So, nope, she was going to wipe him straight from her mind.

She turned into the neighborhood where Millie lived, driving slowly through the residential streets, large, red-flowered acacias shading the sidewalks and the small square homes. The sun was shining, birds were twittering happily, and it was going to be a lovely day.

Scarlett took a deep, cleansing breath. *Everything is going to be okay.*

Movement on the porch of a house just ahead caught her eye and she looked over as her car moved slowly toward it, her heart jolting as a lump filled her throat.

Camden West was exiting the small blue house with the black shutters, buttoning the collar of his uniform shirt with one hand and carrying some sort of black bag with the other.

The woman behind him, leaning in the doorway, wore a short strapless nightie, her smile sleepy as she waved goodbye to him. Scarlett recognized her as the same pretty brunette she'd seen him with at the hardware store, the one who had been arguing in Mason's office. He turned and called something to her, turning back around just as Scarlett's car passed directly in front of the house, the smile he'd shot the woman fading as his gaze met Scarlett's. He stopped short, his head turning as his eyes stayed on hers, following the movement of her car.

Scarlett jerked her head forward, her hands gripping the steering wheel fiercely. Her breath released in a sudden gust of pent-up air.

Well, no wonder.

No wonder he ran so hot and cold. Mystery solved.

He was involved with someone else.

He was an *asshole*.

At this rate, as far as she was concerned, all men were assholes. That woman had had no reason to scowl at her when she first saw her at Grady's, but now?

God, she was mad.

So why did she also have to feel so shitty? Why did she feel so *hurt*?

They'd shared nothing but a kiss. Just one meaningless kiss that he'd obviously quickly regretted. And now it was clear why.

Things with him were *complicated*?

No, buddy, they're simple.

And I'm a misjudging fool.

She pulled to the curb in front of Millie's house. The curtain rustled and Scarlett watched as Millie pulled it aside, shooting them a big grin and waving from her window. Scarlett released a slow breath, trying to regain a measure of peace. Her insides felt like she'd been shaken and all her organs were rearranged.

Why do you have such awful taste in men? she asked herself. *Just why?* Maybe she should be asking a different question though. *Why do men* already in relationships *find me so attractive? Gullible?* She groaned internally. God, it was far too early to handle this. She would put to rest any feelings she'd had toward the deputy, which was a good thing. Her daughter deserved all her attention.

Scarlett got Haddie out of the car and then they walked hand in hand to Millie's door, Millie pulling it open before they'd even climbed the three steps. "Good morning," she said with a smile.

"Hi, Millie," Scarlett greeted, handing over the bag she'd packed for Haddie. "There's an extra set of clothes in there and her lunch."

"Awesome." She took the bag and looked at Haddie. "I have a really cool Fourth of July craft to work on with you today. I got started on it in the living room. Do you want to go check it out while I talk to your mommy for a minute?"

Haddie nodded. "Bye, Mommy."

Scarlett smiled at her daughter, a burst of emotion making her feel suddenly weepy. She pulled her forward, wrapping her arms around her precious girl and hugging her

217

tightly for a moment before letting her go. "Go ahead and check out that craft. I bet it's really cool."

"Okay, Mommy. See you in a minute, Millie," she singsonged turning the corner into the living room.

"Is everything okay?" she asked Millie, a concerned frown creasing her brow.

Millie nodded, but she looked uncertain. "It is . . . I just . . . Haddie's just the sweetest little girl, so I wasn't sure whether to even mention this but—"

"I always want you to be honest, Millie, no matter what. If it has to do with Haddie, I want to hear it."

The girl nodded, another flicker of doubt passing through her eyes. "Well, yesterday, we walked over to the ice cream stand a couple blocks away."

"Yes, I told you that was fine."

Millie nodded. "Haddie was very sweet. She has such good manners."

"But?"

"We were walking home, and all of a sudden Haddie let go of my hand and went running across the street."

Scarlett blinked with confused worry. "Why?"

"There's a boy—Roger Green—who lives a block over. He's in a wheelchair. Haddie ran straight for him, and then bent down and said something to him. I was too far away to hear what it was, but . . . well, whatever she said made him start screaming and shrieking. He was so upset, he almost hurled himself straight from his chair." She paused, glancing over her shoulder toward the room where Haddie waited for her. "Whatever she said to that boy scared him silly."

****

Could this day get any worse? Scarlett wondered, glancing around the interior of her car for some wood to knock on. There was none, which, of course there wasn't, because yes, this day probably could get worse. Not because she hadn't knocked on wood—she wasn't that superstitious—but because that seemed to be the trajectory of her life at the moment.

Scarlett pulled into the hardware store parking lot where she had an appointment to meet with Mason so she could pick out the industrial kitchen appliances he was going to order. She got out of her car and walked toward the front entrance. Millie's words repeated in her mind. *Whatever she said to that boy scared him silly.*

Acid pooled in her stomach and she felt tears threatening. What was going on with her daughter? She didn't get it. She hadn't questioned Haddie after Millie had talked to her on the front porch. Frankly, she didn't feel emotionally stable enough to do so. Scarlett took a deep breath, attempting to get her roiling emotions under control as she turned the corner from the parking lot to the sidewalk where the front of the store was. She'd give it the day and ask Haddie about it later. Had she lied about the other little boy at the church daycare when she'd said she didn't mean to hurt his feelings? Was there some streak of meanness in her after all—brought on by the current upheaval in their lives—that Scarlett didn't see because she was blinded by love?

Scarlett pulled the door open and ran straight into someone's chest. He took hold of her upper arms, steadying her as she let out an embarrassed laugh. "Oh my gosh, I'm so . . ." Her words dropped off as she looked up, realizing who it was. *Camden West.*

She'd wondered if this day could get any worse.

Answer? Yes. Decidedly so.

"Sorry," she murmured, stumbling back a step onto the sidewalk.

The door opened wider and another man in a sheriff's uniform with short-cropped salt and pepper hair and deeply tanned skin appeared behind Camden. Camden stepped forward so the man could exit too. Though he was older, he was very fit, and definitely handsome. He smiled widely at Scarlett. "Well, hello." He held out his hand and when she took it, he gave it one firm shake. "You've gotta be Ms. Lattimore." He nodded backward to the store. "Mason was just telling us about the project out at Lilith House, and that he was expecting you. It's nice to have a new face in town. Especially one as pretty as yours."

Scarlett managed a smile. She glanced at Camden who stared at her silently, his gaze piercing. *Jerk.* She raised her chin and looked back at the older man in uniform. "Thank you, sir. You must be Farrow's sheriff?"

"That I am. Lowell Carson. How are you liking our little town so far?"

"I like it. You know, for the most part." She enunciated the last four words as she looked at Camden who was still staring at her. She followed with a tight-lipped smile, which he didn't return. He raised his hand, sliding on a pair of sunglasses.

The sheriff let out a laugh, his eyes twinkling. "Well, I hope the parts that haven't quite won you over yet, manage to do so." He looked at Camden. "Seems this little lady scooped that property right out from under you, didn't she now?" Despite his jovial tone, something minute hardened in his expression. "Darnedest timing. Your offer came in the day Rand Burroughs over at the bank had a heart attack. Lucky for you it was." His smile widened. "Farrow can be suspicious—even downright unfriendly—to outsiders. But once you're one of ours, well, you gotta work real hard to get rid of us. Isn't that right, Camden?" He looked at him, ribbing him in the side. Camden exhibited no reaction to the jab, though if something flickered in his eyes she couldn't tell as they were now concealed behind dark lenses. "Don't hold a grudge regarding the house. I told you it was too big for you anyway."

Scarlett was taken aback by the sheriff's words. Deputy Camden West had expressed interest in buying Lilith House before she had? Why hadn't he mentioned that?

You're just full of secrets, aren't you, Deputy?

A little girl and her mother exited the hardware store, one of the child's eyes covered with a patch, the other turned in slightly.

"I understand you'll be using the property for an event business?" the sheriff asked, pulling her attention from the girl who smiled at Scarlett and began skipping as they passed by.

"Yes, that's right. Weddings mostly, or at least that's the plan right now."

He paused a beat, his smile growing. She swore she saw his wheels turning, but with what, she didn't know. "Weddings. Farrow will look real forward to entertaining new visitors to our town. Isn't that right, Camden?"

Camden remained silent though she thought she saw a miniscule tic in his jaw.

The sheriff rubbed at his chin. "Hmm," he hummed. "Of course, you'll have to file for a business license through the Farrow courthouse. They can be sticklers for any type of innovation within the community, especially that which brings lots of traffic, so you might want to get that filed ASAP."

"Oh, well, I don't think traffic will be an issue. People tend to stagger arrival times for weekend events, and travel in groups. The parties might even bring a little extra tourism to Farrow? And of course, that's only if I'm moderately successful." She gave the sheriff a small, uncomfortable laugh. "But, um, I'll get that filed as quickly as I can."

"If you need me to put a good word in for you, just let me know," he said, winking jovially.

"Thank you, sir. That's very nice of you."

The sheriff glanced at Camden. "Deputy West here tells me there were some critters in your wall the other day?"

Critters. Was that what he'd said to the sheriff when he'd told *her* he'd suspected kids messing around? And if he hadn't really believed someone was using the crawl spaces in the walls to scare her, why had he boarded them up? *Critters*

222

couldn't climb ladders, and critters couldn't open doors. She looked at Camden but he was no longer staring at her, instead his head turned and his gaze focused somewhere across the street. Something felt off here. "Right," she murmured. "Yes. It was so silly of me to bother Deputy West. It won't happen again."

"Nonsense now," the sheriff said. "We're available anytime, even if you don't think it's something serious. Better to be safe than sorry, right? Especially with you two females out there all alone."

He smiled, and though in her peripheral vision, Scarlett saw Camden turn his head toward the sheriff, she kept her gaze focused on the older man. "I appreciate it."

He nodded. "Like I said, if I can be of any help with the council, just holler. And that goes for you and your little girl getting settled in as well."

"That's very kind. Thank you again, sir."

The sheriff gave her another wide smile, tipping his chin and then putting the hat he'd been holding in his hand back on his head. "You have a nice day now," he said, walking past her.

"You too."

"Scarlett," Camden murmured, leaning in as she walked past as though he wanted her to stop so he could tell her something. Whatever it was, she had no desire to listen.

Scarlett raised her chin higher and didn't stop, pushing the door open and calling behind her, "Goodbye, Deputy."

CHAPTER TWENTY-THREE

$\mathcal{H}$addie hadn't left Lilith House in a week. Her mommy was worried about her, she knew that, and she didn't want her mommy to worry, so she'd stayed locked in the house, playing on her iPad or doing crafts that Amelia brought for them to work on together.

She liked spending time with Millie. She felt sort of like her mommy. Millie was light like a bubble. Haddie thought not *only* light like a bubble, but she was shiny like one too. Millie sparkled. Millie was light and fun. Her mommy sometimes forgot to have fun. Haddie thought that probably had to do with her, and that made Haddie sad.

Sometimes she and Millie played hide and seek at Lilith House, running through the long hallways, and pressing into the dark corners, Haddie covering her mouth so Millie wouldn't hear her giggle, and then Millie tickling her ribs and saying, "Gotcha!" when she found her so that they both fell to the ground laughing so hard they had to hold their stomachs.

Lilith House was almost fully awake now, and it liked the sounds of their laughter. Haddie could tell because the bad and the sad felt . . . *less*, and the light felt *more*. It was like every window had been opened so the sunshine poured through the halls, chasing away the shadows. The rooms on the second floor still felt heavy to Haddie and made her bones twinge, but not nearly as much as before.

Today the workmen weren't working at Lilith House, so Millie wouldn't be coming to play with her. Her mommy was mixing colored gels together in the kitchen, creating shades for her cakes, and when Haddie entered the room, her mommy smiled, setting down the tube in her hand next to a bowl that contained the prettiest peach color Haddie had ever seen.

"Hey, baby. How are you?"

"Good. Can I go read in the gazebo?"

A worried look took over her mommy's face and she glanced at the window, then brought her hand up, putting it on Haddie's forehead. She'd been doing that a lot recently even though she'd never had a fever. It was like she expected Haddie to come down with a sickness at any second. She knew it was because after she'd wet herself, she'd told her mommy the reason was that she didn't feel good. That had been a lie, but she couldn't tell her mommy the real reason. Her mommy liked that man. Haddie had felt the . . . glitter in the air between them, like little bursts of popping light that she could feel, but not see.

Yes, her mommy liked him a lot, so Haddie couldn't tell her mommy what he was.

She didn't think her mommy would believe her anyway. *Haddie* didn't even know what to believe.

Her mommy sighed. "I suppose some fresh air would be good. Go on out to the gazebo. I'll be done with this mess"— she waved her hand over the many bowls in front of her—"in about an hour and then I'll call you in for a snack, okay?"

"Okay," Haddie said.

Haddie did go to the gazebo, but after a few minutes, she placed her book down, and walked to the edge of the woods, hesitating, and then stepped through the cover of the trees.

Haddie walked and walked, stepping over pinecones, and around bushes laden with dark, plump berries, learning more about the forest and all the things that lived there.

She placed her hand on a rock sitting in a quiet clearing, still warm from the sun, running her skin over the rough surface, letting her palm linger in the large dip in its center. *A cradle. It looks like a cradle.* She shut her eyes for a moment to block out the distraction of her sight, helping her to focus inward. The weight was strange here. There was mad or sad—she couldn't always distinguish well between the two because often, they were virtually the same—but also . . . lightness. Fear that made her tremble and . . . safety, like when her mommy held her tight after she had a nightmare. *Rescue.* There was life . . . and death. The feelings surrounding this large rock were not together, but they also wove around one another. Sort of like Haddie's memories. Her recollections were all from different *times,* but they all had her mommy in them. Some were happy and some were sad, but her love for her mommy ran through all of them like . . . a thread that connected different squares of a quilt like the ones her gram sewed.

Haddie stood there for another moment trying to make sense of the differing weights, attempting to understand what this particular thread was in this specific place, but she couldn't. After a minute, she turned, moving in a slow circle and gazing around the forest.

She didn't think the thing was near. She couldn't feel its weight even when it was, but the more she'd been in its presence, the more she'd been able to *sense* it in some new way she couldn't describe. It was like its weight drifted around her, just out of grasp, and she didn't know how to latch onto it but could tell it was *there*. Somewhere.

The sun shifted in the sky and Haddie looked up, blinking at the streams of light bursting through the trees. She had to get home. If her mommy came outside, she'd notice she was gone from the gazebo and would worry.

Haddie walked through the woods, taking care not to let the yellow lace of her dress snag on any bushes, walking carefully through the leaves and debris, stepping around the places she felt the weight of a snake, or the nest of mice, or the heavy plants she knew were dangerous to touch. *Everything* had weight and even though Haddie hadn't spent her short life in or near a forest, she found it very easy to measure. The more time she spent there, the more she could tell that different things not only told her of their good or bad intentions, but they told her what they were.

Except the horned thing. Except that.

The snakes in this forest, for instance, were light as long as you stepped around them. But if you got too close, their weight began to change. So Haddie backed away when she was "asked." Yes, all things had weight, but weight could sometimes shift.

She wondered if that was true of people too. She wished she could ask someone. She wished she could ask her mommy, but Haddie knew her mommy didn't feel weight like she did, and Haddie didn't know the words to use to explain it to her.

It made Haddie feel lonely.

It made her feel *different.*

She *was* different. She knew that.

She stepped out of the trees, making a beeline straight for the gazebo, breaking into a run when she'd made it past the house, hoping her mommy didn't choose that moment to look out the window.

Her book was still sitting there, a story she'd just started called, *The Night Fairy.* She reached for it, drawing in a startled breath when she saw movement just under the bench where she'd been about to sit.

Haddie stepped back, squatting down, her eyes going wide when she spotted the tiny tan body of a baby rabbit. "Oh," she breathed. The little thing was curled up on its side, staring at her with wide, scared eyes.

Haddie reached in, scooping up the bunny as gently as she could and bringing it to her chest the same way she'd held the kittens in the hardware store. It whimpered softly. "It's okay," Haddie whispered. "You're going to be okay." The bunny stared up at her for another moment and then closed its eyes as though it had decided it trusted her enough to sleep.

Haddie turned and headed toward the house, calling for her mommy.

"Haddie?" her mommy called back, walking from the direction of the kitchen. She stopped in the doorway of the foyer when she spotted Haddie, her eyes going from her face to the animal in her arms. She blinked. "Haddie, what is that?"

Haddie stood still, stroking the velvety ear of the tiny creature. "A bunny."

Her mother walked toward her, her shoulders lowering as if with a long exhale. She came to stop right in front of her, still gazing at the baby. "A bunny," she repeated. "Oh Haddie. Honey." She blew out another breath and looked off to the side for a moment. "I can't keep taking in baby things from the woods."

"But, Mommy," Haddie cried, pulling the bunny as close as she possibly could. "He's all alone."

"Baby, are you sure his mother was nowhere to be found?"

Haddie shook her head, picturing where the bunny had been left in the gazebo where her book was.

Her mother shook her head, pursing her lips. "It's just . . . we're not an animal hospital, Haddie." Her mother sounded a little mad now but her mommy's weight always stayed the same even when her words sounded mad. Wherever *weight* came from, her mommy's didn't shift like a snake's did. "I'm trying to start a business, Haddie. I don't have time to be nursing sick forest creatures. We're going to have to put it back in the woods."

Haddie's heart felt crushed. "No! Mommy, we can't. It will die if we don't help it. I named it, Mommy," she said on a whim. Maybe if her mommy knew it by name, it would be harder for her to turn it away.

Her mommy pressed her lips together again. She reached out and ran a finger over its ear, sighing. "What's its name?"

"Her name is Mopsie."

Her mother's lips tipped and inside, Haddie let out a sigh of relief. "Mopsie, huh? It's a good bunny name." She sighed again. "I guess our feathered friend is doing well enough that we can take on one more." She reached out, taking the baby gently from Haddie's hands. "Let's go get my computer so we can figure out what baby bunnies eat."

Haddie grinned, following her mommy from the room.

Later, after the baby bunny had eaten a small dose of heavy cream, Haddie's mommy had sent her to wash up and change into her PJs. She pulled on her pink nightgown and walked from the bathroom back into her mommy's room. Her mommy sat in the rocker by the window, the baby bird in his cradle next to her, the bunny nestled in a towel in her arms. All three of them were sound asleep.

For a moment, Haddie simply stood there watching them. They were all so incredibly *light,* the bird, the bunny, and especially her mommy. A tear tracked down Haddie's cheek. She loved her mommy so much that sometimes it felt like her heart would soar right out of her body.

She would not let that man hurt her mommy. She would not.

CHAPTER TWENTY-FOUR

Thirteen Years Ago

ℒoud footsteps sounded on the wooden stairs to the attic and Kandace looked up from the book she was reading on her bed, placing her pillow more firmly over her stomach. Sydney glanced at her, a small worried line forming between her eyes. It sounded like a man was approaching. A trill of fear whirled through Kandace. *Jasper.* Who else could it be?

Kandace's fight or flight instinct kicked in as she sat up quickly, dropping her book to the floor, her head whipping around for a place to flee. She was finally healed, finally sleeping through the night, the pain in her tailbone tolerable enough that it didn't wake her up every time she moved. Sydney sat up too, raising her hand in a relax gesture, giving Kandace a comforting nod. "You've done nothing wrong," she whispered.

Kandace blinked, forcing her shoulders to relax. No, she hadn't done anything wrong, in fact, they'd even earned the rare privilege of a chaperoned walk around the grounds that afternoon, but at Lilith House, Kandace wasn't sure it mattered whether you were guilty or innocent of any particular charge.

The door crashed open and Jasper stood in the doorway, a moaning Aurora in his arms.

Jasper dropped Aurora on her bed and then turned, walked to the door, and slammed it behind him.

Kandace and Sydney both rushed to Aurora's side, Kandace drawing back when she noticed the bandages on Aurora's trembling thighs, blood seeping through the gauzy white material. "Oh my God," she breathed, pulling Aurora's skirt a tad higher. "Aurora, what did they do to you?"

"They caught me looking through the cabinets in the infirmary." Her gaze stayed stuck on Kandace's. *Snuck into the infirmary?* That surprised Kandace. She'd only known Aurora a short time, but *she* was always the one warning Kandace not to take risks. Not here.

"Why did you do that?" Sydney hissed, an edge of hysteria in her voice.

"Just seeing what I could find."

Sydney made a sound of frustration, standing. "I'm going to get you some water," she said, rushing to the bathroom. She looked ill.

"They caught me but they didn't know what I took," she whispered to Kandace, reaching back and bringing something from where she'd apparently tucked it in the

233

waistband of her underpants. "I told them I snuck in for the pain meds." She glanced toward the bathroom and then put the white wrapped item in Kandace's hand.

Kandace glanced down at it, her stomach landing in her feet. It looked like a pregnancy test. Her eyes shot to Aurora's.

"You've been throwing up almost every morning since the . . . cleansing," she said. "You've been falling asleep before lights out."

Kandace was taken aback. "Only a bug."

Aurora shook her head. "Maybe. Please, just take it." She winced when she shifted. "There was another girl in the infirmary when I went through the drawers. I didn't think she'd tell. I thought I was safe. But she did. She told." She closed her eyes. "So stupid. I should have been smarter about it. My dad said I was the stupidest person he ever met and he was right."

Kandace shook her head. "You're not stupid. It's Lilith House that's sick," she spat out. "They make spies out of us. That girl used the information because she had some reason to. I mean, apart from Sydney and me, do you trust any other girl here? I don't. We've all been sent here by someone who believed our lives mean nothing, that we could be disposed of. And *they* use that against us. It's dog-eat-dog *for the utmost for His fucking glory.* It's the only way to avoid punishment or earn privileges."

Aurora let out a small snort. "A short walk outside? Time off from cleaning duty? That's the price of a soul these days?"

Kandace pressed her lips together. She was certain others had sold out for less. It wasn't always so much about the prize, but the character of the person trying to win it.

You learned how noble you were in a place like Lilith House. You learned how much of yourself you were willing to sacrifice for others. And how cheap your price could be.

Aurora had sacrificed for her because she worried she was in trouble. It hadn't been worth the risk because she wasn't pregnant, but just to know someone had her back in here was priceless to Kandace.

Aurora's expression remained miserable and Kandace glanced down at Aurora's thighs again, remembering her roommate telling them that she was a cutter. She remembered the numerous pink scars, the ones she'd put there herself.

"They cut you," she said, her heart in her throat.

Sydney emerged from the bathroom, returning to the other side of Aurora's bed and handing her a glass of water. Aurora sat up slightly and took a few sips before laying her head back on the pillow. "Yes, they cut me. They held me down and took a razor to my thighs. They opened the door so the others could hear me scream." Her face screwed up and tears filled her eyes. Kandace squeezed her hand. Sydney and Kandace hadn't heard her screams because they'd been outside, but of course, they got to see the result of Aurora's punishment. They were witness to her pain and tears.

"Your parents will see these scars, Aurora," Sydney said. "They'll know."

But Aurora just looked at her sadly. "How will they tell them from the ones I gave myself?" Aurora asked. Kandace's stomach sank. She had no answer because Aurora was right. She'd thought it once before when she'd first arrived at Lilith House, and she thought it now: they were the perfect victims. Liars, thieves, whores, and those who practiced self-sabotage as though it was their *job*. By the time they'd shown up at Lilith House, they'd lost all credibility.

Why should anyone believe a word they said?

As Kandace stood, so that Sydney could hold the glass while Aurora drank, the pregnancy test stolen for her felt like a fifty-pound weight in the pocket of her uniform.

CHAPTER TWENTY-FIVE

$\mathcal{S}$carlett moved a box aside, careful not to disturb the layer of dust that might explode in her face.

The sounds of banging echoed from above, making Scarlett smile. They were erecting the final studs in the newly enlarged kitchen and drywall would go up later that afternoon. One step closer. It was already a decent-sized room, but she needed to turn it into an industrial kitchen with more bench space.

Once the walls were complete, the fun part started . . . cabinets, stainless steel countertops, industrial-sized fridges and freezers, two ovens with induction cooktops, instant hot water, upper and lower cabinets, and paint. She could see it all in her head. Practically *smell* the sweetness of the cakes that would bake in the ovens.

Yes, once the kitchen was complete, she'd be in business again. Not *fully* in business, or at least not the business she planned—that was going to take a completed renovation of the house and grounds, a business license, brochures, business cards, a few employees, W-9s and who knew what other tax documents were necessary . . . but at least once the kitchen was complete, she'd be able to cook and bake. Maybe she'd drive into Farrow and see if one of the local stores was interested in selling some home-baked goods. It wasn't that she needed the money, exactly—she'd planned financially— but what else was she going to do?

Not only that, but it was always good to build on her skill set. And perhaps she'd come up with a few new recipes that would really *wow* the brides.

Not to mention baking was her happy place. Creating beautiful and delicious food nourished her soul as much as it delighted those she fed.

It'd only been a month since she'd been in a kitchen— barring the quick batch of chocolate chip cookies she'd baked at Lilith House—and she already felt itchy.

The memory of the chocolate chip cookies brought Deputy West to mind but she pushed him from her thoughts. She had no desire to think about him. With a tad more strength than needed, she pulled a box aside, the weight of the item taking her off balance so she almost fell backward. She caught herself just in time, dropping the box, which fell apart in a burst of dust, spilling its contents onto the floor. Ugh.

Scarlett pushed at the box with her foot, revealing a pile of dark red fabric, the scent of mildew meeting her nose. *Ew.* She recalled the photo on the cover of the Lilith House brochure and wondered if those were extra uniforms meant for the students who'd attended the school. Likely.

Scarlett used her foot to slide the box and its contents over to the side of the basement she'd designated for junk.

Just as she went to pick up the next box, she spied what looked like an old trunk wedged between the pile she was working on and the one just behind it.

Leaning forward, she peered into it, a tingle going up her spine. *A treasure chest* she thought with an internal smile. In truth, it didn't look fancy. It didn't even look cool in that vintage way old things sometimes did, but rather simply ancient and dilapidated. Still . . . something about it spoke to her.

Quickly, she pushed the boxes in front of her aside and scooted the trunk forward. She knelt down on the floor and pried the rusty latch open, lifting the lid. *Books.* On the top was a thick, leather-bound Bible. Scarlett opened the flap but no name was written inside. She set that on the floor and pulled the next book out: *The Chronicles of Narnia.* Were these things that had belonged to one of the young women who'd lived at Lilith House? Perhaps even one of the girls who'd died in the fire? That thought pulled at Scarlett's heartstrings. If she could find a name somewhere among these items, she was sure the girl's family would want them.

Scarlett set the C.S. Lewis title aside, and another one by Mark Twain, and then pulled out a thick stack of papers enclosed in a suede wrap and tied with a leather string. Speaking of ancient . . . this thing looked like it was going to fall apart at any moment.

Scarlett sat back on her butt, leaning against a couple of boxes behind her and set the bundle on her lap, untying the string and unwrapping the suede covering. At the top was a piece of old linen paper filled with writing in a language Scarlett had never seen before. She squinted at it. What in the world? She moved a page aside and looked at the one beneath it. This paper looked more recent and the handwriting was in English, the letters carefully penned. Her eyes moved over the clean, concise lines, taking in the tale familiar to Scarlett.

It was Taluta's story.

The one Camden West had told her as they'd sat drinking lemonade in the gazebo.

Scarlett rifled through the stack, confirming what she had guessed. "Oh my God," she whispered into the empty basement. Taluta had written out the truth of her story and someone had translated it. Scarlett flipped to the end. Taluta's writings ceased, but several pages in English told the end of her story. Because she hadn't been there to do it anymore. She'd been tossed into the canyon and disappeared. *Who?* Scarlett wondered. *Who did this?*

The very last of their tribe died about three years ago and took their language with her.

Scarlett searched her memory but she couldn't remember the name of the old native woman Camden had mentioned. Had *she* translated Taluta's story? And if so, when? And how did it come to be at Lilith House?

Scarlett found the answer in a small black journal underneath the collection of Taluta's papers and the translation.

"Narcisa Fernando," she said aloud, reading the name inscribed at the front in that same neat penmanship. Yes, that was the name she couldn't quite recall. She'd lived in a small house a few miles from here. Hadn't that been what Camden said? She'd sold herbs and such in town.

Scarlett glanced at the journal. Only one page was written in and Scarlett's stomach knotted as she read the words.

Mr. Bancroft hired me to tend to his wife who was with child, and then the expectant mothers of his parish, but really, I am his whore as my ancestors were to this family of devils. The baby he put inside me was taken, his club feet proving the mark of Satan, or so says Mr. Bancroft. But my baby is not of Satan, though his blood father is evil. They put me to sleep and left my baby on a rock in the forest to die. Mr. Schmidt tried to save my baby. He has a spark of decency in him, but the others are too powerful. Tonight, I shall follow my baby boy by my own hand for I have no other hope for escape.

Scarlett let out a heavy breath, her shoulders dropping. *Holy Christ.* Her heart ached. For a moment she simply sat staring, unseeing, at the disorganized junk in front of her. She'd known this house had a past but she hadn't known such cruelty and suffering had filled the halls of Lilith House. A mild shudder went through her. One of the Bancroft sons had made Narcisa Fernando into his unwilling mistress, she'd borne a child of his, and then because of a physical abnormality, he had left him to die in the woods?

Good God, the unthinkable evil of that was almost too much for Scarlett to bear.

Narcisa had been right—her baby's blood father was a monster.

And he'd come by it honestly. His ancestors hadn't been any better, if not far worse.

She looked at the papers enclosed once again in the suede covering, and the journal. Had Taluta, who had once been kept captive in the house, written out her story during the time she was there? That had to be it . . . Scarlett didn't imagine that native people had the type of paper and ink pen Taluta had used. Then later, Narcisa, who'd come to live in the Bancroft house had found Taluta's writings and translated them, leaving the few necessary facts of her own time at Lilith House?

She'd intended on taking her own life. Hadn't Camden mentioned something about a limp? Had she attempted to harm herself but only come away with an injury? A picture entered Scarlett's mind of a woman, arms held wide as she pitched her body from an upper story window. She shook her head, dispelling the image that had to have come purely from her imagination.

Scarlett bit at her lip, a feeling of deep sadness settling on her skin just as the dust in the basement had coated the trunk where two women's brutal stories resided.

With infinite care, Scarlett set the two items down on a clean spot on the floor and went back up on her knees, peering once again into the trunk and pulling out what appeared to be old photos, each encased in a thick paper frame. The first one was of a man in his mid-fifties with silver hair and distinctive sideburns. He sat looking to the side, his mouth set, expression stern. Scarlett pulled the photograph from its covering and turned it over. *H. Bancroft* was printed in the bottom right corner. Hubert Bancroft. Scarlett turned it right side up and stared at the man for a moment, thinking about the things she knew about him, the evil deeds he'd performed, the lives he'd ruined. She turned the picture back over and returned it, face down this time, to its frame.

The next few photographs were of Lilith House in various stages of construction. Scarlett looked through these with interest, noting the things that were different about the house in its infancy, and the things that remained unchanged.

Under those was a photograph that looked just as old as the original Lilith House photos. It was of five figures dressed in what looked like ancient war garb. A deep shiver went down Scarlett's spine. One of the figures wore a horned headdress, two held long, sharp spears, another was dressed entirely in furs, a mask that looked like a pointy bird beak covering his face. Could this be a picture of the man Camden had mentioned to her? The one who had donned an outfit just like this before he died, and now supposedly wandered the woods beyond?

She set it aside, but paused for a moment, waiting for the deeply unsettled feeling to pass before moving on.

The next photograph was of a group of men, all wearing similar white suits standing in front of Lilith House, a photograph she'd seen before hanging on the wall of Sister Madge's office. She studied it close up now, looking at the men who stood shoulder to shoulder, one more austere than the next.

She removed the photo from its frame and looked at the back. *Religious Guild,* was written in the corner in the same handwriting as had been used to identify Hubert Bancroft on the back of his photograph. She turned it back over, her eyes moving from one face to the next. Hubert Bancroft was in the center. She recognized his stern expression and those notable sideburns. Something skittled under her skin, racing up her spine. Were the rest of them the men in Bancroft's ministry? The ones who'd joined him in brutalizing and murdering the natives? She was tempted to use her fingernail to scratch Xs over each of their villainous faces.

Still, as with Hubert Bancroft's photo, Scarlett turned it over and placed it face down in its frame.

The last photo was again of a group of men, all in white suits, standing in front of Lilith House. Only this photo was much more recent.

The sons of Farrow. They've held the moral line for centuries.

Scarlett frowned, looking closer. She didn't recognize any of the men except one, the sheriff, though he looked about fifteen years younger. She turned the photo over but no information was written on the back, not even a date. She flipped it again. This must be a more recent photo of the Farrow Religious Guild. But if so, why were they standing in front of Lilith House? If the photo was fifteen years old or so, then Lilith House had been a reform school. What did these men have to do with that? For some reason—most likely because of the photo that had been hung directly next to the picture of the original Religious Guild in Sister Madge's office—the old nun's words about fallen women came back to her.

I like this depiction, because she's seeking atonement by reaching for the blessing of a righteous man. So many do not, you know. Atone.

Was that what they'd been at Lilith House to offer? Some form of atonement? A religious ceremony wherein the girls might absolve themselves of their sins? And how exactly did *that* work? These were not prophets, nor deities. They were just *men* who'd joined some church group. How exactly were they qualified to offer atonement to anyone?

After a moment, she set the photos on the floor and knelt forward again, peering into the trunk once more. She removed one book, then another until she got to the musty, fabric-lined bottom. Nothing else remained.

Frowning, Scarlett glanced around at the books. Whose had they been? Who had been the keeper of Taluta's and Narcisa's stories? Who had obtained the old photos of Hubert Bancroft, Lilith House, and different generations of the Religious Guild? It all seemed . . . connected in some way she didn't have enough information to understand. She hesitated a moment and then began placing the books back in the trunk. When she got to the Bible, she paused, opening it again and flipping to the back. Still no name. No information about who had once owned it.

Scarlett closed it and then used her thumb to flip through the interior pages, noting the underlined passages and the highlighted portions, one question mark after another in the margins. The reader of this Bible had struggled with questions of faith. She wondered if they'd ever been answered. Scarlett stopped suddenly when she spied something flattened in the middle. She opened it wide, pulling out the item and swallowing heavily.

With trembling fingers, she grasped it delicately, expecting it to crumble, but it didn't. She held it up, bringing it close to her face so she could take in all the intricate details.

It was a bird.

Formed with a strand of grass.

CHAPTER TWENTY-SIX

$\mathcal{S}$carlett knocked on the blue painted door, waiting a minute before turning back toward the street. She'd dropped Haddie off at Millie's with the bird *and* the bunny, and then gone straight to the address where Millie told her the boy in the wheelchair lived with his parents. The child Haddie had evidently made scream bloody murder a few days before. She'd brought it up with Haddie, and though Haddie had looked confused and ashamed—just as she had after the church daycare incident—Scarlett had again, comforted herself with the belief that Haddie wasn't a bully. She'd seek clarification from the boy's mother before addressing it again.

Unfortunately, that day wouldn't be today. No one was home.

Scarlett got back in her car, and pulled away from the curb. She purposely avoided looking at the house Camden had come out of the other day, and headed to the pet store where, apparently, she might want to consider signing up for a frequent shopper discount. "No more rescue pets please, God," she whispered to the big guy in the sky. There was only so much Scarlett could take on, though she supposed it was her fault that she hadn't considered what else came with owning a house at the edge of a forest full of creatures. Perhaps soon, they'd have their own small petting zoo, and wasn't *that* just what she needed?

She pulled into the lot, and as she was walking toward the store, Camden West pulled into a space, got out of his truck, and headed toward the door as well. He was wearing jeans and a gray T-shirt, obviously off duty. They eyed each other, Scarlett slowing her pace so they wouldn't get to the entrance at the same moment. *Crap.* She really hated small towns. The likelihood of running into people you really didn't want to run into were far too high.

She considered turning around and coming back another time, but while she was wary and suspicious of Camden West, and yes, still *hurt*, she didn't quite hate him enough to starve a baby bunny.

His gaze stayed on her, that stupid enigmatic expression on his face that he too frequently wore. He held the door for her for a moment, but she knelt down and pretended to tie her shoe . . . because she was just that mature.

When she stood, he had taken the hint and gone inside. She headed in as well, spotting him in her peripheral vision over in the dog food section. Scarlett asked the clerk to help her find a formula suitable for a baby rabbit, took the first thing he recommended, paid for it, and left the store.

Camden was waiting outside the door.

Scarlett startled slightly, clutching her bag to her chest. As she turned and began walking to her car, Camden followed, walking beside her.

"Baby bunny?" he asked.

She glanced at him. "Yes. I'm running a zoo out of my house these days, Deputy. So you'll understand if I don't stop to chat. Have a good—"

"Scarlett." He reached out and took her upper arm and she stopped short, looking at the place where he touched her. He let go as if he'd suddenly realized she was made of fire. Two high spots of color appeared on his cheekbones. "Sorry," he mumbled. "But I think we need to talk."

At the imploring look in his eyes, she sighed. Despite that she hadn't been prepared to do it *today*, she wanted to talk to him too. He'd lied to her—not about the woman, she wasn't going to bring that up because she did still have some pride—but about Lilith House. He had some connection to it that he hadn't divulged to her and she wanted an explanation. She wanted to know why Farrow's deputy sheriff had sought to purchase Lilith House before her, and why he had personal effects in its basement.

"I live a couple blocks from here," he said, glancing around. "We could sit on my porch if you don't want to go inside. It's more private than this parking lot."

She shifted back and forth from one foot to the other. Mason and his team were already at her house, and they didn't really expect her back anytime in particular. Plus, if she was going to agree to talk to him, he was right, this was not the place to do it. She might not like what he had to say, and she wouldn't be seen standing in the pet store parking lot of her new town fighting with Farrow's deputy. "Okay," she agreed. "I'll follow you in my car."

"Thank you."

Five minutes later, she was pulling up to the curb next to a small, somewhat generic tan house with a picket fence surrounding the yard, while Camden pulled into the driveway. The house was at the end of a cul-de-sac, an empty lot on one side, and a copse of trees on the other. He was right, it was private. She couldn't imagine it got much traffic, if any. She got out and walked slowly up the front path, climbing the three steps, and meeting him on the porch. Inside, three dogs of varying breeds and sizes scratched at the window and whined in excitement at seeing him. Camden leaned toward them. "Go lay down," he called, making some movement with his hand she couldn't see. The dogs looked briefly crestfallen but turned away.

"I'm assuming it was their food you didn't buy at the pet store?"

"I'll go back later." He nodded to two chairs and they both took a seat.

"Tell me about the bunny," he said, taking her off guard.

"The bunny? *That's* what you wanted to talk about?"

"Not only, but that first."

She screwed up her face, shaking her head. "What's there to tell about the bunny? My daughter found it in the woods. It was half-dead and abandoned. I'm its mother now."

Camden pressed his lips together. "She found it?"

"Yes, I mean, what else? She didn't steal it from its den. She knows better and she's not cruel." *Although, you've been wondering lately about that, haven't you?* The thought brought her shame.

"That's not what I meant," he mumbled. "And it's burrow."

"What?"

"Rabbits. They live in a burrow, not a den."

She shook her head, frustrated that they were talking about burrows, and dens, and motherless baby bunnies, rather than things that actually mattered between them.

"I have questions for you, Deputy."

He looked at her sideways. "Yes?"

"That story you told me about Taluta? How did you know about it?"

His eyes narrowed and he looked just as confused as she must have looked when he asked her about the bunny. "The legend's well known around here."

"Not the legend about the indigenous woman who passed away and turned into a red fox. Not even the reports of drumbeats sounding from those woods." She shook her head. "I found all that online. What I didn't find was the brutal background of those stories. There's nothing at all about any of that." Maybe it was local knowledge, lore that somehow hadn't made it on to the Internet, but she needed to know if that trunk had belonged to him as she suspected, or if someone else had owned it. Someone who coincidentally created the same rare and intricate art using reeds of grass, a craft she'd never heard about, seen, or even imagined, in her entire existence.

His gaze slid away from hers and she could see his wheels turning. When he looked back at her, he asked, "Why are you asking about that?"

Scarlett hesitated. *Why play games? Why not just come out and ask him?* "I found a trunk," she said and watched as his body stilled. "I found a trunk that contained the personal account of Taluta, translated by Narcisa Fernando. It also included Narcisa's story. The trunk had books and photos in it, and inside one of the books was this." She reached into her purse at her feet, retrieved a small notebook, and took out the grass art pressed between its pages, holding it up for him to see.

Camden swallowed, his gaze lingering on what she held carefully in her fingers.

"I think this is yours," she whispered. "I think that trunk was yours too. And I want to know why it was in the basement of Lilith House. I want to know why you didn't tell me you were planning to buy the house before I did."

He closed his eyes for a second, exhaling a long breath. When he opened them, he stared at her for so long she wondered if he was going to speak at all. But finally, he said, "That trunk was mine. I used to live at Lilith House. I grew up there."

For a second, Scarlett was shocked silent. "You . . . what? How is that possible?"

Camden scrubbed a hand down his face and then stared behind her, his jaw rigid. "I was born to one of the students

252

who attended Lilith House. I was never given any details, only that she signed her rights away and then left me behind."

Scarlett frowned, her heart giving a small twist. "Oh," she said. "So then who adopted you?"

He shook his head. "No one. The school took charge of me. Ms. West . . . my tutor was the closest thing to a mother I ever had. We were kept downstairs, forbidden from interacting with any of the students. After the fire and school closure, she took me with her to San Diego. I took her name. She got sick, and I cared for her for several years until she died. Then I moved back here to start a life in Farrow."

"You always do that," she said. "You leave things out. Give me half stories."

"What do you want from me, Scarlett?"

"The truth. Why is that so hard?"

He made a small hissing sound in the back of his throat. "It isn't entirely mine to give," he mumbled. He glanced quickly up and down the street. "Maybe we should go inside."

"Why?" She glanced around as he had done. "Are we being watched?"

"I don't think so, but . . ." He swore beneath his breath. "Listen, there are things you don't know."

"Then *tell* me," she said, frustration causing her to raise her voice. "Tell me what I need to know about Lilith House. Tell me who you're worried about seeing us *talking*. Is it the woman whose house I saw you leaving the other morning?" She cringed internally. She hadn't intended to bring her up. The last thing she wanted him to think was that she was jealous and trying to stake some claim she had no right to because of a bit of flirting and one stupid kiss.

"Georgia," he said. "That's the other thing I wanted to talk to you about." He paused. "What you saw . . . it's not what you probably think it is. I . . . she needs someone to be with her sometimes. We're good friends. That's all."

Friends with benefits, apparently. She didn't care, not one bit. At least that's what she told herself.

Although as she thought about it, she wondered how they were good friends if he'd grown up at a reform school and only recently moved back to town. Admittedly, Scarlett didn't know him well, but she knew enough to guess that Camden West didn't make friends all too easily, much less "good friends." The sudden flash of those three rooms in the basement came to mind, the metal beds in each one . . .

"Oh my God," she breathed. "She grew up at Lilith House with you." She remembered back to the day at Mason's hardware store when she'd heard them all arguing in the back. All three of them.

Camden, Georgia, and Mason.

She could tell by the look on his face that she'd just uttered the truth. She could *tell.* Scarlett swallowed, blinked. "Mason too. The *three* of you grew up together at Lilith House? You lived in those basement rooms."

He let out a breath and ran a hand through his hair. "I didn't want to drag you into any of this."

"Drag me into *what?*" She shook her head, her mind reeling, thinking about what the sheriff had said. "You wanted to buy the house. *Why?*"

"Because there might be something inside that will tell us more about who our mothers were and why they left us behind."

Her thoughts were spinning in all directions. "Aren't there records of who attended the school? Surely you could use those to track down the women who, date wise, could have been your mothers? Why do you need the *house* to do that?"

"All the school records went missing sometime after the fire. No one knows if they were lost during the cleanup and subsequent estate sale of the contents of the house, or misplaced . . . stolen. But in any case, they're gone. Poof." His hand rose quickly, fingers flying open as he gestured the word. "It's as if no one ever attended Lilith School."

She frowned again. Weird. Spooky, even. "Okay, so . . . you were going to . . . what? Buy the place and then commence searching behind its walls?"

He looked away from her, using his hand to massage the side of his jaw, his lips set in a thin line. Her gaze moved to the breast pocket of his T-shirt where she saw the distinct outline of what looked like a small, oval stone. *Like the one he picked up at the stream the day he'd kissed her.* It took her off balance for a moment. Why had he kept it? "Something like that," he muttered after a minute, bringing her smack-dab back into the moment. "All three of us were going to live there. To search it, yes, but also, to own it. We were going to make it ours. I was the only one who left Farrow. Georgie and Mason, they waited for me. We'd all waited a long time, Scarlett."

As more of the picture formed, emotions warred within her, mixing, twisting together so that she couldn't separate one from another . . . despondency, indignation, shock, and sorrow.

"That's why you befriended me," she said, her voice rough, a pit opening in her stomach. "It's why you recommended Mason for the job. The house wasn't yours, but that way, you could still have access to it. You could still be present while the walls were torn down, and the floorboards demolished. Mason's been searching even as his crew worked."

The look on his face confirmed what she'd said. To his credit, he obviously felt at least moderately ashamed. But it didn't change the fact that he'd deceived her. Used her. Was that what the flirting had been about? Even the kiss? She'd thought him unpracticed at both, but maybe what he was doing was *pretending.* God, she felt embarrassed. He'd tried to get close to her as a means to an end, but he hadn't quite been able to go through with it. Whether that was because he had a scrap of honor, or whether it was because the lie of his attraction toward her was too difficult to sustain, she didn't know. And really, did it matter?

"It's the reason you installed the lock and sealed up the crawl spaces? You were worried about them searching the house while I was there? They didn't listen to you, though, did they? You fought about it. You were fighting that day at the hardware store. Why? Why did you care? Did you think you'd get caught?"

He cast his eyes downward. He had lied to her over and over and over since the moment they'd met, so why couldn't she feel angry? Why was her overwhelming emotion *hurt*? She let out a long breath and then she stood. He came to his feet immediately as well.

"Scarlett—"

"No." She held up her hand. "I get the picture. I'm sorry I ruined all your plans. Obviously, I can't have Mason working at the house anymore. He's more interested in his own agenda than in seeing my goals for the house to fruition. If I find anything that might help in your efforts to locate your families, I promise to hand it over. I'm sorry for the suffering the three of you endured and I wish you well. But let me make this perfectly clear: Lilith House is mine. I'm going to run a business from there, I'm going to build a life for me and Haddie there. And there's nothing you can do to stop me."

She knew she must be imagining the glint of respect in his forest-green gaze, because his allegiance to his two friends would have prevented something like that. It didn't matter though. She didn't care what he thought of her anymore. Scarlett turned on her heel and marched down his steps, getting in her car and peeling away from the curb.

When she glanced once in her rearview mirror, she saw him standing on his porch, leaning on one of the pillars and watching her as she drove away.

CHAPTER TWENTY-SEVEN

Thirteen Years Ago

𝒦andace grimaced as she leaned toward the shiny silver napkin dispenser, using it for a mirror as she picked a large scab off her cheek, but breathed out a sigh of relief when it came off clean. She stepped back, taking herself in as well as possible, turning right and then left. Her face *finally* looked halfway normal despite the wavy nature of her reflection in the makeshift mirror. Red, shiny, and still flaky here and there, but she no longer resembled Freddie Kruger, thank God for that.

"Let me see you," Aurora said, coming up behind her. Kandace turned, showing her face. "Better," Aurora breathed, dragging the word out with a smile. "*So* much better."

"Told ya," Kandace said with a smile. "Baby's"—she leaned in and lowered her voice dramatically—"ass." But then she clapped a hand over her mouth as a wave of nausea overcame her, turning and taking the two steps to the toilet where she went down on her knees and vomited into the bowl. At least her hair wasn't in the way.

Bonus to having it hacked off by a power-hungry maniac.

Kandace groaned, bringing her head up as she took the paper towel offered to her by Aurora. "Thanks," she said weakly, wiping her mouth and standing, remaining still as the toilet flushed, to make sure the wave of nausea had passed.

"Did you take that test, Kandace?" Aurora asked. Kandace filled the cup on the sink with water and rinsed her mouth. She couldn't bear the thought of toothpaste at the moment. It would make her hurl again.

"No. I already told you. It can't be that kind of bug," she assured her. "I appreciate the risk you took, I really do"—she smiled softly at her—"but . . . it can't be." Aurora looked at her dubiously and she knew why. They both had histories of frequent casual sex. Hell, she probably couldn't list all the guys she'd been with if someone offered her a million dollars to do so. She wasn't necessarily proud of that, but it was a fact of her life. However, she'd had her period right before she got there . . . but not since. Odd because she was usually right on time but . . . stress could do that to a girl, and Lilith House offered stress in spades. Some of it she'd even brought on herself by choosing to sneak around the way she had. And get caught and severely punished. Anyway . . . "No," she repeated. "Not possible."

Aurora's lips thinned, but she nodded. "Take it anyway, for me," she said. "Just to be sure." Aurora placed her hand gently on Kandace's arm.

Kandace sighed. She'd felt fine all day. Tired, but that was to be expected, considering the trauma her body had gone through and that she was *still* healing. "Fine," she said. The girl had gone to the trouble of stealing something from Lilith House for Kandace and so she'd make it worth the risk she'd taken. Worth the blood she'd shed.

Aurora—and to a lesser extent, Sydney—now felt as close as untrusting, cynical sisters could to Kandace, given their strange circumstances. They were both jaded by life, by disappointments beyond normal, yet they hadn't rejected her, and that had kept Kandace sane. Particularly after the beating . . . *They cared.* They'd helped her survive.

She closed the door of the bathroom and unwrapped the test stick, keeping the wrapper so she could put it inside afterward and discard it somewhere where it wouldn't be noticed, like the large dining room trash to be covered in leftover food. She followed the instructions and then placed it on the tank of the toilet, glancing at the negative result before washing her hands and opening the door. "There ya go," she told Aurora. "Now you can rest easy."

Aurora walked over to the test, picking it up by the handle, her expression grim. "It's positive," she said so softly, Kandace barely heard the words.

Her blood chilled as she took a step forward, grabbing the test from Aurora and looking at the two blue lines. *Positive.* "No," she said, shaking her head. She looked up at

Aurora. "I told you. This isn't possible. There's no way." Panic flashed through her. "I . . . Aurora I had my period right before I got here."

"It must have been a false period," Aurora said. "That happens sometimes."

Kandace put her hand on her forehead. She felt sick again. Her head ached. "Oh God," she said. She met Aurora's eyes. "What am I going to do?"

She shook her head, biting at her lip. "You'll have to tell them," she said. "You don't have a choice. Maybe they'll just . . . let you leave."

"Yes," she muttered, but some red warning signal flared inside. Would they? Would they just let her leave? Or would she be punished again? This time far more severely than before?

Her gaze moved to Aurora. "You can't tell anyone. No one at all. Not even Sydney. The fewer people who know, the better."

She nodded but there was something in her eyes that caused Kandace to question her honesty. *No, no, don't feel that way. Aurora hasn't done anything to make you mistrust her.* Kandace looked at the test. *She brought you the test. She was tortured for her efforts. What if it's some sort of setup? For what reason?* She massaged her temples. God, this place was making her crazy. She had to *think.* How could this be?

"I'll get rid of it," Aurora said, taking the test from her.

Kandace started to object, but a wave of nausea suddenly overcame her and she raced for the toilet for the second time that day.

Later, lying in her bed in her darkened room, listening to her roommates rhythmic breathing, she thought of the pills.

Each morning at breakfast, Ms. Harrah came around with a paper cup of vitamins for the girls to swallow with their juice. Kandace, in a small act of defiance, had been palming them and tossing them away with her breakfast trash. *Fuck your vitamins, you tyrants.*

She'd even wondered if perhaps instead of vitamins, at least one of the pills was a low-dose sedative. She'd originally thought her roommates meek . . . tamed. Or broken. But maybe they were mildly drugged.

She tried to picture the pills in the cup. A large, amber one filled with some sort of oil, one small round pill, a larger pinkish oval tablet, and a very small round, blue pill. Birth control? No. No, it couldn't be. She could understand the mild sedative. But why would Lilith House give their students a birth control pill when they were restricted from seeing anyone except each other and the all-female staff? It was illogical. It didn't make sense.

Kandace rolled over. Now she was just being paranoid.

No, she told herself. *I am not pregnant. There's just no way.* The test was wrong. It was the only answer.

Because otherwise, she'd gotten pregnant because she had secretly been tossing the birth control pills they'd been giving her. Which would mean she got pregnant *after* arriving at Lilith House.

And that simply was not possible.

CHAPTER TWENTY-EIGHT

$\mathcal{D}$r. Woodrow's waiting room was cheery and pleasant, a large fish tank taking up the majority of one wall, and a small children's play area in the opposite corner. Haddie walked past the play area, eyeing it disinterestedly, instead heading to the fish tank where she stood in front of it, tracing a bright orange fish's movement across the glass with her finger.

Scarlett took a seat in one of the pleather chairs, turning to the pile of magazines on a side table next to her and half-heartedly rifling through them. She almost gasped when she slid one aside to reveal one of those weekly tabloids she always avoided in the grocery store, to see Royce Reynolds's face staring up at her in living color, the title screaming, *Hollywood's Golden Boy Reveals Battle With Mental Illness.* Scarlett felt her stomach drop.

With a quick glance at Haddie to make sure she was still being entertained by the fish, Scarlett grabbed the magazine, folded the cover back, and flipped through the pages until she found the article. She read it quickly, skipping over some of the words so she could take it all in before her daughter grew tired of the fish and came to sit next to her. In a nutshell, Royce Reynolds had recently completed a stay in a private mental facility and, because he'd been photographed leaving the hospital and widespread speculation occurred, he'd made the decision to open up about his lifelong battle with mental illness in the hopes that it might help someone else who, like him, had spent too many years hiding a condition they could not help, nor control. What Scarlett read between the lines, was that the speculation over his stay at the hospital, specifically the rumor that he was battling drug addiction— and losing—had cost him a big role, and the admittance of his mental illness was at least in some part, about damage control and attempting to get ahead of the story by giving his personal account.

"Royce has spent his life battling an illness that he suffers with, through no fault of his own," his agent was quoted as saying, driving home Scarlett's assumption. "Despite his overwhelming struggle, he has risen to fame and fortune, moving millions of people with his captivating film roles, and working tirelessly on behalf of his many philanthropic interests. He is a true inspiration, and an American hero. Let it never be said that those struggling similarly cannot work around challenges just as Royce has."

She stared at the page, a myriad of emotions swirling within her. Whether or not there was a PR spin going on, Scarlett had every compassion in the world for someone suffering a mental illness, even this man who had lied to and used her, and then sent his wife to deal with the consequences. She didn't care if the majority of citizens thought of Royce Reynolds as an American hero, what she was most focused on was whether or not his unnamed mental illness might have been passed on to their daughter.

Worry sluiced like acid in her gut. Haddie had said mean things to another child. Twice. And then not remembered what she'd done. She'd wet herself and looked petrified when she'd first seen Camden . . . yet had thought nothing of it. *Did any of it—or all of it—have to do with a mental illness like Royce had?*

Just below his agent's quote was another, this one from Royce himself. "We realize this is controversial, and it's not a choice everyone in my position would choose to make, but my wife and I have decided to forgo having children of our own, and instead to adopt our family. I would never want anyone to suffer what I've suffered, and there are so many needy kids in the world."

I would never want anyone to suffer what I've suffered. Scarlett felt mildly ill.

Her gaze lingered on a photo that was dated the week before, of Royce and a fellow actor posing with a fan. Apparently, Royce had just started filming a new movie in Los Angeles. Scarlett brought the magazine closer, squinting. She recognized the corner of the hotel they were standing in front of. Wasn't that the—

"Haddie Lattimore?"

Scarlett jerked her head up, tossing the magazine, front side down on the table next to her and standing quickly.

"Ready?" She smiled at Haddie as she turned, taking her hand, and following the nurse into the exam room.

The doctor entered a few minutes later, an older man in his sixties, completely bald, with a long face, a pair of round spectacles, and an easy smile. "Ms. Lattimore? I'm Dr. Bill Woodrow. Some of the kids call me Dr. Bill. You must be Haddie," he said after shaking Scarlett's hand and moving his attention to Haddie.

He squatted down in front of the chair where Haddie sat, resting his elbows on his knees. Haddie drew back, appearing as if she was trying to press herself into the wall. Her eyes widened and her expression soured.

"Uh," Scarlett said, taking Haddie's hand in hers. "Haddie can be shy, Dr. Woodrow." She squeezed Haddie's hand but Haddie didn't move, seemingly glued to her chair as she eyed the man sideways.

Dr. Woodrow slapped his knees lightly, smiled, and stood. "I understand. I used to be shy when I was a kid too. Now what brings you into my office today?"

Once the appointment was over and Scarlett had buckled Haddie into her seat, she pulled out of the lot, glancing at Haddie in the rearview mirror. "You didn't seem to care for Dr. Woodrow much," she said, trying to keep her tone conversational. Dr. Woodrow had only stayed in the room long enough to get Haddie's history, and take down Scarlett's concerns about the one-time loss of bladder control. The nurse had come in and performed the rest of the tests after that, and Haddie had seemed markedly more comfortable with the young woman.

Haddie shook her head, but didn't elaborate. Scarlett's eyes lingered on her daughter for a moment before she looked back at the road. "Any particular reason?"

Haddie seemed to think about it but then shook her head again. "He doesn't feel good," she finally said. Haddie had said similar things about other people before. *Based on what?* Scarlett wanted to yell. But she didn't think Haddie knew. Again, one of those Haddie-isms Scarlett had to accept, while simultaneously hoping she'd outgrow it or learn to verbalize it. *He doesn't feel good.* Worry twisted through her when she thought back to the magazine article and the fact that Haddie's birth father had a self-professed mental illness.

Do you hear voices, Haddie? Is that why you always seem so far away? Are you too busy listening to them to focus on me? And if so, what do they tell you, sweetheart? Do they scare you?

Unfortunately, the article about Royce hadn't spoken of his specific diagnosis. That might have helped. As it was, she had nothing more to go on. As it *was,* she could only wonder if it was something that might be hereditary, something that Royce Reynolds had passed on to his unacknowledged child.

Haddie's immediate medical test results hadn't helped shed light on the loss of bladder control or the strange behavior. She didn't have an infection, or a fever, or bloodwork that showed anything even remotely concerning. As far as her physical assessment went, her girl was as healthy as a horse.

Scarlett thought of that small snippet of the downtown LA hotel she'd spotted and wondered if that was where he was staying while he filmed.

Do you dare?

Did she dare go to the hotel and hope to spot a member of his security detail who might remember her and pass a message to Royce? The prideful part of her shriveled at the idea. Not only had she signed a contract that promised she wouldn't contact him, but he'd been distant and dismissive toward her when she'd called to tell him she was pregnant . . . scared and alone.

But it'd been enough of a task just to get a message to Royce the first time she'd contacted him. She couldn't do that this time, not only because it'd be unlikely that he'd call her back, but because she couldn't leave the "paper trail." She chewed at her lip. It would be a risk to break the contract in person too. It could mean being sued . . . losing Lilith House . . . her dream . . . the life she'd planned for the two of them.

But didn't this new information *change* things?

Didn't she owe it to her daughter to mother her in the best way she could? And didn't that mean operating under all possible information? Didn't it mean doing whatever it took to make sure she had all relevant details of Haddie's genetic makeup? God, she wished she'd made that part of the original deal. She'd still sign on the dotted line, but she would have insisted on a file of Royce's medical records.

Maybe though . . . maybe there was still a chance she could get them.

If she changed her mind . . . well, she had renovation shopping she could do in LA too.

She tilted the mirror so she could see Haddie better. "Hey, how do you feel about a visit to Gram this weekend?"

Haddie's smile was bright and instantaneous. And that settled that.

CHAPTER TWENTY-NINE

Thirteen Years Ago

The girls filed in, their hands steepled together in front of them in prayer, heads bowed. The air was drenched in the scent of frankincense and myrrh, a smell that Kandace knew would forevermore bring to mind fear and the desperation to be free.

She followed Sydney as she turned at their assigned pew, shuffling sideways, and then going down on her knees on the red velvet prayer bench.

The lights were dimmed, candlelight sparkling from the altar as Ms. Carroll played the piano softly from the left front of the room, a piece of *worship* music that sounded melancholy and full of foreshadow.

Ms. Wykes stepped to the front of the church, clasping her hands in front of her, her gaze traveling over the two pews where they sat. "Good evening, girls," she said, her lips curving upward in a smile Kandace could only describe as wicked. "As you know, the Religious Guild will be joining us for service tonight and you will be enjoying refreshments afterward. These men are pious, upstanding, and very important members of our community and we are blessed by their presence." She looked pointedly around. "As always, I have no doubt you will give them the reverence and respect they deserve."

Kandace's nerves felt raw.

These men had come once before when she'd first arrived at Lilith House. She turned along with the other girls as the doors to the chapel opened again and eight men walked in, single file, just like the first time. Each was wearing an identical white suit, and each looked fastidiously groomed. All of them looked ancient, easily over the age of forty.

Her gaze moved over them. She thought these men were different than the first group that'd joined them for a service. She hadn't paid much attention to those men then. She'd all but rolled her eyes and turned her thoughts away. She hadn't considered who they were or why they were there. Of course, Kandace had been different then. *Then,* she had practically laughed at their ridiculous ceremony and thought what weird, religious fools they were. She hadn't thought to look at them with suspicion. She hadn't thought to wonder what her role in the ceremony was.

Kandace was inquisitive by nature, and her life thus far had ensured she was plenty cynical, but this? This was completely out of her purview. She had to believe that was the case for every girl there. Maybe it was why they were more easily influenced, their learned behavior more . . . pliable. Lilith House left them all flailing for something that seemed halfway solid to grasp on to. Rules. Obedience. It was what Lilith House offered. And if you accepted, you felt at least halfway in control of your own fate.

The nervous fluttering quickened in Kandace's belly. Yes, this was . . . odd. And unnerving. Why did a group of old men want to join a religious service at a girl's school a good distance outside town?

"Why do they come here?" she whispered under her breath.

She didn't realize she'd said it loud enough for Sydney to hear, until her roommate whispered back. "Who knows. They're stuffy, but fine." She itched her neck and hazarded a quick glance behind her. "And them being here means we get dessert."

Ah, yes. There was that. The girls of Lilith House were denied sugar. Except when the men of the Religious Guild paid them a visit. They'd go back to the dining room where trays of decadent sweets would be passed around, the girls allowed to partake in one of the only pleasures they were briefly permitted.

As the service began, and they all bowed their heads in prayer, Kandace took the opportunity to turn her head and peek back at the group of men as Sydney had done.

None of them were praying. All of them were looking around at the girls. She met the gaze of the balding man sitting at the end of a pew and the look on his face was so openly lascivious that Kandace drew back, turning quickly, a shiver racing up her spine. He'd looked at her as though she were naked.

Religious Guild? They didn't seem very godly to her.

They seemed like nasty old men there to gawk at the "bad" girls.

"Gentlemen, if you'd like to give a blessing to our girls, we would welcome it," Ms. Wykes said. "Girls, bow your heads." Kandace obeyed along with the others, and heard the men stand and then saw their legs—all clad in the same exact suit pants so none could be separated from the other—begin walking in front of the pews where the girls sat, heads bowed. Kandace's eyes followed them, trying to determine who was who without lifting her head. But with their identical clothing, and not having seen these men before, she simply couldn't tell. Last time she'd taken the opportunity to catnap. Now she was wide awake. Now she was paying attention.

A man sidestepped through the narrow pew in front of her, placing his hand on her head and then allowing his hand to graze her cheek as he pulled away. Kandace closed her eyes and held herself completely still, resisting the urge to wipe her face as if she could somehow erase his touch. Resisting the urge to raise her head and glare at him. To see who he was.

One of the faceless men had put his hand on her head the first time too. She'd barely noticed.

This wasn't right. Something was very wrong here.

No other men "blessed" her. She didn't think they were really there for that. She saw the other men walk through the aisles, laying a hand on one girl's head. *Like a chosen one.* Most of the girls had their eyes closed in prayer. God, these men were walking around as though the chapel was a whorehouse and they were choosing their evening entertainment.

Kandace thought of the bruises on her arm, the headaches, the strange dreams.

Bile rose in her throat.

No. No, surely not.

How could it be that one of them had . . . touched her and she didn't remember it? They'd been told they were sinners, there to atone for those sins, sitting in a classroom for hours a day listening to Biblical teachings about purity. Instead, they'd been led to the slaughter . . . given birth control pills . . . *Oh God.*

She felt a headache coming on now as a burst of fear traveled from her chest to her limbs. The incense was suddenly overwhelming, clogging her brain and making her feel ill.

This was all wrong.

Her mind spun through the service, through the communion of wafers and wine, the certainty that the men of the Guild were there for reasons that had little to do with a religious event growing by the moment. When it was over, she was barely controlling the shaking of her body. She'd been touched. She'd been selected.

They filed out of the chapel and followed the teachers back to Lilith House where they again congregated in the dining room. The rest of the girls appeared giddy with anticipation for the dessert they were about to be allowed.

She had to give it to Lilith House. They'd turned a group of former alcohol and drug abusers into young women who were practically dancing with excitement over a serving of *sugar*.

Good work, Lilith House. A plus.

How quickly they'd been stripped of who they were with fear, isolation, and deprivation.

And if that were the sole purpose of Lilith House, maybe Kandace could even give them credit for their success, even though their methods were brutal and inhumane.

Maybe *brutal* was the only thing that would work on girls like them.

Perhaps *inhumane* was the only thing that truly got their attention.

But she had a deep, dark feeling that Lilith House's reform methods weren't the only thing Kandace and the other girls had to worry about, not the only thing they had to survive.

Not even the only reason they were there.

No, something more depraved was going on than she ever could have imagined when she'd stepped through the doors of this place.

Several waitstaff entered the room carrying trays of sweets. A delighted murmur rose among the girls as they began selecting their first mini cake, or chocolate truffle, or brownie bite, all served in foil dessert cups.

"Enjoy, girls," Ms. Wykes said. "You've earned this. The Lord wishes you to partake." Her voice held a note of menace, but no one except Kandace seemed to hear it. The other girls were happily distracted by the array of treats.

Kandace selected a bite-sized lemon cake and then performed a sleight-of-hand, tipping her head back, but instead of popping it in her mouth, folding it into the napkin she also held. She forced a smile she hoped was convincing, releasing a satisfied "mmm" as she dabbed at her mouth and then folded the cake-filled napkin into her fist.

Ms. Wykes walked by, her pale lips curving. For a moment Kandace's heart stalled, and then picked up a rapid staccato beat, but the old bitch passed her, continuing on her rounds. Kandace tossed the napkin in the garbage near the wall and then repeated the same series of movements until the girls had emptied the trays.

"You are dismissed, girls. Straight to bed now. Straight to bed."

Fear filled her. *Six men. Six girls chosen. God, she hoped she wasn't right.* She didn't know who the others were. Her head had been bowed. She looked around the dining room, wondering if any of the other girls felt the same apprehension. No, they all seemed . . . happy but . . . listless.

They filed out of the dining room, Aurora, Sydney, and Kandace breaking off from the other girls and climbing the stairs to their attic room. When they'd closed the door behind them, both Aurora and Sydney kicked off their shoes and dropped down on their beds. "God," Sydney moaned, rubbing her stomach. "I ate too much. I couldn't stop myself."

"Once an addict, always—oof." Aurora laughed as Sydney's pillow hit her in the face. She tossed it back. Sydney caught it and put it beneath her head, her eyes drooping. "Sugar makes me so darn sleepy."

Kandace had gotten very sleepy soon after eating the desserts Lilith House so "benevolently" gifted too. She didn't feel sleepy now. She felt wide awake. Wide awake and scared.

You should have eaten the sweets. You should have gone to sleep. Maybe you don't want to know what happens next.

"Same," Aurora said, lying down and turning toward Kandace. Her expression morphed into concern. "Hey, are you okay?"

Kandace nodded. "Yeah. I ate too much too." She rubbed at her stomach. "Ugh." She couldn't risk telling them what she suspected, as she was almost positive the desserts were drugged. Sydney and Aurora would be passed out shortly. They'd be no help to her whether she told them or not. Her blood chilled. She was afraid.

But this was something she had to know. If she was going to do something about it later, she had to know what was happening here.

She made a quick trip to the bathroom to brush her teeth and when she returned, the girls were out cold. They hadn't even changed into their nightgowns. Kandace went over to each in turn, pulling a blanket up to their chins.

Fear enveloped her, and a peculiar sadness she didn't know how to explain. Loneliness maybe. There was no one to help her. Not here. Not anywhere.

She was in this alone.

"You're stronger than you think you are," she whispered to herself.

Quickly, she changed into her nightgown and climbed beneath her own blankets. Minutes later, the lights went out. Kandace lay in bed, the house creaking around her, the wind rushing past the eaves. Her heart beat hollowly, breath quickening when, after about twenty minutes, she heard the soft thud of heavy footsteps on the stairs, climbing closer, closer to the door of their room. It sounded like a man.

Tears threatened, but no, *no,* she wouldn't cry. She had to do this. If someone was going to make this *stop,* she had to know exactly what they were doing first.

Which meant making them believe she was drugged like the others.

The doorknob turned slowly, and Kandace squeezed her eyes shut, willing her breath to even. The door squeaked open, showing a dim shaft of light that she could see even with her lids closed. For a moment, the person standing in the open doorway didn't move. She could imagine him looking from one girl to the next, ensuring they were unconscious. The footsteps sounded again, moving closer to where Kandace lay, pretending to sleep the sleep of the drugged.

Calm, calm, stay calm. Do not move.

At her bedside, the footsteps came to a halt. She could feel his stare boring down at her. Kandace didn't think she could go through with this. She almost opened her eyes. Almost screamed, tried to run, *something.* Her muscles tightened, primed for flight, but then his arms were scooping her up, and she willed herself to go limp again, to allow her body to be carried from the room.

Oh yes, she had been chosen.

278

The man carried her down the narrow flight of attic stairs. The lights in the hallways had either been turned back on or had never been extinguished. She didn't dare crack her eyes. Kandace tried to pay attention to where the man turned, which hallways he took, which set of steps he went down so she knew where she was. *The second floor,* she knew that. A room on the west side at the end of a hall. This room must face the chapel.

The man used his foot to kick the door very softly, three quick taps, and then it was pulled open and he carried her through. The light dimmed behind her eyelids, and the smell of incense met her nose. Was this supposed to be some strange extension of the religious ritual they'd attended earlier? Possibly. Was that how they justified it? She was laid gently on something soft. A bed. Her blood turned to cement in her veins.

"What's he doing here?"

He? Who is he?

"He always kicks up such a fuss over that ugly little girl being taken away," Ms. Wykes murmured. "Good thing he loves the chocolate cake so much. Ignore him. Or don't. You enjoy an audience on occasion, am I right?" There was dark humor in her voice and Kandace's stomach rolled.

"You may leave now," the man said. His voice was deep and smooth. Commanding.

"She must be prayed over first," Ms. Wykes said. "So that her filth does not pass to you. Instead, may you cleanse her wickedness. May she be blessed. May your wife be blessed as well." His *wife?* Was that what this was? Kandace and the other girls were useful as a means to relieve the wifely "burden" of other women considered more worthy? Cold metal touched her forehead—a crucifix? That silver one with the gemstones she carried everywhere?—as Ms. Wykes murmured a prayer under her breath, her voice reedy and thin. Panic rose within Kandace but she remained still.

"Don't leave marks. And do not rouse her," Ms. Wykes said before her footsteps could be heard moving toward the door. A moment later it shut behind her with a quiet click.

Kandace heard the soft sounds of clothing dropping to the floor and her stomach curdled even more. *Run! I can't do this.* But if she let them know she was conscious now, what would they do? They couldn't possibly risk something like this getting out. She thought of the three young women, their children locked in the basement, even now. What had happened to those women? Had they really left their children here? Or was it something far worse?

Her nightgown was yanked upward and it took all of Kandace's courage not to cry out with fear and anger and distress.

This man, this stranger was using her unconscious—or so he believed—body to do with as he pleased. She screamed inside her mind. A shudder ran through her veins.

She didn't expect the slap. The cry of pain and shock came unbidden. She let out a garbled moan, and let her head fall heavily to the side. The man's breathing sped up. She could hear the sound of his hand working on his own flesh. The violence had excited him, as had her cry.

He slapped her again, but more softly this time. "That's right," he grunted. "Take it, you little whore."

Kandace's head was turned to the side, so the man didn't see the tear that rolled from her eye and was soaked up by the bedding beneath her.

He climbed on top of her, his breath moist and heavy as he panted into her neck, calling her vile names as he rubbed his flesh against her. Kandace thought of all the men she'd let use her. She thought of the men she herself had used. She'd never been very discriminating. The things the man was calling her, they were true, weren't they? Her mother had told her they were. Kandace herself had never denied it. What did this matter? It was for an end.

It was so she could take this place down.

Because now she knew.

So she endured.

The pain.

The burn.

Please stop.

Please stop.

But he didn't. He rammed into her, ripped her flesh, tore something deep inside she wasn't sure what to name. Her soul?

No. My soul is mine. It cannot be torn. Not by you.

You're stronger than you think you are.

She dared to crack her eyes ever so slightly and shock flooded her when her eyes met those of the kid, slumped over on a red chaise lounge, his face turned directly toward her.

His eyes were glassy, unfocused, mouth slack, but his gaze was unblinking as he watched her be degraded.

OhGod,ohGod,ohGod. Her shame spiraled. *He always kicks up such a fuss over that ugly little thing being taken away,* Ms. Wykes had said. *Georgia?* It had to be her she was referencing. Was it just about protecting Georgia or were they also grooming him for their religious group? Had he resisted?

He finished with a loud grunt and Kandace squeezed her eyes shut and then forced her facial muscles to relax. As he pulled away, he slapped her one more time and called her filthy, his voice full of disgust. Then he cleaned her quickly—sparing no gentleness—and pulled her underwear up and nightgown down.

He picked her up again and made the journey back to her room where he deposited her in her bed, the door to the room clicking closed behind him.

In the dark, she heard Aurora's and Sydney's quiet snores. Kandace turned toward the wall. It didn't matter what that man had done. The last time she'd had sex, it was because she'd wanted some weed. She'd endured three minutes of sweaty screwing, rolled her eyes as he climbed off, and then happily smoked the drugs he'd offered. Yes, what had occurred tonight wasn't anything she hadn't *allowed* to happen to her dozens of times. It wasn't anything she hadn't given permission for more often than she could count.

So why am I crying?

Tears coursed down her cheeks and for a moment, Kandace gave in to the silent sobs that shook her shoulders.

Yes, now she knew. Even if she still had no proof.

Her hand moved slowly to her stomach, acknowledging that which she hadn't had the courage to acknowledge yet. The tracks of her tears dried, breath becoming even. Her palm moved over the very small bump, the rounding that would only be obvious to her because she knew her own body.

A realization came to her and her eyes opened, staring up at the shadowy beams of the attic ceiling.

She *did* have proof.

She had the child in her womb.

And now she knew. . . it belonged to one of them.

CHAPTER THIRTY

"*My* girls," her mother said, flinging the door open wide and pulling Scarlett and Haddie into a joint embrace. Scarlett dropped her duffel bag on the floor, one arm around her mother, the other around her little girl, breathing in the comfort of her mother's smell: rose-scented lotion and clean laundry.

"Hi, Mom," she said, smiling when her mother finally let her go, stepping back and closing the door.

Her mother knelt down, bringing her hands to Haddie's face. "How's my grandbaby?" she asked.

Haddie smiled. "Good, Gram."

She kissed Haddie's cheek. "Come on into the kitchen," she said, standing. "I made some coffee cake and apple muffins. And I got *you* a new coloring book, miss," she said to Haddie.

Haddie grinned, taking her gram's hand as they went into the kitchen. Her mother's house was small and somewhat dated, but it was spic and span and had the warm feel of home.

"Where's Gerald?" she asked. Gerald was her stepfather, the man her mother had married ten years before. Although Scarlett had been eighteen when her mother married him and therefore Scarlett had never had a real fatherly relationship with him, he was a kind and decent man. Scarlett was happy her mother had found a companion not only to spend her golden years with but to relieve the financial burden she'd carried on her own since Scarlett's father had died.

"He picked up an extra shift."

"He's a hard worker." Scarlett squeezed her mother's shoulder as her mother sat down, and then Scarlett took a seat next to her. Haddie had already climbed into a chair and was taking the brand-new crayons out of the package, coloring book spread out in front of her.

"Unicorns," Haddie said happily, pointing to the book. "They're *magic*."

Scarlett smiled, brushing her daughter's hair out of her face. "I see, baby." Sometimes, so rarely, she was nothing but the purest vision of a seven-year-old child and it made Scarlett's chest ache.

Once her mother had poured coffee for them and dished up the treats, Scarlett glanced at Haddie, immersed in her art. "Thanks for taking her for the night. She's missed you." *She needs the comfort of the familiar, in a sea of recent upheaval.*

"Are you kidding?" Her mother reached across and tipped Haddie's face up, grinning into it. "I've missed this gorgeous face. Miss Haddie and I are going to have a PJ party, make popcorn, and watch a movie. Plus, I want to hear every detail about your new house and what room she's picked out for me."

A shadow passed over Haddie's face but as quickly as it was there, it was gone, and Haddie smiled. "You can sleep in my room, Gram. Mommy says she'll get me a twindle bed."

Gram laughed. "I think you mean a trundle. And boy, that sounds fun." She shot Scarlett a wink.

"I can't wait for you to see it, Mom. I just want to get some of the bigger work out of the way." She didn't mention the fact that she'd fired her contractor and that she'd yet to hire a new one. Her stomach hurt when she thought about how Mason had sounded on the phone. He'd obviously been prepared for the call. Clearly, Camden had told him to expect it. But Scarlett had been unable to deny hearing the crestfallen tone in his voice, and his apology for the deception had sounded so sincere it'd made her cringe. Not only that, but Scarlett was disappointed too. Yes, he'd lied to her, she had every right to fire his ass, but his vision for the house had been grand and inspiring. Of course, now she understood that part of the reason he seemed so in tune with the place, and as though he knew it from every angle, and in every season, was because he *did*. She didn't want to steal Mason's ideas and give them to the next contractor she hired—that would be unethical—but she was definitely going to do something similar to what they'd planned. Mason had understood that the house deserved not to be remade, but to be the best modern version of herself. She straightened her shoulders. She had to move on. She simply couldn't trust him anymore. *Right?*

When she got back, she'd put a call in to the other contractor in town, the one she'd never bothered calling after she'd met with Mason. And she wasn't going to let this slow down the renovation. She was in LA to shop for tile and flooring, and a few other things that she wanted to see in person, rather than just an online picture.

She'd asked her mother to take Haddie for the night, and was going to stay at Merrilee's house who was— unfortunately for Scarlett—out of town on business. Her mother's house was small, but Scarlett could have slept on the couch and stayed with Haddie, but truthfully, she needed some alone time and was grateful Merrilee had offered.

She needed one night to sift through her turbulent emotions regarding so many things. One night away from Lilith House, one night away from Farrow, and yes, even one night away from Haddie. Since the moment she'd moved, it'd felt as if her life was a bottle of soda that was being shaken, shaken, and she needed a short break from it all to relieve some of the pressure.

She wasn't sure yet if she was going to make a trip to the hotel she'd glimpsed in the tabloid photo of Royce. It would likely be an effort in futility. On the remote chance that she did spot someone who was part of his entourage, she doubted she could convince them to give him a message. And moreover, even if he had some of the same people working for him, they'd never remember her from eight years ago. He had legions of female fans trying desperately to pass him a phone number and an invitation all day, every day. Married or not, he probably had one-night stands all the time.

The biggest risk, of course, was that on the off chance that she was successful, she could literally be sued for seeking him out. But . . . it was Haddie's *health* in jeopardy here. Or rather, the possibility—the very real fear—that Scarlett was mismanaging a mental illness because she was worried about being stripped of her payoff.

So yeah, maybe she would sit in the lobby in a pair of oversized sunglasses and at the very least, see if an opportunity arose. She owed it to Haddie and to herself.

After she'd finished her coffee and chatted with her mother for half an hour or so, Scarlett stood, kissing Haddie goodbye, giving her mom another embrace and heading for the door.

Scarlett made the drive to Merrilee's, what should have taken ten minutes, taking an hour. LA traffic was definitely something she didn't miss. By the time she dropped her bag in the living room of Merrilee's condo, it was already three p.m.

She freshened up and then headed out to a nearby tile store, and then a lighting shop, spending the remainder of the afternoon lost in fixtures and materials that would complement the style and the age of the house, while also bringing it up to date. It was exactly what she'd needed. A few hours alone, and a chance to free her mind—however temporarily—of all that was currently weighing on her.

She called her mom and chatted with Haddie for a few minutes, made herself one of Merrilee's microwave dinners, and poured a glass of wine. She almost didn't go to the hotel. She almost put on her PJs and treated herself to an evening of Netflix. But as she stood there in her towel after the shower, she kept seeing that photo of Royce on the cover of the tabloid, kept seeing the headlines in her mind, kept recalling the way Haddie's gaze slid away from her, and the way her daughter had stood there in the driveway, her expression shocked as she peed on the ground. No, she had to do this. She had to try. There might not be another opportunity to get in touch with Royce, no matter how improbable it was.

She dropped the towel, letting out an exasperated breath. She'd put on the black dress and red heels she'd brought, curl her hair, and have a drink at the bar. She was seldom going to be in LA from here on out. She was a single mom with a young child, a centuries-old house to overhaul, and a business to—hopefully—get off the ground. When was the next time she'd enjoy any nightlife at all?

No time soon.

Scarlett pulled on the strapless black dress, slid the heels on her feet, put on some makeup, and performed the rare task of blow-drying and adding loose, beachy waves to her hair. When she stood back and looked in the mirror, she barely recognized herself. It had been so long since she'd gotten ready for a social outing. For so many years, she'd had spit-up on her shirt and bags under her eyes, then applesauce in her hair and yesterday's yoga pants on. Even now that Haddie was older and more self-sufficient every day, she honestly just felt most comfortable at home with her girl, a pizza on the coffee table in front of them, and a Disney movie on TV.

Yes, she loved spending time with Haddie, but she also hid behind her sometimes, used her as an excuse not to put herself out there, not to risk being hurt.

In her secret heart of hearts, she worried no man would ever want her again and so why even go through the motions of meeting one? It would only lead to disappointment.

She'd honestly convinced herself to forget she was still a *woman,* and not just a mom, a daughter, someone's friend or employee. She'd forgotten she was more than the roles she played for others, most of which she loved, but that wasn't the point.

Camden West had reminded her for a few brief moments, and then confirmed all her fears and insecurities. *I won't let it.* No one else got to decide her value. Only her.

You're stronger than you think you are.

She'd said those words to Kandace once, a very long time ago, and for some reason, they rose inside her mind in that moment. She didn't know why. She hadn't recalled that day for years . . . Kandace's tears, her hurt, the way she felt forgotten, and Scarlett's fervent desire to comfort her friend with words she knew to be true. Kandi *was* strong, she just hadn't been able to see it the way Scarlett did.

Standing there looking in the mirror, Scarlett felt an emotion not unlike grief twisting through her. Scarlett felt forgotten too. Not by anyone else, but by *herself.* She'd put herself last for a long, long time, and perhaps that was just the way it had to be, but it didn't mean the realization felt good. It didn't mean things had turned out the way she'd pictured when she'd been a little girl full of dreams of love. A family. Someone to lean on at the end of a long, hard day.

And it didn't mean that putting herself last was what she wanted to model for Haddie. She wanted Haddie to know that she was worthy of claiming joy, of reaching for it. She wanted Haddie to bless the world with all the gifts that were unique to her—no matter *what* that might entail—instead of hiding in the shadow of service to others. That didn't mean that she'd forsake those she loved. It didn't mean she wouldn't care for those who depended on her, and even those who did not. It simply meant that she mattered too. She was worthy of happiness. Every woman was.

Seize the day, Scarlett.

Go. Go now.

She straightened her shoulders. *Okay, then.* "Fallen woman, my ass," she said to her reflection. There were no *fallen women.* Just women who had made mistakes and deserved grace, not judgment. And perhaps that meant starting with the person she was staring at in the mirror.

Scarlett grabbed her purse and headed for the door.

CHAPTER THIRTY-ONE

Thirteen Years Ago

𝒦andace slammed the erasers together, a cloud of chalk dust bursting in the air before her and causing her to cough and sputter. She leaned away, rubbing any dust off her face with her forearm and setting the erasers back on the board.

"Cheap bastards," she muttered. She was well aware of Lilith House's rates—her mother had thrown the information in her face—and so she knew very well they could afford a cleaning staff, but chose instead to use their students for slave labor.

Of course, she knew very well that wasn't the reason housekeepers weren't employed at Lilith House. Oh no, it was to ensure as few as possible were privy to what was really happening there.

Then again, maybe she shouldn't complain. The two hours she spent cleaning classrooms every afternoon was the only alone time she got, and Kandace needed that time to think. To plan. She *needed* that time to attempt to come to terms with the situation she found herself in.

Feelings of dark despair began descending and with effort, she pushed them away, picking up the trash can and emptying it into the larger bag she'd brought with her. She was working hard to keep the panic that lived inside her at bay, but it grew harder with each day.

Because with each day, her pregnancy grew as well. If she remained there for the entirety of her sentence, there would be no way to hide it. No way. Thank goodness their uniform was loose and shapeless, but she couldn't hide underneath that indefinitely. She was already at *least* five months along, though her stomach was still only slightly rounded, due in part to her willowy stature, but also because she hadn't had much of an appetite in the last several months.

Kandace turned as the door opened and Ms. West walked through. "Oh sorry. I didn't realize you were in here," she said. "I just need to grab my lesson plan."

Kandace's heart jolted. Ms. West. Kandace didn't have her for any classes, but in passing, she'd heard the other girls speak well of her. She was an attractive older woman with a black bun and large blue eyes that seemed to continuously dart around. Sort of a nervous type, but who wasn't—other than Ms. Wykes and Jasper—around there? And Kandace knew she was *their* tutor. The three abandoned basement-dwellers. Kandace wondered how she looked at herself in the mirror and still accepted that those children were prisoners there? How did she sleep at night, knowing those kids had been essentially locked away all of their lives? No socialization . . . no parental love. Only shame. In a way she could relate—maybe most of the girls at Lilith House could as well—but certainly not to this extent. And yet Dreamboat was *kind.* Caring. That was a small miracle in itself.

"I'm almost done. Stay if you need to."

Ms. West stepped around the desk, opened the top drawer, grabbed a folder and held it up. "This is all I need. Have a good afternoon."

Panic flared within Kandace. This was her chance. It might be her only one.

"I met them," she blurted.

Ms. West stopped, turning slowly, a look of surprised concern on her face. "I'm sorry? Met . . . them?"

Kandace nodded, placing the garbage bag on the floor and stepping closer to Ms. West. "I just need a minute of your time. Please."

Ms. West glanced toward the closed door. "This isn't a good idea," she said, taking a step away from Kandace. "And it isn't your place to speak to me or any of the staff—"

"I've been thinking," she said, hurrying on. "What's the plan? Does anyone even know of their existence?" She thought of the barely lucid kid staring at her as she'd been violated. *He always kicks up such a fuss . . .* She had a flash of the thick Bible Dreamboat had been reading from. It only made sense. Those emotionally needy kids were being indoctrinated, slowly and consistently exposed to what was happening at Lilith House, Biblical teachings being twisted and skewed to provide a moral justification. Dreamboat was resisting. Protecting that little girl because he was naturally noble. But for how long? How long until they drained any fight in him? How long until all three of them became monsters too?

Ms. West grasped the folder to her chest as though it was a lifeline. "Pay no attention to them. They do not exist," she hissed, but then something broke in her expression. She glanced toward the door and then away. "It's best for them and for you."

"It sounds like it's best for *you.* But not for them. They're *children.* They haven't done anything wrong. They can still be saved."

Ms. West pulled her shoulders back, but she was clearly distraught. "I'm sorry, what did you say your name was again?"

Her heart raced. This was a risk. But what other choice did she have? Her only hope was to verbalize what Ms. West must know but perhaps wasn't admitting to herself, and hope to God she had a scrap of sympathy for those kids. "The only choice is to get them involved in what's happening here. I think you know that's true." Ms. West's face went a lighter shade of pale. "Tell me, have others been taking on more of their education? Teachers you don't trust? You tried to do right by them, didn't you? But others are overruling you now. Those kids are a liability. They're teens now. It's time to think about their future. And their future is a lifetime of what's happening upstairs, isn't it? Or worse."

Ms. West blanched, the folder she grasped trembling along with her hands.

"Oh yes, you know about that, don't you? You all do, I suppose. How could you not?"

"No. I have no idea what you're talking about. Are you unwell? Perhaps a trip to the infirmary—"

"There's really no other choice. Involve them in it so they either buy into the sickness or are so ashamed of their involvement that they never speak a word of it. Insurance."

Ms. West opened her mouth to speak, but Kandace plowed on, taking a step closer. "He's more than that. I don't know about the other two, but he is. I think you know it too."

Ms. West grimaced. She knew exactly who the *he* was that Kandace was referring to. Of course she did. He was special. Anyone could see that, especially this woman who had presumably been with them most of their lives. She took another step forward. "Who are their mothers?" she asked softly. "Help me help them, Ms. West. I think you might be the only one who can. If you give me some information, anything you're able, I can bring back help. I'll say you assisted me. I'll say you didn't know about the guild. I'll swear to it." She reached out, wrapping her hand gently around Ms. West's arm. "Please. *Please.*"

For a moment their gazes held, the older woman's wide and startled, Kandace's pleading. Ms. West released a gust of breath, shaking Kandace's hold off her.

"Like I said, I think you need to visit the infirmary." She turned, picking up a piece of chalk and writing something low on the chalkboard. "Here's the nurse you should ask for when you get there. She's very knowledgeable about psychiatric issues brought on by repeated and long-term drug use." She set the piece of chalk down and turned. "Now please, don't speak to me again, Ms. Thompson. It won't end well for either of us." And with that she clutched her folder and breezed to the door, opening it quickly and letting it fall shut behind her.

Kandace's shoulders drooped, disappointment and frustration making her want to scream. "Psychiatric issues, my ass," she hissed. "What a *bitch*." If that woman wouldn't help them, no one would. They were completely on their own. Except for her.

A sense of deep responsibility overtook her, the unfamiliar need to *protect*. But Kandace had no proof that those kids were even there, nothing to use. "Fuck," she said, kicking the edge of the desk like a helpless child.

What about the pregnancy? You have that. It's proof that one of those men raped you.

Is it?

Now that she was thinking about it more clearly, she realized that if that was *all* she had, it might not be enough. She'd run away. And she'd make accusations that what? Some guy in town knocked her up in some illicit sex racket? They'd say she was crazy. A liar. Nothing new. She didn't even know what the guy who'd impregnated her looked like. She'd been unconscious. Even if she *hadn't* been though, even if she could point her finger directly at the man, she was worldly enough to know it'd go like this . . . *yes, she snuck into town and seduced me. I'm so ashamed to have had dirty, illicit sex with that filthy woman, but it was consensual.* It'd be her word against his, and as it'd been pointed out quite often, Kandace was a known liar. And a whore.

No, she needed more. And she *wanted* more. She no longer just wanted to leave, she needed to save those kids. But then she considered the last time she'd gone searching for truths there. *The scalding water. The steel brush. The welts. The bruises upon bruises under bloodied skin.* Would she survive if *disciplined* again?

Kandace suddenly wasn't sure. Ms. West could go straight to Ms. Wykes now. *Oh God.* She placed her hand on her stomach. What had she done?

She took the two steps backward and leaned against the board, letting her head fall back against it with a soft thud. Hopeless. This was *hopeless.*

Kandace turned her head, her gaze going to the place where Ms. West had written the infirmary nurse she'd recommended to Kandace. *Weird actually.* Why would she tell Kandace the name of the infirmary nurse? She'd been there for months. Only . . . Kandace pushed herself off the board, moving closer to the chalk-drawn letters. It wasn't only one name. It was three. Kandace sucked in a surprised breath, glancing over her shoulder. It wasn't a nurse's name at all. Ms. West had given Kandace the names of the kids' mothers.

Kandace read them once, then again, committing them to memory. Then she picked up the eraser and wiped the board clean.

CHAPTER THIRTY-TWO

$\mathcal{S}$carlett took a sip of wine, the crisp pinot grigio sliding down her throat. This was her third glass in two hours and she hadn't spotted hide nor perfect golden hair of Royce Reynolds or any member of his entourage.

But it'd been five minutes since she'd watched the two men she recognized as part of Royce's security team, chatting in low, serious tones as they walked to the bank of elevators and disappeared into the car at the end that she knew rose to the suites.

Despite the wine buzz, the sight of them had energized her. She hadn't necessarily expected that any of the same people that had been part of Royce's team eight years ago would still be part of it now, but it could not be a coincidence that Royce was—*probably*—staying at this hotel, and she'd just spotted those men.

Follow them.

Scarlett took in a deep breath, pulling a tip out of her purse and setting it on the bar with a nod to the bartender. The wine went to her head as she stood and she faltered slightly, straightening her dress, and walking into the lobby. Out of the corner of her eye she saw a man with a familiar walk and did a double take. Her heart jolted. Was that . . . no. He walked behind a large pillar and when she leaned around it to get a better look, he was gone. Feeling suddenly off kilter, as though two worlds had collided in some unknown way that she didn't understand, she moved toward the nearby restroom door, heading inside where she stood at the long row of sinks, taking deep cleansing breaths as she tried to decide what to do.

"Party? Presidential suite?"

Scarlett turned her head, looking at the girl a few sinks down, leaned toward the mirror, slicking lip gloss on her lips. She eyed Scarlett, her gaze going to Scarlett's dress and down to her heels.

Presidential suite? Scarlett paused but then nodded, noting that the young redhead was wearing a black dress similar to hers. Had she unwittingly dressed for some part she hadn't realized she was playing?

The girl smiled. "We can ride up together." Scarlett followed her from the restroom, and they both headed toward the last elevator where the two men had gone a few minutes before.

The girl entered a code and then pulled out a compact and a tube of lipstick, using the tiny mirror to begin applying pink gloss to her lips. "At least they pay well, you know?" she said.

"Pay well," Scarlett parroted.

Are you sure about this, Scarlett? You're sort of acting like a crazed groupie.

No, this isn't for me. This is for Haddie.

The girl looked at her suspiciously, her gaze sweeping from her feet to her hair. "First time?"

Scarlett widened her eyes and bobbed her head and the girl nodded, her expression morphing into understanding, her eyes returning to the small mirror as she slicked more gloss over her top lip.

"You're lucky, then. It's a tough gig to get. Don't be nervous. They're just looking for a good time. An *anonymous* good time that won't end up all over the tabloids, you know?"

"Oh . . . uh, yes, right," Scarlett said, a burst of nervousness prickling her skin. Tabloids. Which meant Hollywood. Which meant Royce. *Maybe.* Oh God, was this wise? What if he wasn't there but part of his security team recognized her?

No, she was absolutely not going to do this. What had come over her? This was an awful idea. Terrible. She'd been swept along by her fear for her daughter, and then odd timing and a strange coincidence, including her choice of a black dress and—she glanced down at the girl's similar shoes—red heels, but it was time to turn back.

The elevator doors opened directly into the entryway of the suite where a beefy man sat on a stool. The girl linked her arm with Scarlett's. "Hey, Johnny."

Johnny tipped his chin. "Teagan."

"She's new," Teagan said, indicating Scarlett.

He eyed her, but nodded, and they both passed by, stepping through the entryway into the room beyond where men mingled with women all dressed in black like them.

"Have fun," Teagan said, letting go of her arm and walking ahead of her into the thick of the party. Thankfully, the lights were low, and some type of strobe moved around, casting the faces in flickering colored light and ever-deepening shadow. Scarlett stepped forward, tilting her head so her hair covered half of her face. *Bad idea. Time to go.* Scarlett attempted to turn back around and head to the elevator car and then book it out of there, but someone walking by jostled her, causing her to falter and step forward. "Sorry," he mumbled drunkenly, attempting to right her.

She turned her head. "It's okay," she said as he moved past. On the other side of the entryway, the elevator doors slid closed. The men who she recognized walked by her, involved in their conversation, stopping right near the elevator, to the left of Johnny, and Scarlett backed into a shadowy corner, waiting for her chance to leave unnoticed. *Crap.*

She wasn't supposed to be here. Her skin felt overheated. She was an interloper.

You wanted this, didn't you? This is a bold stroke of luck, don't you think?

She wasn't sure.

Seize the day, Scarlett.

A ribbon of purpose wound through her. She was *here*, she might as well see what was what. Music played, something sultry and instrumental, and laughter rose, along with the clinking of ice in glasses.

There was a door to her right and Scarlett heard the unmistakable sounds of sex. She moved away, just far enough that the moaning and skin slapping were mere background noise to the moody saxophone strains, and then stepped behind a man as he walked by, heading deeper into the party. She'd circle around and hope that when she returned, those two men had moved away from her escape route.

There was a bar, green LED under-lights casting the area in a strange, alien glow. Scarlett took one of the glasses of champagne from a tray, holding it up near her face as she entered the room beyond. She did a double take when she saw a famous Hollywood director sitting on a sofa, laughing, a young woman on each knee.

Scarlett looked away, jolting when she saw the man sitting on the other end of the couch, alone, head hung low. He looked up and their gazes locked. Royce Reynolds.

His eyes widened and he stood, moving toward her. "Scarlett?" he asked, voice slurred. His gaze jumped from one feature to another as if he was trying to piece her together, to decide if it was really her. "Scarlett?" he repeated, and she was honestly shocked he'd recognized her much less remembered her name.

"Royce," she said. She couldn't believe this. She was standing there with Royce after all these years. She'd *found* him, she had so many questions, she wasn't sure where or how to start. "I, hi—"

His eyes darted around the room. "I can see them, you know," he whispered, leaning in, his gaze flitting over her shoulder quickly.

Scarlett frowned. "See who?"

"The monsters. Sometimes they're right underneath their skin." He'd lowered his voice even more, and now he grabbed her arm, pulling her to the side, against a nearby wall. "I *see* them." He let out a ragged breath, leaning his forehead against hers. Scarlett froze, shock, and a modicum of fear rolling through her. She smelled the alcohol heavy on his breath, saw the way his pupils were so enlarged they appeared mystical, almost entirely sea-glass green. Clear and startling. Apparently, rehab hadn't taken. This man was not well. "Not you though." He dragged his knuckle down her cheek and for one hitched breath, she swore he was going to cry. "There's only light in you. I noticed it, even then. I saw." He closed his eyes, leaning away, swaying slightly. "This isn't real, is it? It's not. I'm dreaming you again." For a second his expression collapsed, but he seemed to gather himself, opening his eyes and meeting hers. "I've wondered if you had a boy or a girl. I wonder about that, you know. I'm not supposed to, but I do."

She paused, surprised that in his state, he'd even remembered she was the woman—dream or not—who'd had his baby in real life. "A girl," she said quietly. "I had a girl."

A faint smile came to his lips and he leaned back. "A daughter." He was quiet for a minute. "That would be nice," he said. "I'd like that." He looked at her and even through the drug and alcohol haze, she saw fear in his eyes. "Is she . . . okay, I wonder?"

"Why wouldn't she be, Royce?"

"Because she might be like me."

Her heart sank. Yes, yes, she might be. "What does that mean? Please tell me."

He closed his eyes, shook his head. "I don't know. I have no idea. I'd tell you if I did."

He swayed on his feet, reached out and took a drink out of some guy's hand who was walking by. The man started to protest, his eyes widening when he saw who it was, and continued on.

She took a moment to look at him, really look. And what she saw was not a larger-than-life *star*, just a broken, self-destructive man with problems he obviously had no idea how to manage. She felt compassion for him, but she was no one in his life. She was nothing but the figment of a dream. In *real* life, in his sober moments, he'd written her off. He'd written his daughter off. He'd let others take charge of his life, probably with the excuse that they were "protecting him." And more than that, whatever demons he was battling he didn't know how to identify them. "Yes," she finally said. "She's fine. She's perfect." Because she was. She *was*.

Maybe Haddie had inherited something from him, maybe she hadn't. Either way, they were going to play the hand they'd been dealt. They were going to face whatever challenges they were given, *together*.

She suddenly felt so incredibly sad, and all she wanted to do was run away. She shouldn't have come here. This man couldn't help her. He certainly couldn't help his daughter. He couldn't even help himself. An older man appeared, leaning toward Royce and whispering something in his ear. Royce nodded and the man began pulling him away. Royce grabbed her arm. "Don't wake me. Stay. Meet me in my room."

Scarlett felt tears burn the back of her eyes. "Okay," she said. "I'll be there."

He smiled at her. It was Haddie's gorgeous smile, and her heart clenched. His hand dropped as the man guiding him away glanced back at her once and then gave Royce another hard yank. She watched as Royce broke free from his hold, taking the few steps back to her and grasping her upper arms. He leaned in and whispered, "Walk in the water. The dogs can't track you there." Then Royce was pulled away again, leaving Scarlett blinking in confusion as they disappeared into the darkness beyond the pulsing lights. He was delirious. Sick and unhinged.

She turned, tears blurring her vision. A man reached out, his hand sliding over her ass as she jumped away, out of his reach, hurrying forward. "Come on, baby," he called behind her. "Don't act like you're not bought and paid for." Laughter. She scooted around a couple who was embracing, her head thrown back, his face planted in the hollow of her throat. Next to them, a man leaned over a table and snorted a line of white powder off the glass surface.

Out, out, get me out.

Scarlett stepped into a darkened corner where she had a view of the entryway and sighed in relief to see that, other than Johnny, it was clear. The members of Royce's security team—the ones who may or may not recognize her—were no longer there. She stepped away from where she'd attempted to merge with the shadows, when a hand clamped down on her arm and she was pulled to the side, her back hitting the wall. She let out a fearful whimper. A man pressed his body to hers, leaning in close so his mouth was at her ear. "What are you doing, Scarlett?" he grated.

Scarlett froze, the fight response she'd been about to give in to fading as her breath escaped her mouth in a sudden whoosh of air. *Camden?* Shock infused her cells. But how? Why? It couldn't be . . . but . . . she knew his voice, remembered the feel of his body over hers, knew the particular scent of his skin, though she'd only smelled him this close on one other occasion. Oh yes, it was him. She'd thought she'd seen him in the lobby, had recognized the particular way he held himself and she'd been *right*. Despite herself, despite the fear and the confusion of this situation, every part that made her a woman responded to the man pressed against her. And something even deeper than that, experienced a soft wave of *relief* at his presence. She shoved the feelings down. All of them. She couldn't trust herself because she couldn't trust *him*.

Why was he *here?* In LA? At a Hollywood party with call girls? Her stomach soured. He was a *liar* and dammit she'd liked him. She'd liked him more than she wanted to admit. "I'm not working this party if that's what you think. I came here to see if I could find Royce and ask him some questions about Haddie," she admitted. "My outfit gained me

307

admittance, nothing else." Dammit, why was she *explaining* herself to him?

His head came back, eyes intense. "I didn't think you were working this party." He paused. "Did you? Find him?" He looked over her shoulder as if searching the party for the man.

She nodded, her expression crumbling slightly before she gathered herself. "Yes. I did. He was drunk and high. Useless. It was a bad idea. Now what are *you* doing here?"

His eyes scrutinized her face and something gentled in his expression. He reached up and dragged a thumb under her eye. "Scarlett. What happened?"

More tears threatened. She was sad and mad and deeply confused and she just wanted to get out of there. "Why are you here, Camden?" she repeated.

A muscle ticked in his jaw and he glanced up and around. "I followed you . . . I'm trying to protect you."

Protect her? "From *what?*"

His gaze darted around behind her. "I can't tell you. Not here."

A sound of frustration came up her throat. *Enough* of these useless men who couldn't *or wouldn't* help her with the basic truth. "God. I've had *enough* of your *protection.* Let me leave."

He pressed his lips together and then nodded to two more men standing by the elevator. "I'll cover you."

Scarlett paused but she really didn't want to risk being seen or questioned by anyone, so she moved under his arm when he lifted it, and leaned her head into him as though they were having an intimate conversation. They walked together to the elevator where Johnny gave him a nod, barely sparing her a glance. Obviously, she and the other women there were nothing more than entertainment, no more important than if he'd had a beer bottle in his hand.

Three minutes later they were stepping out of the elevator and walking through the lobby. Scarlett had never wanted to get farther away from a place more than she did at that moment. Rain splashed against the floor-to-ceiling windows as she picked up her pace, moving through the revolving door and stepping out into the warm, rainy night.

"Scarlett."

At the sound of her name, she picked up her pace, her heels clicking on the sidewalk as she jogged as fast as she could in shoes not meant for jogging, coming out from under the covering that shielded the valet stand and drop-off lanes and continuing up the deserted side street, the rain mixing with the tears sliding down her cheeks. The rain picked up, coming down in sheets, drenching her immediately. She heard her name again but didn't turn.

She felt him right behind her, easily keeping her pace, and after another minute, she turned, their bodies practically colliding as he came up short. His clothes stuck to his body, showcasing the definition of his muscles and the lean lines of his masculine form. His eyelashes were studded with raindrops, his hair slicked back from his face . . . and he was the most beautiful man she'd ever seen in her life. He looked positively *tortured,* and some ridiculous part of her wanted to comfort him, but from what she had no idea, and the only *why* she could think of was that she was certifiably insane. And partially buzzed, though that was—unfortunately—wearing off.

She'd been thinking about him as she sat alone at that bar though, the wine aiding in breaking through her hurt so that she might look at his actions more rationally. Or drunkenly. That was possible too; she couldn't be sure.

She swore loudly into the quiet street, her voice rising above the slowing downpour.

"Why are you following me?"

"Because I was asked to."

"Asked to? By *who?*" She looked around as though the mysterious *who* might step from the shadows at any moment.

"The guild. I'll tell you more, but not here."

She regarded him. Guild members? From Farrow? Wanting her followed? Okay, yes, she absolutely needed to know why *that* was happening. *If* it was happening. But could she trust this man to tell her the truth? He'd already lied to her. Numerous times.

"If you're merely following me, how'd you get into that party?"

He paused, looked away. "I got a good education in sneaking around unseen," he murmured.

She felt her face screw up. "What does *that* mean?"

He let out a long-suffering sigh. "Please, Scarlett. I'll tell you more," he repeated. "Can we go somewhere?"

"Why? Why tell me more? Why *protect* me? Over and over? Why install locks on my house, and show up when I call in the middle of the night, and . . . and . . . feed baby birds in my kitchen, and tell me things I don't think your friends would want me to know? Because that stuff? It really doesn't make much sense if your goal is to get access to my house and eventually run me out of town. Before I listen to anything from you, I need to know . . . was it *all* a lie, Camden? All of it?"

He stepped closer, his chest rising and falling, his masculinity rolling off him in waves. His gaze raked over her body, eyes meeting hers. "Do you think I want to feel the things I feel for you, Scarlett? Do you think it's convenient for me? I can't help this any more than you can. I wish to hell I could."

The breath left her. Her shoulders dropped and a sound came up her throat, part breath, part humorless laugh. *I can't help this any more than you can.* Of course he knew how she felt about him, or at least . . . how her body responded to his. It wasn't exactly a secret. But the admittance of his feelings for her? His confession brought confusion and surprise and yes . . . a whisper of happiness too. "I don't understand," she whispered. "None of it makes sense. Tell me what I got myself into when I bought Lilith House. When I moved my daughter and me to Farrow."

He scrubbed his hand down his face, taking a small step back. He suddenly looked so incredibly weary. He exhaled slowly, running his hand over his dark hair, water flying out around him as the rainfall dwindled to nothing. He looked suddenly defeated. "I'll explain it to you. All of it." He looked down at his clothes, and then at her. His gaze went to her bare skin where she could feel the water droplets sliding over her neck, her décolletage, and pooling between her breasts. Camden looked away and when he spoke, his voice was gritty. "Can we please go somewhere where we can both get dried off? I have a hotel room up the street."

She paused, considering. She had so many questions and he seemed prepared to answer them. Yes, she was still deeply distrustful of him, but as she pictured the way he'd held the baby bird with such reverent gentleness, the way he made beautiful, impossible art with extraordinarily patient fingers and a simple blade of grass, she was filled with the certainty that he wouldn't hurt her—at least not physically. She could ask him to go back to Merrilee's, but it wasn't her home, and she didn't feel taking a stranger there was appropriate. "All right. Let's go. But if you give me some stupid double-talk, Camden West, I'm leaving."

Although his eyes remained grave, his lips twitched minutely before he turned, signaling her to follow.

CHAPTER THIRTY-THREE

Camden rubbed the towel through his hair one last time, flinging it over the shower stall and then leaning his head forward so it touched the glass. He stood that way for a moment, collecting himself before leaving the bathroom.

Scarlett sat on the patio, clad in his T-shirt and a pair of athletic shorts, folded over several times at the waist. She sipped from a bottle of water he'd taken from the mini fridge. He took a minute to stare at her, letting out a slow, controlled breath.

Jesus, he was nervous. He'd never confided in anyone other than Mason and Georgia before. With everything at stake, he knew this was a risk. But . . . God, he felt her goodness. He wanted to trust himself with that. If he couldn't, what else did he have? A life of bitterness and revenge? Constantly feeding that voracious dark wolf inside? No, he wanted to protect this woman who'd unknowingly found herself tangled up in this unholy mess.

Scarlett stood, turning toward him, and for a moment they simply stared at each other, the cloudy LA night sky behind her, the brightest stars somehow managing to peek through the gloom.

He was tempted to look away. Camden had a hard time looking at her the same way he'd always had a hard time staring at anything beautiful. It overwhelmed him, made him want to understand its allure—its layers—so he could somehow carry it with him. And when it was taken away, he'd *know* it, and in this way, it could still be his. Truthfully, he wasn't sure if he liked beautiful things—they always made him feel slightly desperate.

Better not to want much. Better not to yearn for things that would never be his.

He'd had to figure out a way to toughen his skin so that it didn't sting each time he encountered something sharp. And yet, he'd only managed one thin layer. Even all these years later, the longing for things he'd been denied still tore at that insufficient protection over a wound he'd realized would never heal. *Abandonment.*

She came toward him, stepping over the ledge and entering the hotel room. Camden swallowed. There was wariness in her gaze and he wished he could wipe it away, but he understood why it was there. He'd fouled this up. God, he'd made a mess out of everything. "Should we sit inside?" she asked, nodding to the small sofa near the window. He turned, pulling the chair from the desk forward and taking a seat on it while she sat on the couch, pulling her legs beneath her. The room had seemed big when he'd first entered it. Now? Now it felt small and enclosed. Somehow this delicate-boned woman took up the entire space, filling it with her presence, overwhelming him.

He sat back. "I'm going to start with the Religious Guild. But before I tell you about the Guild, you have to know how it was formed. You have to understand the way Farrow operates, the way it always has."

"All right."

Camden took a deep breath, gathering his thoughts. "Hubert Bancroft formed the Religious Guild in Farrow. It consisted of men from the thirteen original families. I told you about what they did to the natives. You read about it firsthand."

"Taluta," she whispered almost reverently.

"Yes, Taluta," he confirmed. "Taluta and her people." Camden allowed his eyes to search her face. He saw the empathy there, just as he had when he originally told her the story. This woman, she cared deeply for others, not just those she knew, but those she didn't. Those who were long dead, their suffering ended, and thank God for that. His shoulders relaxed. It was the reason he trusted her, he realized. No person could carry that amount of compassion for people she'd never met and not have a loving heart. And though he wasn't quite sure he deserved it, maybe she'd extend some of that understanding his way.

"When Hubert Bancroft formed the original guild, each man invited to take part also established a monopoly of trade in Farrow for their particular industry. That's remained the case until today and because of it, Farrow is still small, even intimate you might say. Over the years, the guild has also successfully dominated local government and they exert enough control over the Farrow town council that it works to protect and maintain their interests."

Her gaze slid away and a wrinkle formed between her brows. "Outsiders are unlikely to have success in Farrow and eventually move away."

"The ones who infringe on a guild member's business, yes. Farrow has grown some over the years, but the power structure remains the same. Membership in the guild is handed down through the generations, and those members run the businesses, hold places on the town council, and have their hands in every local election. Nothing happens in Farrow unless the guild says it does."

"So that's their purpose? To retain control of Farrow? It's all about money and power?"

"Isn't it always?"

She expelled a breath. "I . . . yes, I suppose it is."

"The same group of families—ten remaining out of the original thirteen—has retained the wealth and control in that town for generations. It's why it's in their best interest to keep each other's secrets, and the secrets of the members before them."

"There's a religious component too though, fraudulent as it might be."

He nodded, considering all he knew, some he'd experienced, and others he'd ascertained. "The Guild hides behind religion, it always has, generation after generation in one form or another. In actuality, God has nothing to do with their practices, though they've convinced themselves He does. It took me some time to realize that." He sighed, remembering when he'd first come upon that trunk hidden behind a portion of wall in the basement. The stories, the personal accounts from Taluta and Narcisa had helped him understand the true nature of evil. He'd had moments of deep discomfort regarding the things he'd been taught at Lilith House, but the indigenous women's accounts had clarified for him right from wrong, helped him assess the kind of god *he* wanted to believe in versus the one being presented to him every day in the form of shame and mercilessness. Manipulation and religious artifice. Those writings had taught him to think critically.

In essence, and he didn't think he thought this lightly, they had saved his soul.

"They use religion, but they believe in it too. Because of how Farrow operates, because of how it always has, in many ways it's stayed stuck in the past. You might have felt that." *He* only knew because, for a time, he'd gotten away. He'd had a firsthand view into the outside world. For the first time in his life, he'd been able to compare the way other people lived. Georgia and Mason had never experienced that. Sometimes he wondered if it was what made him different, made him question things that they didn't. He'd suggested they all move away, leave Farrow behind forever and start lives somewhere else together. But they'd been resistant. They wanted revenge. And he'd told himself he did too, convinced himself of it. It had only taken one day in Scarlett's presence for that "need" to begin to wither and crumble as *new* dreams, new desires, ones he'd never dared imagine, began to unfurl inside him like the budding of a fresh green leaf. Untouched. Seeking out the sun.

"Is there . . . in-breeding in Farrow?"

He paused. He'd questioned it too, seen what might be the consequences, though he couldn't be sure. He'd wondered if one of the reasons the guild hadn't already forced her out of town was because she was fresh blood. The thought sickened him. "I don't know. I wouldn't doubt it. Those families . . . they stick together, not just in secret-keeping, but in all kinds of ways."

She flinched. "When you say they keep each other's secrets," Scarlett went on, "do you mean like what was done to the natives?" She paused. "That was so long ago, though. Those men are dead and gone."

"Those ones are, yes. But that's where Lilith House comes in."

She stared at him, unblinking.

"I lived at Lilith House all my life, Scarlett. You already know that. I . . . saw things." Shame filled him for his inability to stop the evil he'd witnessed, his failure in preventing other people's pain. Yes, he'd *tried*, but in the end, did it matter? Was that a solace to Georgia? To Mason? It was certainly no solace to the girls of Lilith House.

"What kind of things?" she asked warily. She had a right to be wary. He hated having to tell her the truth.

"The guild, they took advantage of those girls. With approval from the headmistress and a blind eye from the staff, the men drugged them and used them regularly."

She did blink then, her pretty mouth falling open as a disbelieving horror took over her expression. "They . . . raped them?"

He nodded, swallowed. And yes, it was the word he should have used outright. To mitigate what they'd done with softened language made him culpable, even now. "Yes. Yes, they raped them."

"Oh my God," she breathed. "No one . . . no one ever went to the police?"

"No. And if any of the women suspected, they had no proof." He paused. "Except one. Kandace Thompson."

Scarlett blinked again. "You *did* know Kandace." She sat back, her shoulders slumping. "And she . . . she was . . . raped?" The last word emerged as barely a whisper.

He nodded, his gaze locked with hers, a fresh bout of shame washing through him. The look on Scarlett's face was killing him. "Yes. I knew Kandace. We were banned from interacting with the students but"—he smiled a sad smile—"Kandace was not a rule follower. She discovered me, *us*, and she became intent on finding the truth. She found out who our mothers were. She had proof." He shook his head. "She took some files or . . . I don't know. She didn't tell me what she had, only that she was going to bring help. She was going to *take that place down*."

"Oh my God," she repeated, looking shell-shocked. "Did she really run away, Camden? Or . . . did they do something to her?"

"I don't know that either. All I know was that she planned to leave, to escape. As far as I know, she did, but she never came back. A week later, the fire happened." His mind traveled back to the day she ran, how he'd picked the fresh mushrooms for her and left them at the top of the crawlspace where she could access them. How nervous he'd been, how relieved when he'd listened through the walls to them shouting about how she'd gotten away . . . and how she hadn't come back . . . not a day later, not five days later . . . *never* as far as he knew. And he had no idea if that was because something more terrible had happened to Kandace, or because she'd changed her mind about rescuing him.

He'd been abandoned before. He was used to it.

Scarlett sat forward, gripping the couch cushion. "Camden, we have to go to the authorities. We have to—" She shook her head. "Wait, you *are* the police."

"Yes. Like I told you, the woman who tutored us took me with her to San Diego. She gave me her name. I kept in close touch with Georgia and Mason, who'd been taken in by members of the guild. Of course, we call Mason's father his father, but we have no clue. Nor who my father might be. We had a plan. We were going to save our money, buy Lilith House. We were going to find that proof Kandace hid, whether in the walls or in the woods, or maybe somewhere buried in the sheriff's office for all we knew, and then *we* were going to take down the people responsible for what happened there." He eyed her, saw her mind racing to keep up with all the information he was dumping on her. "Mason already worked at the hardware store owned by the family who took him in after Lilith House, and I applied to be deputy sheriff."

"They trusted you?" she asked. "After what they'd done to you?"

He gave a small shrug. "I don't know. It might be part of the reason they brought me on, to keep an eye on me. I know things about them. I saw it firsthand. It's a reason to keep me close, keep me in the fold so to speak. As a *son of Farrow*, they're considering me to join the Guild."

"Oh," she breathed. "And Mason?"

"Mason hasn't inquired. For our purposes, only one of us needs to join."

She pressed her lips together momentarily. "And Georgia?"

Camden shook his head. "The Women's Guild? No. Women, especially women like Georgia, are not . . . thought well of in Farrow, Scarlett." He felt a pang to his heart. They had made Georgia the "type of woman" she was and then castigated her for it. That alone had fed his hatred for years.

He worried his lip for a moment. "That flyer? The one you said you found on the street in Los Angeles? The one with the Lilith House sale information?"

She tilted her head. "Yes?"

"I think I was the one who dropped it."

Her eyes widened. "You? How do you know?"

"Because people from Farrow rarely leave, much less guild members. But . . . *I* was in LA a few months ago. I'd . . .

needed to get away." He looked away, recalling that day. "I'd requested to become a guild member, and attended an informal meeting. They didn't divulge anything useful, just questioned me a lot about my time away from Farrow, but on my way out, I was handed a flyer that held basic guild information. I stuck it in my pocket as I left." He paused. He'd felt trapped, edgy. "I got in my car and just started driving, following the signs to Los Angeles." He shook his head as a sigh emerged. "That restlessness we talked about . . ." He looked up, met her eyes. "It led me here, Scarlett. To you."

Her throat moved as she swallowed. She opened her mouth to speak and then closed it, looking away for a moment. She was quiet for several minutes and he left her to gather her thoughts. Finally, she asked, "How do you even have birth certificates? Paperwork?"

"There are ways to apply for that if you were home birthed and there was no record created at the time. It happens somewhat often in religious communities. But in any case, the guild is in charge of—"

"Farrow public records," Scarlett finished. She brought her hand to her forehead and left it there for a few moments as if she had to physically hold in the information her brain was processing. "The whole school, it was a racket?"

Camden considered that. "I guess you could call it that, but, Scarlett, like I said, these people *believe* in the righteousness of what they were doing, just as the original guild did. I don't know if that makes it better or far worse, but it's just the way it is. Even Jill—Ms. West—justified some of it until the end." His brow dipped momentarily, the complex feelings he still had for her coming to the surface. She'd participated in the heinous things that went on at Lilith House, but then she'd rescued him from it, refusing to speak of it after that, though she always seemed to be a basket of nerves. Sometimes he wondered if it had eaten away at her to such an extent that she'd literally made herself sick. He knew now she worried needlessly. No one was coming after her. Farrow was where their power lie. And neither he nor she were valuable enough to them anyway.

"That's why you became the sheriff's deputy? Why you're trying to become part of the guild? To catch them doing something you can use against them?"

"We'll use whatever we can to try to bring justice to those who deserve it."

"Including yourself. And . . . your friends."

He nodded once.

Scarlett sat back, sinking into the couch. She looked shocked and angry and confused. Overwhelmed.

"Right now, we have no proof. We have nothing."

Her eyes met his. "Especially since I bought Lilith House."

"Yes." It was true. They'd had this grand plan. It'd kept them going. They'd take the town down. They'd own the place where they'd once been made victims. They'd rule it all. Only, the more their plan had taken shape, the more specific it'd gotten, the more lust for power and revenge he'd seen in his friends' eyes . . . and in all honesty, even in the reflection staring back at him from the mirror, the more he'd wondered how alike he and the other guild members really were.

Hadn't Hubert Bancroft once lusted for power so strongly he was willing to forsake others for his own gain? Hadn't he seen that very thing take hold of Georgia and Mason when Scarlett had moved in and upended all their plans? They'd been willing to terrorize her, and her child—young and innocent like *they'd* been when they were victimized—in order to move Scarlett and Haddie out of the way. In order to be rid of them. And then they'd both felt betrayed by him when he'd demanded they stop, when he'd protected Scarlett instead of menacing her.

He'd satiated them by recommending Mason for the renovation job, but that would only be temporary. Then what?

Then what would happen to this woman whose smile made him feel alive for the first time in his miserable life? This woman who set his body on fire, and his heart reeling in some way he couldn't even describe?

He'd tried to feel those things for Georgie, he really had, but he never could manage anything more than deep abiding friendship, and a protectiveness he'd never quite lived up to. God, it made him feel guilty. Because he knew she loved him. She always had.

"You said the guild asked you to follow me from Farrow? Why? Where do I come into this?"

"They're suspicious of you. They're suspicious of your daughter. You—"

"What the hell could they be suspicious about in a seven-year-old girl?"

"Who knows, Scarlett? They're not rational." And they weren't, and he knew Scarlett had every right to be angry. "You have a connection to Lilith House. You knew the one person who got away, whether she's been heard from or not, whether she's presumed dead or not . . ." He watched her closely, saw the flicker of sorrow in her expression. "They're trying to learn more about you before they decide whether or not to let you stay for good."

"Stay for good? How would they force me to leave?"

"They'd come up with a hundred ways. They've done it before, they'll do it again. No one stays in Farrow who isn't wanted there."

"By the guild?"

"By the guild," he confirmed.

She searched his face for a moment. "Wouldn't that be more convenient for you? To let *them* do the dirty work of running me out of town?"

"Yes," he admitted. He'd promised to be completely honest with her and he'd meant it. It *would* be easier. Apparently, though, somewhere along the line, Camden had decided against the easier path.

That day at the stream. Those peace-filled moments with her. The rightness. You know that's when it was. That's exactly when it was.

Scarlett stood, walking stiffly to the sliding glass door of the balcony and walking outside. He followed, and came to stand next to her at the steel railing, looking out over the city. He gazed at her, took in her profile, the slender line of her neck, the way a silken tendril of hair lay across her cheek. He longed to brush it aside, to say something that would wipe the deeply worried look off her face.

"Say something," he said, his words choked.

She turned toward him, her gaze moving from one feature to the next. "I want to help," she finally said.

He hadn't expected that. He'd hoped to God he could trust her with his secrets—with *their* secrets for it was about Georgia and Mason too, it always had been, hadn't it?—but he hadn't expected Scarlett to offer her assistance. His heart swelled, happiness overcoming him. The problem was . . . "Unless you're willing to sell Lilith House to us—"

"I'm not," she said, lifting her chin. "I'm happy to hire Mason back if he'll accept. I'm happy to give you access to any and every square inch of it. You can search the places you think Kandi may have hidden any proof she collected. I'll *help* you do that. You can dig up the grounds if you want—they're going to be re-done anyway, but I am not selling. Farrow needs to be wiped of corruption, its secrets exposed, this antiquated notion of fallen women erased, and whatever else they have going on that you don't even know about, and I want to help with that. But I'm . . . *we're* meant to be there, Camden, Haddie and I. I feel that in my bones. So many things, happening in just the right timing, brought me to Lilith House. Even before the day I found that flyer, that *you* dropped, circumstances beyond my control have been moving me toward Farrow, nudging me along, arranging the precise instances that would eventually take me there. Even the fact that I had the money to purchase it when I saw that it was for sale." He watched her. He'd wondered about that. He knew how much Lilith House had been listed for, and even though it'd been a bargain for what it was and the land it was on, it was still a hell of a chunk of change. It'd taken Georgia, Mason, and him years of scrimping and saving and they were only almost at that magic number that would have meant they owned it outright.

Scarlett hesitated for a minute, looking down and then meeting his eyes. "I told you about Haddie's father and the contract. What I didn't tell you is that Royce's wife paid me off. She gave me a million dollars to sign that contract and never bother Royce again, never mention Haddie publicly." Scarlett bit at her lip. She obviously felt ashamed of having taken money, but all he felt was respect. She'd raised the little girl all on her own, and with how rich he assumed Royce Reynolds was, Scarlett probably could have laughed in his wife's face, and sued him for child support that would have amounted to a lot more than a million dollars. He probably made that in a weekend. Scarlett was proud, and he could tell that because of it, she believed she should have accepted Royce's dismissal with dignity and asked for nothing.

"You were owed that money and more," he said.

She let out a breath, turning her head and looking out at the city for a brief moment. "Maybe Haddie does, but not me. I put a little aside for her, but mostly, I'm planning on using it to renovate Lilith House and the surrounding grounds, to start my business."

"That's for Haddie too, Scarlett."

She tilted her head, giving a small acquiescence. "I've been trying to look at it that way. It hasn't come easy."

"Hey," he said, reaching out and using a finger to turn her face back to his when she'd looked away. "Let yourself off the hook. What you're doing, it's for both of you. Scarlett, you deserve your dreams."

For a moment she closed her eyes, her lips turning upward in a sad smile. "Thank you," she said. "Thank you for that."

He paused, recalling something he hadn't remembered until right that moment. "She told me about you," he said.

"She?"

"Kandace. She told me about a friend of hers. I think it was you. It had to be you."

Scarlett's smile was soft but mildly puzzled. "She did?"

"Yeah. Kandace wanted us to meet. She said she'd arrange it if she could."

Her eyes softened and she let out a small gust of breath. "I almost don't want to believe she did because that would mean—"

"I know," he said gently.

She looked up at him with so much concern, but also trust. "Was it hard for her, Cam? If the girls were treated badly, Kandi would have tried to *do* something. *Oh God.* Were they . . . did they—"

"She did do something. She cared. She was the first one who ever did. She took risks."

"You liked her." She smiled softly.

"She was the first person, other than Mason and Georgia who saw me. Looked out for me. So, yeah. I liked her."

"I'm glad, Cam. I'm glad she found you." *Me too. Because that's what she did. She found me.*

He started to withdraw his finger where it still rested on her chin, but instead, brought his hand closer, cupping her cheek. He felt nervous suddenly. Apprehensive, yet also strangely calm. He stared in her gray-blue eyes. *Peace.* He'd found it there. The old fears fell away, the ones that had never been real yet had lingered all the same. Until now. Until her. "I'm sorry I lied to you," he said softly. "But the way I feel about you, the things you do to me, Scarlett . . . nothing about that is a lie."

Her eyes widened, searching his and then she leaned closer into his touch. Her skin felt like warm satin. He stepped forward, so drawn to her, it was as though his body acted before he'd even decided to move. He had been, he realized, from the very first moment he looked at her. Scarlett stepped forward too, tilting her face upward and gazing at him.

Camden's heartbeat quickened, that electrifying sense Scarlett's closeness always elicited growing stronger just beneath his skin. It buzzed through his veins, causing every molecule to quicken inside him. It felt good. God, it felt good. He lowered his mouth, brushing it softly against hers. "Do you want this?" he asked.

"Yes," she said. "I want this. I want you."

His heart sped, body hardening. He let out a pent-up breath of need. "You're sure?"

She let out a gentle laugh, but it quickly faded. She brought her hand to his forehead, moving a lock of hair aside. "Yes, I'm very sure," she said tenderly, obviously understanding why her consent was so vital to him. He'd seen the opposite, portrayed as natural when it was anything but. The trauma still lived within him.

She went up on her tiptoes, kissing his forehead, her lips lingering there. "Take me to bed, Camden."

CHAPTER THIRTY-FOUR

Camden held her face tenderly in his hands as he came over her, pressing his naked skin to hers. Scarlett stared up at him, mouth parted, eyes wide and searching, so beautiful she stole his breath from his body. He groaned, bringing his mouth to hers, the heat of his hardness pressing against the silken skin of her stomach. He kissed her, slowly, tenderly, their tongues dueling sweetly as her thighs came around his hips. He felt his self-control dwindling and struggled to secure his grasp. She made him feel like liquid inside.

As if she sensed his effort, she broke from his mouth, running a thumb over his bottom lip as she gazed up into his eyes. "Let go," she said, her voice breathy. "I want you to let go, Camden. Please."

His heart swelled. *This woman.* This woman seemed to know him, to read his fear and his struggle. To understand that, for him, sex could hold pitfalls, ambivalence, and doubt.

His introduction had been anything but natural. He wanted to find out who he was, to explore his desires, to feel safe enough to do so, *known,* and that had never been a possibility before now because he'd never shared his secrets with a woman. Instead, he'd struggled along, having a few emotionally unsatisfying experiences before he'd moved back to Farrow, always half there, as though he watched his body from the outside, observing, but never truly participating.

Camden didn't feel that way now.

He felt intensely present, almost overwhelmingly so. This slender, delicate woman made him weak in the knees and the thought made him want to smile.

Scarlett opened her eyes wide and looked at him, her expression filled with trust. It honored him, that trust. It helped him relax, helped him give in to the lust rising inside him like a tidal wave.

Camden leaned up, looking down where his hand rested on her naked thigh. "A heart," he said, running his thumb over her birthmark. "It looks like a heart."

She laughed softly and he raised his head, his lips meeting hers.

He kissed her and it wasn't tentative, it was wild and warm and wet. Just like those moments spent with her at the stream, everything about it was sweet and *right.* Her thighs gripped him tightly, bringing their cores closer and the wave rose higher. There was nothing but *her,* the taste of her on his tongue, the soft scent of her skin. Wildflowers and rain. And God, he wanted to make this good for her too. He wanted this to mean as much to Scarlett as it did to him.

After all, she'd been mistreated as well. She'd been used and lied to. And then abandoned. She deserved to feel cherished.

He'd been taught what was holy and what was not, the idea of unmerciful divinity drummed into him like a gong ringing constantly in his head. Loud. Brutal. But none of those teachings had ever felt *true*, not in his gut, not in his soul. Because Camden had sat in silence in the shaded woods, listening to the peaceful trickle of water. He'd seen the miraculous unfolding of a brand-new day. He'd held innocent life in his hands and watched as it first floundered, then healed, finally flying away in a rapturous flapping of wings, rising into the open sky. He knew what was holy because his heart had told him, and he had listened to its soft singing.

He felt that holiness now, as this beautiful woman trustingly and wholeheartedly offered him her body—and her heart.

He brought his hand to her breast, teasing the nipple with his thumb until she moaned and arched and breathed his name, his own breath coming ragged and fast. He pulled his mouth from hers, closing his lips around one stiff peak and tugging gently. He was rewarded with a soft cry that made him swell and ache and press against her, seeking relief.

"Yes," she breathed. *"Yes."*

She writhed beneath him, pressing upward, inviting. Heat burned in his belly, his loins, her hand moving between their bodies, wrapping around his hardness so that he moaned, gasping out a strangled sound of pleasure.

She stroked him slowly, almost languidly, raising her head so she could see her hand on his flesh. He followed suit, watching as she pleasured him, and it was far too much and not nearly enough. "Scarlett," he groaned, a tortured laugh moving up his throat as he placed his hand over hers and removed her grasp. "Later," he gritted.

She blinked at him, and then a knowing smile tilted her lips. "Yes," she murmured, as she parted her legs and guided him inside.

He sucked in a breath at the first wet grasp of her body, their eyes meeting in the dim light. Her lashes fluttered and they stared at each other, the moment so intimate he didn't know if he could bear it, and yet never wanted it to end.

He began to move, his body demanded it, gliding in and out of her in long fluid thrusts. His head lowered, moving to her breast where he took a nipple in his mouth and began sucking to the rhythm of his hips. He was drowning in her, drowning a slow, sweet death. Scarlett gasped and he felt the pull of her muscles deep within. He could feel her ragged breaths against his neck, hear her tiny mewls of pleasure.

Her desire fueled his and with a groan of surrender, he gave in to the lust, letting it sweep him away, moving faster, pleasure rising. He gritted his teeth, holding himself at the brink until he heard her cry out, her body shuddering around him as he came in long rolling waves of ecstasy.

Camden pulled her with him as he rolled to his back, not willing to let her move away, their breathing growing quieter as their heartbeats slowed, a smile of joy spreading across his face. Nothing had ever felt more right.

CHAPTER THIRTY-FIVE

Thirteen Years Ago

𝒦andace wrapped the towel around her body quickly as Sydney entered the bathroom, yawning. "Morning," she said sleepily heading to the sink.

"Good morning," Kandace said, scooting past her so she could dress quickly in the bedroom. Aurora had left a few minutes before, heading down to the dining room. Kandace turned her back to the closed bathroom door, pulling her underwear, bra, and uniform on quickly. Thank goodness the uniform Lilith House made them wear was oversized and unshapely. She was definitely showing and Sydney, who'd been sharing a room for months now and had seen Kandace in various stages of undress, would notice. How could she not? Maybe it was safe to confide in Sydney, but Kandace wasn't going to take the chance.

Kandace had accepted her pregnancy, accepted the horrific circumstances under which she'd conceived. But it was still so surreal, so *impossible,* that she could almost pretend it was all just a great big mistake. A false positive or a . . . chemical pregnancy or something like that.

A tiny tap from within caused her to swallow, fear rolling through her.

No, no mistake. She was pregnant and even now, her child was consistently reminding Kandace of his or her existence.

Sydney exited the bathroom as Kandace was slipping her shoes on. "Another joyous day at Lilith House," she muttered. "At least there's dessert to look forward to tonight."

Kandace froze, straightening. "The Guild is coming to the service? I thought that was next week." She'd thought she had time to come up with a plan . . . some sort of plan. Feign illness perhaps? But no, wouldn't they want to examine her if she pretended to be suffering from some malady or another? It would be unwise to go anywhere near the infirmary right now.

Sydney nodded as she pulled on her uniform. "Ms. West mentioned it yesterday. I guess they have something else to do next week so they moved it up." She waved her hand around as though *they* weren't the point. It was the trays of dessert that came along with them that meant something.

Oh God. Kandace's muscles tensed. If one of them chose her, he'd know. They'd all know.

But if no one did, she'd have an opportunity to break back into Ms. Wykes's office. She had *names* now. Specific names to search for. Did she dare?

All through the day, Kandace turned the question over in her mind. *Do you dare? Do you dare?* No one knew she was aware of the sleeping medication in the desserts. She hadn't even told Aurora. She knew Ms. West hadn't mentioned speaking to her because no punishment had been forthcoming. Not only that, but Ms. West had given Kandace information. Why would she rat on Kandace, when Kandace could rat on her too?

It was time. It was time to use the information she'd been given. It was time to put things in motion that would result in the closure of Lilith House and hopefully more than several prison sentences. It was time to help the kids in the basement, and to ensure that what was happening now did not continue.

You're stronger than you think you are.

Kandace pulled in a slow, steady breath. Okay then. It was time for Kandace to prove it.

This was her opportunity and she had to take it. She might not get another.

****

The men filed in, Kandace's hands trembling as she clutched the back of the pew in front of her. *Please, God, please don't let me be chosen tonight.* Her heart galloped as they went through the motions of the opening prayer, sweat breaking out on her brow when the men stood up to "bless" the girls, their footsteps echoing in her brain like her own death walk. If it was true as she suspected, that one of them had impregnated her while she was drugged and unconscious, she could ruin them all.

And Kandace didn't think they'd allow that to happen. No, she knew they wouldn't.

One of the men was moving slowly her way, approaching the end of the aisle where she stood, head bowed, heart pounding wildly, a prayer on her lips, but not directed toward any god Lilith House believed in.

Please, please. Don't let me be chosen.

An arrow of guilt speared her. Begging God to spare her being chosen meant she was praying for another girl to suffer unknown indignities that she would never even remember. And the fact that she wouldn't know what happened to her, in Kandace's mind, made it worse, not better. She pressed her lips together, tears gathering behind her closed lids. She gripped the pew in front of her to disguise the shaking of her hands. She didn't know what to pray for and so she simply repeated in the quiet of her mind, *Help me. Please help me.*

No touch came. She let out a controlled breath, attempting to slow her rapid heartbeat. The man moved away, obviously having chosen the classmate next to her—Lucille, the girl who'd been responsible for her "cleansing." She wanted to feel some measurement of satisfaction, but she didn't. Couldn't.

No one deserved what these men were doing to them.

And she understood these girls—their opportunism, their poor judgment, their greed, their lack of empathy, and their jealousy. She was one of them. She'd displayed all of those things too. She was no worse, but she was also no better. She had no right to judge.

Later, Kandace lay in bed, listening to the drugged snores of Aurora and Sydney. She didn't know if they'd been chosen and so she waited. The house squeaked, quiet footsteps echoing through the walls as girls were carried from their beds. No one climbed the stairs to the attic.

Kandace slid quietly out of bed, keeping her nightgown on as it was the only other clothes she had except for her uniform. She slipped her shoes on and made her way down the rickety set of steps, her muscles tensed at every squeak and creak, praying that if she was heard, it would be assumed that it was one of the men retrieving one of their "blessed ones." She didn't think she had to be overly quiet. Tonight, Lilith House was a bevy of activity, and they all believed quiet was unnecessary.

As she slipped around the corner, tiptoeing down the third-floor hallway, she caught movement out of the corner of her eye. Kandace's heart lurched and she pulled herself into a doorway, pressing herself against the hard wood, her rounded belly showing past the jamb. She held her breath as a man, carrying a girl, moved from one hallway to another, his head turned in the opposite direction. The girl in his arms looked small and frail and Kandace clapped a hand over her mouth when she saw that it was the young girl who lived in the basement. The one with the dark curls and the hair lip. The one who couldn't be more than fourteen years old.

Fury dripped through her, making her feel nauseous but what could she do? *I'm trying to help you, I swear,* she said silently to the unconscious girl. *I can't now, but I will.*

"Dreschel," someone's voice greeted the man in passing, but out of her line of vision, both of their footsteps—*thank God*—moving in the other direction. *Dreschel. I'll remember your name. I won't forget.*

When the footsteps had faded, Kandace stepped out of the doorway and raced ahead, slipping down the back stairs, and moving swiftly down the hall, back pressed against the wall, head moving in both directions to ensure no one caught her.

When she'd made it to Ms. Wykes's office, she pulled the pin from her hair, making the series of moves she'd mastered at this point. She had the door open in seconds. Sweating, her breath coming rapidly, Kandace slipped inside the room, closing the door softly behind her, engaging the lock and exhaling slowly. The Tiffani lamp on Ms. Wykes's desk was on, the stained-glass shade deep red, green, and blue, casting the office in a somber glow. For several minutes she simply stood there listening, a few creaks and squeaks from above making their way to her ears.

She grabbed the wooden chair near the wall and slipped it under the knob, tilting it so she'd have time to . . . what? What was she going to do if she'd been unknowingly seen and Ms. Wykes and Jasper showed up again? She had no escape. The most she could do was find a weapon . . . her eyes darted around . . . the paperweight on the desk, or the pointy umbrella in the stand near the door. This time, she'd at least go down swinging.

Kandace rushed to the file cabinets, picking the lock of the first cabinet, and quietly pulling the drawer open. She rifled through the files, finding the first name in her memory, a surge of excitement causing her to inhale sharply as she pulled it from the drawer. She quickly found the second and third, moving to Ms. Wykes's desk where she opened the first folder and gazed at the picture of the pretty young woman. God, she looked just like Dreamboat with those soulful eyes and full lips. Something caught in her throat and she swallowed it down, using her finger to quickly scan through her information. She'd been from New Jersey . . . *Camden, New Jersey* . . . Kandace scanned the page finding only basic information, but when she flipped the first page over, she let out a soft, "Oh." She'd shown up pregnant. They'd contacted her family and they had requested that Lilith House facilitate an adoption. *Shown up pregnant. Like Kandace had "shown up pregnant"?* Kandace turned the page. God, her chest hurt. This girl who looked no older than sixteen had given birth at Lilith House under the medical care of Dr. Bill Woodrow. Her eyes scanned the sloppy writing, pulling out the words that told the story of what turned into a traumatic birth. Shoulder dystocia . . . lack of oxygen . . .

Was that it then? They'd believed Dreamboat to be mentally impaired? He wasn't . . . though she supposed by the time they were able to ascertain that, his life had already been decided.

Kandace exhaled, closing the file and opening the next one. This girl appeared about the same age. Same story, she'd been pregnant when she arrived, Lilith House had been in charge of facilitating the adoption of the unwanted child. Birth presided over by Dr. Bill Woodrow, the baby girl born with a cleft palate. *Georgia,* her mother had been from Georgia.

Kandace moved her mind away from what was being done to that baby girl right that moment. Kandace's gaze stopped on two scrawled words under Dr. Woodrow's notes: signs of sin.

Sin? Who did that refer to? The mother or the infant? And either way, *really?* A doctor, a so-called *medical professional,* diagnosing *sin?* A deep shiver moved down her spine.

Kandace closed the file and opened the next one, noting the photo of the blonde and turning the page. Pregnant. Adoption facilitated by Lilith House. Dr. Bill Woodrow again making note of: signs of sin. Signs of sin. Signs of *sin?* What *was* this? Kandace flipped back to the photo of the girl, the blonde from Mason, Ohio, thinking of her boy. *Sin?* The fact that he had different colored eyes? All three of them had been deemed sinful, unadoptable, for some physical quality none of them could control and relegated to the basement of Lilith House for it? Why hadn't they simply killed them? Was it because they weren't quite throwaways, not *quite,* just like the girls of Lilith House who served a purpose despite their sinful natures?

God, what had it been like for them? To be openly pregnant at Lilith House? To give birth there and then not be sent home, perhaps because your own family still didn't want you? Still thought you needed "redemption"? Had they been trotted out—or maybe strung up just like her—in front of the other students? Used as examples? *Of course they were.*

Sickness overwhelmed her. She had no adequate word for the evil story these folders told.

A small squeak sounded outside the door and Kandace's breath stalled as she froze, waiting to hear the doorknob rattle. It didn't. She let out her breath. She needed to get out of there.

Kandace glanced back at the open drawer. She couldn't put these back inside. She needed them. They were her proof. She'd take them to the authorities, to the girls themselves if she could find them, the girls who likely believed their children were with loving families.

She began to stuff them under her nightgown, but hesitated. Before she left this room, she had to know what was in them. If she was caught on the way back to bed, if they were taken, the information had to be in her brain where no one could touch it.

Trembling now because she'd spent too long as it was, she quickly opened the folders and looked at the final pages. All featured a similar police report signed by Sheriff Carson.

Though Camden's mother had arrived—and given birth—a year before the others got there, the girls had all run away from Lilith House together. *What the hell?* Kandace scanned the lines, skipping some and reading others. There was a search, it was feared they'd been injured or they'd met with foul play. It was short and concise. The search had gone on for three days and then the case had been closed. Apparently, no one had put too much effort into finding three previously drug-addicted screwups who had shown up pregnant, signed their babies away—product of sin that they were—and then hit the road.

A small bump came from within and Kandace brought her hand to her belly. A certainty fell over her. If she revealed this pregnancy—*no*. A streak of protectiveness shimmered through her. Yes, there was *more* than just herself to consider.

She had to escape. She had to take these folders and leave Lilith House the second she could.

Kandace stood quickly, gathering the folders. She turned and closed the file cabinet drawer, re-engaging the lock at the top. Then she removed the chair from beneath the door handle, placing it back where it'd been. She tucked the folders in the back of her underwear so they lay flat against her back. She held her breath as she quietly turned the knob, opening the door a crack and peeking out. The hallway was empty. Kandace turned the lock from inside and then shut the door as silently as she could, only releasing the air from her lungs when she'd started walking hurriedly toward the stairs.

She cringed when she made it to the second floor where she knew she'd been taken that night, and heard a man's grunt coming from a room close by. *Oh God.* Kandace gritted her teeth and turned the other way, hurrying to the staircase and climbing to the third floor, and then to the attic above. She slipped into the quiet of her darkened room, relief flooding her. She'd made it. She was safe. And she'd gotten just what she needed.

Kandace removed the folders from her underwear and walked quickly to her bed, slipping them beneath the mattress. She'd have liked to read them more closely, but the room was dark and she didn't dare turn on a light. There would be no more risks tonight. She had a feeling, she'd used up all her luck for the moment.

She got beneath her covers and lay there, thinking about the absolute evil she'd discovered. The girls, their children, supposedly marked by the sin of their parents. She could hardly wrap her head around the fact that these people had convinced themselves of such a thing. Not only convinced themselves, but *fucking* acted upon it.

Yes, Kandace needed to leave. But she needed a plan. She was in the middle of nowhere. She didn't even know which direction to head. And even more concerning, she had a feeling the three girls who'd escaped had tried that too, only they were never heard from again.

Another chill went through Kandace and she brought her hand to her swollen belly again. "I'm going to figure this out," she whispered into the silence of the room. "I'm going to get us out of here."

She didn't know how, but she'd just made a promise, and she intended to keep it.

CHAPTER THIRTY-SIX

$\mathcal{S}$carlett opened her eyes, turning toward Camden in the dark and finding his side of the bed empty. She sat up slowly, catching sight of him standing at the balcony, his masculine form outlined by the glow of city lights. As her eyes adjusted, she saw he wore only his boxer briefs and held a water bottle at his side. She took the opportunity to watch him unaware, to drink in the athletic grace of his body, the beauty he seemed almost completely unaware of. She understood why now. He'd practically reached adulthood without ever being taught of his appeal. Instead, he'd been isolated, shamed, a terrible vision of what sex was presented to him in his tender, formative years. He was damaged, yes, but he was also strong. Stronger than he realized. He was good and honorable. Loyal.

Scarlett got out of bed, wrapping the bedsheet around herself and approaching him from behind. When she slipped her arms around his body, he startled slightly, then chuckled, the sound low and deep. She turned her nose into his back, breathing him in and then kissing the smooth skin of his shoulder.

"I didn't wake you, did I?"

"No. Well, maybe. I think I sensed you were gone, even in my sleep."

He smiled down at her as she dropped her arms and came around his side. He lifted the bottle of water, still half full and offered it to her. "Thirsty?"

She shook her head and he draped his arm around her, pulling her into his side. "What are you doing out here all alone?"

She heard his smile even though he was turned away. "Just reliving what we did in that bed in there."

"Yeah? What part are you at?"

"I'm stuck on the moment you did that swirly thing with your tongue."

She laughed. "That swirly thing, huh? You liked that?"

"*Like* doesn't seem like quite the right word."

She laughed again, dragging a finger down his chest. "You know, there's a small chance you can relive it in body, not just in thought."

He grinned and her chest constricted. Even in the dimmest of light, he was so beautiful he made her heart ache.

"Come back to bed," she invited.

He followed her into the room where they made love again, the sounds of the city drifting softly to them from the open balcony door, the cool night breeze whispering over their heated skin.

Camden gathered her in his arms and they lay in silence for several minutes, his fingers running up and down her arm. She sighed. "I assume this isn't what they meant when they asked you to keep tabs on me," she said wryly.

Camden let out a soft laugh that quickly faded. "No." She looked up at him, his features etched in worry. "What's going to happen when we get back?" she asked. She hadn't wanted to burst their happy little bubble with talk of guilds and missing girls, but it was reality, it was *his* reality especially, the one he'd lived most of his life, and this was no time to bury their heads in the sand for too long either.

Camden sighed, unwrapping his arm from around her and sitting up. He swung his legs over the side of the bed and leaned forward, stretching his neck. "We can't be seen together, Scarlett."

She sat up halfway too, bringing the sheet to her breasts and leaning back on one elbow. "We can't be seen . . . why not?"

He looked back over his shoulder so she could only see his profile. "Because if I have any hope of becoming a guild member, a woman like you wouldn't make an acceptable prospect."

Hurt spiraled through her and it took a moment to swallow down the lump in her throat. He turned before she could speak. "They're not my rules. But I have to play by them if I have any hope of gathering the information I need, if there's even any information to gather."

Scarlett took a deep breath. She had to be reasonable about this. She had abandonment issues; she acknowledged them. But she couldn't let her own self-doubt get in the way of the bigger picture. Camden had been honest with her when it could have cost him everything to do so. He'd trusted her not only with *his* secret, but with the secrets of two people he'd grown up with. Two people who craved the same justice he did. She chewed her lip for a moment. She wanted to help, but she also wanted to be clear about where she stood. Especially if it was going to mean pretending she didn't know him in public.

"The woman whose house I saw you leaving that morning, you said she's a good friend—"

"Georgia." His back was still to her so she couldn't see his face.

"Yes, Georgia." She paused, considering her words and in the end just diving in. "She considers you hers." She'd seen the look on her face both at the hardware store, and as he'd left her house the morning she'd driven by. She'd replayed it in her mind. Far too many times.

For a moment he was silent, still, but finally he nodded. He looked back over his shoulder and she saw the conflict in his expression. "Sometimes I think she's right to, you know?"

Scarlett's ribs tightened.

"It seems like . . ." His words faded away, as though he didn't know how to finish that sentence.

"Like you owe her?" Scarlett asked. She tried to imagine what it must have been like for them, those three against the entire world, bonded in a way she probably couldn't even imagine.

Camden let out a staggered breath. "I don't know," he finally said. "Someone does." He paused for several moments. "We were told one of the reasons our mothers gave us up was because we were born damaged. Our mothers' sin was passed along to us in the form of something physical."

"Something physical?" She frowned.

"Georgia was born with a cleft palate. The man who became Georgia's guardian paid for her surgery. Mason has heterochromia."

"Those are signs of sin?"

"In Farrow they are."

She shook her head, trying to wrap her mind around what he was telling her. This was all so unbelievable. So . . . outside anything she'd heard of before. Were there other places like Farrow? Towns still lost in time, operating under archaic, irrational beliefs like the ones that had fueled the Salem Witch Trials? Even *laws?* Did they really believe such things? Or were their physical abnormalities an easy excuse to treat them in any manner they pleased and in whatever way was convenient? "And you?" She'd seen every perfect strip of him. "What in the world is your *sign of sin?*"

"I don't know. I never knew what mine was. I worried." He paused. "I wondered if it was something they knew but never told me, some illness I couldn't see or feel but that might one day show itself. I don't know." He scrubbed a hand down his face. "In any case, even beyond the disability, Georgia suffered the most, more than either of us, just by virtue of being female." Something dark came into his eyes and Scarlett's heart went out to him. And Georgia. She didn't have to wonder what sort of treatment Georgia received from the members of the guild. From those who were accessories to the crimes taking place inside the walls of Lilith House. She understood why Camden was torn about his feelings for her. He didn't want to hurt her more than she'd already been hurt.

She crawled forward, sitting on the edge of the bed next to him and turning his face to hers and saying very gently, "You can't force yourself to feel something you don't, any more than you can stop feeling the things you do. I had to accept that." She turned her gaze from his momentarily. "It's why I didn't try to force Haddie's father to be part of her life. Love by force or . . . obligation . . . guilt . . . is not love."

He turned his face into her palm, kissing the hand that lay on his cheek. "I know," he breathed.

"So try to stop feeling guilty for not loving her," she said gently.

Camden raked a hand through his hair. "Dammit, I do love her, Scarlett. Just . . . not like that." He whispered it like a confession. "The things I feel for you, the things I want . . . I could never feel them for her, no matter how hard I tried. It's like . . . that fate you talked about. That *pull*. I feel it every time you're in the room. I have since the moment I laid eyes on you." He exhaled, taking her face in his hands and leaning his forehead on hers.

She understood his conflict now, understood why he'd said it would be easier not to feel the things he felt for her. If only feelings could be planned and organized to suit what was most convenient. Or perhaps that would be the most tragic thing in the world.

"We can't help the way we feel," she whispered back. "Like you said about nature. It just *is.*"

He gazed into her eyes for a moment and then he kissed her mouth, her eyelids, her nose, and she laughed softly. He smiled back. "Will you tell me more about why you sought out Royce and what happened when you saw him at that party?"

Scarlett sighed, sitting back. She drew her legs up and told him about Haddie's doctor's appointment, about reading the article on the man her daughter shared genetics with, about spotting the hotel in the background of the photo. She described Royce's behavior, his obvious inebriation, and the way he'd seemed to believe she was nothing more than a dream. "I can't say whether he was just highly intoxicated, or whether I was seeing signs of his illness, or both. But either way, I knew I wasn't going to get any answers from him. Not in the state he was in. Probably not ever."

He appeared to digest what she said, finally asking, "Does it matter?"

"What? Whether or not he has a mental illness?"

"No, whether Haddie has a predisposition. What will you do?"

Scarlett shrugged. "I would know better how to treat her."

"It seems like you're doing just fine, Scarlett."

Her first reaction was to bristle. He was being almost . . . dismissive and not acknowledging the seriousness that her daughter might be suffering from a mental illness. Or if she wasn't now, that she might in the future. But as she looked in his eyes, she realized that his was the reaction she should hope for. She should *hope* that someone, anyone for that matter, learning that Haddie had a mental illness, would react with calm reassurance, rather than feverish hysterics. He'd never judge her, she realized. He knew exactly what it felt like to be judged and determined as less.

She took a deep breath, letting it wash through her. He was *right*. So what if her daughter's Haddie-isms were based on some genetic abnormality? Then . . . she'd love that abnormality. It was part of what made her *her*. Did she really need some label when she was only seven years old? A label that might or might not come to fruition? And if some specific diagnosis became helpful later, whether because she suffered from something genetic, or for some random curveball life threw at them, then she'd deal with it. She laughed softly. "God, I'm an idiot." She smiled at him. "Thank you. You're kinda good at advice."

He moved forward, taking her in an embrace. "Yeah?" He grinned. "Did I earn one more round of that swirly thing?"

Her laugh was cut off by his mouth meeting hers.

CHAPTER THIRTY-SEVEN

Ever since they'd returned from Gram's house, Haddie had been thinking about the horned thing she was so frightened of. She'd been thinking about the way he'd eaten all the Skittles, and then started skipping the green. She'd been thinking about the little boy in leg braces, and the one in the wheelchair. She'd been wondering about a lot of things. And Haddie wanted to find the answers. She wanted to understand the things that were only starting to be clear. She thought . . . she thought it might be very important. Haddie set her iPad aside, going into the hallway on the second floor where her mommy was hanging long strips of wallpaper with blue and gold flowers on it. Her mommy had been smiling a whole lot since they got back from LA, but she wasn't smiling now. Haddie didn't think the wallpaper was going very well for her mommy because she was muttering bad words under her breath and the one strip she'd hung was crooked and half falling down. She tapped her on the back and she jumped, laughing as she spun around to see Haddie standing there. "You okay, baby? You didn't hear what I said, did you?"

"Yes, Mommy."

"Oh. Well. Don't repeat those words, okay?"

"I won't. Can I play outside?"

"I don't know if that's a good idea. It rained earlier. The grass is all wet . . ."

"I'll wear my rain boots."

Her mommy looked at her for a minute before sighing. "Okay, but promise me you'll stay in the yard, only to the edge of the woods, okay?"

Haddie nodded, her fingers crossed behind her back. She hated to lie to her mommy, but this was *important*.

"Okay." She glanced at the piece of falling-down wallpaper. "I'll probably leave this to Mason's crew before I waste any more of this expensive wallpaper. I think I should stick to baking." She smiled. "I'll be in the kitchen working on the computer and I'll leave my headphones off and the window open. If you stay out back, I'll hear you if you need me, all right?"

"Yes, Mommy."

Ten minutes later, wearing her green dress with the tiny white flowers, and a pair of yellow rain boots, Haddie exited Lilith House through the back door. The air felt steamy from the rain, a soft mist rising from the ground, growing thicker at the edge of the woods, curling toward her like reaching hands. Haddie glanced at the open kitchen window, checking to make sure her mommy wasn't looking as she ducked into the cover of trees, allowing the cool, misty fingers to swirl around her limbs.

Despite the hazy ground, she spotted the acorns immediately. She'd seen them when they got out of the car and started walking toward the door, and she'd been thinking about those acorns since then. They'd been left for her, she knew they had been. The horned creature had used her idea and left a trail for Haddie to follow.

Haddie stepped tentatively over the pine needles on the ground, following the acorns farther into the woods. At first, they were spaced close together, and then farther apart. Eventually, they tapered off completely and confused and slightly frightened, Haddie turned in a full circle, wondering what she should do.

The mist had risen off the ground and now it whispered through the trees, creating a world that felt both dreamy and strange. Straight ahead, a pair of horns appeared, their outline parting the fog and then being swallowed up once again as the creature moved forward. Haddie gasped, her feet primed to turn and run. But no, she'd come here for answers and she had to be brave.

The horns appeared and then faded into the mist, emerging again seconds later, even easier to follow than a trail of acorns. Haddie gathered all her courage, moving forward, following the creature that had no weight.

Haddie moved through trees, first so thick she had to weave between their massive trunks, and then spaced farther apart. She got caught up on brush, her legs and arms scraped and poked. She followed the thing *up*, her legs growing weary, and then *down,* her rainboot-clad feet slipping in the dirt, though she caught herself before she fell.

She followed for a long time, her muscles growing weary, the sky beginning to grow dim, the creature waiting for her, but keeping just far enough ahead that Haddie could never see it clearly.

Where are you leading me?

Follow.

A shiver of excitement raced through Haddie. She'd heard it. Not in words, but in intentions. She'd *heard* it.

The first glints of starlight appeared, the sky overhead colored in a hundred different shades of blue.

Her mommy was going to be very worried.

Haddie was worried too. But she'd come this far, and she couldn't turn back now.

The creature wanted to show her something.

It was . . . saying something . . . and she could almost hear like she had before, but not quite.

Through the mist, Haddie spotted a small hut-like house between two tall trees. She stopped, peering at it, wondering if that was what she was meant to see. But no, the creature had passed right by the dwelling and moved somewhere beyond. Haddie took in the weight of the structure, measuring it. It felt light. A peaceful place, though she also felt its emptiness. Someone had lived there once, but not anymore.

Haddie continued on.

The ground grew rockier, large boulders replacing the trees. The creature had disappeared, replaced by the soft pounding of drums from . . . somewhere. Haddie couldn't tell where the sound came from because it echoed off the rocks and the walls of the canyon ahead, bouncing all around so it was everywhere at once. She could see the edge of the cliff that fell into it stretching around in a giant circle. Though there was no fog out in this wide space, the canyon was so deep, Haddie couldn't see the bottom from where she stood.

The moon was big here, big and yellow and round. High in the sky, bats circled, their inky wings outlined in moonglow. A bunny hopped out from behind a rock, spotting Haddie and going still, its little nose twitching. He and Haddie measured each other, then satisfied, both turned away, focusing back on their own business.

Haddie eyed the cliff again, lost in uncertainty. What was she supposed to do from here? She glanced down, and that's when she saw the red-hued rocks, each about the size of her fist. They had been formed in a trail, just like the acorns. Just like her Skittles. Haddie took a step forward, then another, moving to the final reddish stone directly on the edge of the cliff.

Haddie picked it up, holding it in her hand, feeling the very slight warmth in her palm. Warily, she leaned forward, peeking over the edge of the cliff.

Down.

Startled, she looked around, searching for the one who'd said that word. Demanding.

Again, she peeked over the edge. It was very, very far down. Did the thing want to hurt her? *Kill* her? Her breath came short and she stumbled back, her feet slipping in the gravel and coming out from under her, pitching her forward. With a cry of fear, she threw her body sideways, landing on her stomach, the air knocked out of her lungs.

For several minutes she lay there, gripping the ground and sucking in lungfuls of dusty air. When she'd finally managed to calm herself, she began to push back from the edge, the rocky ground scraping her bare legs.

Something caught her eye on a ledge below. A reddish rock. Haddie stilled, glancing around at the windless night. She scooted herself forward just enough to hang her head over the edge, her hand finding a prickly plant and wrapping around its strong root.

She eyed the reddish rock on the small ledge below, her gaze moving to a similar one on a wider ledge beneath, plants and brush growing near the wall of the cliff.

Haddie's bones squeezed tight, growing leaden in her body. She cried out softly, her head falling limply over the edge of the cliff, her eyes glued to that second ledge. This place was like that room on the second floor of Lilith House. It had *weight*. She didn't know if the weight was bad or sad, it wasn't like that with places. *Places* weren't clear like people. Places held their weight *different*.

Haddie caught her breath, lifting her head, willing the feel of the weight to leave her bones, but remain in her mind. She'd been practicing that lately, and sometimes it worked. Mostly, it didn't, but Haddie didn't want the weight of *badness* to make it so she couldn't *move*.

That scared her, and she didn't want to be scared. She wanted to be brave.

She peered below the weighty ledge. There were no more rocks beneath.

Haddie paused, lifting her head higher and peering around again. The distant sound of a drumbeat started up again. She couldn't tell if it was moving closer or farther away.

Haddie looked down again. She knew what she had to do. She knew she had been led here for a reason. Haddie came up on her knees, gathering every ounce of courage in her small, skinny, seven-year-old body. And then Haddie turned around, lowering herself backward over the cliff.

CHAPTER THIRTY-EIGHT

Georgia sat on the couch, legs drawn up, arms linked around them, a scowl on her face that Camden knew hid her hurt. He sat down next to her. "Georgie," he implored. "Look at me."

She turned away. "You shouldn't have told her," she said. "I can't believe you told her."

Mason cleared his throat from where he sat on the easy chair across from the sofa. "He had to, Georgia," Mason said.

She whipped her head toward him. "Now you're on her side too?"

He let out a breath. "There don't always have to be sides," he said. "What was Camden supposed to do? Deny what she'd already discovered?" He glanced at Camden. "He has feelings for her. He trusted her. And she wants to help."

"Help, my ass!" Georgia said. "What can she do to help?"

"She can give us complete access to the house," Camden said. "The property."

"We could have had complete access to that property ourselves if you'd have let us do whatever it took to get rid of her."

"God, Georgie, listen to you," Camden said, his voice a low growl of frustration. "Do whatever it took to get rid of her? You sound like Ms. Wykes."

Georgia let out a gasp. "How dare you? Until five minutes ago, you were just as on board with this plan as we were."

He ran a hand through his hair. "Yeah, well, things changed." *My priorities changed.*

"Yeah, because Scarlett Lattimore opened her legs for you. What a good *guild* member you are."

"For the love of God, stop this, you two," Mason said, standing up and lacing his hands behind his head as he paced. "This is ridiculous. Georgia," he said, turning to her. "I'm sorry, but I'm with Camden. Our plan . . . it needs to be adjusted. We can still seek answers, justice. That's not going to change, okay? That part is bigger than just us. But I don't want to be ruled by vengeance either. I want . . . more." He looked at her so adoringly that Camden glanced away. He sometimes wondered if Mason ever admitted his longing for Georgia, even in his own head. What he did know was that Mason was inspired by the work he was doing on Lilith House. It'd become a passion project for him, not only because he was good at what he did, but because it was filling something inside him to be given reign over the structure that had imprisoned him for most of his life. He was turning Lilith House into something different than she'd been, inspired by the vision he had for her. Camden could see that it provided a cleansing for Mason, one long past due, one taking the place of what they had previously planned. This one feeding the good wolf inside, he could see it in Mason's eyes. "Don't you want more, Georgie?" Mason asked softly.

She glowered at him. "You want more than us?" she asked. "Suddenly we're not enough for you anymore?"

"You've always been enough for me, Georgia," he said softly. "But I also want to be happy." He looked at Cam. "I've never seen Cam happy . . . until now. And I want that for you too. I want that for me," he finished. "We deserve to have a life, Georgia, things that bring us joy and satisfaction. Things that don't only revolve around Lilith House and the damage done to us."

"That's easy for you to say," she choked, her face still turned away from them. Camden's chest gave a hard knock. He glanced at Mason and they exchanged a look of empathy. Yes, she'd had it harder than both of them, not just at Lilith House, but after that when she went to live with the head of the guild, Clarence Dreschel. That man had paid for her surgery, and then promptly exacted payment in the form of another slice of her innocence, which she'd only divulged to him and Mason when they'd begun setting their plan in motion. He would give anything to change it, to change all of it. He'd give anything to have had the power then to rescue her. But he'd been a kid too. Traumatized. Confused. And

God, he admitted it, so desperately relieved to have been swept away from Farrow.

"I still hear his cane on the floor," she said, her gaze faraway. "Coming toward my room."

He went to sit back down next to her. "I'm sorry, I'm so sorry. Nothing like that will ever happen to you again. You'll always have us, Georgia. We're family. We will never ever desert you. But, look at me." For a moment she ignored him, but then her face turned his way. She had tears in her eyes. "We—all three of us—have to make it our end goal to build lives that are bigger than what happened at Lilith House and even after that. We have to, Georgie, or we'll turn into the very people we're trying to punish. The people who hurt us so badly."

"It's always been us. Just us," she whispered miserably.

A tear slipped down her cheek and Camden wiped it away. "Maybe it doesn't have to be. Maybe that's not healthy, Georgie. There are others out there who will love you too."

Georgia let out a humorless laugh. "How could they?" *Oh, Georgia.* She still saw herself as that damaged, unwanted girl. An ugly reject. An unlovable castoff. He had seen himself in a similar light for a very long time. It had been an awakening, a long-awaited miracle to find out he wasn't the loathsome mistake he'd been taught to believe he was. To discover that a person like Scarlett Lattimore could find him worthy. But it was *his* decision to choose her word over the lies of all those who had manipulated him so terribly. And he hoped to God someday Georgia and Mason would be able to do the same.

"Easily," he said softly but with great surety. He looked at Mason, who watched them from where he stood. "I think it was a mistake to think that by recreating our situation on our terms, it would give us power, help us move on." He bit at his lip for a moment. "I think instead it would've just left us stuck in the past. Forever those three invisible children. You deserve more, Georgia. We all do."

Georgia let out a slow breath, giving him the ghost of a smile.

Mason came to sit down on the other side of her, wrapping his arms around her shoulders. He nodded to Camden who did the same.

After a moment, Georgia let out a sniffy laugh. "You're crushing me."

Camden sat up on a smile, his phone dinging from his pocket. He stood as Mason grabbed a tissue and started blotting at Georgia's eyes as she let out a teary laugh.

Camden looked down at his text, everything inside him stopping cold.

CHAPTER THIRTY-NINE

Camden raised his fist, banging on the door. He heard footsteps rushing toward it and a moment later Scarlett flung the door open, her expression frantic.

"How long has she been gone?"

"Hours." She wrung her hands together. "I told her she could go out and play in the yard." She shook her head. "This is my fault. I got distracted with the damn wallpaper and then some designs I was working on and by the time I looked up, it was getting dark. I went out to call her in and it was like she'd just . . . disappeared." *Oh Jesus, Scarlett.* Her face crumpled and Camden stepped forward, taking her in his arms, but just as quickly letting go. Time was of the essence.

"We're going to find her." The alternative was too unthinkable.

She bobbed her head, swallowing, her face awash in misery. *Fuck fuck fuck!* He felt sick with worry, desperate to find that little girl. "I went out to the woods. She's always been so cautious. I couldn't imagine that she went farther than the tree line. I called and called . . ." A small sob came up her throat but she quickly gained control of herself. "I didn't dare go any deeper into the woods and get lost myself."

"Okay. Listen, we're going to have to form a search party."

"My God, Cam, this is exactly what happened to Kandace. She walked out into those woods and was never seen again."

"That's not going to happen." And yet even as he said it, a ball of lead formed in his gut. *Don't go there. Chances are she just wandered away and lost her bearings. She's out there right now, curled up under a tree, waiting to be rescued.*

Cam brought his phone from his pocket, but Scarlett grabbed his forearm, halting him. "Can we trust them, Cam? They might be behind Kandace's disappearance. What if—"

He ground his jaw. "We have no choice. We need lights, equipment. We need as many hands on deck as possible if we have any chance of finding her."

She bobbed her head again, her eyes filled with terror. He wanted to yell, to claw at something, to run out into the woods right this second and start screaming bloody murder for Haddie to please, *please* come home. And he knew what he was feeling was nothing compared to what Scarlett was experiencing.

He'd only dialed three digits when the door swung open. They both whipped around to see Haddie, disheveled and covered in dirt, the hem of her dress mostly detached and hanging down around her dusty calves, standing in the doorway.

Scarlett let out a strangled yelp, flying to where Haddie stood and going down on her knees in front of her. For a moment, Camden watched as Scarlett ran her hands over Haddie's face, over her head, down her shoulders and over her hips, her hands visibly shaking as she checked her child for injury.

"Mommy," the little girl said, and her voice was surprisingly strong and clear.

"Haddie, Haddie," Scarlett repeated over and over. She drew her into her arms, clinging to her for a moment before pulling back. "Where were you, baby? What happened? Did you get lost?"

Haddie glanced up at Camden, her gaze lingering on him for several beats, a wariness coming into her eyes before she looked back to her mother. "Bones, Mommy," she said breathlessly. "I found bones."

****

The sky was smudged with shades of pink and amber, the sun a pale ring in the morning sky when Camden pushed the vegetation aside, startled to see, not the rocky side of the cliff as he expected, but instead the opening of a cave. He leaned away, looking up to where Scarlett lay at the edge, peering over to where he'd carefully lowered himself, and then slowly, painstakingly made his way down the very narrow path to the ledge below.

Haddie sat several feet safely behind her mother, having directed them through the forest and to the hidden opening where she'd seen the bones. She'd been insistent on leading them back to this spot, but Scarlett had been even more insistent that they get her cleaned up and wait until daybreak to make the long trip through the woods. "There's an opening here," he called up to Scarlett. "Just like she said." How had she known? From the top, it looked just like any number of other small ledges on the basin of this deep canyon, bristly brush growing from a crack in the rock.

Scarlett nodded, her eyes wide. "Can you see them?" she called. "The bones?"

A noise distracted him and Cam turned, gazing in the opposite direction, the soft sound of what he thought was a drumbeat coming from nearby. He'd heard that sound before, remembered it from his childhood. He felt *watched.* His head turned in the other direction, and then slowly returned to Scarlett. "I'm going inside," he said.

"Please be careful."

He nodded once, and then moved the brush aside again, crawling into the cliffside cave. He saw the bones immediately, just as Haddie must have, dark red fabric, rotted and falling apart, only partially covering the skeleton. Camden swallowed, sadness welling up inside of him. It was a Lilith school uniform. She had been one of its girls.

Kandace, it had to be Kandace.

He crawled forward, kneeling next to her for a moment, bowing his head. He didn't know what to say, though he had this sense she was listening. "Thank you," was all he could manage. *For noticing us. For caring. For trying so hard to do the right thing.*

How had she died? He'd heard the staff whispering later. They'd said she escaped. Were they lying? Had her body been hidden here? Or had she somehow managed to find this opening as Haddie had? Did she crawl inside this space to hide? To die?

His gaze shifted as he looked around the cave, trying to spy the leather bag he'd taken for her, the one she was going to use to carry the files. Camden, walking on his knees, moved around her bones, giving as wide a berth as possible, cognizant that this was a crime scene, but also mindful that Kandace had given her life for the proof in that satchel, and he was not going to leave it behind if it was here. "Where did you put it?" he murmured? Or had it been taken from her?

He heard Scarlett call his name again, but crawled forward, the light growing dimmer the farther he ventured. He stopped for a moment, his eyes adjusting, Camden stopping short when he saw what lay at the far end of the cave.

Two more sets of bones. These ones far more ancient, any clothes they'd once worn, disintegrated to dust. He let out a harsh exhale. The bones appeared to belong to a man and a woman, turned toward each other, bodies close, fingers laced. They'd died in a lovers' embrace.

It couldn't be . . . *but it had to be.*

Taluta and her warrior?

The air left Camden and he turned back. He had to get out of this small space where so much death had occurred. He crawled past Kandace, pushing the brush aside, and pulling himself carefully from the cave, onto the small ledge.

"Thank God," he heard Scarlett say from above. "You worried me."

He walked up the path, his heart stopping each time he slid a bit, causing gravel and dirt to fall over the edge into the abyss below. He didn't even want to think about the fact that a tiny girl like Haddie had made this climb as well. He still couldn't fathom how or why she'd decided to look in the spot where so many bones waited to be found.

Scarlett had scooted back and Camden hoisted himself up and over the edge, pulling himself to his knees, and brushing the dust from his shirt. She moved forward, grasping him, holding on tightly, her heart beating as swiftly as his. He gripped her back and they stayed that way for a moment, clutching each other on the side of the cliff. When she pulled away, she asked softly, "It's her, isn't it?"

"I think so, yes."

Scarlett's shoulders dropped and she let out a soft moan. "My God. All this time."

Haddie approached, looking behind Camden where he'd sworn he'd heard the soft sound of a drum. Whatever animal or peculiarity of nature made that echoing rumble hadn't changed or gone away in the thirteen years he'd been gone. "You found them," Haddie stated.

Scarlett turned, gathering her daughter to her. "Yes, baby, we did." She took her face in her hands and leaned her forehead on hers. "I didn't realize that canyon was so deep."

She shivered visibly and her voice broke as she said, "You could have been badly hurt."

"I had to, Mommy," Haddie whispered. "I felt them there."

Camden frowned, wondering what the little girl meant by that, but Scarlett simply released a slow exhale, seemingly unsurprised by the comment, if not confused.

Camden walked forward, going down on one knee in front of Haddie. Scarlett glanced at him questioningly but moved aside. He smiled at the child. She looked like Scarlett, except for her coloring, and those wide, almond-shaped eyes that somehow seemed young and ancient all at once.

"Haddie, can I ask what you mean when you say you could feel them there?" He could sense Scarlett's eyes on him, and her wariness. It comforted him. She would step in and let him know if his questions were out of line, or if he risked scaring the little girl.

Haddie glanced at her mother and then back to Camden. "Some people . . . or places feel heavy like . . ." She scrunched her nose and looked off to the sky behind him. "Like a storm is coming, only on the inside. In my *bones.*"

He tried to understand, wanted to be the person he would have wanted if someone had questioned him when he was a child, trying to unearth things which seemed desperately inexplicable to his young mind. "Like . . . pressure?" he asked.

"Pressure?" she repeated.

"Yes, like when something heavy is pressing down on you."

She nodded, her eyes opening wide as if with excitement. "Yes, pressure. Heavy. Achy. Some people, some *places*, are so heavy, I can't move."

Camden watched her for a moment. He didn't know what to think of what she was saying, but he also wanted to get the information from her while she seemed inclined to give it. Perhaps it was the side of him that had worked law enforcement for several years now, or perhaps it was more that he had grown up escaping to these woods every chance he got. He'd sensed things here too, things he could never explain, things that made him feel strange. And he also wanted this little girl to trust him, Scarlett's daughter.

Maybe Haddie's words were simply the way a child would explain her fear and confusion. Things that were scary to her caused pressure to build inside. He thought about how Haddie had appeared frightened of him the first time he'd been in her presence. So frightened she'd wet herself. "Am I heavy, Haddie?" he asked quietly.

"No," she said softly, shaking her head. "You're light. Like my mommy. Only . . . *different*." She appeared to think for a moment. "She's light like air. You're light like fire."

She stared at him with a surety he'd never seen before in a child's eyes and tenderness filled him. Whatever she'd been afraid of that day, it hadn't been him. He felt inexplicably honored by her words. Humbled. *Relieved*. "Thank you, Haddie."

He stood and so did Scarlett. She took his hand in hers, squeezing it gently. "What do we do now?" she asked.

Camden looked behind him, squinting out into the canyon. "We call the authorities. We get as many people here from outside Farrow as we possibly can."

CHAPTER FORTY

$\mathcal{I}$t had been two days. Two days since the state and local authorities had come to lift Kandace's body out of the hidden cliffside cave, along with the ancient bones found deeper within, those believed to belong to an indigenous woman named Taluta, and her husband.

In that time, it had been verified that it was indeed Kandace Thompson's body that had long lain in wait, and that she had sustained two gunshot wounds, one to her shoulder blade, and the other, surely the fatal blow, to her upper torso. In those forty-eight hours, Scarlett's emotions had swung wildly between heartbreak and deep anger, knowing that her friend had died alone in a dark cave, and that somebody had known how and why all this time. *Murdered. At seventeen.* Her family had cast her away, and this was what happened. *Kandace, I'm so sorry . . . for what you went through . . . for how it ended. I'd give anything to go back in time and help you.* God, she ached.

Things were unraveling. Scarlett could feel it, and yet a sense of doom pervaded, sucking the air from the room. This town had long-held secrets. They weren't going to let go of them so easily.

She had to help ensure they didn't have a choice. *Light exposes darkness,* she reminded herself. *It always does.* And Kandace's remains might just be that beacon. Her friend deserved that justice, among many others.

Camden had spent the night with her, slipping from her bed and leaving Lilith House quietly in the pre-dawn hours so as not to wake Haddie in the next room. Scarlett continued to catch her daughter shooting Camden curious looks, despite his commitment to follow her lead into the dark forest upon her word alone, and despite that he'd listened so kindly, so intently, as she'd attempted to explain the Haddie-isms Scarlett was well acquainted with. But Scarlett figured that was normal. Her daughter had never once seen her with a man. It was a new, and possibly upsetting, experience for her. It would take time. And it would take smoother waters before Scarlett had the luxury of addressing her new relationship with her child. Now was simply not the time.

She smiled softly as she walked past the open bedroom door where Millie and Haddie were playing, Haddie teetering across the floor in an old pair of Scarlett's heels, Millie swinging one of Haddie's dress-up boas around her neck and saying something in a French accent that made Haddie giggle.

Scarlett's cell phone rang and she pulled it from her pocket, hurrying down the hall and sitting on a window seat overlooking the woods as she answered the unknown number. "Hello?"

"Scarlett? This is Dru Dorrington, formerly Thompson." She gave a small laugh. "I was a Kaufman and a Hadlock between the two."

Scarlett was glad the woman couldn't see her grimace. She'd been married twice more in the years since Kandace had gone to Lilith House and never come home? Didn't it seem right that one should run out of chances to obtain a license after failing at marriage half a dozen times or more? "Thank you so much for getting back to me, Mrs. Dorrington. I really . . . I just wanted to give my deepest condolences."

"Call me Dru, darling. And thank you. I'm so glad you called. I'm just stunned. I don't know how to feel. Murdered. My Kandace." She paused. "I can't say it was a shock to learn she'd run away, nor a shock to learn she'd got mixed up in something ugly that cost her life. But . . . there's relief too. I can bury her now. Lord knows, I'm more experienced buying white dresses than black, but I'll have to stretch my wings." She gave a short laugh that felt like a needle pricking Scarlett's heart.

The woman hadn't changed. She didn't need to imagine what it might have been like to be raised by a such a mother. She knew very well from Kandace. *Heartbreaking.* "I can't imagine what you've been through not having any answers."

"Well," she sighed. "I imagine you can. You were her friend too. She cared very much for you, in case you didn't know."

"Thank you, Mrs.— Dru."

"I'd given her one final chance. All this time, I imagined she just decided not to take it. I'd resigned myself to the fact that we would never know how she got caught up in foul play. Farrow's sheriff implied drugs. I . . . well, I had no reason to disagree. Kandace . . . she made bad choices."

Scarlett's skin felt suddenly icy. She didn't think drugs were the reason Kandi had been killed, but there still wasn't any proof. And *whatever* choices Kandace might have made, she didn't deserve to be murdered. All she could do was wait and hope that those not involved in the crime would uncover *something.* In any case, it was clear to her that this would be the last time she spoke to Dru . . . she'd already forgotten her last name, which was well enough. Why use brain space for something that would inevitably change in the very near future?

"She was smart and vibrant," Scarlett said. "She was stronger than she ever knew." *Than* you *ever knew.* "And she had her whole life in front of her. Someone should be punished." And if she had even one word to say about it, someone *would.* Scarlett brought one knee up and rested her arm on it as the sun shifted shades, lemon to gold.

"Yes, of course," Dru said dismissively. Scarlett pictured the incredibly beautiful woman flipping her hand in the air like she remembered her doing. "Oh, one other thing," Dru continued. "The medical examiner called this morning and well, there's no need to make this public, but . . . as her friend, I think you should know."

"What is it?"

"He believes Kandace gave birth at some point."

"Gave birth?" she asked, confusion clear in her tone.

"Yes. Something about marks on the pelvic bone. It wasn't just that she was pregnant, but that she experienced a birth. He can't pinpoint the timing, just that."

Scarlett's mind spun. "How could that be?"

"Well, that's why I thought I'd tell you. It couldn't have been while she was at the school. They would have contacted me. I'm assuming they would have sent her home immediately. They were . . . very religious. So it had to be before she went there. I admit there were long periods of time I didn't see my daughter. She'd run away . . . then come back, get into trouble . . . her life . . . well . . ." She sighed. "Anyway, did she ever say anything to you about a pregnancy?"

"No," Scarlett answered. "But you know, we were out of touch for long periods sometimes too."

"Can you imagine," Dru went on, "that somewhere out there, I might have a grandchild, and I'll never know him or her?"

Scarlett wasn't sure what to say to that. Her mind was spinning too fast to string her thoughts together. She managed to chat with Dru for a few more minutes, the older woman promising to send Scarlett the funeral information as soon as Kandace's body was released. Scarlett hung up, staring blindly out at the forest, the forest Kandace had once run toward, her life slipping tenuously through the hands of time whether she knew it at that moment or not.

Kandace had given birth? It couldn't have been in the cave. No tiny bones were found. And if an animal had carried the baby away, surely Kandace's own bones would have been at least partially disturbed too. No, from the descriptions of the three sets of bones in that small area, the dead had lay completely undisturbed.

Until Haddie had discovered them . . . *felt them there.*

Could Kandace have given birth prior to being sent to Lilith House? It was possible, she supposed, but she also knew that one of the reasons Kandace's life had spiraled the way it had was because of drug use. Kandace didn't make the best choices for herself, Dru had been right about that despite the casual, blameless way she'd spoken of it, but try as she might, Scarlett just couldn't see the girl she'd known partying on without any care for the innocent life she carried.

Maybe you didn't know her as well as you think, Scarlett. You were only fifteen the last time you saw her. You'd drifted apart.

Yes, all true. And *still*, the doubt persisted.

So if she didn't give birth before she came to Lilith House, and if she didn't give birth in that cave, then could she have had a child under this very roof? Scarlett brought her arms around herself, a sudden chill wafting across her skin.

Other girls had given birth at Lilith House. Three of them, at least.

She looked around at the peeling walls. "What happened here?" she whispered.

Scarlett wandered down the hall, pulled by the sound of Haddie giggling. Her lips tipped as she came to the doorway where the girls were still playing. Millie was dancing in front of the window, using a ray of sun as a spotlight just as she and Kandace had once done.

She was laughing, her dimple flashing, eyes alight with unabashed joy. Scarlett smiled softly. In that moment, Millie reminded her so much of Kandi—the way she moved, the way she threw her head back—but that was possibly because she'd been in Scarlett's thoughts for the last few days. She was seeing things she wanted to see. Clinging to a friend who had lost her way. *Then lost her life.*

Millie spun around again, tipped her head to the side, and winked at Haddie, laughing.

Scarlett's heart stalled.

Oh my God.

It can't be. She *can't be* . . .

Scarlett *knew* that smile. It flashed in front of her and in her *memory* as well. The glimpse of a soul she'd once known and loved. It *wasn't* just wishful thinking, recalling a face she'd missed for years.

No, that effervescent, enthralling grin . . .

It was Kandace's smile.

CHAPTER FORTY-ONE

Thirteen Years Ago

Camden whipped around, letting out a slow breath when he saw it was her. "Hey," Kandace said.

Camden lowered the small animal in his hands to the ground, his expression bleak. "Hi," he said quietly.

Kandace stepped closer, peering down at the small thing he'd placed on the forest floor. A baby bird. "Is it—?"

"Yes. It was too late." Camden cast his eyes downward as though in apology for not saving one of God's creatures.

"You can't save every baby animal you find," she said. He'd told her it was like the baby animals came to him, but she knew that couldn't be the case. Injured animals could no more seek him, nor anyone, out than they could call an emergency vet. It was just nature, harsh and unforgiving to the weakest among its inhabitants. And that happened to be the young and the helpless. Kandace was pretty sure injured baby animals could be found everywhere—for anyone—if they took the time to look. Camden, little dreamboat that he was, thought the animals were delivered straight to him because he took immediate responsibility for them. *Sweet, sweet kid.*

"I know," he said, but he didn't appear to be convinced of his own words. Kandace took a seat on a low rock next to the one on which Camden sat, the dead baby bird lying at his feet. The forest grew a smidge brighter as the sun rose higher in the sky. She squinted toward the row of trees that separated the forest from the Lilith House grounds, her baby giving a strong kick from within. Kandace pulled her uniform away from her body as much as possible. She didn't want Camden to know this secret. There was no reason.

It was her turn to take responsibility for the innocent.

"You shouldn't risk this," he said after a moment. "Coming out here. You should stop. They'll catch you eventually."

"I know." And she did. The risk she was taking was monumental. Yes, there was no reason for him to know about the baby, but she did need his help for something else. He was the only one she believed she could trust. "I won't be coming out here anymore. I'm going to leave. It's time."

Dreamboat's head came up, lips parting, but for a moment he simply blinked at her. "What?"

"I have to." Kandace squinted off behind him for a moment before meeting his eyes. "I have proof," she told him. "I think they did something to your mother, to Georgia's mother, and to Mason's. I don't think they left of their own will."

He blinked again, his forehead creasing as he shook his head. "Why?"

"I don't know exactly, but with what I have, there will be an investigation. People will be questioned. You'll be taken away from Lilith House."

With those words his gaze snapped to hers, but what she was telling him seemed to have rendered him mute. "Listen, Dreamboat, you know they're abusing us here. I believe they abused your mother too."

He looked down, two spots appearing high on his cheekbones. He looked ashamed and Kandace wondered if he remembered being in the room with her as she was being raped or not. Her own shame spiraled inside her. If he didn't . . . she preferred to leave it that way. When she spoke next, she gentled her voice. "I think the town is in on it, or at least its officials. They have to be. And they're getting away with it." She reached out and put her hand on top of his where it lay on his knee. His gaze went to it, thick eyelashes creating dark crescent moons on his cheeks. She heard movement somewhere nearby, the snap of a twig or the crunch of a leaf and though they both looked in the same direction from which it'd come, each looked away after a moment of silence.

For several minutes he didn't say a thing. He appeared deeply conflicted. When he looked up at her, she saw that there wasn't only uncertainty in his gaze, but fear. "I found an old trunk in the basement," he said.

"A trunk?" she asked, confused.

He nodded. "It was behind a portion of wall in one of the smaller storage areas. I was . . . looking for other hidden panels like the ones that lead to the crawl spaces and I found it."

"Okay," she said, her brow dipping.

He swallowed and then he told her about what he'd found inside it. He told her the story of Taluta and Narcisa and the testimonies they'd left in a hidden trunk behind a secret wall.

"Holy God," she breathed. "Ms. Wykes . . . she says a demon native roams these woods."

He paused, seeming to consider what he was about to say. "I've heard the drums," he whispered, shaking his head. "I don't know what it is, but I've seen the shadow of . . . something." His eyes bored into her. "And if he seeks vengeance, he has a right to it."

Kandace shivered, her eyes moving to the dark forest beyond.

"I know what you're talking about," he said, grabbing her attention once again. "The abuse you mentioned. I know what they do at Lilith House." He looked down again, embarrassment filling his handsome young face. "They tell us it's God's will and that fallen ones must be redeemed."

Redeemed? Was that what they called rape and torture these days?

"But . . ." he said, shaking his head. "I read Taluta's story, and Narcisa's and . . . we read the Bible, God's word . . ." His brow dipped, his frown deepening as he rubbed at his temple. "The things written in the Bible don't match up with what they tell us God desires. It's like . . . they got it all wrong. It's like, they don't understand."

Oh, Dreamboat.

"They did," she whispered. "They did get it all wrong." And so had she. She'd gotten it all wrong too. Her baby kicked again and she adjusted her body to hide the movement of her midsection. She'd thought she was strong, brave, *invincible,* but she'd been no such thing. Recently, as she'd lain in bed at night, she tried to figure out the exact moment when everything went wrong. The hour that, if she'd made a different choice, she wouldn't have ended up where she was. And just the night before, she had. It was her mother's sixth wedding day, when the judge had become her stepfather. She'd been upset, angry, and so she'd decided to go to a party with a guy she knew was bad news in every sense of the phrase. She hadn't cared. That day, she relished the idea of letting him bring her down in whatever way he might. Scarlett had called her as she was heading out the door— she'd known it was her mother's wedding day and she'd called to see how Kandace was doing. Whatever she'd heard in her voice, whatever she'd sensed about Kandace's mood, she'd asked her to come over and visit.

But visiting Scarlett was too safe and offered no promise of self-destruction. And so, she'd said no. She'd said no, and that night she'd tried cocaine for the first time, which led to theft and rampant promiscuity and other behaviors she didn't want to think about at the moment. That was the night she'd veered crazily off course.

That was the hour it all went wrong.

But if she'd said yes to Scarlett . . . if she'd gone to her instead of to that party . . . she would have left better, not worse. Because Scarlett had loved her. Not because she was family. Not because she had to. No, she'd loved her as a friend, without strings or obligation. She'd found her worthy. She'd hoped Kandace would see in herself what Scarlett had seen in her.

When she escaped, she was going to tell Scarlett that her words had carried her through so much. She was going to try to be the person Scarlett believed she could be. In the meantime, Kandace was going to hold on to that moment like a promise.

They had both been quiet for the last few minutes, each lost in his and her own thoughts. When Kandace looked up at him, she smiled. In some inexplicable way, he reminded her of Scarlett. They both had the same deeply sensitive heart, the same steady presence, the same overt *trustworthiness.* "I've got this friend, Dreamboat, and she's just your age. If I can arrange it, I'm going to make sure you meet. I think you'd get along. She's brave like you. I *act* brave, but it's a show. You and this friend of mine? You're the real deal."

He offered her a small, confused smile, but it quickly dwindled. "You're brave too, Kandace. What do you need me to do to help you escape?"

CHAPTER FORTY-TWO

$\mathcal{S}$carlett pulled up in front of Millie's house, getting out of the car and beginning to walk toward the front door when she spotted the woman pushing a stroller toward her on the opposite side of the sidewalk. The woman smiled and Scarlett looked closer, realizing that the stroller she was pushing was for a special needs child, and the boy sitting in it—who looked to be a pre-teen—was clearly disabled.

"If you're going to visit Vicky Schmidt, she won't be home. She attends a church meeting every Thursday at five. We usually take our walk a little earlier and we see her leaving." She smiled, ruffling the boy's hair. He craned his neck, his mouth opening as he gazed at his mother with clear adoration.

"Oh, thank you," Scarlett said, changing direction and walking toward her. "Do you, by chance, live in the blue house a few blocks over?"

"Yes. Do I know you?"

"No. I'm Scarlett Lattimore. We, um, moved to town very recently. Millie babysits my daughter, Haddie, and she mentioned you."

"Welcome to town. I'm Dotty and this is Roger."

Scarlett smiled down at the boy whose arms were folded inward, head slanted, tongue protruding through the same open-mouthed smile. He was obviously non-verbal. "Hi, Roger." When she looked at his mother, she said, "I just wanted to say I'm sorry in person. Millie told me Haddie made Roger scream. I don't know what came over my daughter that would cause her to upset him like that. She's usually kind and very accepting—"

"Oh, Ms. Lattimore." Dotty laughed, shaking her head. "I don't think Millie understood. Haddie didn't upset Roger." She ran a hand over her son's brown hair again. "He does that when he's excited or . . . overcome with happiness." Her smile widened. "It's loud, and can be disconcerting if you don't know him well, but it's joyful. Haddie didn't hurt him. Far from it. Whatever your daughter said made him overwhelmingly happy."

Scarlett blinked in stunned wonder, her spirit lifting to hear what this mother was telling her. "Oh, I see." She let out a breath, putting her hand over her heart. "I can't tell you how relieved that makes me feel." *Oh, Haddie, I'm sorry I doubted you. Again.*

Dotty gave her another grin. "I'd like to know what it was Haddie said so we can repeat it. Daily. He so rarely has a reaction like that. It was precious to me." She gazed down at her child. "Roger is a handful some days, but he's a gift." She met Scarlett's eyes. "He was taken, you know, a few days after his birth." She swallowed, obviously reliving the memory.

"Taken?" Scarlett whispered.

"By a wild animal. I was napping and my husband was with him in our backyard. They'd said he needed sunlight . . . for his jaundice. He only turned away for a moment, but when he turned back, Roger was gone. The sheriff never could quite figure out what it was. There were no tracks . . . nothing. But . . . there had been other abductions like it in Farrow. Animals take babies sometimes, you know, just like they take cats and small dogs. Especially when they're hungry."

"Oh my God," Scarlett said, putting her hand over her heart to imagine the horror of a moment like that for a new mother. The pictures that must have come to mind. The absolute torture she must have experienced.

"But he was found. Obviously."

Dotty bobbed her head. "Yes. A hunter out near Lilith House heard an infant wailing. When he investigated, he found Roger, cold but unharmed in the little shed behind the property. It was like God Himself had delivered him to safety." Her gaze became distant. "Like I said, there had been animal abductions before, but they seemed to stop after that." Her eyes came back into focus and she looked at Scarlett, smiling. "Anyway," she said, "despite the challenges, I don't take a moment for granted."

"No, of course not," Scarlett murmured, gazing at the boy.

A wild animal took him. She could believe in the possibility.

But if so, what kind of creature *returned* him?

Maybe Dotty didn't care. She had her boy back and that was all that mattered. Scarlett mustered a smile for her. "I'll have to ask Haddie what she said to Roger so I can let you know. It was so nice to meet you both."

"Yes, I'd love that. And likewise. See you around town."

Scarlett turned, watching as Dotty pushed her son's modified stroller away, returning to her car. She took a moment to shake off the unsettled feeling that crawled under her skin at the mere *thought* of a baby being taken by a wild animal. But she couldn't ponder on that, not now when there were critical and urgent questions that needed to be asked.

Whatever your daughter said made him overwhelmingly happy.

Scarlett took a moment to let herself enjoy the relief flowing through her spirit on *that* front, at least. Haddie hadn't been cruel. On the contrary, she'd brought the boy joy. She'd said something that elicited such a strong reaction from him, he hadn't been able to contain his elation.

Scarlett started her car. The worry that clouded her mind returned as she pictured Millie in her mind, recalled the moment she'd stood watching her from the hall, the surety that had filled her heart.

How could it be true though? *How?*

You might be imagining things, Scarlett.

Yes, it'd been an overwhelming few days. Her mind could very well be playing tricks on her. She remembered losing her dad when she was just a little girl. She remembered how after his death, she saw him everywhere. In the man walking on the sidewalk as their car drove by. In the profile of the cashier at the grocery store right before he fully turned her way. She suspected it was a common phenomenon when you lost a person. And for all intents and purposes, she had just experienced the loss of Kandi all over again. But she had to find out if there was any merit to the feeling that had gripped her just an hour before. She had to speak to Millie's mother. Immediately. This could not wait. She owed it to Kandi.

Scarlett pulled up at the church, her heart sinking when she noticed that there were only a few cars in the lot, Vicky's not one of them. She glanced at the clock on her dashboard. Six thirty-seven. *Damn.* If the meeting had lasted an hour, then everyone, including Vicky, would be gone by now. She got out of her car, walking toward the building. Likely, she'd passed Vicky as she headed for home, and Scarlett would have to drive back to her house if she wanted to speak with her. But first, she'd check inside the building just to make sure.

She pulled the green door open, the scent of incense meeting her nose, the cool solemnity that all churches seemed to hold greeting her. At first, she thought the room was empty, but then she spotted a woman sitting in one of the pews, head bent forward in prayer. Just as Scarlett noticed her, the woman turned toward her. Vicky Schmidt.

A look of surprise came over Vicky's face as she stood, turning toward Scarlett.

"I didn't see your car in the lot," Scarlett said as she approached.

Vicky shook her head. "I got a ride with Sister Madge. My car's in the shop." Her brow dipped. "Is Millie okay?"

"Yes. Millie is fine. No, she's more than fine, Vicky. She's so lovely, and Haddie is so lucky to have her caring for her."

"Oh, well. Thank you. She's always been a happy child. Highly spirited, if you know what I mean."

Highly spirited. Like her mother? A lump formed in Scarlett's throat and she swallowed around it.

"I came to ask you something and"—she bit her lip, glancing to the side—"I understand that this might sound odd and . . . personal, but . . . I have to know."

Vicky frowned. "Okay."

"Millie said you and your late husband had her later in life. But . . . was she actually adopted?"

Vicky's gaze flickered with surprise, two spots of color rising in her cheeks. "I'm sorry?" she asked, her voice cracking. "Whatever gave you that idea?"

Scarlett came closer, watching Vicky's face. "Millie looks very much like someone I once knew. The body they found in the woods two days ago, Kandace Thompson? She delivered a baby before she died." She paused, her voice lowering to a mere whisper. "I'm wondering if that baby was Millie."

Vicky let out a small gasp, sinking down into the pew. Scarlett's heartbeat quickened as she came around the bench to sit next to the woman.

Vicky gripped the back of the pew in front of her. For several weighty moments, she stared up at Christ, hanging on the crucifix at the front of the church. "We tried so hard to have a baby," she finally whispered brokenly.

Scarlett stilled, a silent moan rising inside. She'd been *right. Oh, Kandi, oh my God, what happened?*

"Year after year after year. I wondered what I was being punished for." She looked down, her hands twisting in her lap. "Then one winter this tiny baby was left on our porch, the umbilical cord still attached." She looked at Scarlett, tears glittering in her eyes. "Like an answer to our prayers." She looked down again, her voice growing stronger. "I knew it belonged to one of those girls. It must. And I knew what happened to children born at Lilith House. But that tiny, tiny baby, she appeared perfect. No mark of sin."

Horror settled in Scarlett's stomach, Camden's story rushing through her mind.

"Someone had taken her from there, they'd left her on our doorstep rather than leaving her in the woods or keeping her hidden behind its walls."

Scarlett fisted her hands, her nails digging into the tender flesh of her palms. *They'd known. They'd all known.*

"I stayed in for months and when I came out, I had the baby. She was still so very small. No one doubted she was a newborn. I told them all we were too nervous to tell of my pregnancy after our many losses. My husband went along with it, God rest his soul." She did the sign of the cross. "He was a decent man."

Scarlett's mind raced, and acid burned her throat. That phrase . . . *he was a decent man.* She'd heard it before in connection with Mr. Schmidt. She'd read it in Narcisa's letter: *Mr. Schmidt tried to save my baby. He has a spark of decency in him, but the others are too powerful.*

Had Narcisa, once a midwife, delivered Kandi's baby as she lay dying? And then—very old herself and unable to care for a newborn—delivered it to the one decent person she knew of in Farrow? A small sound came up Scarlett's throat, born of shock and horror. "Narcisa," Scarlett breathed.

Vicky's gaze darted to her and then away. "I suspect, yes. I'd secretly bought oils and herbs for fertility from her. The church wouldn't have supported that sort of medicine, but I did it anyway. I was desperate, so I sinned." The last words emerged as a mere croak, her cheeks coloring in shame.

"We have to tell, Vicky." She reached out, putting her hand on hers where it rested on the pew. Her skin was cold and papery. "Millie, she has family, people who deserve to know she exists." *That Kandace lived on in the eyes of her child.*

Vicky looked down where Scarlett's hand covered hers. "Yes. They should know. Amelia's people. I'm sick." She looked back up, her eyes on Christ again. "I have cancer. Perhaps I've been punished after all. Perhaps we all have."

A noise sounded and Scarlett looked up to see Sister Madge standing near a side door. Her expression was somber, eyes filled with sadness as she looked at Vicky. "I told her," she said to Sister Madge.

The old nun approached, such blatant sorrow in her eyes that Scarlett's chest squeezed. "Yes, dear. You had to. You saved that little girl. You did right by her, and now you must do right by her again. We all must repent for the roles we played."

Scarlett watched the nun, a breath of relief ghosting from her lips. Although her overwhelming emotion at the moment was shock, she also felt a modicum of breathless triumph. *Hope.* Millie, Kandi's daughter, could very well be the key to bringing the truth to light. And that truth involved Camden.

"I believe, Victoria, that we must call the police. Immediately. All of this, it's gone on far too long." She turned her head, looking at Jesus as Vicky had done, joining her hands in prayer. "Forgive us, Father," she whispered mournfully. "Oh, please forgive us."

Vicky was weeping quietly now, her head hung. "Come, dear," she said to Scarlett. "Let us leave Vicky to her grief. I'll come back and drive her home after we've made the call. I believe it's best that we do not contact the sheriff." Her face registered conflict. She knew he was part of the guild. She knew he was corrupt.

Scarlett pulled her cell phone from her pocket. "We can use my phone."

"I'm afraid the church doesn't have wireless service," she said, a sad smile coming over her face. "Oh, we're desperately out of touch, aren't we?" She sighed. "I have the number for the state police in my office. We can call from there. You must tell the police what you know about your friend. Perhaps a DNA test . . ." She frowned. "Oh, dear, it's going to hurt so many people." Still, she turned and began moving toward the door. Scarlett stood, following. She appreciated that the old woman was going to do the right thing, despite that she had played a part in the town's corruption. At the very least, she'd aided and abetted with her silence alone. Despite her words, and despite Scarlett's hope that she was being truthful, she walked a few paces behind the old woman, as frail as a bent tree branch. She was far too feeble to do anything physically to Scarlett, but she wasn't going to give her the element of surprise should she try.

She looked back, offering Scarlett the glimmer of a smile. "I drove out to Lilith House just a little bit ago, to offer my condolences on your friend, and see if there was anything the church could do to aid in your comfort."

"Oh," Scarlett frowned. "We must have just missed each other. Millie was there," she said. "Did you see her?"

"No, just that pretty little girl of yours." She opened the door to her office and Scarlett left it open wide. Sister Madge sat behind her desk and took out an old-fashioned phone book that appeared to be for the state of California, flipping through the pages. There was a Saran Wrap covered plate of cake bites on the edge of the desk and Sister Madge used one hand to push them toward Scarlett. "For the youth group sleepover tonight. I suppose I'll have to cancel it now . . ." She unwrapped a corner. "Those girls do love their sweets. Have one. Something sweet to temper the sour. A comfort for the soul." She smiled, sad and wistful. "You know better than anyone how food ministers, don't you, dear?"

Yes, Scarlett liked to think she did. *Something sweet to temper the sour.* Of course, in this case, *sour* seemed to be an understatement. There was a lump in her throat. She didn't really want a bite of cake, but for the sake of politeness, when the old woman went back to flipping through the phone book, looking for the state police number, Scarlett took one small cake, placing it in her mouth and chewing slowly.

It might have been good. Scarlett was so preoccupied by what she was going to say to the police, to Camden when she got hold of him, that she didn't even register anything about the sugary treat.

Cam. Kandi. So many possibilities swirled through her mind. The state police would come back. They'd question Vicky further. Would they run a DNA test on Millie? Her thoughts felt strange. Suddenly disconnected. She massaged her temple.

"Vicky overheard Haddie telling Amelia about the horned beast she follows through the woods."

"What?" she asked, frowning when her words came out slurred. The old nun wavered in front of her and she shook her head.

"Mm." Sister Madge licked her finger slowly and then used it to flip another page, her gaze trained on Scarlett. "She's seen him. She knows where he is. They'll be after her now."

After her? A fog descended and she felt suddenly overcome with wooziness. *Haddie? After Haddie?* Sister Madge replaced the phone in its cradle, leaning in and staring at her. Scarlett gripped the side of the desk, the room going blurry.

Sister Madge stood, walking around the desk slowly. Scarlett attempted to rise, but her legs buckled from under her. The nun came to stand above her, her face stark white and wobbly. "All you vile, fallen women," she heard her mutter.

Oh God, oh no. They'll take Millie. They'll hurt Haddie. It was her final thought before Scarlett floated away.

CHAPTER FORTY-THREE

$\mathcal{S}$carlett moaned, attempting to lift her head as the world slowly came back into focus. She tried to move her hands but they were tied behind her back. Fear dripped down her spine. The fog cleared minutely and she pulled herself up with effort, scooting backward against whatever was directly behind her, pressing into her back uncomfortably.

She opened her eyes, the world shifting into focus. She was in a stark, monastic bedroom, a bed against one wall with a large, metal crucifix hanging above it, a dresser on the opposite wall, devoid of any knickknacks or personal items.

A tabby cat sat on the windowsill casually licking its paws.

Scarlett gave her hands another tug, glancing behind to see that she was tied to a silver radiator.

Sister Madge's bedroom down the short hall from the office where she last remembered sitting. It *had* to be. There was no way that frail old woman could have dragged her any farther than this. Panic howled through her. She'd drugged her. With a cake bite meant for the . . . what had she said? *Youth group?* Disbelief and sickness welled up inside of her and her panic increased. She pulled harder at whatever was holding her hands to the radiator, grunting with the effort. Her limbs still felt heavy, weighted.

The radiator rattled, tipping slightly back and forth but it didn't give. Her brain cleared a little more and she turned her head around, looking for something, *anything,* that she could use to get free.

There was nothing. She stilled for a moment, listening, trying to ascertain if Sister Madge was still in the house. When she didn't hear anything, she began yelling. "Help! Help!" over and over until her voice gave, her throat raw and painful.

Tears came to her eyes and for a moment she let the terror overwhelm her. They were going to hurt Millie. They were going to hurt Haddie. *Oh God. Oh God. Are they already there? Do they have the girls?*

You have to get free, Scarlett. You have to warn them. If you don't, there's no telling what they'll do. Not just to them, but to you.

Where do you think Sister Madge went? To drive Vicky home? Yes, but then she'd head straight to get someone better equipped to deal with you. Or your body . . . once you're dead.

They'd have to kill her now. They would have no choice. Her time was ticking.

Scarlett rocked the radiator with her hands again, using every ounce of strength she could muster to pull and push, pull and push, faster and faster, using the appliance's weight against it. She cried out, her shoulder throbbing each time it wrenched farther from her body. Tears streaked down her face and she let out a yell of defeat and pain, bringing the radiator to a halt.

A light scratching sound came from behind a door next to the dresser and Scarlett stilled, her breath catching as a shadow moved beneath the frame. The scratching came again, a soft papery-sounding laugh as the doorknob began to slowly turn.

Scarlett pressed herself into the radiator, turning her face as though awaiting a blow. The door clicked open, swinging inward slowly. Something only partially human lay on its stomach on the floor, up on its forearms, its grotesquely burned face staring at Scarlett, mouth turning upward in a hideously wicked smile. It had a pair of sharp, silver shears in its disfigured hand. Scarlett's whole body jolted, fear pinging over every nerve. She let out a strangled sound of terror, pulling on the radiator again, then pushing, creating the same rhythm she'd tried before, only this time more powerful, more intense, all the strength of her revulsion and horror behind her.

The thing she thought had once been human began crawling toward her, its piercing golden eyes wide and unblinking. "We have rules here," it said in a scratchy voice, the shears hitting the floor heavily with each drag forward. Scarlett pulled and pushed at the radiator with all her might. It smacked into her brutally as it came forward and jerked her shoulder backward relentlessly as it rocked back. Her upper body screamed in agony. "You have not been granted permission to leave. She said I should stop you if you tried to get free."

The thing was a woman, Scarlett could see that now. Its snowy-white hair patchy and stringy, attached only in clumps to the burned and mottled skin of her scalp. She dragged herself toward Scarlett, and Scarlett let out panting yelps of pain as the radiator clunked and loosened. Back, forth, back, forth.

She cried out, her shoulder at risk of coming out of its socket.

Haddie. Haddie. I won't let them hurt you. At the thought of her daughter, she upped her effort, gritting her teeth, pulling and then pushing with all her might, her entire body slamming and rocking along with the loosening radiator. *HaddieHaddieHaddieHaddie.*

The burned woman was almost to her, reaching, her mouth stretched open, revealing small yellow teeth. Her legs ended at the knee, her calves and feet burned away.

With a roar of pain and one last burst of all the strength she had in her still-drugged body, every molecule of herself infused with the fierce love she had for her baby girl, she wrenched her shoulder out of its socket, the radiator breaking free from the floor and crashing heavily against the wall.

The burned woman reached her, grabbing her ankles, lifting the shears and bringing them down on the top of her foot. The shears sunk into her flesh, and then the woman tore them out, raising them again.

With a scream of pain, Scarlett pulled her foot back, blood flowing from the wound as she attempted to stand. The woman grabbed her ankle again, twisting it so that Scarlett smacked back down to the floor before she could get her bearings enough to stand.

"We started that school," the burned woman said. "We reformed those girls!" She brought the shears down again, stabbing into Scarlett's calf. Scarlett screamed, then wrenched her leg away just as the woman pulled the shears out of her flesh again. Scarlett tried to push herself up with one arm, her other hanging uselessly by her side, but couldn't get enough leverage to do so.

Instead she pulled herself backward, trying again to stand while the woman dragged herself up Scarlett's legs. She was only half a person, old and horrifically injured, but she seemingly had the strength of ten men. Scarlett cried out, her head falling backward as she hit the side of the bed so hard the wall behind it shook and the crucifix fell, landing on the mattress above.

"When the lightning strike hit, I locked those doors and Jasper blocked them. He was a faithful servant." She pulled herself farther up Scarlett's body as Scarlett writhed and fought, attempting to kick her weighted legs from beneath the woman's body, delivering blow after blow to her head with her one good arm. The woman's face was almost directly over hers now and Scarlett could see the evil in her golden eyes, smell the brimstone on her breath. She reached blindly above, her fingers brushing the cold metal of the crucifix. "The Lord wanted them *all* to burn," she yelled, spittle flying from her mouth. "But he spared me! He spared me for my righteousness!"

403

This woman, this living demon, hadn't been spared from anything. She'd been made to suffer, to go slowly insane if she hadn't been halfway there already, locked away in some dark corner. It hadn't been a lightning strike that started that fire. Or if it had been, it was brutal human evil, and *only* that, that had caused the subsequent deaths. Scarlett's fingers grasped metal, curling around one slim edge of the cross from which Jesus hung.

The woman raised the shears again, her mouth opening in an unholy scream, exposed tendons stretching, but Scarlett brought the crucifix down, arcing it toward her back, the long metal spike of the vertical portion of the cross spearing through her skin and coming out the other side of her chest right where her shriveled heart lay.

The woman's eyes widened, her head snapping back, arm frozen above. The shears dropped to the carpet next to Scarlett's head with a soft thud and the woman's body went limp.

With a cry of horror, Scarlett pushed her off, suddenly as light as a bag of bones. She crumpled to the carpet, and shaking, Scarlett pulled herself to her feet. She wobbled before righting herself, a river of blood trailing behind her as she gripped her elbow in her hand, holding her dislocated shoulder still as she limped out to the office.

She picked up the phone, but there was no signal. Throwing it back down, she fled for the door, turning the lock, and flying outside, tripping down the stairs, but catching herself before she fell. *Haddie. Haddie. I'm coming.*

Scarlett's breath came in sharp pants as she ran from the back of the church to the parking lot, glancing behind her every few steps, half-expecting that shriveled monstrous thing to come rushing at her like a flying ghoul. She glanced at the church door, but no, she could trust no one here. *I should have known. I should have known.*

Her car key was in her pocket. Thank the Lord above. She pulled it out, her hands shaking as she put it in the ignition, and screeched out of the lot.

She didn't remember much of the drive, only that she prayed the whole way there. When she burst through the front door of Lilith House, she almost ran smack dab into Mason. His eyes went wider than they'd been, the look on his face turning her blood to ice in her veins.

His gaze moved from her foot to her bloody clothes to her face. "Oh my God, Scarlett. What—"

"Haddie!" she screamed.

"Scarlett!" Mason said. "It took them."

She whirled toward him, her heart hammering. "Who? Who took them?"

He grabbed his head. "I don't know what it was. My crew had just left. I thought it was one of them coming back for something." He shook his head, his expression haunted. "I only saw its shadow. It took Millie and Haddie. It had horns. Jesus, it had horns. But it was *walking*." He shook his head as though trying to wake from a bad dream.

Terror zigzagged down Scarlett's back. "When?"

"Just now. Right before you got here. I tried to call Cam, but he's not answering. I don't know whether to call the sheriff."

"Don't call the sheriff. Call the state police. Tell them there's been a kidnapping. And keep trying Cam. I need you to stay here and keep calling Cam. As soon as you get hold of him, tell him where I am. Please, Mason, I need you to do that. I'm going after them."

Mason grabbed her as she began to turn. "No, Scarlett, you don't know what that thing is! And you're hurt—"

"I'm okay. It has my girl, Mason."

Mason let go of her, his hand dropping. Scarlett tore the hem of her long shirt with one quick yank, taking it in her teeth and ripping that in half and wrapping it around her bloody calf and tucking in the end, and then doing the same to her still oozing foot. With a grunt of pain, she pushed her feet into the tennis shoes that were sitting by the door. "It has my girl," she repeated to Mason, and then Scarlett turned and she ran as fast as her injured foot would carry her, heading for the woods.

CHAPTER FORTY-FOUR

Thirteen Years Ago

$\mathcal{T}$he guild was on its way. She'd walked by the kitchen and smelled the unmistakable scent of cake baking. Her stomach rolled. Who would have ever guessed that the smell of dessert would trigger her heart to race as a feeling of dread filled her chest?

She forced herself to calm. This was her chance, as there might not be another. She'd gotten lucky their last few visits and hadn't been chosen, but her luck would eventually run out. Possibly tonight. And though she might have been able to hide her rounded stomach before in the dim lighting while lying on her back, there was no hiding it now.

No, tonight was the night. It had to be.

Kandace walked stoically to her room, Aurora shooting her a worried look as she entered. "The guild is here," she

407

said, looking pointedly at Kandace's stomach, still hidden beneath the roomy, square uniform, and the oversized black sweaters they'd been given now that the temperature had dropped.

"I know," she said. She hadn't told Aurora about what the guild was doing when they came to "bless" the girls of Lilith House. It was better for Aurora that she didn't know. But Aurora, friend that she was, worried about someone discovering Kandace's secret, and the more people who saw her, the more likely one of them would be extra observant.

She walked to Aurora and grasped her hands. "It's going to be fine. And remember, *whatever* happens, do not worry."

Aurora's gaze held to hers as she searched her eyes for several seconds. Finally, she nodded. *I have a plan*, she wished she could say. *But it's too dangerous to discuss it.*

She squeezed Aurora's hands and then let them go. She wished she could tell Aurora she'd been a good friend when she'd needed one. She wished she could thank her for being the one person she could trust in this hellish place, that if she'd ever doubted her, she shouldn't have. She couldn't risk a goodbye, not now, but she'd be sure to tell her all those things when she saw her again.

A friend—just one true one—could save your soul. And the gift of friendship lasted forever, its lingering grace there to draw strength from even when you were alone. Kandace knew that now.

"I'll see you at chapel," she said. "I'm going to go early and say a few extra prayers."

Aurora nodded and Kandace offered her a smile, infusing all the gratitude she could in it. Then she closed the door behind her and made the slow walk downstairs and outside where the building was waiting to be filled by the fallen women of Lilith House and the *good* men who were there to offer atonement.

She slipped inside the door, a prayer on her lips that she had arrived before anyone else. The room was empty. Kandace exhaled a breath of relief, rushing forward and going directly to the cabinet at the back where she'd watched Ms. Wykes remove the communion wine so many times.

She glanced back, toward the closed chapel doors, before opening the cabinet and removing the corked bottle. Sweat gathered on her forehead and her hands trembled as she reached into the pocket of her uniform and brought out the piece of folded paper, unwrapping it on the floor in front of her, and then creating a makeshift funnel as she tipped it over the bottle and let the powdery grounds of the dried mushrooms flow into the wine.

She'd broken into her mother's room so many times, and yet she'd never been nervous. She realized now that perhaps she'd hoped to be caught, hoped for . . . what? The attention that accompanied the disappointment? The small burst of satisfaction she'd received by doing something that caused her mother to actually *look* at her? To see her, if even for a moment? And even if that version of herself had little to do with who she actually was? Yes, she realized now that was exactly what her goal had been. She'd fooled herself into thinking the stakes were high then, when she had no concept of the meaning. God, how naïve she'd been, thinking she was clever, in control of her life. She hated Lilith House with every ounce of her being, but she also had to feel thankful that she'd grown up. She'd been redeemed after all. By the power of her own will.

And by the grace of friendship.

Kandace crumpled the paper, sticking it back in her pocket, and then shook the wine, recorking it and placing it back in the cabinet.

Footsteps sounded outside the door. Kandace stood, rushing off the platform and swinging around the first pew. She went down on her knees, joining her hands in front of her in prayer just as the doors swung open and several staff members entered. *Please God, please let this work. Please help me get away.*

The staff ceased talking when they saw she was there early, instead slipping quietly into a pew on the other side of the room. Soon the other girls arrived, along with the staff members present. Kandace's limbs shook with nerves, the baby in her belly kicking her rib so hard she made a small sound of discomfort, covering it with a cough. *Gentle, little one. I need your cooperation tonight. Just a few more hours and we'll be free.*

Ms. Wykes's heels sounded on the floor, that unmistakable click slide that signaled her particular gait. Kandace gripped the pew in front of her tightly, holding herself steady.

The guild members filed in and the blessing began. Kandace cringed when a cold hand was placed on her head. She'd been chosen. *It doesn't matter. I'll be gone.*

When it came time to take communion, Kandace reached up and guided the silver chalice to her bottom lip, careful to let the liquid slide back into the cup before it'd touched her skin. She watched in silence as the guild members, the staff, and each of the girls drank from the poisoned wine. *I'm sorry, girls. I'm sorry for this, but it will be worth it for all of us in the end.*

After, in the dining room, the first student started vomiting the minute she'd swallowed her first bite of cake. The others quickly followed suit, girls running for the garbage cans, sprinting for the bathrooms.

Kandace slunk back into a corner, watching the mayhem, a lump forming in her own throat, not of physical illness but of sympathy for what was her fault. She saw Ms. Wykes double over in the opposite corner, and the sight strengthened her resolve. *This is the only way.*

Several staff members went running from the room, their faces stricken, perspiration shining from their pallid skin.

She heard the sounds of running footsteps from above. Somewhere upstairs, Kandace knew the guild members were fighting for use of the old-fashioned bathrooms as well.

She slipped out of the room, the moans of pain growing distant as she headed in the opposite direction of the first-floor restrooms. Kandace sprinted up the back stairs, her loud footsteps hidden by the mayhem in the rest of the house.

She slipped into her room, her breath coming in sharp pants, throwing on her sweater, and grabbing the leather bag the kid had managed to pilfer from the stash in the basement and hide in the crawlspace in the wall. She reached under her mattress and retrieved the files she'd need to bring the authorities straight back to Lilith House. The proof that would open an investigation into how three unnamed children were living in the basement of the house. *No. Not living. Hidden.* The proof that would lead to one person talking, and then another, until every vile thing that had ever happened at Lilith House was exposed and prosecuted.

As she began to stuff the stack of files into the bag, one slipped, falling to the floor in a scattering of papers. Kandace swore softly, bending to gather them up, her hands shaking. As she scooped them forward, something met her eye. She picked up the piece of paper that identified Camden's birth mother, her gaze zeroing in on the block of scrawled words she had missed in her original haste to gather what she needed and leave Ms. Wykes's office. More detail about Camden's birth and—

Kandace heard a bang from somewhere below and shoved the paper into the folder, stuffing the stack into the bag, standing quickly, and strapping the satchel around her body. She'd have to decipher all that later when she had the time. She bent, retrieving the tennis shoes Dreamboat had also found and pulling them onto her feet. She had a long trek ahead of her. She needed to be far, far away by the time they cleaned up the mess of their sickness and realized she was gone. If she was very lucky, that wouldn't be until morning.

Kandace glanced around the attic room one last time. How different she'd been when she'd first stepped into this space. How completely, utterly different. She ran a hand quickly over her bump, gathering her resolve. *Ready? Let's do this,* she said, slipping out the door and heading down the stairs.

The retching noises echoed in the halls as she descended from one floor to the next, finally making it to the main foyer, and opening the front door. The cool breeze of the night air greeted her, a breath of pure freedom. It was this night she would melt into. Disappear. No longer would the smells of Lilith House assault her: incense and hypocrisy. Evil.

Outside, the sky was awash in vivid shades of orange and red, golden rays streaming into the trees like a beacon. *Come forward. Safety lies this way. True salvation.* She heard it as a whisper, a promise. Hope filled her, so sudden and so intense that she almost cried. She moved toward that bright light, jogging down the steps and moving toward the woods.

"Stop, whore. And hand over those files." The voice behind her was gritty with rage. Kandace halted, terror crushing the hope that had risen within only moments before. She turned slowly as the man in the pristine white suit ran a hand over his mouth. His other hand held a weapon. As she stared, two more men stepped out the door. They hadn't gotten sick? Why hadn't they gotten sick? Kandace's heart cried out, the agony of defeat hitting her full force in the gut. *Oh God, oh God.* They stepped toward her, the intent clear on their faces.

Kandace turned, and she ran, her hands held forward, reaching for that promise of salvation.

CHAPTER FORTY-FIVE

Camden entered the sheriff's department, saying a quick hello to Shara who worked at the front desk. "Is the sheriff here?" he asked.

"Yup. He's in his office."

With a short nod, Camden walked past the desk and headed toward the back. The body of Kandace Thompson had been autopsied that morning and apparently the sheriff had just received the results. He'd called Camden in to discuss them.

Camden felt tense, edgy. The discovery of Kandace's body could be the very thing they'd been waiting for, the investigation that might very well expose the crimes being committed in this town for far, far too long. Her body had been transported to a lab in Los Angeles where her mother and stepfather lived, far away from Farrow and the corrupt hands that might intervene to hide evidence.

He heard the sheriff on the phone inside his office so instead of knocking, turned the knob quietly, creating a small gap from which to peek in and catch the sheriff's eye at his desk, wait for a nod to enter, or a signal to wait outside. But when Camden looked through the small opening, the desk was empty. He opened the door wider to see the sheriff standing with his back to the door, the phone held on his shoulder, a gun in one hand and a metal file in the other as he filed away what Camden assumed was the serial number. He froze. "It doesn't exist, Gene," the sheriff said. "Not anymore." *Gene.* Gene Miller? The guild member who ran the Farrow insurance company? The sheriff held the gun up, inspecting the spot he'd just filed, placed it into a box and then set the box inside the file cabinet he was facing. "Nope. Gonna bury it. Relax, Gene." He listened for another minute, answered whatever question Gene asked in the affirmative, saying a quick goodbye, and then beginning to turn. Camden pulled the door quickly, and then began pushing it open just as the sheriff turned around.

He smiled, disconnecting the call. "Camden, come in."

Camden entered slowly, his heart racing. The sheriff rounded his desk, taking a seat and indicating Camden should sit down too.

"How are you, Camden? How are Georgia and Mason?"

He stilled, sensing something beneath his words. "They're fine, I guess."

The sheriff smiled broadly. "That's good to hear." He paused for a moment. "By the way, I noticed how you went out of your way to comfort the Lattimore woman the other day after her kid found the body—damn thing that was, by the way. I still don't understand what a little thing like that was doing scaling the side of a canyon. But in any case, you be careful how much time you spend with her, you hear? I asked you to keep tabs on her activities, not what's under her skirt. I wouldn't want you getting caught up with someone unacceptable unless *unacceptable* is what she's looking for." He chuckled softly. "Type of woman like that, little kid depending on her, she's gonna try to trap you if you let her."

Camden's hands fisted on his thighs. "Yes, sir. I'm aware of her type."

The sheriff's smile grew. "Course you are." He turned his gaze to a folder on his desk. "I received the full autopsy results from the victim recovered two days ago, Kandace Thompson." He paused for a moment. "I sure do wish you would've let us handle it first," he said, his smile unmoving. "Instead of calling in outsiders. We would have preferred to complete the autopsy right here, in our Farrow lab. The guild won't look favorably on your choices."

Camden let out a breath. "There didn't seem to be a way around it, sir, since Ms. Lattimore knew the victim and her mother. Strangest coincidence."

"Strange indeed," he said. "That's what happens when those not vetted by the guild move to town. We should've stopped that. We'll have to see what can be done about it now."

Dammit. Camden's gut churned, but he nodded. "Was there anything more found in the autopsy report, sir?"

The sheriff smiled, quietly watching him for a moment. "The gunshot wound to her torso caused her death."

Yes, he'd figured that. He still felt sick. They'd shot her. They'd chased her through the forest and shot her like an animal.

Hey, Dreamboat. He saw her smile and a ribbon of sadness wound through him. She'd tried. She'd done her best to exact justice.

The sheriff sat back, lacing his hands over his flat stomach. "The girl obviously ran into some trouble. Whoever helped her run away must have shot her. We figure it was about drugs. The root of all evil. She had a history and all." He eyed Camden. "Something similar happened before, if you didn't know. Three girls ran away from Lilith House, back to their life of depravity and fornication. They were never seen again."

Three girls. No, he hadn't heard about that. Hadn't found it anywhere in the crimes database for the town of Farrow. *Why?* Because it hadn't been considered a crime at all, but just three runaways, missing of their own accord? Or had the sheriff known enough to hide that from him? Camden sat frozen, watching the man in front of him lie to his face, accuse others of what he himself had done. He cleared his throat. "No, sir. I didn't know about that."

"Of course, you didn't. You would have been, what? Two or three when that happened I guess. In any case," the sheriff went on, sitting forward, "I just wanted to let you know. Case closed. Shame the choices people make."

Camden hid his disgust with a clearing of his throat.

The sheriff stood, his chair creaking and rolling backward. "Well, now that that nasty little business is over, I'm going to go make myself some tea. Would you like a cup?"

"Uh, no, sir. Thank you. I'm just going to catch up on a little paperwork, and then follow up on some calls from a few folks in town."

"There ya go," the sheriff said, clapping him on the back and then squeezing his shoulder. He made eye contact, held it for just a beat more than felt comfortable. "There ya go," he repeated, removing his hand. They both exited his office. The sheriff walked past Camden, entering the kitchen just down the hall. Camden heard him whistling from inside. He turned quickly, grabbing a tissue from a box on the sheriff's desk, heading directly toward that drawer, and removing the box. He used the tissue to pick up the gun, the serial number already shaved off, but maybe, *maybe*—God willing— containing prints not only from the sheriff, but from Gene Miller too.

"I was hoping I was wrong."

Camden whirled around to see the sheriff standing in the doorway of his office. "Dammit, Cam, I really hoped I was wrong. About all three of you. But mostly about you." He shook his head, looking truly sorrowful. "You just can't wash the sin away, can you? It's embedded in your marrow. From those women who conceived you."

"I don't think you know the meaning of the word sin, Sheriff," he said softly. "I don't think any of you do."

The sheriff sighed. "You're wrong, son. No one knows the meaning of sin better than us. We've been attempting to cast it off since Farrow began. As my son, my blood, I thought you might come to know that. I thought you might be able to fight the evil inside you."

Camden's mouth parted. *As my son.* He was the sheriff's son? His blood. His head swam. He swallowed. "That's why you let me come back," he murmured. "It's why you let me have the job."

"Of course, son."

He felt lightheaded. Off balance. *Son.* "You hid me in the basement of Lilith House for most of my life," he said, his voice breaking on the last word.

The sheriff's jaw hardened momentarily. "They wanted to leave you out on that rock in the woods. *All* of you. I didn't allow it. They told me I'd come to regret my compassion, said evil only begets more evil, but I was stubborn. I'm sorry to say I should have listened to them."

"Who was my mother?"

"Your mother was a sixteen-year-old whore who had track marks on her arms." He smiled, and it was disgusting in its callousness and lack of shame. He had raped that sixteen-year-old he called a whore. "Pretty thing though. Real pretty. I blessed her every time. Only me. It's how I know you're mine. She shouldn't have run. I would've kept her."

Kept her? Like she was an animal?

"What was her name?"

"Can't say as I recall."

Breathe in. Breathe out.

"Georgia's and Mason's mothers?" he asked, and it sounded like his own voice came from a great distance.

The sheriff eyed him. "I don't remember the specifics, just that they fell pregnant. Too low a dose of birth control, Dr. Bill figured. He replaced it with a stronger type after that. Unfortunately, those two were born . . . damaged as well."

Damaged.

"What's my damage?"

The sheriff cocked his head to the side. "Why, none, son. None at all. We thought you'd suffered an accident of birth, but"—he swept his hand toward him—"clearly that's not the case. It's why my hopes were so high. So high."

Camden heard the disappointment in the sheriff's words. He shook his head, screwed up his face. So many questions, so many, and yet he knew the clock was ticking. He had to get out of there. If the sheriff was telling him this, it was because Cam had become dispensable. He wasn't going to let him simply walk out the door. Not now. Whatever roles he'd played in this town were over.

Still, he had to *know.* This might be the last chance he got. He recalled what the sheriff had told him just fifteen minutes before about the three runaways. "Our mothers. They left? With us?"

"They did. One of them must have heard you. Babies aren't the quietest of creatures. They figured things out somehow, hatched a wicked plan, snatched all three of you and they ran."

They ran. Camden's head pounded. He'd *dreamed* it, or at least that's what he'd thought it'd been. A dream. But no, it was a *memory.* A memory of being carried through the forest, a mirror in his hand. *Why did she make me carry a mirror?* Some strange superstition? Or was it simply a toy he'd brought along, clutched in his grasp, his own eyes wide, jaw slack, as he stared back at himself?

God, the memory made his head hurt. He'd been so young. He was likely misinterpreting most of it. "You killed them," he said in a monotone. "You had to because we were proof of what you'd done."

"The right thing is not always the easiest thing, Camden. Farrow men have always known this. If more of my blood than hers filled your veins, you'd know it too. You'd believe."

More of my blood than hers. Thank the Lord. Thank the Lord above he had more of his mother in him than this sick, twisted bastard who stood before him now.

"We tracked those girls down. They'd hidden you in that forest, but we found you, brought you home, made things right."

Home. Lilith House. He didn't trust himself to speak.

"But we *failed* in our mission thirteen years ago. We let that girl get away. And because we fell short, evil gained strength. Our Women's Ministry was struck down and engulfed in flames. And *still,* because of what we didn't do, our town, Farrow's people, our very way of life has been *cursed.* Just like the Bancroft family who died off when those natives escaped their God-ordained fate! That beast roams the woods, it *grows* in ever-increasing power, it plagues the children of even our most pious citizens with unearned signs of sin, it *returns* them to us when we attempt to cast them off."

Cast them off? He recalled the whisperings he'd heard of a scattering of animal attacks on infants. But that had been while he was gone, and nothing of the sort had happened since. There was no evidence to substantiate those rumors, and nothing at all in the sheriff's database. Now he knew why. And in that moment, he realized the truth that had only skated around the periphery of his mind, too terrible to comprehend. Camden swallowed, horror filling his veins, horror and rage. They'd tortured young girls for their own pleasure, they'd *murdered,* they'd left babies to die in the woods and they believed their sin was *unearned?* And that the punishment was delivered by some horned devil, emboldened by their failures, and out to exact his long-awaited justice?

Perhaps he—*it?*—deserved the vengeance he sought.

But he wasn't the only one.

"Only ten families now," the sheriff went on. "My own wife *barren.* We needed you. Farrow needed you. We thought you were lost to the outside world, but then you came back of your own will and hope was renewed. You were to replenish, not to replete!"

Like hell.

The anger flaring inside fueled him, primed his muscles. The sheriff must have noticed the hot burn of fury in his eyes because he removed his weapon and reached for his phone. Camden didn't waste a moment. He leaped forward, smashing the gun into the sheriff's cheekbone with all his might. The sheriff howled, blood spurting as he whirled sideways and gripped his desk. Camden raced past him.

The sheriff lunged for him but missed, and a loud boom filled the hallway, a gunshot smashing into the door at the end of the hall, wood splintering. Camden swore, ducking as he rounded the corner, another gunshot ricocheting off the wall next to him.

"There's no way to get out of town, Camden!" the sheriff shouted. "We won't let you leave Farrow. Come back and admit your crime. Accept your punishment. You killed that girl, didn't you? Camden!"

Shara peeked her head up from behind the desk as Camden raced by, her eyes wide with fear. He flew out the front door, jumping into his truck and peeling out of the lot just as the sheriff appeared in the doorway, taking aim once again. The shot went wide, the sheriff bringing his phone to his ear as Camden turned out of the lot, speeding toward the road that led to town.

He beat on the steering wheel, swearing savagely. He was a liability now. The coverup they'd planned on wouldn't work without his cooperation. So now they'd try to pin it on him somehow. Goddammit! The entire guild was going to be after him, rifles at the ready, prepared to shoot him down and blame him for Kandace's murder. And they'd come for Georgia. For Mason.

"Fuck!" Mason was at Lilith House. With Scarlett. Scarlett and Haddie and Millie too. Georgia would be at work right now.

The split in the road approached. Drive to town to warn Georgia, or drive to Lilith House where the rest of them were, completely unaware of what he'd just set into motion?

A bead of sweat rolled down the side of his face. He didn't know what to do. There was no good answer. At the last minute, he yanked the wheel, heading toward Lilith House.

CHAPTER FORTY-SIX

$\mathcal{S}$carlett ran/limped through the woods, her head whipping back and forth as she called Haddie's and Millie's names. Her breath came in quickened bursts of panic. Something had her baby, something dangerous and unnamed. An animal, or even a demon. She could believe that now, after being attacked by the thing that must have once been a woman and now lay dead in a heap of bones in an old nun's bedroom.

She stopped, taking a moment to catch her breath and listen to the sounds surrounding her. The trill of a bird. Leaves and foliage rustling in the cooling breeze as evening began to descend. The scampering of something close by. But nothing that told her where Haddie and Millie might be. Not the crunch of bones, or the tearing of flesh. She let out a terrified whimper as she raised her uninjured arm and clamped a fist over her ear, pounding once, as though she might beat out the visions her thoughts brought forth. A small sob escaped her throat but Scarlett drew her unharmed shoulder back, moving forward.

She was not going to fall apart. Not when her child needed her. Not when Millie, *Kandi's child*, needed her.

Scarlett followed the path Haddie had led them on to find Kandi's bones, cradling her useless arm to her chest. She had no other idea, no other way to go that would be based on anything except panicked wandering.

The pain of her injuries made her feel woozy, but her fear was bigger, and far more pressing.

She didn't know whether it was wise to continue to call Haddie's and Millie's names, so she stopped. What if it only alerted the thing that had taken the girls as to Scarlett's whereabouts? What if it helped the thing avoid her?

She ran on, weaving through the trees, and stepping over fallen branches as the day fell to dusk, washing the woods in an ethereal pale peach glow. The rustling noises picked up, the bird calls increasing in their noise level and enthusiasm, and a little girl in a pale pink dress with a green satin sash stepped from behind a tree. Scarlett gasped, a small cry emerging as her heart jumped and she raced forward, toward her daughter.

With another cry, she went down on her knees in front of her, bringing one shaking hand to her shoulder and then pulling her forward breathlessly, wrapping her arm around her. "Haddie, Haddie, oh my God, Haddie. Are you okay? Baby, are you okay?" She pulled back, her head whipping around. "Where's Millie? Haddie, we have to—"

"Mommy. You're hurt."

Scarlett bobbed her head. "Yes. But I'll be okay. I have to get us all out of here. Now."

Scarlett stood, leaning down to pick Haddie up, to run, to find Millie, to escape whatever had taken them deep into these darkening woods.

"Mommy," Haddie said more forcefully. "Come with me."

"Come where? Baby, we have to find Millie. You can tell me later—"

"Millie's that way," she said, pointing her finger in the direction from which she'd come.

Scarlett nodded, her breath coming just a little easier. "Is she hurt?"

"No, Mommy. She's with him."

Her blood chilled. "Him? Who's him?"

"Him. He's light, Mommy. Very, *very* light. So light I couldn't feel him at first. But I can now. I learned. Please, Mommy. Come *see.*"

Scarlett blinked down at her daughter, taking in her pristine dress, her hair still in the same mint-green barrettes she'd clipped in that morning, white sandals slightly scuffed but otherwise undamaged. It appeared her daughter was not only completely fine, but might have been carried gently through the forest. *But how is that possible?* She held out her hand. "Take me to Millie," she said.

Haddie smiled, grasping her hand, and pulling her along. They only walked about three hundred feet through the carpet of pine needles, rounding a bend and coming upon

427

a large rock between two massive trees. "You can come out," Haddie called. "I found her. I found my mommy."

All of Scarlett's organs felt as though they'd turned to stone as she stood, clutching her daughter's hand, waiting with bated breath for what was about to appear with Millie, but *trusting*, trusting Haddie because she was obviously not afraid.

Millie stepped out first and Scarlett sucked in air, lifting her injured arm as much as she could and holding out her other hand to the girl. Millie smiled, rushing forward. "I was scared at first too," she whispered.

Scarlett looked up, stilling, staring, squeezing both Haddie's and Millie's hands tightly as . . . something else emerged. At the sight of it, she drew back, pulling the girls, a cry of fear on her lips. He had *horns* only . . . no, they were perched on a small cap of what had once been the animal skull, fashioned into a type of hat. He was draped in leather and fur, and fabric pants that were far too short. He had an ancient-looking drum strapped around his neck, and despite its obvious age, the bleached leather was still stretched taut. Her eyes darted from one thing to the next, trying to make sense of what she was seeing.

He was a man . . . just a man. Not an animal or a demon. As he moved forward, his shoulders were curled inward, head angled downward and to the side as though he was the one fearful of *her*.

"It's okay," Haddie said softly. The man slunk closer, finally lifting wide, scared eyes to her, peeking up from under his shaggy dark hair and offering her the shy smile of a small child. Scarlett made a tiny sound of shock and confusion, stumbling backward a step. She let go of the girls and clapped a hand to her mouth momentarily, breathing as she attempted to get her bearings.

Scarlett dropped her hand. "How?" she asked. "How?"

"I don't know, Mommy," Haddie said. "But he's light." Haddie signaled him to come forward.

The man let out a soft, snorty giggle, lowering his head again bashfully and moving closer.

Scarlett couldn't stop staring at him.

What in the world is your sign of sin?

I don't know. I never knew what mine was. I worried. I wondered if it was something they knew that they never told me, some illness I couldn't see or feel but that might one day show itself. I don't know.

It was Camden, but not. It was his brother, his *twin.* He had to be. But how? *Why??*

"Oh my God," she murmured aloud, the story she'd read in Narcisa's own pen forcing itself to the forefront of her mind, the way they'd left her baby in the woods to die because of a disability. Had they done the same with Camden's brother? If yes, why one but not the other? Her thoughts spun crazily. This man was obviously mentally impaired. Had there been some sort of trauma at birth? Had one twin been deprived of oxygen, while the other's condition remained unknown? Had *this* boy been deemed completely worthless like Narcisa's baby, while his brother was shoved in the basement of Lilith House, believed to be sinful, but ultimately useful, just as Narcisa and some of the other natives had been? The ones they'd used as their whores and their slaves.

Valueless. But exploitable.

A moan of pain and fury emerged. Oh the evil. She couldn't bear it. It kept coming. It kept blindsiding her.

"What's your name?" she murmured.

He smiled shyly, but turned his head. "He doesn't talk in words," Haddie explained. "Not many anyway. But he *can* talk," she insisted.

Scarlett shook her head. "How, Haddie?"

She seemed to think about it for a minute. She glanced at Millie momentarily and then back at Scarlett. "Some people . . . are on different channels."

Scarlett frowned, glancing at the childlike man. "Tell me."

Haddie wrinkled her nose. "Like how Sofia the First is on Disney channel, and Word Girl is on PBS. You have to switch back and forth. If you're only on Disney, you can't watch Word Girl. It's not even there. It's like it doesn't exist, but it *does.* It *is* there, it's just on another channel."

Scarlett glanced at the man, at Millie, and then back at Haddie, giving herself a minute to digest what Haddie was saying. The moment in the church daycare came back to her. *You're nothing. Nothing at all.* That's what Haddie had said about the boy with the leg braces. She shivered, goosebumps causing her skin to prickle. Was it possible that since that moment Haddie had learned to . . . somehow communicate with people who otherwise couldn't? Who operated on a different sort of . . . channel?

"Did you say something to the boy who lives near Millie that let him know you understood him?"

She bobbed her head. "*Yes,* Mommy. I wanted him to know I was on his channel."

Scarlett struggled to understand but she knew one thing: *This,* this was the inner world she'd been wanting to share in. She *could not* mess this up. She had to be the mother Haddie needed. She had to *try* to understand, to believe in her even if it didn't make sense. Cam's reaction to the possibility of Haddie having a mental illness handed down by her father suddenly flashed in her mind.

"Does it matter?"

"What? Whether or not he has a mental illness?"

"No, whether Haddie has a predisposition. What will you do?"

"I would know better how to treat her."

"It seems like you're doing just fine, Scarlett."

He'd been right. Haddie didn't need treatment. She needed understanding and love. Acceptance and . . . awe. *She's so incredibly precious. And she's spreading that gift . . . that light . . . everywhere she goes.*

Even in a forest with a man who'd been left to die. Scarlett's heart overflowed with love.

She nodded over to the man. "Did he tell you why he took you?" she asked Haddie.

"He didn't take us," she said. "I called for him and he came."

"Why?"

"That nun came to Lilith House," Haddie said, her expression going somber, eyes dull. She blinked and her eyes cleared. "She was heavy, Mommy. So heavy I couldn't *move.* I made myself move though. I did it."

Tears gathered in Scarlett's eyes even while dread trickled down her spine. Sister Madge had told her she'd visited. She'd told her she'd dropped by to offer condolences. However, she'd gone to take, not give. "That's good, baby," she choked out.

Haddie nodded. "She left, but I think she's coming back, Mommy. I think she's bringing others. They want to hurt you, and me, and Millie too. They want to hurt us bad." She looked over at the man, blinking his forest-green eyes at them, his lashes long and lush. "He knows this place. He's going to help us," she whispered.

CHAPTER FORTY-SEVEN

Camden didn't bother knocking. He threw the door to Lilith House open, rushing inside. Mason came bounding down the stairs. "Cam! I've been calling you."

"Where are they?"

Mason reached the foyer. "Jesus, Cam, it took them. It had horns. Scarlett, she—"

"Mason. Calm down. Tell me where they are," he gritted, his heart constricting so tightly he could hardly breathe.

"They're in the woods. The thing, it took Haddie and Millie. Scarlett got home and went after them. Someone hurt her, Cam. She was real banged up."

The thing? "When?" His voice sounded like it was coming from very far away, panic dripping through his veins. It had them? *It?* And Scarlett was hurt?

"Just ten minutes ago. If you run—"

He grasped Mason's upper arm with one hand, holding the box in his other. He'd need to hide it quickly. "We have to call Georgia, and tell her to hide." He'd prayed the entire way there—all twenty-four minutes of his far-too-speedy drive—that the guild was busy gathering, organizing, rather than going directly after Georgia. He prayed *he* was their priority. They'd figure out where he'd gone quickly enough and then they'd come after him. Here, to Lilith House. "Then you come with me. We'll go after them together." He pulled his phone out, but Mason held up his hand.

"I already called her, Cam. I told her something bad was happening. I told her to come here."

Fuck! "Call her back. The guild is after me. They're on the way. *Here.*" He didn't have time to tell Mason anything other than that.

Mason swallowed, pulling his phone from his pocket and dialing Georgia's number. After a few seconds, he hung up. "Not answering."

He raked a hand through his hair. "Goddammit!"

"I thought it was best, Cam, that we gather here, start searching for Scarlett. I didn't know any—"

"It's okay." Georgia had answered. She was all right. She knew there was a situation. He just hoped to God she was ahead of the others. "Wait for her, Mason. Then you hide too. Both of you. You know this house. There are a million places to choose. We'll come back for you. Just stay hidden." He thrust the box at Mason and Mason took it. "Use this if you need to. There are two bullets in the gun. You know they won't let any of us leave town." The weapon was evidence—

all they had—but Mason's and Georgia's lives were more important.

Mason nodded solemnly. "I know. I'll wait for her. We'll be here waiting."

Camden nodded once and then he ran for the woods, drawing his firearm as he ducked into the trees.

Where are you, Scarlett? God, please let them all be okay.

The sky had been a vivid peach as he'd made the windy drive to Lilith House, but now had faded to a pale pink streaked in yellow. It made the woods feel peaceful and for a moment Camden almost believed nothing bad could happen here. He stopped, listening, but when he didn't hear anything he continued forward, not attempting to be quiet. If he was going to make up the time between when Scarlett had gone into these woods, and when he followed, he was going to have to run. Scarlett was hurt, and she didn't know this land, not like he did. He could only hope that she'd traveled cautiously and he could catch up with her. Then they'd both search for Haddie and Millie together and whatever might have taken them.

He couldn't consider what it was. Not now, not when he was helpless to do anything about it. Old fears surfaced, stories of horned demons, Satan's creatures roaming this forest, and he forced himself to push those terrors aside. His girls needed him. His. *His* girls. The thought bolstered him, dissipating the fear with something stronger. Love. Scarlett had calmed that restlessness he'd lived with all his life. Given him a purpose greater than spite. And he had to find them. He *had* to find them.

The forest dimmed another shade, drifting from pink to purple, and behind him, he heard the distant roar of trucks. The forces had arrived and he only had a twenty-minute lead. *Please let Georgia have made it to the house before them. Please let both she and Mason be secreted away in one of the many hiding places they knew well.*

The guild would see their cars, but they'd see his and Scarlett's too. There was nothing he could do about that.

He began to turn toward the stream where he'd first kissed Scarlett. She knew that route, she'd take it, wouldn't she? A fox darted out in front of him very suddenly, causing him to emit a short yell as he stumbled to a stop. The fox stared at him, wide-eyed and then darted in the other direction, stopping, looking back once, and then disappearing into the darkening forest. Camden paused for a moment and then, for reasons he couldn't quite articulate to himself, he followed it, moving in the opposite direction from which he'd been going. Toward the canyon where the bones had been found.

He ran through the trees, his breath coming short, gun gripped in his hand. "Camden." He heard his name, said in a hushed whisper and spun around, lowering the gun to his side.

"Scarlett?" he gasped.

"Here." He moved toward her voice, a strangled moan of love, of relief, of thankfulness coming from his throat when she stepped out from behind a tree. He rushed forward, taking her in his arms and she yelped in pain. He let go, stepping back and looking down to see her arm hanging at her side, blood splattered on her clothes. "Oh hell, Scarlett, you're—"

"Yes. Cam, you have to come with me. I heard their trucks. They're here. Sister Madge tried to kill me, or not her but some, oh God, one of the teachers burned in the fire I think. She had these *shears*. This is her blood on my shirt, not mine. Sister Madge knows about Millie. I discovered something very important. I have to tell you everything. Everything."

"Whoa, whoa, slow down, Scarlett, it's okay. I'm here. We'll go through all of that later. Right now, we need to find Haddie and Millie."

She bobbed her head again. "Haddie and Millie are fine. They're back there. We heard someone coming. We didn't know who it was. I came to see. Thank God, it's you. Thank God, Cam."

Haddie and Millie are fine. Relief all but punched him in the gut. "I wish you'd led with that," he said, taking a moment to pull her—gently—into his arms again, holding her for only a moment before letting go. "Mason said something took them," he said. "An animal or—"

"No, no, no. That wasn't right. There's something I have to show you. Cam. You have to prepare yourself."

She held out her hand and he took it, unease causing goosebumps to form as he followed her through the woods. But he took comfort that her distress was not apparently caused by whatever she led him toward. She was afraid of what was currently outside these woods. The threat didn't come from within. Although the sky had deepened further, the moon was peeking through the gaps in the trees, shining down and outlining the forest in muted golden light.

With trust, Camden followed Scarlett to a more open area, a large rock between two trees. "It's Camden," she called and a moment later Millie and Haddie rushed out. He went down on his haunches, opening his arms and pulling them both into his grasp. They squeezed him back and, for a moment, the world was right. They all were safe. Safe and—mostly—unharmed and he was with them.

A horned creature stepped out from behind the rock and Camden released the girls, coming to his feet and drawing his weapon. Scarlett stepped forward. "No!" she cried as the thing slunk back, presenting his shoulder as he dropped his head in submission. Camden lowered his weapon. "No, Cam," Scarlett said. "He's a man. He's . . . he's your brother, Camden." Camden stepped back. His *brother? What?* "I think he found those horns and that fur in the cave. I think it belonged to the indigenous man, Taluta's husband. It's old, Cam, old and falling apart." Camden's head swam. She was saying words but none of them made sense.

The man raised his head, shuffling forward. He looked shyly up at Camden, a smile blossoming across his face. Camden stumbled back, a sound of shock and disbelief coming up his throat. "Bemme," the man said, looking around and then pointing at Cam. "Bemme. Bemme. Bemme." He looked happy, exceedingly so. Camden blinked, moving closer. "Bemme hep bobby."

"He's your twin, Cam."

"How?" he whispered. "I don't understand." But he could see that Scarlett was right. He had a twin. A *brother.*

Before she could answer though, the truth hit Camden in the gut. He almost doubled over under the blow. "They left you out here," he said. "They left you and they kept me."

"It had to be that woman," Scarlett said. "Narcisa. They left her baby out here to die, and then they did the same to him." She glanced at his brother. "She couldn't save her own baby, but she saved this one." She paused, her gaze moving between them. "He's probably been out here alone since she died."

The man approached him tentatively, reaching up and placing his fingers on his arm, pulling gently and then dropping his hand, looking away fearfully as though he had just behaved badly and waited for the repercussion.

"He wants to give you something," Haddie said. He looked at the little girl, something dawning. No wonder she'd reacted to Camden the way she had when she first saw him. She'd seen this man first. She must have been scared and confused about why Camden had his face.

Her statement repeated in his muddled mind. *He wants to give you something.* "What?"

She shrugged. "I don't know. But it's important." The man let out a burst of garbled words and Haddie's face scrunched up as she regarded him intently. "Something hidden that he found."

Hidden. By Kandace? Camden let out a shaky breath. The proof she'd collected? God he hoped so.

He heard the shouts of men in the distance and a light swept through the sky, something large that would illuminate the woods in front of them. They weren't close enough yet for it to find them in the nighttime shadows. But they had to *go*. They had to hide. The how and why of his brother's existence, the disbelief that was still pinging through him would have to wait to be addressed.

"Come here," he said to Scarlett. "This is going to hurt, but I have to do it. You need use of your arm." Fear clouded her gaze but she nodded, turning, and offering him her shoulder trustingly. He took hold of it, pausing and gathering his own strength. It killed him to hurt her, even if it was necessary. "On the count of three. One, two." He wrenched it back into place as she let out the softest of groans, her face contorting in pain. He could tell it had cost her not to scream out loud. But her shoulder was back in place. With a grimace, she rotated it slowly, bringing her arm up, testing its use.

"Thank you."

Camden gave one quick nod. "We're going to split up," he said. "You have to take the girls and get them out of here."

Scarlett shook her head. "No. We should stay together."

"There's too many of them. I need you to listen to me." He pointed. "You go that way. They'll expect us to come out at the road, but you're not going to do that. Follow the stream. It leads to another wooded area that lets out on a trail five miles from here. There's an emergency phone attached to a pole. You'll see it. Call the state police. Get them here." He handed her his gun and though she glanced at it warily, she took it from him. "Don't hesitate to use this," he said. "If you have to, shoot to kill."

She gripped his shirt. "What about you?"

"I'm going to lead them in the opposite direction. I think I can stay ahead of them with his help." He looked over at his brother who smiled bashfully when he caught his eye.

"Bemme," he whispered softly. It was obviously his name for Cam though Camden had no idea what it meant.

He took Millie's hand in his, squeezing it and offering her what he hoped was a comforting nod. Then he bent down to Haddie. "If you feel anything strange, at any time, you tell your mommy, okay?"

Haddie nodded very seriously, holding her pinkie up in front of him. It took him a beat to realize what she was doing. *Pinkie swear.* He lifted his hand, linking his finger with hers, meeting her eyes and shaking. Haddie let go, throwing her arms around his neck, hugging him. Camden shut his eyes momentarily, drawing strength from the moment, from the unexpected affection of this special child.

The shouts grew louder, another arc of light sweeping overhead. He stood, pulling Scarlett to him, breathing her in and kissing her forehead. "I love you. Now take the girls and go."

Tears filled her eyes but she nodded. "I love you too," she said, kissing him hard once on the mouth. And then Scarlett took Millie's and Haddie's hands in hers, turned, and headed toward the stream.

God, please, keep them safe. Bring them back to me.

CHAPTER FORTY-EIGHT

*C*amden and his brother ran through the woods, the man next to him, though obviously mentally slow, was surprisingly swift and agile. Camden allowed him to take the lead, running a step behind so that his brother could show him which way to go.

Camden knew these woods relatively well, but this man had lived in them his whole life.

His *brother*. It was still almost too impossible to believe. But Camden didn't have the luxury of examining his emotions now, on this topic or any, so he pushed them to the background. They would be for *later*, if in fact they got one.

He heard the men behind them, still distant, but coming from every direction now, fanning out to cover a larger ground. *Hurry, Scarlett. Hurry.*

When they'd gotten to a small clearing, Camden stopped, signaling his brother to put his hands over his ears, preparing him for the loud noise he was about to make. Then Camden let out a series of deep yells as though he'd injured himself somehow. A second later the men's voices rose in pitch, bodies crashing through brush, coming straight toward them, though still a good distance away.

They ran on, faster now. The man turned left, racing through the trees, jumping easily over downed logs and rocks as though he had each one memorized. And maybe he did. As he ran, he chanted, low and mostly indiscernible, mixing what Camden assumed were Serralino words with garbled English, adding more credence to what Scarlett had said about him being raised by Narcisa Fernando. The horns he wore on his head bobbed and weaved as he ran and Camden had the insane urge to laugh out loud. He'd been afraid of this unknown "creature." Afraid of the faraway drumbeat and the glimpse of animalistic features, afraid of the low grumbly chanting he'd heard coming from the woods. He'd been fearful not because his gut had told him to be scared, but because Ms. Wykes had made certain he was. Did she know? Did she know that the "thing" roaming the woods was just a shy, abandoned boy? He didn't want to think about it. The awfulness, the pure malevolence of that was too big to hold.

The man slowed and Camden did too, as the dilapidated house once belonging to Narcisa Fernando came into view. "Hum," his brother said, but he turned away, appearing not to want to enter. *Home*. Camden had understood that one.

This had been his home. Narcisa must have rescued him from the forest and raised him there. Then she'd died and he'd been alone. All these years, he'd been alone. Camden walked forward, looking back at his brother. His twin followed slowly, cautiously. Was he acting nervous because there was something Camden should be concerned about too? Or was he simply afraid of the place where he had perhaps found his mother—for that's what she'd been—deceased in her bed? Voices. The far-off barking of a dog. He paused, listening. They had bloodhounds. *Fuck.* They had Roland Baker's hounds, a younger guild member, part of the ten remaining original families, who lived on several acres on the hill above town. He'd seen him in with the sheriff on multiple occasions. Camden figured his father had been one of the men who chased Kandace into the woods that night. He wondered if the family had taken to dog training in case anything similar happened again.

We failed in our mission thirteen years ago. We let that girl get away. And because we fell short, evil gained strength.

No. *They* were the evil. They always had been.

Camden hoped to God the shouting had caused all of them to turn in his direction, away from Scarlett, but he had no way to be sure. *Walk in the stream, Scarlett. Hear those dogs and walk in the stream.* He hoped she knew that the dogs wouldn't be able to catch their scent in the water but his ribs constricted with worry. He recalled what she'd said to him the night he'd helped her feed the baby bird.

I'm a city girl who never owned a pet. I know very little about animals, wild or otherwise.

Maybe she'd picked that information up in a movie or something though. He had to hang on to hope. It was all he could do. "Hurry," Camden said, pointing into the forest where the hunters grew ever closer. The man blinked at him, looked back and then moved toward the house. He stopped at the doorway and rocked for a moment, doing that strange chanting again, a sort of self-soothing.

Camden pushed the door open and then took him by the arm. "Come on. I'm here."

His brother smiled. "Bemme," he said, stepping over the threshold.

It smelled like dirt and mildew inside, and struck him as a long-vacant place that had been left in a hurry. He looked at his brother, eyes darting around nervously and wondered where he'd been when they carted Narcisa's body away. Had he watched them from some shadowy corner, chanting quietly, not understanding what was happening or why he was suddenly alone? He couldn't let himself picture that. He couldn't. "Hurry," he said again.

His brother did move then, stepping forward and going down on his knees, pushing a threadbare rug aside, and prying a board from the floor. He reached underneath, bringing something out, and then stood, handing the item to Camden.

It was the brown leather bag, the one he'd given to Kandace so many years before. He pulled the flap back and looked inside to see a stack of folders, the proof she'd obtained about their mothers. It was what she'd died for.

He itched to know its contents, but he didn't have time to look at it, not now.

His lungs burned. He smiled at his brother. He wished he could ask him where he'd found it and when. But he

445

couldn't, and so he settled on, "Thank you." He pulled at his arm. "Hurry," he said again because the man seemed to know that word.

His brother pulled back, pointing to something near the wall. A trunk. He said a word that Camden could not decipher, pulling him to where the storage container sat. "Hurry," he said again. His brother dashed to the trunk, flung it open and grabbed something inside. Then he returned to Camden handing him the small piece of fabric.

An embroidered baby hat. And stitched on it was the name Alonzo.

"Alonzo?" Camden asked, pointing to him.

Alonzo gave a grunty giggle, looking shy, but infinitely pleased.

"Alonzo," Camden repeated. He pointed at himself. "Camden."

"Bemme," Alonzo said softly.

Good enough. "Canyon," he said but Alonzo just tilted his head, staring at him in confusion.

Camden let out a breath of frustration just as it dawned on him what Alonzo would know it as. "Novaatngar," he said. *The dark place.*

Alonzo's face lit with understanding. He nodded and they turned to the door where Camden spotted a tall spear leaning against the corner wall. He grabbed it. They could use any weapon they could get their hands on. They rushed through the door, heading back into the woods as Camden strapped the bag around his body as Kandace had surely done in these very woods thirteen years before. He was even more in awe of her at that moment, considering what she achieved. *You were so, so brave, Kandace. You deserved so much more than this life gave you.*

"Hurry!" he said to Alonzo and Alonzo ran, Camden on his heels, the noise of their hunters drawing closer in pursuit. If they could get to the canyon ahead of the men, they could change direction and follow the outer rim and eventually meet up with Scarlett.

And the state police.

Camden followed his brother's lead, avoiding the shadows, trusting Alonzo to lead him to the canyon. They'd need to make it there well ahead of the hunters if they were going to get far enough away that they wouldn't be seen in the sweeping light. They had hounds, and the hounds could follow their scent, but the dogs would also slow them down. The edge of the canyon offered little cover, but it would be the quickest way to travel, open ground where they could straight-out sprint.

They just needed to get to that trail and hope a squad car waited. *You can do this, Scarlett. I know you can. Walk in the water. Walk in the water.*

The trees thinned, the shadows of boulders rising around them. They were almost there when Camden heard a buzzing behind them. Alonzo and Camden slowed as the sound of the buzzing increased, dipping and rising, drawing ever nearer. It was an engine. A dirt bike, possibly two. *Fuck!* He hadn't imagined they'd ride dirt bikes into a thick forest, much less travel at the speed at which he could hear them coming. There were a hundred ways the driver could be injured or thrown. Or, most likely, crash headfirst into a tree.

It meant they were desperate.

There was no way they could outrun a dirt bike and it was coming fast. Camden grabbed Alonzo, shoving him in a large east-facing crevice between two boulders. The approaching light wouldn't find him there. They'd have to pass him and look back to see Alonzo, and Camden didn't intend to let that happen. He'd create a distraction. They were coming for him anyway, not his brother. He took the bag from around his body, and strapped it to Alonzo. Then he handed him the spear. "Hide," he whispered. Alonzo squatted behind the boulder, gazing up at him with wide, fearful eyes. He'd obviously known that word. "Hide," Camden repeated, putting his hand on his brother's shoulder.

The dogs were behind the dirt bike, but there was too much open space here for Camden to hide for long. Even if the dirt bike rider missed him, the dogs would be close on its tires and would scent him out, and he'd give his brother's hiding spot away. The dogs wouldn't be tracking Alonzo, nor would they have an item from which to do so. For all intents and purposes, his brother didn't exist. He was nothing but a ghost, a horned "demon" haunting these woods.

Sadness gripped him, but so did a dreadful sense of acceptance. Scarlett would come back for Alonzo. He had no doubt of that. She'd use the files Kandace had collected and she'd exact justice. A strange peace descended. He trusted her, knew her strength. Her conviction. She would fight for him and for Kandace. For Alonzo and all the others who'd been sacrificed at the altar of Lilith House. Sacrificed by the men of Farrow.

With one final nod at his brother, Camden ran ahead, putting as much distance between Alonzo's hiding spot and himself as possible. He ducked around one rock and then another, slowing as he walked out into the wide-open space, heading for the edge of the canyon.

Novaatngar. It was where it had all started, wasn't it? And perhaps it was right that it was where it would end.

Camden went down on one knee, choosing a rock from the ground around him, clutching it in his grip, and then waiting. The engine grew louder, coming closer, its headlight appearing through the trees moments before it darted out of the woods. Camden took aim and threw the rock with all of his might.

The driver jerked, flying off the bike and landing with a loud thud on the ground, the person who had been riding behind him, throwing himself off and rolling. The dirt bike continued forward, zipping past Camden on his right and soaring over the edge of the canyon. Camden stood, breathing hard, adrenalin pumping, as the man who'd been behind the driver, staggered to his feet. The sheriff. It was the sheriff. His father. *Their* father. The other man—Dr. Bill Woodrow Camden now saw—remained still, his head twisted at an unnatural angle, his neck likely broken. Dead. Over his shoulder, Camden heard the very distant sound of the bike hitting the ground far below.

The sheriff raised his firearm. "Raise your hands, Deputy West. It's over. You have to take responsibility for what you did to that girl. You killed her, didn't you? Where'd you hide the weapon, Camden? The one you used to murder her? Will we find it in your vehicle? Your house? Maybe with those friends of yours?"

He heard men crashing through the woods toward them, the light sweeping overhead but still a good distance away. The dogs were even farther back. The younger guild members would be slightly behind their fathers, slowed by the tracking hounds. How far away were they? Ten minutes? Fifteen at the most? Then there'd be thirty men, if not more. The Farrow Religious Guild, all of them.

He prayed that Mason and Georgia had hidden safely. They'd be able to use the gun for evidence later, but it would be flimsy on its own. He could think of a hundred ways the sheriff could twist things, make it look like Camden was the guilty party. They'd been doing it for centuries, and getting away with it. Justifying evil in the name of God.

No, Scarlett and now Alonzo were the only hope.

As if he'd read his mind, the sheriff said, "The dogs scented her, son. They're on her trail. Tell us exactly where she's headed and I'll let you live."

No, he wouldn't. There was no way he could. Not now. They'd have to kill him, Camden had no illusions about that. His gut churned. *The dogs scented her. They're on her trail.*

Run, Scarlett, Haddie, Millie. Please run.

"I don't know where she is," Camden said.

"We'll find her, Camden. Whether you help us or not. We need that little girl to assist us in locating the devil. We need her to help us kill it so we can save our town."

It. This man's *son,* though he didn't know it. Believed he had perished in these woods as an infant after they'd left him to die. "I came out here to search, but I didn't find them." All he could do now was buy time, wait for the men to bypass Alonzo so the man could slip away, and then let them do with Camden as they would.

He didn't want to die, God, *he didn't want to die,* not now when he felt like his life was truly just beginning, but he was prepared. He wouldn't go fearfully. He'd face death the way Taluta's warrior had done: with honor, even gravely injured, he'd carried her broken body up the side of a cliff to a hiding spot where they could die on *their* terms. Camden had done all he could. He had to trust that those he loved would take it from here.

The sheriff sighed, glancing behind him where the sounds of the men's voices grew more distinct. "I wish you could understand, son. The world is a fallen place, draped in darkness. Some men are tasked by God to keep that darkness at bay. Farrow's sons have always known this." He swept his hand around, indicating the canyon. "It's been that way since the township began. It's the way it will always be. We failed but we will reconcile. We will always cast out sin. I'm sorry you couldn't grasp that and become one of us. I truly am."

Without waiting for a response from Camden, the sheriff raised his gun and fired. Heat blossomed between Camden's ribs, and he doubled over, clutching a hand to his abdomen where he'd been shot. He staggered, blinking at the sheriff who stood stock-still in front of him, watching. His ears rang, the close sound of voices, the more distant barking of dogs

451

becoming muted, then fading away completely. The sheriff raised his gun again, aiming, when a blur of movement caught Camden's attention. He looked behind the sheriff, his eyes growing wide. The sheriff, having apparently heard the movement, looked over his shoulder, his scream rising into the night as a monstrous creature flew from the darkness, a spear raised in its hand, its horns outlined in shadow, its voice raised as it chanted the chant of the dead.

The sheriff fired wildly, the shot missing as the creature continued in its rush forward. It raised its arm and then lowered it, the spear plunging into the sheriff with a sickening sound of wetness. The sheriff emitted a yell that quickly faded into a gurgled whoosh of air. The creature kept running forward, driving the sheriff backward with the long spear as he helplessly flapped his arms, flying past Camden and directly over the edge of the cliff.

For a breathless beat, Camden's eyes met the sheriff's as he desperately grabbed at the spear that wouldn't help him. The creature had let go and now stood at the edge of the cliff. They both watched as the sheriff dropped, his horrified shriek echoing, fading, and finally ending abruptly as his body hit the canyon floor far, far below.

The voices grew louder, lights brightening. Alonzo moved back and ducked near a large boulder and Camden fell to his knees, his hand still held to his wound. He was bleeding to death. He'd die here.

The men burst from the cover of trees. One of them caught sight of Camden and pointed. "There he is!" They all turned in his direction, raising weapons when a flash of lightning ripped across the sky, startling them and momentarily diverting their attention. In its wake, their light blinked out, the distinct sizzle and pop of a dying bulb rising into the night.

Several men swore loudly, but there was enough moonlight for them to see exactly where he was and they continued to advance. Thunder roared and Camden swayed as he attempted to catch his breath and rise to his feet. If he was going to die, he refused to do it kneeling before these monsters.

But before he could, a dark, horned shape rose to their right, looming. Several of the men let out startled yells, all of them whipping their weapons toward the creature. With a low growl, it ducked and ran behind a boulder, gunshots ricocheting off of the rock.

"There it is! Did you see it?"

Camden watched as the man they thought was a horned beast darted between objects, ducking and weaving, the shifting pockets of moonlight making it appear as though he was everywhere at once. He began chanting as he moved, the sound rusty and chilling, even though Camden knew the gentle source. He threw his voice in one direction and then in another so that it echoed first on one side of the canyon, and then on another. He knew this place, understood how it worked. He was everywhere and nowhere at all.

The men turned wildly, trying to figure out where he was coming from, firing haphazardly, moving as a group, first one way, then another, yelling one command, and then directly following that, another that contradicted the first.

A second blaze of lightning lit the sky, merging Alonzo with his shadow and making his moving form appear ten feet tall. One man screamed. Thunder rumbled, shaking the earth. Their voices grew higher, more unsure, and woozily, Camden drew to the side as they came closer, right to the edge of the cliff.

He's herding them. Oh my God, he's herding them.

With one final booming chant that ricocheted from one side of the canyon to the other, Alonzo appeared from behind a rock, fur-covered arms held wide, head lowered, charging. A few more shots went wild, as the disoriented men turned, the one closest stepping off the cliff and grabbing for the one in front of him. They grasped at each other, floundering in their panic, pulling, falling, their screams billowing upward like the howls of a multi-headed devil descending to hell.

Camden let out a gasp of shock, leaning over as far as he dared and witnessing the men he'd watched rape troubled girls plummet to their deaths, their bodies bouncing off of the jagged rocks of the cliff wall before landing in a heap below.

He rolled to the side, struggling for breath. A fox sat quietly, its eyes trained on the place where the men had disappeared. It turned to him and their gazes held, its ancient amber eyes glinting in the moonlight. Camden blinked as she turned and ran toward the forest, disappearing into the shadows. A few cool raindrops fell, misting his skin.

Barking. Voices. Shouts. The dogs were still coming, being led by the smaller group of younger guild members. They were almost there, driven faster by the chorus of their father's screams. Five minutes, if that.

Alonzo appeared, horns tilted, shoulders slumped. "Bemme," his brother said softly, picking him up. He tossed Camden over his shoulder, grunting with the effort.

Then Alonzo ran, huffing with exertion, Camden held firmly against him, the press of his body and the leather bag he still wore staunching the blood flow, but the bouncing movement causing him immense pain. They were far enough away now that they were shrouded in darkness. He heard the sounds of dogs, of mayhem and confusion, but the voices didn't follow.

Camden raised his head and in the glow of their own light, he saw the group of younger men, standing at the edge of the basin, peering into its dark depths. The dogs were barking, straining at their leashes, but coming up short as the edge of the cliff plunged below. The scent they'd been told to track stopped there. Alonzo had picked him up and carried him. There was no scent to follow. As far as they knew, he'd gone over the edge along with the others.

Alonzo stopped next to a large rock, going to his knees, and rolling Camden from his back. Camden hit the ground with a huff, sitting up as slowly as he could, propping himself against the rock and assessing his injuries. The gunshot wound oozed blood. He felt hot and cold at the same time, drowsy.

Alonzo sat next to him, breath coming harshly, eyes wide with uncertainty. Camden pulled himself up, reaching out and taking his brother's hand. The slight rainfall had cleared completely, over before it really began.

His brother smiled at him. It was a tired smile, but pure, filled with the open adoration of a child. "I'm going to be fine," Camden lied.

"Bemme."

Camden squeezed his hand.

"Bet me," Alonzo said more slowly, breath still staggered with all the effort he'd expended.

"Bet . . . me," he said, a breath causing him to pause between each syllable. *Bet-ah-me.*

Bet-ah-me.

Better me.

Oh. *Oh.*

No. It was the other way around, Camden could see that clearly.

The world swam around him, and Camden felt a gurgle of blood coming up his throat. He lay down and Alonzo followed suit. Camden curled onto his side next to his twin. Perhaps they'd lain this way once before in their mother's womb.

His hand hit the ground and his fingers curled, grasping a fistful of earth. *. . . till you return to the ground, for out of it you were taken; for you are dust and to dust you shall return.*

Everything slowed. The earth. The clouds. The heavens.

He thought of the dream that was really a memory, of his mother running with him through the woods—with *them,* for it wasn't a mirror he had been looking into, but the eyes of his brother. She'd somehow found them *both* and attempted to escape, but like them, she'd been hunted. Caught. She'd hidden her children first though, and the guild had found

Camden, but not Alonzo, for they hadn't even known to look for him. Narcisa must have handed Alonzo over to their mother and then saved him for a second time when things went so terribly wrong.

He'd never know all the answers and maybe that was okay, because he knew this: he hadn't been abandoned. None of them had. They'd been *stolen*. His mother had been brave, her last act selfless. She was more than the poor choices she'd once made. So much more. It was the last thought Camden had before the world faded, the dirt falling through his fingers, grain by grain, until there was no more.

CHAPTER FORTY-NINE

$\mathcal{M}$ason sat in the small space behind the hidden wall in the storage area of the basement. He draped an arm over his knees, listening for any sound that might reach his ears from above. Nothing came except the creaks and groans that he still knew well, even after all of these years, as though he somehow shifted right along with the house. His heart beat swiftly, every nerve prickled. He'd waited for Georgia. He'd waited, but she hadn't shown up before they did, the men of Farrow who came in cars and trucks, touting rifles and handguns, dogs barking excitedly in one of the pickup beds. They'd mobilized quickly. Mason had stood at the window and watched them unload, gritting his teeth with fear and rage, hoping fervently that Georgia had seen them driving toward the road that led to Lilith House and held back.

They'd started walking to the house, two hounds straining on leashes, and Mason had booked it to the basement where he'd holed up behind the secret wall, listening as they searched the house, and then hearing their footsteps move toward the front door and spill out into the forest. Whatever item they'd given the dogs to trace, it hadn't been his. Apparently, they had other priorities, namely Camden and Scarlett who the dogs must have tracked to the forest. But that wouldn't be the case for long. They'd come for him next. And Georgia. He was certain they had the roads blocked off. Just like Camden had said, there would be no leaving Farrow.

If they could manage it somehow, there'd be no *entering* Farrow, either.

He'd risked calling Georgia once he'd heard the door of Lilith House slam, but it went straight to voicemail again. He'd turned his off too and stuck it in his pocket, lest his phone give him away by lighting up.

Mason itched to *move,* to come out of hiding and search for Georgia, perhaps leave the house and make his way to the edge of the road, wait for her car. Would they have posted someone on the road? Either at the turnoff from town or at the beginning of the long driveway that led to Lilith House? Both?

As he sat there, Mason ran through escape scenarios, all his possibilities, trying to figure out the safest thing to do. There was only the smallest modicum of light in the hidden space, only enough to see the outline of his own legs, and the box that sat next to him, the one Camden had shoved in Mason's hands. A gun. *Use this if you need to.*

Mason opened the box, removing the weapon, and then pushing the portion of wall aside. He climbed out of his hiding spot as quietly as he could. Would they have left someone behind to guard the house in case anyone tried to return? Likely. Maybe that person was outside, walking the perimeter? Or maybe they were stationed in the foyer, sitting as quietly as a mouse.

Mason crept through the basement, climbing the stairs noiselessly, toward the slip of light below the door. He remembered each place to step to avoid the creaky boards, just as he and Cam had done so many times in their youth for one reason or another, just as he and Georgia had done the night they broke in and tried to scare Scarlett from the crawlspaces in the walls. He couldn't use those crawlspaces now. Camden had nailed them shut, and even if Mason tore the boards away, the nail holes and damage would expose the once-hidden entries.

With utmost caution, Mason opened the upper door, slipping into the hallway and using the back stairs to climb to the second floor, stopping every few minutes to listen to the sounds around him. He heard a series of strange squeaks and they caused him pause, but Lilith House was undergoing several structural changes, ones he'd overseen himself. Her sounds might be slightly different now than when he'd lived there, but he had no way of knowing for sure. He entered a dark second-floor bedroom at the front and went to the window, sticking the gun in his waistband, moving the heavy, moth-eaten curtain aside, and peering out.

The darkened woods spread out around him, but from this higher vantage point, he could see the dim faraway glow of the spotlights they must be using, moving slowly forward.

He stared up at a particularly bright star and took a moment to make a silent wish for Camden and Scarlett and those two young girls, out there being hunted like animals right that very moment.

He saw movement below and moved quickly, stepping to the side of the window just enough that his body was hidden, but he could still see below. A man walked by, he couldn't tell who it was from this angle, but he saw the rifle in his hands.

He had to *do* something. He had to intercept Georgia if she was on her way. Mason turned, exiting the room and walking quietly down the hall until he got to the railing overlooking the foyer, gas lanterns burning brightly. He leaned forward. *Empty*. He let out a long, silent breath. How long would it take him to make it through the backwoods to the main road? Thirty minutes? Mason began to turn toward the back stairs when movement to his left caused him to whirl around.

Clarence Dreschel, the head of the guild, and the man who'd been Georgia's guardian, stood in the doorway of a bedroom across the open space, his cane in one hand, a gun held in the other. A delighted smile stretched across his angular face. "Hello there."

Mason stared, his hand itching to move toward his waistband where he'd stuck the gun.

"We hoped you'd come out," Clarence said, taking several steps forward, his cane tapping on the hardwood floor. "I've been waiting. Quiet as a mouse." His lips stretched into the semblance of a smile. "The dogs will be tired when they return. It would be thoughtless to make them go from floor to floor searching this monstrosity of a house." He tilted his head slightly, eyes moving across the walls. "We should have burned this place down years ago. It fostered so much evil, so much sin."

Rage blossomed in Mason's chest, because he knew the sin this man was referring to was not his own. The *evil* Dreschel recognized belonged to everyone but himself. The things he had done to Georgia . . . Mason should have exacted his own revenge on this man years ago instead of waiting for some plan between the three of them to come to fruition. He'd always talked himself out of it, saying Georgia deserved the satisfaction of the retribution they exacted. And that he'd be no good to anyone—least of all Georgie—dead or in prison. *How do you kill men who think they're gods? Who rule a kingdom of evil?*

Mason's gaze moved from one direction to the next, weighing his options for escape. Clarence Dreschel was a good shot. He'd been an avid hunter, just like many of the guild members, before the accident that had hurt his leg. Perhaps his skills were rusty though. Would Mason have time to drop, retrieve his weapon, and get a shot in before the old guy did?

"Let him go." Mason's head swiveled to the right where Georgia had just stepped around a hallway wall. *Georgia. No.*

Clarence turned too, whipping the gun in her direction. He let out a huff of breath, shaking his head. "Georgia. You should have stayed hidden. Goddammit, girlie. I might have helped you."

Georgia laughed and Mason heard the edge of hysteria laced within. His hand moved slowly toward his weapon. "You might have *helped* me? Is that right? Well fuck your *help*, old man. I'd rather get shot in the face than accept anything from you," she hissed. "I'd rather die than let you lay a finger on me ever again."

His lips stretched. "They were right. You're an abomination. You all are."

Even from where Mason stood, he could see the angry red spots that rose in the man's face. Without wavering, he turned the gun on Mason. Everything slowed. Mason saw Georgia's mouth open in a scream as she dove toward him. He saw the old man squeeze the trigger. He felt the impact of her body as both he and Georgia went flying backward, hitting the floor, the jolt stealing his breath and resuming time in a loud, painful rush of air and screaming nerve endings.

Mason yelled, struggling to make sense of what had happened, pulling himself out from under Georgia who lay on top of him. Blood. So much blood leaking from a hole in her chest. She'd jumped in front of him. She'd been shot. She'd taken the bullet meant for him.

She turned her head to where Clarence Dreschel stood, the gun still pointed at them. "You're the abomination," she said, and then the sound of two more gunshots exploded, causing Mason to yell out, falling, his ears ringing. He watched the old man hit the wall behind him, screaming as one hand came over his groin, blood soaking his khaki colored pants, spreading rapidly, and the other clamped over his neck, more blood spurting through his fingers. He slid down to the floor, his screams fading to gasping, gurgled whimpers, curling in on himself, the gun he'd dropped skating far across the floor.

Mason tried desperately to orient himself, his head whipping back and forth. Georgia had taken the gun from his waistband as they collided, and then she'd shot the man who'd shot her. Her tormenter. One of many. A pool of blood spread out around the old man's dying body, soaking into the floorboards of Lilith House as his pitiful cries grew weaker, so faint they could hardly be heard.

Georgia fell backward, the gun in her hand clattering to the floor. He bent over her body, pressing on her wound. "Georgie," he breathed. "Georgie. You're going to be okay."

She smiled up at him. "I'm okay now." Her smile twisted and her face grew paler.

"We've gotta get you help. I'm going to carry you—"

"Mason," she grabbed his shirt, pulling him closer. "It's okay. This is right. It's how it was meant to be."

"What?" He moved to stand so that he could pick her up, carry her to his car, drive her to a doctor in town. "No, Georgia. No."

But she shook her head. "There's no one to treat me. They'll let me die. I'd rather die here with you. Stay with me, Mason. Please."

"You're not going to die. No way—"

"Mason, I told on her."

He pressed harder on her wound. "Told on who? It doesn't matter. We have to get you out of here."

"Kandace. I heard them talking and I told the guild her plan. They didn't drink the poison. It's my fault. I was jealous." Her voice cracked and a tear rolled down her cheek. "I thought . . . she'd come back and take you . . . away from me. You. Cam. You were . . . all I had. All I've ever had."

Oh God. Oh, Georgia. He swallowed. "It doesn't matter, Georgie."

She shook her head and it appeared that the small movement pained her, her expression turning into a grimace. "It does matter, Mason. It does. All this time . . . I hated them for what they did to me but I . . . hated myself more. The fire . . . all those girls . . . it wouldn't have happened if not for me. I did all . . . of that. Me, Mason. It was my fault. And in the end, you were taken away anyway. And I was left with *him*." She tilted her head minutely toward where Dreschel lay unmoving. "But maybe I deserved it."

"Oh, Georgia, no. You were just a young girl. You were confused, hurting. You had no way to know what they'd do, or how it would all end up. None of us did. I've always loved you, Georgie. I always will. There's nothing you could ever do to lose me."

Her lips tipped into a smile and she brought her hand to his face. He leaned into it as she gazed at him, seeming to really see him for the very first time, though they'd known each other all their lives. "Oh, Mason. Always living in someone else's shadow. I did that to you, didn't I? I'm so sorry. You deserve more. You always did."

"We all did, Georgie. Don't leave me. Let's find out—"
He choked on his words as her hand fell from his face and her body went limp in his arms.

CHAPTER FIFTY

$\mathcal{S}$carlett stopped, letting go of Haddie's hand and reaching out to grab Millie's arm. The girl was a few steps ahead of her and she came to a halt, turning. Scarlett put a finger up, indicating they should take a minute, bending over and placing her hands on her knees for a moment as she caught her breath. Even in the dim light of the moonlit forest, and despite that her shoes were soaking wet from having waded in the stream for miles, she could see that blood had saturated the cushioned fabric, turning it pink. Her wounds had opened. She didn't dare take the time to stop and attempt to re-bandage them though. She needed stitches, but she didn't think she was at risk of bleeding to death, and so they'd keep moving.

"What's wrong?" Millie whispered.

"Nothing. Just a quick rest." She swallowed, looking behind them, her eyes moving through the shadowy trees.

It'd been hours since she heard the gunshots echo off the canyon beyond them, mixed with the brief bout of lightning and thunder, two hours that she'd been whispering prayers that Camden hadn't been hit. She had a sinking feeling in her gut though. There had been so many shots, and soon after, they'd seen the lights moving in the other direction. That couldn't be good.

No, don't think that. You have to stay hopeful. For the girls. For them.

She'd heard the dogs barking a short time after they'd split up with Camden, and fear had nearly made her double over. They were being *tracked*.

Walk in the water. The dogs can't track you there. Royce's seemingly nonsensical words came back to her then. She didn't know what it meant, didn't know how his inebriated rantings could possibly be connected to what was actually happening to them, but nonetheless, she'd led the girls to the stream, and they'd walked in the water.

"Let's go, Mommy," Haddie said, taking her hand again. She drew strength from the solid feel of her daughter's hand in hers, the warmth, and Scarlett stood straight, nodding at them both as they continued on through the trees.

She was so incredibly proud of Haddie and Millie. So proud. They'd traveled miles and miles—through water when they'd heard the dogs—over rough terrain, under deeply stressful conditions, and they hadn't complained once, neither of them. And here *she* was, the one asking for a rest. They needed it though. They needed a few deep breaths to complete the last leg of their journey.

God, she hoped they were close. She hoped she'd followed Camden's instructions properly. If she had, they should come out of this thick blanket of forest at the edge of a trail. And somewhere on that trail was an emergency phone that would bring help.

"Let's go," she said.

They began jogging again, Scarlett's feet screaming with so much pain she wanted to cry out from the agony of each step, but she didn't. She wouldn't let them know. She wouldn't put her burden on them as they were burdened enough as it was. They moved as fast as possible through the dense woods, but not so fast that they couldn't see objects in front of them. It would do no one any good to trip and break an ankle.

"Mommy," Haddie said, pointing ahead where the trees opened. Deep relief fell over Scarlett when they stepped out of the tree cover onto a hiking trail. She pulled both girls to her and let out a soft laugh of triumph. They squeezed her and rejoiced under the light of the moon.

After a few moments, they began walking, traveling on the edge of the trail so that if they needed to seek cover again, they could do so immediately.

"There," Millie said, and when Scarlett looked where she was pointing, a small sob came up her throat. It was a tall pole next to an enormous pine, an emergency satellite phone box attached to it.

They ran for the phone, Scarlett's hands shaking as she opened the box, lifting the receiver. A dial tone sounded in her ear and she let out another quiet sob. Scarlett dialed 9-1-

1, tears streaking down her face as she told the operator where she was and what she needed. She forced herself to speak clearly, not to give in to the hysteria bubbling inside of her, and to explain that the operator must not alert anyone from the Farrow Sheriff's Department. State police. *Only* state police, and on a private channel.

The operator asked her to hold on for a moment and when she came back, she said, "Ma'am, there's an overturned logging truck on the highway leading to Farrow, and the spot where you are. I'm going to have our officer take the back road. He'll be there as quickly as possible."

"Hurry, please hurry."

Scarlett hung up, taking a few steps and lowering herself carefully to the ground, holding her arms out for Haddie and Millie. They rushed forward, each curling up to her, their heads on her shoulders, hidden in the shadows of the massive tree.

They waited that way until a light cut through the darkness, a person approaching on the trail from below. Scarlett stood quickly, pulling the girls to their feet, and holding her finger to her lips and then indicating they should follow her behind the trunk of the tree.

They huddled there together, Scarlett peeking out, watching as a man in uniform walked closer, squinting up the trail, his flashlight held out in front of him. Haddie pulled at her shirt. "It's okay, Mommy," she whispered. "He doesn't want to hurt us. He's going to help."

Scarlett released a gust of breath. "Okay, baby." They stepped out of the trees and began waving to the officer.

When he caught sight of them, he hurried forward, his eyes moving over the three of them, lingering on Scarlett's feet for a beat. He put an arm around her shoulders, holding her up. "Don't worry, ma'am. I'm going to get you three help. Are you able to walk to my car? It's just about a quarter mile from here. I couldn't drive any closer."

She leaned on him. "Yes. Yes. We can walk."

They began moving down the trail, when a noise sounded in the brush. The officer let go of her, pulling his weapon out and pointing it at the sound. *No. No. We're so close. Please, God. Please.* Scarlett stepped back, her heart drumming, drawing the girls close to her side as they took cover behind the officer.

A second later, a man came stumbling out of the trees, his arm wrapped around another man as he supported his weight . Scarlett let out a strangled gasp. "Camden!" She rushed toward them and he opened the arm not around his brother, the ghost of a smile tilting his lips. His brother blinked at her.

"Oh my God! You've been shot." She ran her hand over his chest. So much blood. So much blood. "Oh my God."

"You made it. You did it," he breathed, and even through the exhaustion evident in his voice, she also heard the pride.

Tears streaked down her cheeks as she took them in. They both looked half dead, one from his injury, one from fatigue. Cam was shirtless, with his uniform button-up wrapped like a tourniquet around his chest. His brother had a brown leather satchel strapped around his body. "So did you. You both did. Oh my God. Hold on. Hold on for us."

Camden looked at the man he was leaning heavily on. "His name is Alonzo. He saved my life."

They'd walked miles and miles. That *had* to mean Camden would survive his wound. *Please.* Scarlett reached for Alonzo's hand and brought it to her cheek. "Thank you, Alonzo. You did so well."

The deputy swept in, shooting the man in the fur and horns a curious look before ducking and putting his shoulder in Camden's armpit so he could support him as Alonzo stepped aside. "Come with me," he said, and the six of them staggered the quarter mile to the squad car.

Alonzo got in the front seat and the officer lowered Camden into the back and Scarlett, Millie, and Haddie piled in on the other side, Scarlett wrapping her arms around Camden and holding him tight as the car drove off. Camden reached forward and put his hand on his brother's shoulder, leaving it there. Alonzo turned his head and Scarlett saw the curve of his gentle smile.

She put her head on Camden's shoulder, Haddie's body pressed against her, Millie right on the other side. The lights of the squad car cut the darkness as they turned onto the main highway, heading in the opposite direction of Farrow.

They were going to be okay.

They were *all* going to be okay.

Never had Scarlett believed her life would lead her to this moment and all that had unfolded since she'd first bent down on a city street and retrieved a fallen flyer. But now, with her fatigue pulling her under, with all she loved tucked into her sides, Scarlett clung to the tenuous hope lying just beneath the deep-seated exhaustion and fear.

Her purpose had been bigger than she'd ever imagined. She was too tired to wrap her head around it now, but somehow she sensed, deep inside, that Kandi had been part of all that had come to pass. She moved her eyes upward, out the window where the trees of the forest whizzed by, the miles between them and Farrow ever growing. "Thank you," she whispered. "Rest now, my brave friend. We're all together." She laid her head on Camden's shoulder and Scarlett rested too.

EPILOGUE

In the Aftermath

Haddie smiled, running her hand over the cat as it arched its back and rubbed itself against her leg. "Good boy," she said, scratching his head until he purred. After a moment, Haddie stood, squinting off into the distance, hoping to see Alonzo at the edge of the woods. The light shifted, but it was only the trees swaying in the autumn breeze. Alonzo had come to live with her, her mommy, her new daddy, and Millie too, but the big, gentle man spent as much time in the forest as he did at Lilith House with them. Haddie knew it was because he had been raised there and it was where he felt most at home, but Haddie still missed him when he was gone. Her heart would always leap with joy when she saw him step from the woods, often with a hurt baby in his hands, his compassionate eyes filled with concern as he handed it over. "Hat hep bobby," he would say. *Haddie help baby.*

And then together, they'd take the tiny thing to her mommy, whose eyes still widened as she brought her hand to her chest and laughed that laugh that meant *you have got to be kidding me.* Then she would sigh and say, "Well then. Let's see what we can do."

Or if she was in the middle of baking or decorating one of her cakes, or getting ready for a bridal party to arrive, she would call Camden and he'd take the creature to the pretty little shed at the edge of the woods that he and Haddie and Millie had painted together. She and Millie even made a sign that they proudly hung on the front: *Ruby Sugar Baby Animal Rescue Center.*

Her mommy's business had opened the year after they escaped the men in the forest and had become very busy over the last few months. Her mommy said it was because all her advertising was finally paying off, but her daddy said it was because her mommy was the most talented person he knew, and she'd made Lilith House into a magical place any bride with good taste would fall in love with. Haddie agreed with her daddy. Her mommy's cakes were so pretty they made Haddie gasp every time she saw one. And Lilith House was beautiful with all its new paint and floors and balconies, and shimmery lights. Every time a bride entered, her eyes got big and she'd look around like she'd never seen a place like it before.

Haddie loved the brides. She loved their dresses made of white lace and shiny satin. She loved the way sparkles glittered around them and their grooms the same way they did around her mommy and daddy. She and Millie—who was her sister now—would peek at the brides from around doorways and out windows as they took photographs in the gazebo and walked through the flowers and trees, holding hands and smiling at each other.

Lilith House must love them too. The screams in the walls had faded. The rooms felt light. The house was happy that love lived there.

Haddie knew that there was lots of dark in Farrow. She'd felt it that first day. But now, many places felt light, as if the darkness had been swept away. Mommy said that her new daddy had become the biggest sheriff, and that he was finding all the bad and making them leave Farrow. Her new daddy was very tall, so that's maybe how he did that.

A man appeared at the edge of the forest, large and horned, and Haddie's face broke into a grin. "Alonzo!" she called, grasping the hem of her dress and rushing toward him as he whooped with joy and ran toward her.

****

Camden grinned as he watched Alonzo race toward Haddie, that deep, snorty laugh filling the air as he picked her up and twirled her around, her yellow dress flying out around her. They were close. Even closer than he and Alonzo, but that was because Haddie understood him on a level no one else did. Haddie had a gift that surpassed his understanding. She confounded him. And awed him. He couldn't wait until she was old enough to explain the things that went on inside her extraordinary mind. She didn't have the words yet, but perhaps, in the same way she'd learned to speak to Alonzo, that was a language she'd need to teach them when she was able.

They'd initially enrolled Alonzo in several programs where he could interact with others like him, but he'd become withdrawn, even depressed. He'd never lived in the outside world and he didn't take well to it. His brother very obviously felt most comfortable, most *himself* in the woods, so they let him come and go as he pleased. He was still "home," but he was no longer alone. He had all the love and affection he could handle and sought it out often. Thanks to Ruby Sugar, he had all the *cake* he could handle as well and that seemed to be quite a bit.

Haddie took Alonzo's hand and they began conversing in that unique way of theirs, hurrying toward the shed near the back tree line to tend to the healing creatures the way he once had.

Inside the house, Camden headed for the kitchen. Scarlett was taking a bride and her mother on a tour of the grounds and he spotted them out the window, standing by the gazebo, chatting and laughing. He picked up one of the first apples that had come from the small orchard they'd planted, and bit into it, smiling as he chewed. If they booked—and he was confident they would as almost a hundred percent of the people who traveled to view Lilith House in person did—Scarlett would need to hire another few employees.

Glancing down, Camden noticed one of Scarlett's lists sitting on the counter. He grabbed a pen and added two line items to the bottom:

Be ready at seven for dinner in town with the sheriff.

Do the swirly thing to your husband.

With a self-satisfied smile, he set down the pen, noticing the pile of mail nearby, a letter from Georgia on top. She could have emailed him, of course, but whenever he suggested it, she laughed and asked if he could blame her for being "old school."

He opened the envelope, scanning her letter quickly. Because of the files Kandace had stolen and then hidden, he, Mason, and Georgia had all been able to locate and contact their mothers' families. Each of them had sadly assumed their daughters were dead and had been shocked to learn they'd birthed children.

Georgia had healed physically from the gunshot wound she'd sustained, the one that had been removed by the doctor a town over who Mason had managed to get her to in the nick of time. Emotionally . . . well, that was still ongoing. But testifying in the trials of the few remaining men who'd been arrested in connection to what happened at Lilith House and in Farrow had helped her heal.

Georgia's grandmother was especially involved in Georgia's life. Georgia was in the South spending a few months with her. Her letters, including the one he'd just read, sounded . . . hopeful. More hopeful than Camden had ever known her to sound. Mason had moved to LA six months before and was working with a company who restored old homes. His mother's family had embraced him as well, though from afar, and Mason sounded happy too.

Camden's family had flown to California immediately upon finding out he and Alonzo existed. There had been an overwhelming reunion and although Camden was still getting to know them, they were good people he knew would be a constant in his life. In Scarlett's and Haddie's and Millie's lives, along with the baby on the way.

He'd let his mother's family know it was because of her—because of the knowledge that she'd tried so hard to rescue them—that he'd gathered every ounce of his strength that night he'd been shot, and continued on.

The trials for the crimes of the remaining guild members—the ones who hadn't perished at the bottom of Novaatngar—and guilty parties in the town of Farrow, were still being splashed across news articles nationwide. He believed justice would be served, at least that which was handed down by man. He also firmly believed they'd have an additional price to pay when their time on earth was done.

Camden set Georgia's letter on the counter, turning his head to gaze out the window at the forest beyond. He still pictured the way the sheriff—his father—had flown off that cliff. Had the sheriff wondered why God had forsaken him and sent a horned demon to drive the spear of an ancient people straight through his heart and toss him into the canyon where their ancestors had once been cruelly murdered?

As far as Farrow, where evil had once presided over it, now new people were moving in. The town was growing, though slowly. Some were still apprehensive to begin a life in a place that held so much tragic history. In ways both big and small though, the remaining citizens were reinventing their town, and he loved what it was becoming. Scarlett's business was helping in that effort. It brought traffic, tourism, happy events. It was a small slice of heaven in what had once been the midst of hell.

Ruby Sugar. Right there at Lilith House. Kandace would have liked that. She would have liked that a lot. Her daughter grew more beautiful by the day and despite the grief of losing the woman who'd raised her, Millie was thriving. She was an integral part of their newly-formed family.

They'd found something else among the proof of who their mothers were that Kandace had smuggled out of Lilith House. The proof that had it not been for her, would have never come to light. A letter, dried blood staining the edges of the piece of paper, had been placed inside the bag later, one penned in Kandace's own shaky hand. Last words that had probably been written as Kandace lay moments from death after just having delivered Amelia in a cave on the side of a cliff. A cliff where an ancient midwife had made a perilous climb and attended Kandace in her final moments. She had not died alone.

Dreamboat,

I tried. I tried so hard. Somehow, a boy who looks just like you carried me. He's strong and gentle. He saved me. They both saved my baby. She's beautiful, tiny but perfect. I wish I could tell you everything. I wish I could know my daughter. I wish. But I'm fading now. I did all I could. I hope you know that someday.

Promise me you won't stop being brave. No matter what, promise me you won't hide your heart, even if that seems like the easier thing to do.

You're stronger than you think. That's what Scarlett told me and she was right. She was right about me, and I'm right about you.

You're stronger than you think.

Forever,
Kandace

Is anything forever?

He'd once asked his wife that very question. Kandace's final words had helped him find the answer. Love. Human resilience. The power of grace over condemnation. The God-given ability that resides in every human heart to distinguish right from wrong, truth from falsehood, and love from pain.

Camden's life was overflowing with love. In two beautiful girls who were his daughters by heart. The unexpected brother who had lived through multiple tragedies yet still laughed. *Loved.* A wife whose heart was simply and undeniably heavenly. Matchless.

It was all around him, every single place he turned. *Forever.*

ACKNOWLEDGMENTS

This is the twenty-first acknowledgments page I've written, and finding the right words to express gratitude to those who helped me tell a story never comes easier. I couldn't have arrived at this point without:

Angela Smith and Marion Archer who tell me gently what needs to be better, and then provide specifics on how I might do that. Many a plot hole are filled because of them.

Karen Lawson who polishes my final manuscript until it's shiny and Sharon Broom who ties it up with a bow.

Ashley Brinkman, JoAnna Koller, and Elena Eckmeyer who offered up their valuable time to read my first draft and provide beta feedback.

My agent, Kimberly Brower. There are lists and lists of things I could not do without you.

My reader group, Mia's Mafia for your love and enthusiasm for my stories, even the strange ones.

And to all the readers, blogs, Instagrammers, and book clubs, who review, recommend and support my books—my appreciation is unending.

To my husband who reads my work with a critical eye and a loving heart. I am so incredibly lucky to have you as my partner in all things. *Forever.*

ABOUT THE AUTHOR

Mia Sheridan is a *New York Times*, *USA Today*, and *Wall Street Journal* Bestselling author. Her passion is weaving true love stories about people destined to be together. Mia lives in Cincinnati, Ohio with her husband. They have four children here on earth and one in heaven. Her works include the Sign of Love collection (Leo, Leo's Chance, Stinger, Archer's Voice, Becoming Calder, Finding Eden, Kyland, Grayson's Vow, Midnight Lily, Ramsay, Preston's Honor, Dane's Storm, and Brant's Return), the standalone romance novels, The Wish Collector, and Savaged, and the romantic suspense duet, Where the Blame Lies, and Where the Truth Lives.

The standalone romance novels, Most of All You, and More Than Words, published via Grand Central Publishing, are available online and in bookstores.

Mia can be found online at:
    MiaSheridan.com
    Twitter, @MSheridanAuthor
    Instagram, @MiaSheridanAuthor
    Facebook.com/MiaSheridanAuthor

Made in the USA
Middletown, DE
15 July 2024